C000005072

"I'll shoot you in th
"What if you hit my
What did the gunman d
he overcome Mother?

He frowns. "It doesn't matter where I shoot you as long as it's not immediately fatal. I know you heal fast. Now, stand up. Hands behind your head."

I comply. "How do you plan to escape with me as a prisoner? Since you know I can heal quickly from a gunshot wound, you probably know I'm faster and stronger than you. Do you really think you can walk out of here, avoiding the security detail, with me in tow? Take your eyes off me for a second, I'll disarm you and break your arm in the process."

Sweat rolls down his brow. "Stifle it. Turn around. Keep your hands behind your head."

"You're making a mistake." I can't believe he overcame Mother. Taking me by surprise is one thing, but overcoming Mother, a battle-hardened, magic-wielding, full-fledged skaag, is next level.

"We have your parents downstairs. You don't start doing what you're told without giving me lip, they'll get hurt."

Dad shouts from downstairs, followed by a loud thud, but no gunshot. I drop my hands and dart toward the intruder. Before he can pull the trigger, I'm on him, wrenching the gun up and to the side. Burning pain lacerates my right shoulder, and the crack of the gun is deafening. I'm more surprised than hurt because the sleeper's prowess courses through my veins.

Praise for Dragons Walk Among Us

"An inspirational and socially relevant fantasy."

~ Kirkus Reviews

"…Dragons Walk Among Us imparts further lessons on different kinds of prejudices and assumptions and the process of replacing knee-jerk, judgmental attitudes with understanding."

~ D. Donovan, Senior Reviewer,
Midwest Book Review

"This enjoyable story is well-crafted with a female protagonist that is not just lovable but adorable. Allison Lee's struggles are real and the author writes social issues that resonate with young adult readers, including bullying and the need to belong."

~ Readers' Favorite

"A perfect balance of fantasy, suspense, excitement and fun!"

-5 star review from Indies Today

The Blood of Faeries

by

Dan Rice

The Allison Lee Chronicles,
Volume 2

The Blood of Faeries

Cover Art by *The Wild Rose Press, Inc.*

The Wild Rose Press, Inc.
PO Box 708
Adams Basin, NY 14410-0708
Visit us at www.thewildrosepress.com

Publishing History
First Edition, 2022
Trade Paperback ISBN 978-1-5092-4648-9
Digital ISBN 978-1-5092-4649-6

The Allison Lee Chronicles, Volume 2
Published in the United States of America

Dedication

Dedicated to my father, who always believed.

Chapter 1

I hide on my bed wrapped in a warm blanket, leaning against an oversized kitty cat stuffy. My bedroom of the last seventeen years should be a safe place, but instead, I'm a stranger. I have my mother to thank for this liminal feeling. After abandoning me at birth, she's back and doing her damnedest to ruin my life. You'd think she'd take her time putting her stamp on the household, having just rejoined the family.

But that's not her style.

My mother is a juggernaut. As if it's not enough I'm a monster because of her, she's turned my bedroom into a hotel room. I like everything out where I can see it. Mother believes order will break down if anything is even one millimeter out of place. My clothes are folded with military precision inside icky plastic drawers stashed in the closet. Even my camera, my lifeline to sanity, is hidden away. I prefer to have my camera out on the desk next to my laptop where I can see it.

Most bizarre of all, the room even smells clean. I can probably detect cancer with my sense of smell, but I have to admit my room doesn't stink. All I can smell are the outdoor scents coming in from the open window. How does Mother do it—magic, maybe? I wish I possessed magic capable of rendering the chanting from the street inaudible. As it is, I have to keep reminding myself the racket is the soundtrack of my life; it's just white noise. I'm tempted to close the window, although I'll still hear the crowd with it closed.

A soft rapping against the door causes me to tremble. Oddly, I didn't register footsteps in the hallway. I really am out of it.

"Allison, the meeting is about to begin," Dad calls.

"I'll be down in a minute." I throw aside the duvet and stare at the door. Decorating the door is kaleidoscopic color being sucked down a blackhole like water whirlpooling down a drain. Barely discernible in the riot of colors is the band's name, Dark Matter Electrica—my favorite group. It's the only aspect of the room that still feels one hundred percent mine.

"Promise? You won't try sneaking out the window again?" Dad asks.

I roll my eyes. "I promise."

"I'm serious, Allison. You need to know the ground rules, or they won't allow you to go back to school," Dad says in his stern professor voice.

"I know, Daddy." I swing my legs off the bed. "I'll be down in a minute."

I wait until he retreats down the hall for the stairs before jumping out of bed and causing a loud thump everyone will hear downstairs in the dining room. I slam the window shut, decreasing the "white noise" a decibel, and stomp across the room to the study desk at the foot of the bed and inspect myself in the mirror hanging on the wall. I scowl at the sight of my blue hair. I miss my forest green hair, but my green mop had become synonymous with Allison Lee, the monster girl, since The Incident—our euphemism for the series of events that among other things gave me awesome prosthetic eyes, reunited me with my monstrous shapeshifting mother, and introduced the world to not-from-this-planet dragons. I also saved humanity from an invasion of skaags by collapsing an interdimensional portal. Skaags are shapeshifters capable of morphing into giant alligator eel abominations. I happen to be half-skaag, I guess. My dad is human.

Thanks to social media, the 24-hour news cycle, and a podcast produced by my best friend's ex, I'm a global celebrity. I hate it. At this point, all I want is not to be recognized whenever I step out of the house. Regardless of my hair color, I'm readily identified all the time. I need to up my game and go all secret agent to be incognito, but I don't want to have to be someone else to fly under the radar.

On the plus side, my shoulder-length hair is disheveled. That along with my ratty black T-shirt and sweatpants that are threadbare at the knees give off the vibe I want.

The "I don't give a goddamn" vibe.

Leaning over the chair and desk, I flip open my laptop and fire up a messaging app. I chicken peck out a text to Dalia.

—*Time for "the meeting." Wish me luck.*—

I wait a minute for a response. Oh well, she's probably out for a run or something; it's a nice day. Before I turn for the door, the computer pings, and her response appears on the screen.

—*Make sure they let you return to school. Good luck!*—

I scoff and tap out a response.

—*What if they insist I have a bodyguard? Don't need or want.*—

—Make sure he's hot.—

A series of smiley face emojis with heart eyeballs follow the words.

My lips tug upward.

—Call you after.—

I shut my laptop, feeling a little better. My BFF always knows how to lighten my mood. I'm about to head downstairs, but I stop at the sliding doors to the closet. I open the closet and snatch my camera off the top of a disgusting plastic drawer. I enjoy the device's weight in my hands. Smiling, I cross the room to set the camera on my study desk.

****

I sit at the dining room table in between Dad and Mother.

"Dressed for the occasion, I see," Mother remarks and sniffs loudly.

Since her sense of smell is as sensitive as mine or even more so, Mother might find me stinky. Luckily, I'm inured to my BO, thank goodness. Otherwise, I'd go crazy.

Of course, Mother might be sniffing the air to see if she can smell the dragon in the room, not that she can while his draconic form is incorporeal. Mother is a dragon hunting monster, and sitting across from us is Dr. Radcliffe, a dragon masquerading as human. His humanoid form is an elderly, slightly avuncular university professor, a profession he performed before The Incident at Tahoma University, where my dad works as a professor of computer science. Since The Incident, Mother and Dr. Radcliffe have an uneasy truce. He keeps Mother's identity secret in exchange for her not killing him and his handful of draconic followers on Earth.

The real Dr. Radcliffe is a colossal, golden-scaled dragon of the European variety with massive green wings and equally green tubes dangling from his snout like a drooping mustache. Right now, the dragon rides the slipstream, a dimension or wormhole or whatever connecting universes throughout the multiverse. What's trippy is I can see the dragon—all glimmering and fading in and out of existence—while it rides the slipstream. No one else can see it, not even Mother. Even trippier is the dragon passes in and out of the room and everyone in it, including me. A foreleg impales my chest. The Black woman sitting next to Dr. Radcliffe is inside his draconic abdomen. It's best not to dwell on these things.

I face Mother. "I'm inside my home. Unlike you, I don't wear pantsuits."

With bright, blood-red lipstick applied with a surveyor's precision, Mother could be a CEO or CIA assassin. She can almost pass off as human except the sclera around her irises is far too thin. A closer examination of her orbs reveals no color delineation between the pupils and irises. Her eyes are twin soul-churning black abysses surrounded by thin white ovals. What's weird is no one notices her eyes, not even my squad or the dragons or my dad, all who know she is not human. Agent Deveraux, the head of my protection detail, who sits across the table from us next to Dr. Radcliffe, believes my mother is human. The agent standing at Deveraux's shoulder is none the wiser too. How crazy is that?

I chalk it up to Mother's magic and everyone being afraid to call her out when it comes to her true identity.

Even me. I hate being a half-skaag, a monster girl, an abomination, but I still value my life. Cross Mother on this, and she'll crack my skull like an eggshell.

"You can at least pretend to care about your future, Allison," Mother says.

"I want to go to school, believe me." I slide to the right until my shoulder bumps against my dad's to be as far away from Mother as possible.

Mother clenches and unclenches her hands, which rest on the table, then lowers them out of sight. "Shall we begin?"

Agent Deveraux arches an eyebrow. "If the two of you are done sparring." She looks at both of us in turn. "Well, are you? We all know this will go faster after the two of you stop bickering."

Father whispers into my ear, "You don't always need to have the last word."

I turn to Agent Deveraux and nod. "I'm as ready as I'll ever be."

Mother gives me a sidelong glance I catch in my peripheral vision. Her lips form a toothless smile. Undoubtedly, she heard Father's whispered words to me. "We're ready to proceed."

Agent Deveraux nods and gives us a forced smile. "Excellent. Before we get started, I'd like to introduce you to a new member of your protection detail." Deveraux indicates the man standing at her shoulder. "This is Derek Brodie. He'll be filling in for Jim Haskell for the next week or so."

"What happened to Agent Haskell?" Mother asks.

"He's on sick leave."

"That's too bad." Mother leans forward, the chair creaking. "This new man…what's his name?"

"Derek Brodie," Brodie says.

"Agent Brodie doesn't seem up to the task of protecting my daughter. He's scrawny."

Deveraux's lips form a straight line, and I suspect she's fighting the urge to grind her teeth. Smirking, Dr. Radcliffe leans his elbows against the table and steeples his fingers. Brodie blanches, and his eyes, which are a little too far apart for his face, go wide. He is a pipsqueak compared to Agent Haskell, who is built like the Empire State Building on steroids. Still, I could tear off his arms without breaking a sweat, and the same goes for Agent Brodie's arms.

"I assure you Agent Brodie is fully qualified for this assignment," Deveraux says.

"We all know Allison is capable of protecting herself," Dr. Radcliffe says. "As I have stated previously, the agents are here to intimidate malefactors with their presence. Think of the agents as protecting"—the professor uses air quotes—"the crazies from Allison."

Dad raises his hand, making a placating signal. "Please, forgive my wife. We're sure Agent Brodie will perform his duties admirably. We're lucky to have him on the protection detail, and we wish Agent Haskell a speedy recovery."

Deveraux smiles stiffly. "I'm glad to hear it. Shall we move on?"

I shift in my chair and cross my arms before my chest. Moving on means the spotlight will shift off Brodie onto me.

"Of course, we're all anxious to learn the protocols in place for Allison returning to school," Mother says.

Dad nods in agreement.

Deveraux dismisses Brodie, who retreats from the dining room to the front hallway.

"First off, I want it known I don't agree with Allison returning to school," Deveraux says. "It is safest for Allison, her fellow students, and the school staff if she remains at home."

"What?" I bounce in the chair. "I don't want to do more remote school. I did it last year. It sucks."

"Do not worry, Allison, you will be returning to school," Dr. Radcliffe says with an indulgent smile.

"Good," I declare.

Deveraux jumps right in on the litany of protocols I must follow to attend school. I miss part of the spiel because I'm distracted by the front door opening, undoubtedly Agent Brodie letting himself out. From outside comes a cacophony I had managed to ignore, but with the front door open, I can hear with absolute clarity dozens of distinct voices declaring I'm an abomination who will burn in hell. The protesters clogging the sidewalk and street in front of the house are a mob ready to burn a witch at the stake.

Not all the crowds that gather in front of our house protest my existence, but most do. Some groups think I'm the second coming or a representative of an advanced alien civilization sent to lead humanity to the stars. My fans are as horrible as my detractors. I wish they'd all leave me alone, so I could go back to living my life.

I try to listen to Agent Deveraux, but it's hard. I can't turn off my preternatural hearing. I do get the gist of what is expected of me, though.

"Those idiots are going to follow me around in a car?" I ask. "God."

"If by those idiots you mean the security detail, yes." Agent Deveraux frowns. "I must insist you stop referring to my agents in a derogatory manner."

"I only have to let them follow me to and from school? They won't go inside?"

"Correct. As you know, the protesters are only allowed to gather on the street between the hours of nine a.m. to seven p.m."

"They shouldn't be allowed to gather at all," Mother says.

"I can have you relocated to the base if the protesters are bothersome," Deveraux says.

I'm about to jump out of my seat, but Dad places a firm hand on my shoulder. "That won't be necessary. We understand you're doing your best given a difficult situation."

Deveraux nods. "I simply ask, Allison, you arrive at school before nine a.m., which shouldn't be a problem since classes start eight forty-five. That way, you will avoid the protesters in the morning. After school, you are to return home promptly. The security detail will make sure you get inside the house without being molested."

Deveraux requires me to sign paperwork affirming I agree to follow the instructions of my security detail. I sign each line with a flourish, if not with the intent of obeying anyone's commands.

The meeting breaks up, and I'm feeling pleased. Dr. Radcliffe hangs back after Agent Deveraux leaves the room. He looks at me meaningfully, both the man and the translucent dragon, whose head projects down from the ceiling.

"What?" I snap.

"Allison, I hope you understand how hard I worked to keep you in your home and for you to return to school. Agent Deveraux is looking for any excuse to lock you away at Joint Base Lewis-McCord. Do not, my dear, do anything to set her off. My work heading the U.N. Draconic Task Force is taking me to New York and D.C. I might not be available to smooth things over if you...do anything untoward."

"I'll do my best." I cross my arms before my chest.

Chapter 2

I sit at my study desk, earbuds in, bobbing to the electronic beat of Dark Matter Electrica piped in from my ancient music player. The music helps drown out the shouting of the far-right nationals gathered outside on the street. They don't want to kill me so I can burn in hell, which is a nice change of pace. They want me to join their movement to help overthrow the government. Although our politics don't coincide, I'm less a fan of the government with each passing day. The few times I've been allowed outside the house, either to hang out with friends or to have my prosthetic eyes serviced, the conspicuous agents shadow my every move. It's stifling, and so is having to check in with the oh-so-wonderful Agent Deveraux every week. Sometimes I want to turn into a skaag to show those agents what they're "protecting" and the demonstrators what they're protesting, and then fly away into the sunset. Of course, doing anything like that will upset Agent Deveraux and win me a one-way trip to a lock-up on the military base.

That is unless I want to go rogue, which I don't. I want everything to go back to the way it was before The Incident. I want the protesters and agents to go back to wherever they're from. I want to go back to being the semi-anonymous girl at school. Most of all, I want Mother out of the house and out of my life. I wish I had never encountered her, even once.

I admire photos I took of the cherry tree in the front yard in the morning's wee hours displayed on my laptop. A glacial blue sky punctuated by pink clouds is behind the green leaves and branches playing out in fractal patterns. My computer dings. A text message from Dalia pops up and fades away in the screen's top right-hand corner.

I open the messaging app. I wish I could text as easily on my phone as my peers do, but I can't. All my dad allows me is an archaic pay-as-you-go flip phone, which makes texting a hassle, so the only thing the phone is good for is making calls. It's shocking how old school Dad is about tech, considering he's a frigging computer science prof.

—*Saw Leslie and Jason at cross country practice. They want to hang out.*—

I smile. Getting out for a little bit will be great. My room is like a cage, and there are still three weeks to go until school starts.

—*The protesters don't have to leave until 7.*—

—*I'll set something up for after 7. Cool?*—

—*Sure.*—

—*What about Haji?*—

My lips straighten. I jab out my response.

—*What about him?*—

—*Should I invite him or not?*—

I sigh and run a hand through my hair. I still haven't forgiven Haji for appearing on Devin's podcast, *Skaags and Dragons*. Devin is Dalia's ex and a complete bottom feeder. He has turned his involvement in The Incident into a podcasting empire by spinning apocryphal tales about me, the monster girl. It was quite a coup for the slimeball to interview Haji, who shared kisses with me in the wreckage of an automobile after I had saved Mauve, who happens to be a dragon, from my mother. I warned Haji not to go on the podcast, but he did anyway. I've scarcely said a word to him since. That was at the start of summer, nearly two months ago.

—It's OK. I'll not invite him.—

—Maybe I should forgive him.—

—He regrets going on the podcast.—

I rest an elbow on the table and start chewing on my lower lip. I'm glad he regrets going on the podcast, and maybe it's time to bury the hatchet. But am I ready? Maybe it doesn't matter if I'm not prepared. I should meet him now before school starts, so we can clear the air somewhere other than the hallways of Cascadia Prep. I'm about to type out a response when my door creaks.

Ripping out my earbuds by the cord, I spin in my chair to face the intruder, expecting my dad. Only it's not him in the doorway. A man dressed all in black points a handgun at me and raises a finger to his lips for silence.

Keeping the gun trained on me, he steps inside the room and quietly shuts the door. Inside me, the sleeper stirs, powerful and ravenous. I can break this man, this would-be assassin or whatever he is, but I need an opening. Even fueled by the sleeper's supernatural might, I doubt I can cross the room and disarm him before he pulls the trigger. I can transform, but that stratagem falls in the realm of last resort since my skaag form is bigger than the bedroom. Transforming might destroy the house.

"Stand," the intruder demands.

"Why should I? Are you going to shoot me?" I'm

more worried about Dad than I am for myself.

"I'll shoot you in the leg." He adjusts his aim.

"What if you hit my femoral artery? I'll bleed out." What did the gunman do to Dad? How in the world did he overcome Mother?

He frowns. "It doesn't matter where I shoot you as long as it's not immediately fatal. I know you heal fast. Now, stand up. Hands behind your head."

I comply. "How do you plan to escape with me as a prisoner? Since you know I can heal quickly from a gunshot wound, you probably know I'm faster and stronger than you. Do you really think you can walk out of here, avoiding the security detail, with me in tow? Take your eyes off me for a second, I'll disarm you and break your arm in the process."

Sweat rolls down his brow. "Stifle it. Turn around. Keep your hands behind your head."

"You're making a mistake." I can't believe he overcame Mother. Taking me by surprise is one thing, but overcoming Mother, a battle-hardened, magic-wielding, full-fledged skaag, is next level.

"We have your parents downstairs. You don't start doing what you're told without giving me lip, they'll get hurt."

Dad shouts from downstairs, followed by a loud thud, but no gunshot. I drop my hands and dart toward the intruder. Before he can pull the trigger, I'm on him, wrenching the gun up and to the side. Burning pain lacerates my right shoulder, and the crack of the gun is deafening. I'm more surprised than hurt because the sleeper's prowess courses through my veins.

I tear the gun from his hand, which falls with a thump to the carpet. Rage and hunger not entirely mine alone muddle my thoughts. Kill this tool. Feed upon his flesh.

The man pistons a fist into my face, serving to enrage the sleeper further. I grab him around the crotch with one hand and hurl him against the wall. He slumps to the floor next to the door with a dazed expression plastered on his face.

My right arm goes numb, and blood moistens my deltoid. I hold up my left hand, palm outward. "Stay down. I don't want to hurt you." I leave out the fact the sleeper desires nothing more than to eat him alive.

Snarling, the man crouches, pulling a knife from a boot sheath. He hurls the weapon with frightening accuracy. I duck to keep the blade from piercing my throat. Growling, I charge him, leading with a left hook. My fist crashes into his jaw, breaking bones and snapping tendons. The blow slams him into the wall, twisting his neck unnaturally to the side. He falls to the floor and does not move.

Breathing hard, I stare, willing him to show a sign of life. "Oh my God. What did I do?"

I'm vaguely aware of shouts from downstairs. I try to concentrate on the shouting to keep me in the here and now, but hunger pangs knot my abdomen, and the sleeper's savage desires promise to erase my burgeoning guilt at what I have done.

****

"Allison. Allison, wake up." Fingers burrow into my shoulders.

"What?" I mutter, blinking my surroundings into focus to discover I'm on the floor in the middle of my bedroom. Only something isn't right. My right arm throbs, red stains the carpet, and a metallic tang permeates the air. "What happened?"

Mother stands over me. Even in the aftermath of whatever happened, she looks ready to walk the fashion runway.

"Was I shot? There was a man with a gun. I hurt him." I turn to face the door. I glimpse my listless assailant slumped against the wall. "What have I done?"

"Look at me, Allison," Mother says, utterly calm and commanding. I'm unable to tear my gaze away from her hypnotic apertures. "You killed the man in self-defense. That is all. Do you understand?"

"I killed him in self-defense. That is all."

"Excellent. Proceed to the shower. The bullet passed straight through you. It's barely more than a graze. As long as you clean the wound thoroughly, you'll be right as rain in a few hours."

"Yes, Mother."

I stand, and she rises with me. I turn to the entrance and, noticing my would-be assassin, wonder who he is. A firm voice much like my mother's echoes in my skull: *That's not important right now. Do as you're told.*

"What about Daddy?" I ask as I open the door and step into the hallway. At the top of the stairs, an agent stands guard. From the bottom floor come voices, not one my father's. "The gunman told me he has accomplices."

Mother's red lips twitch upward in a ghost of a smile. "Your father is fine, Allison. As you may recall, I don't like Agent Brodie. He will no longer be part of your protection detail. Now, go shower."

****

Red water sheets down my right arm. The shower scalds my skin, and steam fogs the stall's glass door. A modicum of relief assuages my burgeoning guilt over the gunman. I hurt him...killed him, but I didn't surrender to the sleeper's primal urges. I'm still mostly human.

Someone opens the bathroom door.

"Who is it?"

"You forgot to turn on the fan," Mother says, and the fan begins droning.

Mother fusses around the bathroom. I can't tell what she's doing through the fogged glass. I'm tempted to wipe away a patch of mist, but I don't want Mother to see me nude with the blood-stained water running off me.

"I'm removing the clothes you were wearing. I'm afraid they will be taken away by Agent Deveraux's people. I've brought you fresh clothes."

Without warning, Mother opens the shower stall.

"Boundaries! Hello?"

Mother studies me with a mortician's detachment. "Make sure you scrub the wound, Allison, and don't take too long. Your father is putting off Agent Deveraux, but she's growing impatient. She won't wait much longer before insisting on seeing you whether you're presentable or not."

****

In a windowless room in the JAG Office on Joint Base Lewis-McCord, I sit between my parents at a conference table across from Agent Deveraux and several older men in the military uniforms of high-ranking officers. The room smells musty, and the youngest officer wears too much cologne.

I glance at the flat screen affixed to the nondescript wall next to the door. "Will Dr. Radcliffe be joining us?"

Deveraux looks up from the folder opened before her on the table. "I'm afraid not. He has meetings in D.C. that can't be rescheduled."

I sink in the chair. The draconic leader had warned me he might not be able to help me if I screwed up. Since the failed kidnapping attempt, my family has been forced to live on base under constant military protection. We're essentially prisoners.

"Can I still go back to school?"

"The short answer is yes," Deveraux says.

"Yes!" I bounce in the chair, my lips parting into a ten-gigawatt smile.

"Thank goodness," Dad says.

"Have you learned anything about Agent Brodie or his accomplice?" Mother demands.

The officers look abashed, but Deveraux flashes a toothless grin. "That is still under investigation."

The officer wearing too much cologne adds, "You'll have to forgive us, ma'am, if we're not forthcoming about the abduction attempt. It's a matter of national security."

The other two officers nod, faces grim.

"That's convenient," I murmur.

Deveraux arches an eyebrow. "You have something to say, Allison?"

Dad nudges me in the side.

"No. I just want to get back to school. Real school. I don't think I could survive a year of remote."

The oldest officer clears his throat. "Yes, well, there is one condition. We have prepared a cover story for what happened to account for the gunman's death. Basically, your mother killed the gunman in self-defense and defense of you. This will play better in the media and with the public than if you killed him."

"Oh, yes, I'm the monster girl." I turn to Mother. "You already knew about this?"

"Of course. It's for the best," Mother says. "I believe it is Dr. Radcliffe's idea."

"It's Radcliffe's idea," Deveraux confirms.

"All we need you to do, young lady, is sign this memo." The officer passes a letter on DoD letterhead across the table.

Smirking, I take the paper. They have no idea Dr. Radcliffe and my mother have duped them. They think Mother is an ordinary human. They have no idea my mother is the skaag Druk, an implacable killing machine feared throughout the multiverse.

"Take your time reading it," the officer says and offers me a pen.

Chapter 3

The blaring alarm clock startles me awake. Groaning, I roll in bed and paw at the bedside table, fingers questing for the diabolical device. Efforts in vain, I open my eyes to what should be a dark bedroom. Only it's not for me. My prosthetic eyes have superior light gathering capability, so all the lights might as well be on and the blinds pulled up to allow in the noonday sun.

I turn off the alarm and glimpse the time.

Seven-thirty.

a.m.

I stifle a yawn and slip out of bed. There is no way I'm going to be late for my first day of junior year. My first day of real school since The Incident. I'm not going to allow the fact I lay awake half the night obsessing over how I will react to seeing Haji at my front door this morning make me late. There's nothing to worry about; Dalia will be with us to referee.

In the center of the room, I come to a dead stop. A swath of wall to the right of the door holds my gaze. Only I see more than the wall. I see the gunman's crumpled form with his neck twisted at a grossly unnatural angle. My stomach grumbles, and I taste sourness.

Blinking, I shake my head, and the dead man disappears. *He shot you. What you did was in self-*

defense. Nothing more. Nothing less. Yet, no matter how many times I remind myself of that, I can't shake the feeling I'm becoming my mother, a killing machine. Sure, I had been shot, but did that justify losing control, allowing the sleeper to emerge violent and unfettered? I could have overpowered the gunman with a fraction of my half-skaag strength, but instead I had punched him with full force or close enough to make no difference.

I head to the shower, hoping scalding water will wash away some of my guilt. All it does is pinken my skin. I return to my room to dress and am pulling on my black skinny jeans when my gaze falls on the hole in the wall the bullet made after passing through my deltoid. The bullet had lodged in a stud and was removed as evidence. Dad plans to patch the hole, but I don't know if I want him to. I need the reminder of what happens when I lose control. The doorbell rings, seeming insanely loud this early in the morning.

"Seriously?" I murmur and check the clock.

Seven forty-five. Strange. My squad shouldn't be here until closer to eight fifteen.

"Timmy is at the door," a man's voice with a British accent emits from speakers in the hallway and the living room.

"Why is Timmy outside at this hour?" I snatch the oversized white shirt off the bed and pull it on. Then I'm striding from my room, galloping down the hall, and running down the stairs. I'll die if Mother does something bad to Timmy. He's just a harmless kid, albeit a strange and extremely annoying one. As I round the stairs into the entry hallway, I call to Mother, who is in the kitchen, "I got it! I got it!"

"Excellent. I find that boy insufferable," Mother

says.

The doorbell jingles again. A few seconds later, the British butler announces, "Timmy is at the door."

A growl rumbling in my chest, I skid across the wooden floor coming to a halt before the front door. I plaster a cheery smile on my face and open the door. I shiver as the cold air caresses my cheeks. I make a mental note to wear my heavy winter coat to school. Timmy stands on the stoop dressed in a T-shirt, shorts, and garishly blue high tops. His blond hair sticks up like porcupine quills. Behind sporty glasses, his blue eyes are bright and excited. The cold seems not to affect him. Sometimes I wonder if Timmy is human. I sniff, detecting along with a smorgasbord of other scents, Timmy's distinctively human little boy body odor, which is an amalgamation of urine and sweat partially obscured by soap.

"Hi, Allison! Can I take a selfie with you?" Timmy hefts a phone.

"Shouldn't you be getting ready for school right now?"

"I am ready, and it only takes me five minutes to walk to school. Plenty of time for a selfie."

"Okay, but didn't we take one a few days ago?"

"We took one last week, but I need a new one because I have a bet with this boy, Toby, I can get another. I have ten bucks on the line. You don't want me to lose, right?"

"You don't post these pictures on that website, do you?"

Timmy scrunches up his eyes, causing his glasses to slide up the bridge of his nose. "Website?"

"I don't remember what it's called. My security

detail warned me about it. People post pictures of me there, so I'm easier to spot even after I change my hair color, whatever. It makes it super hard to avoid reporters."

"What? No way! I don't do that. I wanna win the ten bucks. Then I'll have twenty. Can we take a selfie? Can we? Can we? Please."

"Just a sec." I wave aside the hand clutching the phone he thrusts in my face. I stare over his head past the cherry tree with its branches stirring in the breeze to the dark sedan parked across the street. My jaw tightens. At least the protesters aren't here—yet. I'd hate for Timmy to come over with them clogging the sidewalk and street. "Okay. Let's take a picture."

I take a knee, and Timmy sidles up next to me.

Timmy snaps a picture. "Come on. Happy face. Happy face."

I flash the best smile I can muster this early in the morning. Timmy snaps a couple more shots. We say our farewells, and I head inside to gobble up breakfast before my friends arrive.

The savory scent of garlic chicken sausage and the rich aroma of coffee fill the dining room. My gaze settles on the place setting next to the head of the table, a plate with three chicken sausages and a steaming mug of coffee. Without warning, my stomach rumbles as loud as a trumpeting elephant, and my abdomen knots. The grimace distorting my features has nothing to do with food or hunger. Mother sits at the head of the table wearing a slate gray suit, not a single strand of her mid-neck length black hair out of place.

"What smells so good?" Dad remarks as he walks past me toward the kitchen. "Oh, look, Allison, your mother made breakfast." He pauses next to Mother to give her a peck on the cheek. Her lips perk upward. "You're so sweet, dear."

"Your oatmeal is on the stove, Raymond," Mother says, glancing at my father. She turns her attention back to me. "Sit, Allison. Eat. You don't have much time before your friends arrive."

"You didn't have to make coffee," I say stiffly and pull out the chair that scrapes against the wooden floor. I sit and snatch a sausage off the plate. I take a bite of the sausage, smacking my lips and chewing with my mouth open.

Mother looks at the fork and knife next to the plate, then back to me. "You don't have to eat like a barbarian."

"I'm in a rush," I say between bites.

Her jaw muscles quiver.

I snag the second sausage and shove half of it into my mouth.

"Proper etiquette costs you nothing, Allison."

"This oatmeal smells great. Thanks for making it, hon," Dad declares as he strides into the dining room, holding a bowl with steam rising from it. He sits next to Mother.

Mother smiles, this time showing teeth. "I'm so glad you appreciate it, dear." She pats his hand and turns back to me, eyes narrowing. "It's so wonderful to have my efforts appreciated. Allison, why don't you try your coffee? You won't be able to stay awake at school without at least one cup."

Dad looks at me expectantly as he eats his oatmeal. "Try it, Allison. I had a cup in the kitchen. Your mother is getting good at making coffee."

Reluctantly, I grab the mug, which radiates heat. Dad's words aren't the ringing endorsement he thinks. I sip the brew and scowl. The coffee is almost scalding but as weak as tap water. I'm about to give my unfiltered opinion when the doorbell rings.

Seconds later, the ever-irritating English butler announces, "Dalia and Haji are at the door."

Before I can even set the mug on the table, Mother is halfway across the dining room, heading for the entry. "I'll let your friends in, Allison. I expect you to finish your entire breakfast before leaving."

I'm about to leap from the chair and race her to the front door when a hand resting gently on my wrist stops me. I stare at Dad. He squeezes my wrist.

"She's going to embarrass me." The words coming out like a snarl.

Dad smiles. "Relax, Allison. Finish your breakfast, and drink your coffee. That will make your mother feel appreciated."

The front door's hinges squeak.

"Hi, Mrs. Lee. It's a cold one out this morning."

Haji's voice short circuits my anger. I'm not ready to deal with him. Not now, not yet. Telling Dalia he could tag along with us was a mistake.

Laughter drifts from the living room.

"What's wrong?" Dad asks.

I rip my hand from his grip and stand, nearly upending the chair. "She's telling jokes."

"She's getting quite good at it," Dad says.

"You'll laugh at anything."

"Allison, wait. At least drink the coffee."

I turn back to the table and seize the mug and gulp down the weak brew, battling my gag reflex the entire time. I slam the cup onto the table. "Satisfied?"

Dad says something, but I'm not listening. I'm storming to the living room on a mission to save my friends from Mother's terrible jokes. Dalia's laughter is brittle, but Haji sounds like he's having a good belly laugh. Figures he'd find Mother funny. Her jokes are the variety that make dumb dad jokes seem hilarious.

I enter the living room to find my squad on the couch. Dalia has the decency to look stiff, but Haji doubles over with laughter.

"What kind of meat does a vulture eat?" Mother asks.

"Seriously? You haven't figured out that's a terrible one yet?" I stand inside the entryway. "Let's go. Before she breaks out the rest of her standup routine."

Dalia leaps from the cushion, shoulder-length neon pink hair bobbing, and makes a beeline for me. "Allison! Ready?"

Haji is slower to rise, but he's stopped laughing. Even he thinks the vulture joke might not be funny.

"Definitely," I say. "Let's roll."

"Just in time," Dalia whispers.

I wince and mouth, "She can hear you."

Dalia's cheeks redden.

Mother looks from us to Haji and back again. Her lips droop into a severe frown, and her voice is deadpan when she asks, "Don't you want to hear the punchline?" No one answers for a beat too long. "What? Are my jokes truly as bad as my daughter claims?"

Dalia faces her. "No. No, they're funny. What was the joke again?"

Mother arches an eyebrow.

"I got it! I got it!" Haji says excitedly. "Dead meat.

What kind of meat does a vulture eat? Dead meat."

He can barely contain his giggling as he says this.

"I'm so glad you find the joke funny, Haji. I made it up myself."

"I do love a corny joke," Haji says, adding at motormouth speed, "Not that your jokes are corny."

"Don't worry, Haji, I understand your sentiment, and I won't bite you...unless I'm famished." Mother turns back to me with a twinkle in her eyes. "You see, Allison, my jokes are improving."

Chapter 4

My compatriots and I set a fast pace down the concrete path riddled with cracks. A stiff breeze picks up, carrying the stench of car exhaust and the earthy scent of decaying leaves. A handful of leaves fall from the cherry tree next to the sidewalk, making a twirling descent to the splotchy brown and green grass to join their fallen brethren. It's early for the leaves to drop— maybe as much as a month—but a heatwave stretching from June through July had taxed all the flora.

The security detail, two burly men in dark trench coats, sit in an idling black sedan across the street.

"How typical," I mutter and dart across the street.

"Allison, wait up," Dalia calls.

I stop in front of the sedan and slam my palm against the hood, glaring at the goliath Agent Haskell in the driver's seat and his average proportioned partner. The men exchange startled looks before turning their attention back to me.

I flip them the bird. "Don't idle your car!"

Grimacing, Haskell lowers his window. "I turned on the engine just before you stepped out the door."

"Can't you drive an electric or at least a hybrid?"

"I can ask," Haskell says lightly.

"Good." I pound the hood once more for good measure then cross the street to rejoin my squad.

"Was that smart?" Haji asks.

"What?"

"Pounding on their car," Haji says.

"Flipping them off," Dalia says.

"I didn't get much sleep last night, and the agents are annoying on the best of days. Okay?"

Without waiting for a response, I set off down the sidewalk lined with deciduous trees. The leaves are in various phases of turning from green into yellows or oranges or reds. The fresh air is invigorating, and I force myself to slow my pace. I shouldn't be so waspish this early in the morning. I haven't even had to face down protesters or reporters yet.

My friends catch up by the time I hang a right onto the main drag chock-full of vehicles belching greenhouse gas from tailpipes. The security detail stalks us in the sedan.

Haji tries to maneuver between Dalia and me, but my BFF sidesteps over until our shoulders are touching. With a soft sigh, Haji slides in next to Dalia.

"You've changed your hair," Haji says. "I like it. The blue looks good."

"I don't. I wish I could keep it forest green, but that makes it too easy to pick me out in a crowd."

"I liked your hair orange," Dalia says.

"I would've kept my hair orange except for that stupid website," I say.

Dalia nods sympathetically, and I think Haji does too, but I'm doing my best not to look at him, so I can't be sure.

"Sometimes...sometimes I think I have to totally change my style not to be recognized. Like—" I shrug "—wear a dress or something."

"That I have to see," Haji says. "Do you even own

a dress?"

"Please, Haji, how can you even ask that question? You know she doesn't own a dress," Dalia says. "Changing your style up a bit might help. You're coming to the march, right?"

"CO2 Free Seattle? Of course." I'm mildly scandalized Dalia thinks I might not participate. She is heavily involved in the local climate movement, often helping to organize our peers to join the various protests around the area.

"Well, if you want to be super inconspicuous, you can wear one of my dresses."

"I think it would be a miniskirt on me."

Haji goes googly-eyed at this remark, so I pointedly turn my gaze straight ahead, concentrating on the sidewalk and taillights.

"That's true, but think about it," Dalia says. "Throw on some dark sunglasses to go with the dress, and no one will ever guess it's you."

"You're definitely going to go to the march?" Haji asks.

"That's what I said," I reply.

"I want to be sure." Haji says, words running over each other. "You know, with the security detail following you around and—" His voice drops to a whisper. "—your mother, I don't want to make assumptions. I plan on running a story about CO2 Free Seattle in *The Weekly*. If you're not going to photograph it, I'll have to ask Leslie. *The Weekly's* readership expects top-shelf photography."

"I'm going to the march, Haji. I'll take pictures for the paper."

"Blog, you mean," Dalia says snidely.

"*The Cascadia Weekly* is not a blog," Haji declares. "A better term is online periodical."

My friends continue sniping at each other as we come to the crosswalk leading to Cascadia Prep across the busy street. Behind a stand of Douglas fir is a squat blue and white building. Good old Cascadia Prep.

News vans are parked up and down the road. Dread slithers along the back of my neck, leaving behind its slimy residue, at the sight of a gauntlet of reporters congesting the sidewalk. A few of my peers are already giving interviews. My prosthetics zoom like camera lenses, and I inspect my peers. Only passing acquaintances. I wonder how many lie about our relationship to get their faces on TV.

"Fantastic," I mutter.

"Don't worry," Dalia says. "You'll be fine. They aren't allowed on campus, remember? Dr. Radcliffe saw to that. With your blue hair, we'll breeze right past them into the building before they even know you're there."

"I hope so," I say.

The light changes, and we cross the street. The black sedan is stopped at the light, the security agents eyeballing me. I wish they'd do something useful, like clear out the media.

As we step onto the sidewalk, someone calls, "There she is! Right there with the blue hair!"

The reporters rush toward me, armed with cameras and microphones, like prehistoric hunters moving in for the kill after following a trail of fresh blood. Microphones and cameras are shoved in my face as reporters scuffle and shout questions. I squint against the flares of firing flashes. A video camera lens zooms in on my face like the cyclopean eye of a diabolical artificial intelligence. Squealing, a reporter in a skirt and high heels topples from the sidewalk into the shrubbery—the poor bushes crack under her weight. I try to break free from the snarl, but the journalists surround me in a feeding frenzy.

"Is it true someone attempted to kidnap you?"

"How did your mother overcome the assailants?"

I chew on my tongue to keep from snarling that I snapped the neck of the man who attacked me with my bare hands. The insalubrious memories and questions cause the well of guilt in my gut to overflow. Why did I lose control? Why?

"Allison, is it true you closed the gateway?"

"Do you know magic?"

"Are the huge alligator eel pictures circulating in the media and online of you?"

I almost shout: that's my mother; she's at home right now. Maybe you should go harass her. But I keep my lips zipped.

"What's your relationship to Dr. Radcliffe, leader of the U.N. Draconic Task Force?"

"Let me through. I have class."

"What was that?"

"Speak up, Allison. I can't hear you."

"Are you responsible for the destruction of the suspension bridge at the Grove of the Patriarchs?"

"Let me through!" I yell.

Instead of being discouraged, the reporters press in even tighter, shrieking their questions. The disgusting amalgamation of their body odor, morning breath, and cheap coffee grabs hold of me like a riptide. I clench my jaw. I desire to toss the mob aside like straw dolls, but I don't dare. Doing that means unleashing the sleeper, and this time, innocent people will be hurt or die for simply asking irritating questions.

A hand takes hold of mine. I nearly pull away, but it's Dalia. My squad. My fam. She doesn't know I've become my mother. If I lose control, she'll see I'm a killing machine unable to stop myself.

Haji pulls up beside Dalia and bellows in his impersonation of a sports broadcaster. "Look! Holy cow! That's a dragon! It's Dr. Radcliffe!"

You'd think veteran journalists would be too jaded to fall for such an obvious ploy, but they're too ravenous for anything vaguely draconic not to look. Dalia drags me through a gap in the scrum. We take the stairs two at a time to the doors and enter the relative sanctuary of Cascadia Prep.

When we reach the school's common room, the throng of journalists is a bitter memory. What I face now, standing at the room's periphery, is as daunting— nearly one thousand five hundred of my peers, or near enough to make no difference. Most stand around confabulating, but a few of them stride through the crowd as purposeful as honeybees gathering pollen. The activity takes place under the watchful gaze of a blue titan, the school mascot, painted on the far wall.

"Oh, wow," I whisper.

"What?" Dalia asks, beside me.

"I haven't been around this many people for like…it seems forever," I say.

"Since The Incident," Dalia says.

"Yeah. I don't want to go in there." I swear people are giving me sideways glances. "Someone will recognize me. I'll be mobbed. Again."

We retreat down the hall, and Haji, smiling broadly, rejoins us. We huddle next to the blue lockers lining the hallway.

"You look as pleased as a well-fed cat," Dalia remarks.

"I'm rather proud of myself." Haji points at the ceiling. "Look. There's Dr. Radcliffe."

Haji laughs, and even Dalia cracks a smile, but I don't join in their mirth.

"How did they recognize me by my blue hair? That website?"

Haji nods grimly and fishes his phone out of his pants pocket.

"Don't you ever visit monsterspotting.com? It's all about you." Haji turns the phone so I can see the screen.

"As if I want to visit any website that's all about me being a monster." My mouth drops open. Displayed front and center on the website are my face and blue mop. "Timmy! That little brat. He took that picture of me this morning. He was in it. He cropped himself out."

Haji taps the screen with his thumb. "Let me see who posted this."

"You let him take another selfie with you?" Dalia says. "I warned you about him. It's weird for a little boy to want to take pictures with you all the time."

"I'm a celebrity. I don't like being one, but I am." I shrug. "He told me he doesn't post any pictures to that website."

Haji shows me a screen full of thumbnails of me with my hair dyed in different colors. "All uploaded by user tinytim123."

"That punk. Next time he comes over, I'll let my mother answer the door."

We meander around the hallways trying to avoid prying eyes until the bell rings, announcing it's time to head for class. Haji sets off for his first period class while Dalia and I tromp to trigonometry. Upon entering the classroom, I catch a whiff of Mr. Leonard's forest-scented cologne. Technically, he's not supposed to wear cologne, but he does sweat a lot.

"Allison," Mr. Leonard says in his chocolatey voice. He smiles broadly to show off perfectly straight, bright white teeth. "My celebrity pupil. Welcome. Welcome. How are you today, young lady?"

I give my best fake smile. "Great, Mr. Leonard."

He spreads his arms expansively. "Take a seat wherever you like. Dalia. Welcome."

I fight off the urge to cringe as I head to a desk in the back of the classroom. That's one great thing about my prosthetic eyes. I can sit anywhere and still read what the teachers scrawl on the whiteboards. I unsling my backpack and flop down at a desk, chair squeaking. Dalia sits at the desk next to mine.

When my peers start trickling into the classroom, their gazes inevitably lock onto me like flies drawn to carrion. Some are polite enough to look away, but others openly stare like I'm an exotic animal on display at the zoo. A gaggle of girls comes in, and they have a whispered conversation about me. Of course, I can hear every word. It's hard not to listen when you're the topic of conversation. It's nothing bad—just offhand remarks about my hair.

Dalia takes her schedule from her backpack and distracts me by talking about all our classes together. Still, every time someone whispers my name, I look. I can't help it. That's the problem with heightened senses.

Finally, the desks fill up, and Mr. Leonard addresses the class. "Greetings, pupils. Welcome to your first day of the new school year. Before I get started, I want to acknowledge we have a celebrity in our class"—the teacher's gaze settles on me—"Allison Lee."

My face flushes. Everyone turns to stare at me.

Chapter 5

By lunchtime, I'm ready for the school day to be over. Trigonometry with Mr. Leonard was the morning's worst period, but my other classes weren't cakewalks. I sit in the corner of the common room at a circular table with my friends. Dalia sits between Haji and me. He seems to have accepted the arrangement as he bites into his peanut butter and jelly sandwich with gusto, but I suspect he's tempted to drag his chair around the table to sit next to me. I try to enjoy my turkey meatballs kept warm by an insulated container, but Haji isn't the only one eyeing me up. I swear everyone stares at me. It's like their eyeballs have grown tentacles and are slithering over everything leaving behind gooey trails, including on me.

"What class do you have after lunch?" Haji asks between bites of sandwich.

"Photography," I say with a wan smile.

"That's great," Dalia says. She's hardly pecked at her vegetarian lunch. "You love that class." She digs through her backpack, pulling out the class schedule. All the classes we have together are highlighted in pink. "Our next class together is AP English with Mrs. Achebe." Dalia looks at me quizzically. "Mrs. Achebe?"

I shrug.

"She is super strict," Haji says.

"You've had her class already?" Dalia asks.

"Jason told me. He has her for second period."

Jason is a senior, a cross country phenom and my one-time heartthrob. Not that long ago the mere mention of his name would set my heart thundering and my mind whirling through wild romantic scenarios.

"Strict is great," I say. "All eyes front and center on the whiteboard. No rubberneckers staring at me."

"Has it been that bad?" Haji asks.

"What do you think?" I scarf a meatball without tasting it.

"Excuse me. Allison? Allison Lee?"

My mouth gapes like an open garage door when I see who speaks to me.

"Can I take your picture?" the matronly school resource officer asks, hefting her supersized smartphone.

My gaping mouth obviously shows off the partially masticated meatball resting on my tongue.

The officer's cheeks flush. "Sorry. I wouldn't even ask, but the guys at work have been nagging at me about it for weeks."

I clamp my mouth shut and start chewing. My initial reaction is to say no way, but respect for the municipal muscle is so ingrained I can't get the words out. Maybe it's the gun and taser strapped at her waist or the gleaming badge pinned to her chest jamming the words in my throat. The firearm draws my gaze. I massage my right shoulder where I was shot.

"Officer Elliott, aren't you supposed to be doing paperwork or something?" Leslie looms over us like a Valkyrie.

Officer Elliott starts and fumbles her phone,

snagging it before it plummets to the floor. She cranes her neck to glare at Leslie, who stands at least six feet.

"What did you just say to me?" the officer demands.

"I'm introducing myself, Officer Elliott," Leslie says with a smile that's fool's gold. "I'm Leslie Walker. You've probably heard of my father. George Walker. He was elected to the city council in the special election."

"Nice to meet you," the officer splutters and waddles off.

Sometimes it pays off to have the most entitled, meanest White girl in the school as one of your friends. We weren't always friends. We used to be rivals for Jason's affection and the position of top photog in school. Leslie won the boy, and I'm okay with that. Jason is still a friend, but it would've never worked out between us in a romantic relationship. Leslie and I still compete to be the best photographer, but the rivalry has turned from cutthroat to friendly.

Leslie watches the officer trundle away, then pulls the last chair at the table over next to me and sits, eliminating the possibility of Haji maneuvering beside me. "Did she seriously ask to take a picture of you?"

I nod. "Thanks. You're a lifesaver."

"That's so unprofessional." Leslie shakes her head.

"How's your dad like being on the council?" Haji asks.

I bite into another savory meatball.

Leslie shrugs. "We don't talk much lately. He's busy with his business and being a big shot politician."

"How are your classes, Leslie?" Dalia asks.

Leslie flashes a sour smile. "Calculus is going to be

hard."

We talk about our morning classes while polishing off our lunches. When the five-minute warning bell sounds, we're all packed up and ready to head to our classes, even Haji, who had been steadily eating the whole time. When he stands, he is as tall as Leslie. When did that happen?

"You have photography next, right, Allison?" Leslie asks.

"I do. I've been looking forward to it all day. Finally, a class that's fun."

"That's my next class, too," Leslie says. "Let's go."

I walk through the halls within Leslie's magical aura. Our peers notice her before recognizing me. Instead of mobbing me, they bask in Leslie's radiance. I don't know how she does it. She takes it in stride, I guess. I'd find being her exhausting.

"Hey, that's not cool. You should ask first," Leslie barks at the school's hotshot wide receiver who is about to take my picture with his phone.

"Sorry. Can I take a picture, Allison?" he asks.

I shake my head in the negative, and to my surprise, he lowers his phone and slips it into his pocket with a shrug. "Sorry. That was rude of me."

We enter the photography lab, a room full of long desks with thirty-inch widescreen monitors, with a minute to spare and sit together at the front of the class. People trickle in, filling the seats.

"Did you make it to Artist Point with your dad?" I ask. Artist Point is a spot near North Cascades National Park famous for its photogenic beauty.

Leslie shakes her head. "No. He's pissed I refused

to stop hanging out with you. He thinks the association will be bad for his political career."

"Oh, jeez."

"Don't worry about it. He's been a total jerk since being elected," Leslie whispers and falls silent as Mr. Eldridge, the photography teacher, strides before the class.

Leslie's words leave me feeling remorseful my being a monster has disrupted her relationship with her father, but I'm also reminded I'm not the only person struggling with family for one reason or another. Of course, my mother is a monstrous killing machine, but still.

"Greetings, class," Mr. Eldridge says with a voice made raspy from years of smoking before giving it up a decade ago. He is bespectacled and tall, almost gaunt with a cue ball for a cranium. His opening remarks abruptly end when he gasps for breath and retreats to his desk. Leaning heavily against the desk, he struggles to breathe.

"Mr. Eldridge? Are you okay?" I ask.

Leslie already has her phone out and looks prepared to dial. Mr. Eldridge holds up a hand and gives a thumbs up. He speaks in an indecipherable whisper. Murmurs of concern resound around the class.

Mr. Eldridge maneuvers himself to sit on the edge of his desk and takes a deep breath. "Apologies for that. As some of you might be aware, I was absent for most of the second semester last year. In February, I underwent surgery to have part of my left lung removed. Cancer."

"Oh my God," I gasp. I knew Mr. Eldridge had missed large portions of last school year due to chemotherapy, but the surgery is news to me. Leslie puts a hand on my shoulder and squeezes reassuringly.

Mr. Eldridge gives a strained smile. "I'm happy to say that today I'm cancer free. Unfortunately, my lung capacity isn't what it used to be. Not yet. Sometimes I become short of breath, but don't worry. I'm okay. In fact"—he claps his hands—"I feel better than I have in months. Now, let's move on and discuss the expectations for portfolios this semester."

My excitement builds as Mr. Eldridge talks about ideas for portfolios, occasionally fielding questions from students. He finishes his spiel without losing his breath again, and I can believe he truly is okay, and his class will remain a safe place where I can express myself through photography. My portfolio will document the various climate actions around Seattle, starting with CO2 Free Seattle.

When the bell dings announcing the end of class, I'm pumped to start working on my portfolio. I'm swinging my backpack over my shoulder when Mr. Eldridge meanders over.

"Allison, do you have a moment?" he asks.

I glance at Leslie, who waits for me. "I'll catch up."

Leslie nods. "Great class today, Mr. E."

My friend glides out of the classroom, and I turn my attention to the photography teacher. He looks older than I remember, his skin drawn tight over his skull, and his scalp is liver-spotted. How much life did cancer steal from him?

Mr. Eldridge smiles and sits on the table's edge. "I want you to feel comfortable in my class, Allison. Safe. More generally, I want this for all your time spent at school and in every aspect of your life. I know over the past year…to put it lightly, life has thrown you some curveballs. If you need someone to talk to about what happened or what you're going through…I want you to know you can talk to me. I won't judge you." Mr. Eldridge smiles, warm and genuine. "That is to say, I'll do my best not to judge you. I'm a good listener."

"No!" I say. He can't know about what I have done. He can't.

"Okay." He holds up his hands. "That's okay."

"Since The Incident, I want some normal. That's all."

"I won't bring it up again, but my offer stands in case you change your mind. And don't worry. I'll do my best to make this class your slice of normal."

"Thanks, Mr. Eldridge," I say, and I'm about to leave, but I pause. "Are you okay? With the cancer?"

"I am, Allison. You don't need to worry about me."

"Honestly?"

"My policy is to never lie to my students."

After school, I'm walking home with Haji since Dalia has cross-country practice. The fall afternoon is warm, and a gentle breeze rustles the turning leaves. We cut through the school grounds to avoid the news vans parked out front. We end up stopping at a red light at the first intersection, but we thankfully evade the press. Cars driven by boys hyped up on too much testosterone peel out while making right turns. A school bus rolls by, and I'm heartened to see it's a new electric—quiet, odorless, and best of all, green.

The light turns, and we're off. I'm tempted to set a fast pace Haji will struggle to maintain, but I don't.

Despite still being angry, I can't make myself drive him away. I fear it will feel like kicking a puppy or something. He's not my boyfriend any longer, but he's still a friend. If I want to keep him as a compadre, I need to figure out how to make this work. Besides, if I can stand the security detail following me around like a bunch of creeps, I can tolerate Haji.

"Was your first day back as bad as you expected?" Haji asks.

"Yes and no." I give him a quick synopsis of my day.

He waves aside my concerns. "It can only get better, you know. Once the novelty wears off, everything will go back to normal. People forget. Just like what happened with your prosthetics. No one mentions those anymore."

"I hope so," I say without conviction.

"Well," Haji says, sounding pleased, "Keb called me after school just before you showed up. He wants to schedule me on the podcast to talk about magic."

"I hope you told him no."

"Yeah, yeah, of course."

"Haji, you said no, right?"

"I didn't say yes."

"You know I don't want you to do more interviews with Devin." I stop in my tracks and glower.

Haji stares at me with an aggrieved expression. "But the episode won't be about you. It's about magic. I said I wouldn't do it if your name comes up in any context. I swear."

"And Keb said Devin won't utter a word about me, right?"

"Yeah, of course. You know Keb. He's

trustworthy."

"Keb is great, but he's not the one asking the questions. Keb will say one thing and honestly mean it, but Devin will do whatever he wants. You know that."

"Allison…"

I get up into his personal space and crane my neck to stare into his kind, clueless brown eyes. I put my index finger underneath his nose. "What did Devin ask you last time? Oh, I know. What's it like having sex with a monster? Something like that, right?"

"I didn't answer that question," Haji splutters.

"How could you? You never had that experience. You better not go on the podcast."

"But…"

I storm off without listening to his retort.

Chapter 6

I stride along the roadway as if in a tunnel deep in the earth. Conflicted thoughts and emotions rebound through my mind like scores of basketballs. Beneath it all is a feral undercurrent of rage and hunger. Since the sleeper first stirred inside me nearly one year ago, I'm always ravenous. Every day my craving for meat is metastasizing like a cancerous carbuncle.

Before The Incident, Haji had only been a friend— a certified member of my squad, part of my family. Haji, Dalia, and I were as close and inseparable as any three friends can be. But I never thought of him as boyfriend material until after seeing a dragon for the first time and having my dear friend Joe point out the gangly boy is head over heels for me. Now I always find reasons to push Haji away no matter how much I adore him. A dull knife saws through my intestines from the inside out. Like everything else about my life, I wish my relationship with Haji could return to what it was before the dragons upended my world. I just want some normalcy in my life. The chance of that happening is minuscule, but a girl has got to dream.

"Allison Lee is un…"

Hearing my name, I come to a jittering stop and take in my surroundings. My street is still half a block away, but discernible over the rumbling of vehicle engines is the ranting of a protester in front of my home.

"She's unnatural! She's an abomination and a danger to our community! She is the daughter of Satan, and we demand she go back to Hell!" The speaker must be using a megaphone.

"Wow," I murmur. This is the first time I've heard anyone name the Prince of Darkness as my father. Being called an abomination is typically like a slug to the solar plexus, but the pain is dull today. The wound caused by Haji considering going on Devin's podcast is still so fresh it overwhelms all the other injuries. And honestly, the raving protester is rather amusing. Daughter of Satan? Get out.

"Daughter of Satan! Go back to Hell! Daughter of Satan! Go back to Hell!"

Being told to go to Hell by what sounds like one hundred people or more gets under my skin. Death by hundreds of needles and all that. I push the chanting from my mind, instead focusing on the task at hand. Get home while avoiding the protesters and not revealing my surreptitious route to the security detail.

I meander down the sidewalk, trying to catch sight of the dark sedan. As I near my street, I spot a sedan parallel parked along the road. Agent Haskell watches me from the driver's seat, his eyes hidden behind reflective aviator sunglasses.

Haskell and his partner look like movie extras from Bad-Guys-R-Us. I hate having those creeps following me around everywhere, watching my every move. I don't need their protection. If anything, they're a danger to me. Agent Brodie had allowed the gunman into the house and held my parents at gunpoint.

Images of the gunman, his neck twisted at an

unnatural angle, flash through my mind. If it weren't for the stupid protection detail, that man would've never gotten inside the house. He was only able to because we trusted Agent Brodie. I could be living my life without mountainous guilt burdening me twenty-four seven for having killed. I loathe the agents.

Instead of turning down my street, I stay on the main drag and break into a full-tilt sprint. Let's see those losers catch me now. I cover the distance to the next street over and dart down it in five seconds or less.

A dog walker strides toward me, chaperoning no fewer than half a dozen dogs of sizes varying from a toy poodle to a Great Dane. Half the canines lunge at me, yapping. I veer into the road to avoid them and immediately bank hard to the right to evade an oncoming car. A horn blares as I leap over a parallel parked SUV to land on the sidewalk without breaking my stride.

By my estimation, I'm turning into the neatly kept front yard of a lime green craftsman with purple trim in under fifteen seconds. Hanging before the porch is a brightly colored pride flag. An elderly gentleman in a three-piece plaid suit lounges on a rocking chair by the front door.

"Hi, Mr. McGregor," I call.

"Mind the fence," he barks.

I vault the six-foot-high fence into Mr. McGregor's backyard. The first time I did this, I misjudged the jump, caught my trailing foot on the fence, and did a face plant onto the grass. I wasn't hurt beyond a battered ego, but I missed crushing Mr. McGregor's prized rosebushes by inches. Careening through the yard, I'm careful to avoid the numerous flowerbeds like they're landmines. I leap the back fence onto the ill-kept grass of my backyard with an ear-to-ear smile plastered on my face. Fond memories resurface of running cross country with Dalia back before my half-skaag abilities revealed themselves. Now, I can outperform Olympic athletes at everything from the shot put to the marathon. Even the protesters' rabid chanting out front can't dampen my mood, at least not much.

I eyeball the roof, considering leaping onto it to enter my room through the unlocked window, but it's not worth the effort. Mother will detect me with her hypersensitive ears, and the protesters might spot me. Sighing, I head for the back door, entering the house through the mudroom.

How can Mother stand listening to protesters all day? Patience is not one of her strong suits, at least when it comes to me. The TV blares from the dining room, the volume on high. Why does she bother turning the volume up so loud? Her hearing is at least as sensitive as mine, so the TV won't drown out the protesters, and even with the distraction, she can discern whatever is on the tube with the volume so low a "normal" person would hardly hear a thing. She's probably doing it to seem ordinary. That's just like her—trying to fit in by acting like a complete weirdo.

"Allison, stop playing games and come greet your mother. We need to keep up appearances, even in private. It's good practice," Mother says.

I let out a huff and slink into the dining room. Mother sits at the foot of the table, watching the cable news. Before her is a white dinner plate splattered with blood—probably the remnants of a raw steak. How she manages to choke down the meat without getting even a drop of blood on her pristine clothes or lips is beyond me.

"Hello, Mother. I had a great day. I hope you did too," I say, rushing past her on my way to the hallway.

"Not so fast, young lady," Mother says, patting the chair next to her. "Sit down and tell me all about your first day back at school. Was it bad? You came through the backdoor. Does that mean you evaded your security detail? Agent Deveraux won't be happy about that. If she decides to move us on base again, I won't tolerate it. It will get in the way of your training, and your father cannot teach classes at the university if we're confined to the base. Without that dragon here to smooth things over, I will be forced to take control of the situation."

My shoulders sag at the dose of reality that is like a cooler full of ice water poured on my face. Nothing gets past good old Mom. I'm about to tell her off and escape to my room, but then the newscaster announces, "Our next guest is none other than Dr. Frederick Radcliffe, director of the newly formed U.N. Draconic Task Force and, as I'm sure all our viewers know, a dragon from another planet."

To say my curiosity is piqued is a severe understatement.

Mother faces the TV. "Sit, dear. We can discuss your escapades after listening to the interview."

"Fine." I take a seat. She wins this round.

"Where's Dr. Radcliffe?" The newscaster looks off screen. His face betrays a modicum of panic.

Dr. Radcliffe is always one to defy expectations. A year ago, on a remote beach on the Olympic Peninsula, Radcliffe had been willing to hand me over to Mark

Cassidy, a skaag who had been my mother's boss, in exchange for the location of an interdimensional gateway. Him handing me over wasn't part of the plan. Memory of his betrayal makes me clench my jaw so tightly my teeth ache. Haji and Devin aren't the only males in my life who often seem as wonderful as an infection of flesh-eating bacteria.

"Is something bothering you, Allison?" Mother asks.

"Of course not," I say through gritted teeth. "I guess the interview isn't happening."

"Patience, Allison, patience. The dragon never misses an interview and loves unique entrances."

"Sorry, sorry," Dr. Radcliffe's voice comes from off screen. "I was slapping the flesh, kissing babies, and signing autographs. You know, I am a great baby kisser. Maybe I should run for president? No, no, Thomas, do not bother standing."

The reporter's face scrunches up. "Run for president? That's impossible. You're an alien. A dragon."

The tall, spindly doctor leans over and gives the journalist a friendly pat on the shoulder. "That is a joke, Thomas, a joke. I try never to take myself too seriously." Dr. Radcliffe sits and faces the camera, smiling. His face is long and thin, almost gaunt, and his gold-rimmed spectacles glimmer in the light. His dragon form is invisible even to me over the TV since while he rides the slipstream, his true form is hidden to almost everything, including cameras. "I do love kissing babies. That is not a joke. That is a fact."

"This is almost too painful to watch," I mutter.

"The dragon is trying to put the humans at ease."

"As if acting like a complete freak will put anyone at ease."

Unlike my mother, Dr. Radcliffe knows how to act halfway normal since he's been doing it for close to seven hundred years if you believe him. But since The Incident, with its consequence of the dragons' existence being outed, Dr. Radcliffe has abandoned his persona as a stuffy university professor for something more akin to a larger-than-life carnival barker.

"I hope you can give us insight on one question I hear people speculate about all the time," the newscaster says.

Dr. Radcliffe nods.

"How many dragons are on Earth right now?"

The view transitions to a close-up of Dr. Radcliffe's face. He looks every bit the elderly history professor I remember from the Chapel Library—a little overfriendly in a creepy way. Of course, whenever I see him in person, there is a giant, golden dragon projecting out of his body and passing through everything around it like an apparition.

"I am not at liberty to share that information," Dr. Radcliffe says with a twinkle in his eyes.

"We know there are more dragons," the newscaster says. "There is video evidence of a silver dragon. And this other creature"—he looks down at his notes—"a, what is it—"

"A skaag. Yes, I am aware of the video."

"Perhaps we can play—"

"There is no need," Dr. Radcliffe says. "I was there on the beach. The dragon in the video is named Ion. As has been reported exhaustively, she was killed by a skaag."

A knife's edge of grief slices into my heart. I was there when Ion died. She was a bully who constantly threatened to eat my friends and me, but I discovered she wasn't that different from me before her death. She was frightened and alone and stricken by terrible losses. And in the end, her ultimate sacrifice helped ensure my survival on the windswept beach.

I shift in the chair, surreptitiously watching Mother. She gazes at the screen, her unnerving eyes rarely, if ever, blinking. She is the skaag who killed Ion by decapitating the dragon using her massive fang-filled maw. I shudder at the memory and at the searing knowledge I am just like her. I have killed. I've wished the lie Mother had killed the gunman is the truth so many times I can almost fool myself, but deep down I can't escape the fact I'm a murderer.

The camera angle changes to a view of the reporter and the doctor.

"Well, that's you and Ion. That's two dragons. There is also photographic and video evidence of a copper dragon, bringing the total up to three confirmed dragons. There are also reports of a green dragon flying westward about one hundred miles off the coast of Washington state. That's four dragons we know of. I ask you again, how many dragons are on Earth?"

A green dragon…Tatsuo. The one-eyed dragon had been the size of a jumbo jet. Numerous scars covered his jade scales from the many battles he waged against skaags over the centuries. His size and ferocity didn't save him from Mother.

As far as I know, only three dragons remain on Earth. There's Dr. Radcliffe, obviously; Mauve, who since The Incident has become one of my best friends in the world; and Tanis, who is elderly even by dragon standards.

"I have no comment beyond this," Dr. Radcliffe says, steepling his hands underneath his chin. "Ion died protecting humanity from skaags. Have no doubt; skaags are a dangerous scourge. Should these monsters arrive on this planet en masse, I fear for the future of humankind. That threat is one reason I have spent these past months partnering with the United Nations to form the U.N. Draconic Task Force. Quite frankly, I am here to talk about the task force. Right now, we are laying the groundwork for the infrastructure required to keep humanity safe. For example, the gateways skaags use to traverse the slipstream give off phantom radiation. We need to build detectors capable of—"

"We'll get to the task force in a moment," the newscaster says.

"Oh, I wanted to hear more about that," I murmur.

Mother laughs mirthlessly. "About the dragon's phantom radiation detector? A pipe dream is my guess. Humans will argue about funding it for years before attempting to build it, if ever."

"Knowing when skaags are going to show up seems important to me," I say.

The newscaster continues. "First, I want to give you another chance to tell the world how many dragons are living alongside us. People everywhere want to know, Dr. Radcliffe. Surely, you can understand that?"

Dr. Radcliffe leans back in his chair, smiling condescendingly. "You are a persistent little man, Thomas. Persistent." Thomas frowns. "I can assure you there are far fewer dragons on this planet than there are humans. In fact, we dragons pose no threat to humanity.

We want to help humanity prosper. I am very passionate about this. That is why…"

Mother's cell phone blares an absurdly loud cosmic ringtone. Without warning, she turns off the TV. I suspect she has the controller squirreled away in a pocket.

"I was watching that," I say. "It was just getting to the interesting part, the task force. Hello?"

"Calm yourself, Allison," Mother says, glancing at her smartphone. "I must answer this. It's Devereaux."

Glowering, I stand and am ready to escape to my room, but Mother says into the phone, "Agent Deveraux, I was expecting your call." A pause. "Oh, you're right outside. Yes, Allison is here with me." Another break, and Mother glares at me. "Yes, I thought you'd want to talk to her. I'll meet you at the door. See you in a sec."

Mother ends the call and looks at me, her lips perked up in a predacious smile revealing the barest hint of white teeth.

"Deveraux wants to talk to me? Give me a break. It's not my fault those losers can't keep up with me."

Mother reveals even more teeth. "Remember, whatever happens to the lovely Agent Deveraux is your fault, Allison."

The doorbell rings followed by the disembodied butler voice announcing the agent.

Mother stands. "Don't you dare leave this room, Allison. I want you to see the consequences of your actions."

"Consequences? Whatever. I'm going to my room."

I'm halfway out of the chair when Mother's hand

presses down on my crown with crushing force. She shoves me down in the chair. I don't resist because a fraction more pressure will break my neck or crack my skull.

Mother removes her hand from my head. "You will stay, daughter."

I draw a jittery breath, sweat beading over my face. "Yes, Mother."

Chapter 7

"Agent Devereaux, I must apologize for my daughter's behavior. I'm at wit's end."

The door clicks shut. Their footsteps tick along the hallway floor. I don't want to face the agent or Mother, but the urge to flee out the back door is a fleeting one. I don't know what Mother has in store for Deveraux, but I hope my presence will ameliorate her baser desires.

I shift in the chair until I'm facing forward, staring across the table at the wall. Clenching my hands, I place them on my lap, hidden from view by the tabletop. My fists are so tight my arms shake. Like Mother, I don't want to go back to the base, but Agent Devereaux shouldn't be hurt for doing her job.

"Allison, you did wait," Mother declares upon entering the dining room with Devereaux trailing behind her.

I force myself to relax my hands and give the women a terse greeting.

"Forgive my daughter for being so rude." Mother gives the agent an apologetic smile. "I'm glad she didn't try sneaking out when I answered the door."

Agent Deveraux sits across from me and glowers. She wears a gray sports jacket over a white blouse. In her hands is a small tablet she sets on the table. Mother sits next to me. I suppress the desire to switch chairs to be farther away from her.

Deveraux lifts the tablet and manipulates the screen with a finger. "Allison, is it true you deliberately evaded your security detail at three fifty-six p.m. today?"

"No!"

Deveraux glares and arches an eyebrow.

"You did enter the house through the back door," Mother says.

"I didn't purposely ditch anyone. It's not my fault they can't keep up with me."

Devereaux reads off a report about my actions from Agent Haskell. "Are you claiming this report is false, Allison?"

Unable to meet the lead agent's grim stare, I drop my gaze to my lap.

"You signed an agreement laying out the protocols you must follow to remain living at home and attending school." Deveraux sets the tablet down on the table. "If you can't follow the rules, you will be confined to the base. Is that understood?"

"Yes," I murmur.

"I can't hear you, Allison."

"Speak up, dear," Mother says all sickly syrupy.

I turn in my seat to face Mother. "Do you have to be so fake all the time?"

Mother places her hands against her chest. Her nails are painted the same bloody red as her lips. "Fake?"

"Jesus," Deveraux says. "Can the two of you save the histrionics for when I'm not around for once?"

I round on Deveraux, who massages her left temple with her fingers. "I don't need protection. I'm a monster. Besides, the security detail is useless. They let the gunman sneak inside the house. I killed him. I didn't mean to, but I killed him."

Deveraux drops her hand to the table with a loud smack. "That's why you should be on base. On base, we have total control over who has access to you."

"Agent Brodie allowed the gunman inside! Your agent! Part of the security detail! Have you learned anything from him? Have you? Brodie threatened to kill my father." I'd keep fuming, but I'm hyperventilating.

"I'm not privy to the details of the investigation, and as you were told before, the results of the investigation might remain classified due to national security concerns," Deveraux says, expression exasperated.

"How convenient."

Deveraux's nostrils flare. "I assure you, Allison, nothing about anything that has happened since the kidnapping attempt has been convenient for anyone. Now, as I can tell you have no intention of abiding by the agreement you signed, you leave me no choice except to recommend you are confined to Joint Base Lewis-McCord."

"What?" I involuntarily pound my knuckles against the underside of the table. "No. No way."

"Agent Deveraux, I know my daughter is far from the ideal protectee," Mother says. "She tries my patience daily, but perhaps she deserves a second chance in this instance. It was her first day back at school in nearly a year. I'm sure it was an overwhelming experience for her."

Deveraux leans back in her chair. "No." She shakes her head. "I can't in good conscience allow that. Her actions put the public, my agents, and herself in danger.

I'm…what are you…"

Mother leaps from the chair and vaults across the table, landing beside Deveraux, who is halfway out of her chair. Mother grabs the agent's chin, forcing her mouth open, and slams her against the wall, knocking over the chair in the process.

"Mother, stop!" I stand, but I'm too frightened to intervene. I can't prevent Mother from doing whatever she wants, and I fear anything I do might provoke her to even greater violence.

Deveraux paws at her waist for a holstered pistol, but she's so slow. Mother regurgitates thick maroon saliva that she spits into the agent's mouth. Deveraux beats her fists against Mother, but she is too weak to escape. Mother makes a series of guttural sounds ending in a long hiss. As the hiss fades, the agent stops struggling, and her face goes flaccid.

"What did you do?" I ask.

Mother releases Deveraux, who placidly rights the chair and sits. The agent's gaze is listless. Facing me, Mother places her hands on the table and leans over until her head is on par with the agent's.

Deveraux's head lolls precariously to the side. Her expression is slack, and drool dribbles down her chin.

"I warned you I might be forced to take action, daughter. I'm not as skilled as that dragon at manipulating the human mind. My manipulation might leave the good agent irreparably changed." She smiles. "Or not."

"Please, don't hurt her."

"It's too late, daughter. Either she's already damaged, or she's not."

My hand goes to my lips. What have I done?

Wasn't killing the gunman enough? No, this is Mother's doing. "You didn't have to scramble her mind. We could've talked to her. Convinced her to change her mind."

"Perhaps that dragon could have, but I am not him, daughter. Agent Deveraux, are you listening?"

Deveraux's head straightens, and her expression morphs into one of extreme concentration, but her eyes remain glassy. "Yes."

"Excellent. Do you plan to have Allison Lee and her family confined to the base?"

"Yes."

"No, that is not what you intend to do."

"What is it I intend?"

Watching Mother strip Deveraux of all her faculties makes me nauseous. Even worse is the dread Mother might have done this obscene magic on me, and I'd never know.

Mother's smile doesn't waver as she speaks. "You intend to allow Allison Lee to remain in her home and continue attending school. You are satisfied her actions this afternoon were the innocent mistakes of an angsty teen. When she told you she will never attempt to avoid the security detail again, you believed her. Do you understand?"

"I understand."

"Repeat your instructions."

Deveraux recites Mother's words.

"Will she…" I say, but Mother holds up a finger for silence.

"You will stop listening for now."

I breathe in sharply as Deveraux's expression slackens, and her head droops to the side like an unused marionette. Mother straightens, looking down on me.

"Is there anything you'd like to ask the agent, daughter?"

I almost tell Mother to ask Deveraux about Brodie and hate myself for the fleeting thought. "Will she be okay…normal…after…after this?"

"I don't know, daughter. The human mind is weak, and my magic is a blunt force. Rarely have I manipulated the human mind. Often, the subjects degrade over time, but not always." Mother walks around the table. "Maybe she'll be lucky." She sits next to me. "Are you sure there's nothing you wish to ask?"

"Release her, please."

"Very well." Mother makes a series of indecipherable guttural and hissing sounds.

At the spell's conclusion, Deveraux immediately reanimates. A mask of confusion descends upon the agent's countenance then disappears. After that briefest of hesitation, she chides me for my actions and warns me never to avoid the security detail again. Mother escorts her from the dining room to the front door.

I remain seated, afraid Agent Deveraux isn't herself any longer.

Mother returns, acting as if nothing has happened. "Should we check if that dragon is still being interviewed?"

I stare, disgusted by her blasé attitude. She might have ruined a woman's mind, and she doesn't care. Part of me wants to demand why she doesn't have any guilt, but she will only deflect the question by claiming it is all my fault. Mother might be able to take the shape of a human, but she doesn't possess an iota of humanity. What truly frightens me is what that says about me.

"Have you ever done that to me?"

"Would you believe any answer I give you, daughter?"

Mother turns on the TV, but the interview with Dr. Radcliffe has concluded.

I stand ready to retreat to my room to process what I experienced.

"Oh, before I forget," Mother says. "We'll be heading into the wilderness Saturday morning."

I stiffen. Heading into the wilderness is a euphemism for Mother training me in all things skaag. Disrupting the training is the one thing confinement to the base is good for. Seeing what she did to Deveraux gives me a clue as to how we can disappear as a family into the wilds of Washington every couple of weeks without a single question asked by the security detail or anyone else. The only time the routine was interrupted was when we were on base.

"I need to go to the climate march this weekend. For school."

"For school?"

"Photography class."

"There will be plenty of other climate marches, Allison. You need to master your abilities. Through mastery, you will gain control of yourself."

****

After a disgusting spaghetti dinner overcooked by my mother and a vain attempt to plead with Dad to intervene on my behalf regarding the weekend excursion, I sprawl in bed venting to Dalia over the phone. My head rests against my cushy kitty stuffy.

"Mother insists I go into the wilderness with her this weekend. Can you believe it? I told her about CO_2

Free Seattle. She doesn't care. She says there will be other marches. I don't care what she says. I'm going."

"Allison, I hate to say this, but…your mom is right. There will be other marches. Maybe you don't want to…you know, piss her off."

I snort. "She needs to understand I have a life outside doing what she says when she says it. Besides, Mauve is coming."

"Mauve won't want you crossing your mother," Dalia says, her voice rising an octave.

"I know." Having been nearly killed by Mother makes Mauve exceedingly cautious. Only my throwing dirt clods and screaming at Mother kept her from prying up Mauve's scales to deliver a fatal blow. "It's just…living with her is…"

"Rough," Dalia says.

"That's an understatement."

We laugh. We have to be careful what we say because the government monitors all my phone and electronic communication.

"So how was the walk home with Haji?" Dalia asks.

"You won't believe what he said."

"What?"

"He's considering going back on that podcast."

"On my ex's? No way."

"Umm…yes."

"He's so clueless. Listen, Allison, I'll talk to him. Lead him to the light. Did he say what the interview is about?"

"He says it's all about magic."

"Riiiight."

"Dalia?"

"Yes."

"Don't say anything to Mauve about my mother wanting me to train this weekend. Okay?"

"I won't. You're coming to the march, then?"

"Are you kidding me? Of course!"

Chapter 8

Wednesday afternoon Dad picks me up early from school and takes me to my appointment with Dr. Jane Woolworth at the glass and steel Robotics Technology Center on the Tahoma University campus. We take the elevator to the second floor and navigate the hallway to Dr. Woolworth's sleek lab.

"Allison, come in, come in," Dr. Woolworth greets me from in front of a large flat-screen computer monitor. The cheer is gone from her voice when she adds, "Dr. Lee."

Graduate students work throughout the lab, either at computers or on sensitive electronics for prosthetics. I don't recognize any of them from my previous visits.

"Hi, Dr. Woolworth." I flash a genuine smile. I'm happy to see her, and my prosthetics are supposed to be inspected once a month. I missed my last appointment due to the kidnapping attempt.

"I'll wait outside," Dad says.

"That's probably for the best," Woolworth says coolly.

Before Mother moved back home, Dad was over here all the time helping out Dr. Woolworth. I thought maybe the help was in reality hanky-panky, but little did I know Dad and Mother had been surreptitiously keeping in contact all those years.

Dr. Woolworth rolls a stool out from under the

table. "Sit, Allison."

As the doctor retrieves a tablet from the tabletop next to an ergonomic keyboard, I take the offered seat.

"I hate it you missed an appointment." Woolworth jabs the tablet with an index finger. "Your prosthetics are cutting edge." She looks up and smiles wanly. "I know there are extenuating circumstances…it's not your fault. I wish…I wish the government allowed me to properly care for you. You're my patient."

She stops manipulating the tablet to wipe her eyes. Luckily, she doesn't wear make-up. She doesn't need to because her stunning complexion is all natural.

"Is something wrong, Dr. Woolworth?"

"Nothing. How embarrassing. I'm being unprofessional. Let me run the diagnostics."

"Okay." I smile.

Five minutes later, Woolworth announces, "Your prosthetics check out with flying colors." She sets the tablet down on the table. "I'd like to do a complete visual inspection since"—she takes a deep breath—"well, I assume you were roughed up since you were almost kidnapped."

I breathe in sharply. Visual inspection means she intends to remove my prosthetics. I'll be blind. What if someone tries to nab me again? How will I defend myself? How will I protect Dr. Woolworth, whom I trust implicitly? I glance around the lab jampacked with scientific equipment. Any of the half dozen or so graduate students might be a plant. Presumably, they've all been checked out by my security detail, but Agent Brodie was a traitor.

"We don't have to do it today if you don't want to," Woolworth says. "It's not due for another three months."

I chew on the inside of my lower lip. If the sleeper wakes, I won't need to see to detect attackers. I'll be able to hear and smell them, but tripping hazards all over the place may cause me trouble.

"Let's do it another time," I say.

****

A constant drizzle falls from a gloomy sky as I walk home alone from school on Friday. Dalia is at cross country practice, and I haven't seen Haji since our argument on the first day of school. To be honest, I'm glad I haven't seen Haji since he told me he's considering going back on the podcast. I have nothing to say except to insist he decline the interview. Of course, he won't decline it. He can't. He loves the limelight almost as much as Devin and Dr. Radcliffe.

After dodging road spray kicked up by zipping cars, I reach my street to find Agent Haskell and his cohort waiting for me in a silver sedan. Haskell flashes me a toothy grin, and I flip him the bird, which makes him smile wider. Far down the street, the protesters are gathered in front of my house in two opposing packs screaming vitriol at each other. Ragged chants come from the groups: one declaring I'm an angel, and the other decrying me as a spy for a foreign government. How can I be a spy when everyone knows who and what I am?

"Allison! Allison, check out the car."

I turn to stare at Agent Haskell. He has rolled down the driver-side window. His left arm hangs out the window, and he pats the door.

"It's a hybrid," he calls.

"I told you to ask for an electric."

"You said an electric or a hybrid. This is the best I could do on short notice."

"You should've demanded an electric."

Haskell rolls his eyes. "Some people are never satisfied, Allison. Don't be some people."

"Whatever."

Haskell rolls up the window, and the car darts down the street. By the time I near my house, the agents are next to the vehicle waiting for me while facing down the protesters. Maybe some of them are fans? One woman holds a swaddled, bawling infant with a cleft lip overhead, pleading I bless the child. The poor kid's face is covered in raindrops.

The whole scene makes me cringe, which isn't unusual, but the baby makes me want to cry. He...she...doesn't deserve that treatment. And what does the mother expect me to do? Even if I am an angel, can't she see I've fallen from grace? I'm a killer, not a healer.

Agent Haskell positions himself ahead of me as I stride toward the crowd. His partner takes up the rear.

"Keep to my shoulder," Haskell says. "We'll get you through this."

The mob gives way to the agent's bulk to avoid being run over by a man nearly the size of a small tank. The crowd's screams buzz in my ears. Sometimes I can make sense of what they're saying, but mostly it's a riotous din. Even worse is the stink of all the bodies, a reeking fusion of BO, fast food, and soiled diaper. My after-school appetite is ruined.

Signs are thrust in my face experience has taught me not to read, but no one touches me. I'm not sure if it's fear of arrest—Haskell once body-slammed and cuffed a man who spat on me—or me that keeps them at bay. There's footage on the Internet of me ripping the door off a wrecked car with my bare hands and numerous videos of my mother in skaag form nearly killing Mauve. People may disagree on whether I should be loved and hated, but they all agree I'm dangerous. If they knew I killed the gunman who attempted to kidnap me, they'd be terrified.

Haskell steps aside after breaking through the crowd. Ahead of me is the beautiful cherry tree and the house. I break into a run for the front door. Even inside the house, the screams of the mob, and above all, the baby's wails are audible. I can pretend the shouting is white noise, but the child's crying is glass scraping over my gray matter.

****

After the protesters disperse, I'm finally able to settle down at my desk to hammer out homework. Earlier, I couldn't concentrate while listening to the baby wail. What kind of mother treats her child that way? Hasn't she heard of diaper rash? That kid needed a diaper change.

Staring back at me on my desk is a well-worn book with a giant scarlet A on the cover. Facing down the besieging crush today has left me feeling like Hester Prynne. Not that my newfound empathy for Hawthorne's character will stave off the book's soporific qualities. I have fifty pages to read and an essay to write before class on Monday. If I read in bed, I'm afraid I'll fall asleep before finishing five pages.

I crack open the novel and catch a whiff of moldering paper. Not the most disgusting thing I've smelled today, but not pleasant either. My parents' soft footfalls on the carpeted hallway distract me before I've even read a single complete sentence. Anticipating their arrival, I stare at my door decorated with the psychedelic Dark Matter Eletrica poster.

There is a soft rap against the door. Dad must be leading the vanguard since Mother's style is to barge in without preamble.

"What? I have tons of homework to do. Mrs. Achebe is one hundred percent pure hard ass."

"Is that your English lit teacher?" Dad's voice is muffled.

"Yes. Now, go away."

"Raymond, we don't have time for this," Mother says. "Open the door."

"Patience, dear. We need to respect her need for space."

"I am extremely patient with her, Raymond. My mother would have cracked her skull open and eaten her brain months ago for her transgressions."

"Yes, well, thank goodness you're not your mother."

The door opens a crack. The upper half of Dad's face appears in the opening.

"Daddy." I scowl and heft the book. "I. Am. Busy."

"Have you seen Haji at school lately?"

"Haji? No. Why?"

The door opens, and my parents step inside. Dad lifts the cell phone to his ear. "Allison says she hasn't seen him. Would you like to talk to her?" He is silent for a beat. "Yes, I agree that's a good idea." Dad offers me the cellphone. "It's Mrs. Patel. Haji is missing."

The paperback slips from my hands onto the desk.

"Missing?"

"Yes," Mother says tersely.

Dad nods. "He didn't show up at school on Wednesday. His parents haven't seen him since Wednesday morning."

"He's missed three days of school? No way." I stand and snatch the phone from my father. "Hello, Mrs. Patel. I can't believe Haji missed three days of school. He's way too much of a goody-goody."

"Oh, Allison, it's good to hear your voice." Mrs. Patel is tremulous. "Have you seen my boy? We're worried sick about him. Like you say, he's not one to miss school. Not my Haji."

"I haven't seen him since Monday."

"Monday. Oh. Did he say anything about his plans?"

"He did. We had an argument." I give Mrs. Patel a brief synopsis of our fight. As I speak, I can't help fearing my pushing him away drove Haji to do something foolish. That's stupid self-recrimination, but I can't help it.

"Oh, that boy Devin is bad. I don't like him," Mrs. Patel says. Neither does my mother, judging by the rude snorting sound she made when I mentioned his name.

"Have you talked to Dalia?"

"Yes, she saw him Tuesday at school. Nothing unusual about his behavior except she had the feeling he was avoiding you. That must've been due to this argument you had with him."

I take a sharp breath. I'm certain Mrs. Patel doesn't mean anything by her comment, but it's like a punch to the throat.

Dad puts a hand on my shoulder and gently

squeezes. "It's okay, Allison. Everything will be okay."

Mother stares at us unnervingly. There's nothing motherly about her appalling orbs.

I look away from Mother, taking a deep breath and gathering my thoughts. "Have you contacted Leslie and Jason? Haji always checks up on Leslie to make sure she's going to photograph the local sports scene for the *Weekly*."

"Oh, yes. That's a good idea. Do you have their numbers?"

I give Mrs. Patel Leslie's number. "I don't know Jason's number, but Leslie will."

"Thank you so much, Allison. If you hear anything about my Haji, please call right away."

"I will, Mrs. Patel."

We say our goodbyes and end the call. I hand the phone back to Dad, and we embrace. We stay like that for a long time. I suspect Haji's interest in magic may have led him into trouble. Human magicians shoot up heroin, after all, to feel the magic.

"Can we talk about tomorrow, now? We need to make a final decision on the location of Allison's training. I have several in mind," Mother says as tone deaf as a wrecking ball.

I scowl at Mother aghast. Dad and I break our embrace.

"Perhaps, we can discuss that in the morning, dear?" Dad says.

"What? Haven't I allowed you enough time to comfort her, Raymond? She's obviously not upset about the boy. Look at the way she's staring at me."

"I'm not training tomorrow," I say, words staccato. "I'm going to CO2 Free Seattle."

At the march I'll be able to connect with Mauve and run my theory by her that Haji's interest in magic has gotten him in trouble. Anything related to magic is not something we can discuss in detail on the phone with the government listening in.

"I'm afraid I insist," Mother says.

"Maybe you should give her a break this weekend. It's her first week back at school, and her friend is missing." Dad says.

I step back and sit on the edge of the bed.

"Give her a break? Really, Raymond? Is that what you think? That our daughter needs a break? If skaags find another gateway to Earth, they will hunt her down. General Bale wants her dead. You know there are oaths I can't break, even for Allison's sake. She must be capable of defending herself."

I jump up. "I collapsed a gateway on the skaags. I don't need any training to do it again."

Mother scoffs. "You only survived due to Dalia's foolish bravery."

I stomp my foot I'm so mad. It's true, Dalia foolishly reached into the gateway between dimensions and pulled me out, but I caused the collapse. I discharged electricity, causing the causeway through the slipstream to implode upon the skaag expeditionary force. I did that without any training or help from Mother. She had been AWOL.

Dad turns to me, his expression sorrowful. "Allison, your mother is right. You need to train." I'm about to scream, but he cuts me off. "Please, let me finish. I know you want to go to the march and that it's for school, but there will be other marches. Sometimes it seems like there's one every week."

"No, there's not," I mutter.

"What if Haji's disappearance is somehow related to The Incident? You need to know how to defend yourself," Dad says.

"I know how to defend myself. I killed the freaking gunman right here in this room."

Mother gives me a condescending smile. "You *killed* the gunman, daughter, and you allowed him to shoot you—very poor form. I incapacitated Agent Brodie without him discharging his firearm, which he had pressed against your father's head."

****

Incessant buzzing drags me out of my slumber. Bleary-eyed, I stare at the glowing red numbers displayed on the alarm clock—six a.m. Why is my alarm going off?

"It's Saturday," I whisper.

Desperate to silence the beeping before it alerts my mother, I roll and simultaneously stretch an arm toward the alarm clock. My fingers are pawing over the clock, searching for the button to turn off the alarm when I slide off the bed. I yelp just before my rump strikes the floor with a thud. Stifling the groan, I stand and turn off the alarm. If the electronic beeping hadn't alerted Mother, my crashing to the floor did.

Rubbing my aching butt, I otherwise remain still, listening. Sure enough, the stairs softly creak, and feet thump against the floor in the hallway. The sounds are so soft an ordinary human wouldn't notice.

"Allison? Are you okay? I heard a bang."

Does that woman ever sleep? "I forgot to turn off my alarm last night. That's all." I yawn loudly. "I'm going back to bed."

I flop onto the bed, causing the springs to squeal.

There's a long pause. I'm sure Mother is trying to decide if I'm lying to her. She's always suspicious of me, whether I'm up to something or not. Of course, I am up to something, but that's not the point. A normal person would allow their daughter to go to the climate march instead of dragging her out into the wilderness to transform into a lightning bolt spewing monster.

"More sleep will do you good. We have a long day of training ahead. I'll wake you in an hour and a half."

"Okay," I say.

After waiting until I'm sure Mother has meandered back downstairs, I slip from bed and retrieve my clothes, including a pair of zebra-striped sneakers. Once I'm dressed, I grab my sling bag with the camera inside from my study desk. I admire myself in the mirror, giving my hair a close inspection. I was up until one a.m. dyeing my mop afraid the entire time the results would be a total failure. I miss my forest green hair, but fire engine red makes me look wicked. I snag a pair of sunglasses off the desk and slip them into the pocket of my black hoodie. Draping the bag over my shoulder, I slink across the room to the window and pull up the blinds. The dusky cityscape of houses and green spaces sleeps beneath an indigo sky smudged by clouds so dark they're almost black.

I open the window, shivering as the cold air blows across my face, bringing with it an earthy, autumnal scent. I place my hands on the frame and hoist myself up and out the window onto the roof as silent as a ninja assassin.

Chapter 9

I gently shut the bedroom window, fearing the entire time I'll screw up and make a sound that will attract Mother. A fine mist moistens everything, including me. Spongy moss grows on the shingles in green rectangles. The combination of cold temperature and relentless damp sets my teeth chattering. All in all, it's a quintessential Pacific Northwest morning. I need to head out before my hoodie is soaked through. I make a mental note to stash a raincoat underneath the bed for the next time I plan to sneak out of the house.

I creep toward the edge of the roof. I'm about halfway there when my right foot slips out from under me, and the world whirls, and I windmill my arms to keep from falling. The sling bag thumps against my back. I slam my foot onto the roof to regain my balance. The thud reverberates around the quiet neighborhood.

"Yikes," I whisper.

Not moving a muscle, I listen for any sound indicating Mother coming to investigate. Five feet separate me from the window. Throw the window open, scramble inside, shut the window, and leap into bed underneath the covers. I can do that before she comes upstairs.

An engine roars to life from somewhere across the street, followed by the distinctive thump, thump, thump of a motorcycle. I grind my teeth. Mother could be coming up the stairs this instant. The motorcycle crackles as it drives toward the main drag. Not daring to breathe, I listen for any noise from inside the house. Nada.

I let out a long hissing breath, and my entire body sags with the release of tension. Mother likely heard me stomp against the roof and misinterpreted the sound. That must be it. She heard the noise but wrote it off as my dad or me getting out of bed or one of those odd old house sounds. If she suspected I was sneaking off, she'd be busting into my room right now. Or…my gaze shifts to the edge of the roof. No. She wouldn't go outside through the back door and wait for me to jump down like a predator ambushing prey, would she? Of course, she would.

I bite my lower lip so hard I grimace as I shuffle to the roof's edge and survey the damp grass below. Mother isn't lying in wait, so I stop clamping down on my lip.

"A nice quiet landing," I whisper and leap off the edge.

I bend my knees on impact. A jolt runs through my legs, and dull pain briefly radiates from my hips, but at least my landing is relatively silent. I glance around the yard, half expecting Mother to appear at any moment. When she doesn't, I stand and run toward the fence, vaulting it into the front yard. Crouching low, I scurry toward the street, not coming to my full height until the cherry tree partially obscures me.

I cross the street and tap on the driver-side window of the security detail's sedan. Looks like good old Agent Haskell and his partner are watching late-night comedy on a smartphone. Haskell startles, spilling hot coffee over the console. His eyes scrunch up and his lips curl into a snarl.

I give them a dramatic wave. "Good morning, agents."

I start down the street, thinking some coffee will hit the spot before heading downtown.

****

An hour later, I step off the bus with a spring in my step in Seattle downtown, fully caffeinated from two huge cups of dark roast at The Obsidian Roast. Even though there are nearly ninety minutes until the march officially kicks off, people are everywhere: meandering or congregating on the sidewalks in the shadows of brand-name boutiques, overpriced cafés, and massive department stores. A few people spill over into the streets. The exploiters might have money, but we have people power. I smile. Fresh excitement along with the sun bursting through the cloud cover burns away my gloom. CO_2 Free Seattle will make a real statement today, and I'm going to take some wicked photos for my school project.

I join the crowd moving along the sidewalk, listening to people chat and admiring the slogans on the signs some people carry: There's No Planet B, Woman for President, Too Hot 4 Me, Wash Away the Green Sheen. I'm so inspired I pull my camera out and start shooting, concentrating on the sign bearers. I check the LCD on the back of my camera until I dial in the proper exposure. The filtered sunlight beaming through the branches of trees lining the sidewalk creates wonderful chiaroscuro.

One of my subjects notices me taking her picture. I

lower the camera and smile, which usually puts people at ease. Her expression becomes quizzical, and her gaze shifts to the phone clutched in her hand. Fearing she might recognize me despite my fire engine red hair, I make my getaway through the crowd before the woman decides to take my picture and posts it on monsterspotting.com. I fish my coke bottle sunglasses out from a pocket and put them on.

My phone tickles my abdomen from inside the hoodie's pocket. Pulling out the device, I slither through the crowd to stand next to the window display of a luxury clothing boutique. The sparkly dress in the window makes my head throb. Who would be caught dead in that skimpy rag? Flipping open the phone, I turn away and lean against the window. I read a text from Dalia asking my location.

I chicken peck out a response.

—*Already downtown. Get over here. Crowd gathering. Dope vibe.*—

Dalia's response is nearly instantaneous.

—*The march is at 9. I need coffee.*—

I flex my stiff left hand.

—*You can get coffee over here. Hurry. The march will be lit!!*—

—*On my way.*—

I close the phone, and I'm about to slip it inside my hoodie when I decide I had better confirm Mauve is coming. If Haji's interest in magic has anything to do with his disappearance, we will need her help finding him. I open up the phone and bang out a text.

—*You're going to make it up today, right?*—

—*I'm on the bus. I should be in Seattle downtown before nine.*—

—Fantastic. See you soon.—

I stare at the screen. The temptation to tell Mauve my concerns about Haji is strong, but I slip the phone back into my pocket. My texts are monitored, and we don't want anything coming out that might turn the attention of my government minders on Mauve.

I slide through the crowd toward the street, pause at the curb to check for traffic, then step out onto the roadway. I don't see the security detail, but I'm sure they're around here somewhere, keeping tabs on me. That's good because I don't want to get in trouble again with Agent Deveraux. I don't think Mother has permanently scrambled her mind yet, and I don't want that to happen.

I lift the camera to my eye, zooming in and out to capture the marchers in front of luxury shops. Once I frame an acceptable composition, I blaze away—three shots, bracketing, of course. From my left growls an internal combustion engine. I step back up onto the sidewalk before a loudspeaker blares: "Do not block the street."

A police cruiser slowly rolls by, lights flaring blue. Some of the younger protesters shout vitriol. A group of twenty-somethings in grungy yet chic clothes all flip off the cruiser's rear end. Instinctively, I step out into the street, bring the camera up, and fire, zooming out while pressing the shutter button several times in rapid succession.

Stepping back onto the curb, I check my shots on the LCD. I smile when I see the group with their middle fingers extended on the sidewalk and the slightly blurred police car in the distance. The picture will look lit as a black and white.

"Hey, you. Camera girl! With the red hair!"

One of the guys I photographed sneers at me. His hair looks dyed black, and eyeshadow gives him raccoon eyes.

"Why are you photographing us?" he demands.

"I'm documenting the climate march." I smile.

"Are you with the paper or something?" He lurches toward me.

I stand my ground. I don't want to be in a scuffle. I can see the headlines now: Monster Girl Batters Young Man at Climate Protest. Lucky for both of us, a woman in a plaid miniskirt grabs his forearm.

"Leave her alone, Drake. She's just a high school girl."

Drake looks at his friend, his expression softening. He turns back to me. "No more pictures."

I turn away, rolling my eyes, eager to be gone in case the confrontation attracts attention. Pulling up my hood, I retreat to the edge of the crowd to wait for my friends.

The crowd grows, and more municipal muscle arrives, presumably to block off streets and prevent property damage. The police don't make me feel any safer. You can only watch so many videos of minorities being brutalized and shot by the police before determining law-enforcement props up the injustice systemic in America. They'll happily arrest anyone for defacing a storefront owned by some corporation making egregious profits by exploiting child labor and spewing more carbon into the atmosphere than a third-world country. Yet we protesters—the young people who are having our futures slashed and burned for quarterly profits—are a danger to society.

The crowd clogging the street moves from the path of the express bus pulling up to a stop. I can't help smiling when I see Mauve's copper-scaled head and neck projecting through the vehicle's roof. Her serpentine tail, flicking to and fro, trails out the bus's backend. The draconic body parts randomly flicker to nothingness then reappear. A beam of sunlight sets her scales ablaze, causing me to squint. My prosthetics need a second to readjust to the intense light.

Brakes squealing, the bus stops at the curb. With a loud hiss, the bus doors open, and riders disgorge to join the host. I track Mauve's progress toward the backdoor by her dragon form. The dragon faces me, its sinewy neck reaching as high as some buildings are tall. Its bronze eyes, split by vertical black pupils, meet my gaze. A red forked tongue licks the air and disappears.

When Mauve's golem steps off the bus, I'm giddy at reuniting with the one being who might understand what it's like to be me.

"Mauve! Mauve!" I call as I weave through the crowd.

Mauve smiles, awkwardly trundling between protesters holding signs painted in bright colors. Her draconic form projects out of her, passing through the bus, people, and other obstacles. A cardboard poster decorated with the earth and the words "climate justice for all" bumps her golem on the head, knocking her circular glasses askew. If people saw the real Mauve, the svelte copper dragon riding the slipstream, they'd either soil themselves or start taking photographs with their phones. Instead, all they see is a frumpy woman of indeterminate age with mousy brown hair hacked off at her neck wearing a baggy sweater and wrinkled sweatpants. Mauve adjusts her circular glasses, which make her face appear owlish.

We come together in a tight embrace. Her golem feels as human as anyone. Mauve starts loudly sniffing me, and I push her back to arm's length.

"What are you doing?" I mouth, aware we're in a crowd and noisily smelling someone with the intensity of a bloodhound might be normal for a dragon but isn't for humans.

Mauve leans close to me and whispers. "I smell magic on you."

Chapter 10

"Smell magic?" I whisper. "What magic?"

"I don't know. It's faint yet distinct." Mauve sniffs me. "Subtle."

"You don't know. What do you mean you don't know?" Mother put the magic on me, of course. She's not supposed to cast spells on me. In fact, she promised not to.

Mauve throws up her hands. "Don't shoot the messenger."

She learned that line, *don't shoot the messenger*, from Haji. I have to tell her he's missing, but we need to get to somewhere with a bit of privacy first. Plus, we do need to confirm it is Mother's magic Mauve smells to be safe. There are human magicians running around, and at least one wants me dead.

"Come on." I lead Mauve to a brick façade at the edge of the mob. I face my friend and whisper, "It must be my mother. You know, she had a tracking spell on me. She promised she removed it. So much for promises."

"Pull down your hood so I can get a good snuff," Mauve says. Her draconic neck and head pass through the awning overhead.

In the crowd, someone shouts into a bullhorn. "Where do fossil fuels have to go?"

"Away!" A handful of people reply.

"When?"

"Now!" scores of people reply.

"Where do fossil fuels have to go?"

"Away!" people scream, some waving signs and others shaking fists.

I pull off my hood. No one will notice us. I hope.

"You've changed your hair color," Mauve says, fingering a few strands of my red locks. "I like it."

"I preferred green."

The chanting continues, growing louder with each iteration. Off to the right rumbles an impromptu marching band. An oldster with wild gray hair and a bird's nest of a beard walks by, toking.

"Pretty wild crowd already, huh?" he says, letting out a puff of marijuana smoke.

I raise my eyebrows. "And the march hasn't even started."

"We'll show those squares at City Hall. People power!" He takes a long blaze on the joint. "You want to take a drag?"

"No thanks," I say.

"Suit yourself." He shrugs. "C'ya around. Peace."

The oldster saunters off, leaving us in a haze. Marijuana smoke sets off my overactive sense of smell––*ugh*. Mauve buries her face in my hair, sniffing loudly. Her sparkling draconic chest passes through my head and torso, causing me to blink due to its brightness. When my vision clears, a few people are throwing us sideways looks.

Mauve backs away, grimacing. "The marijuana smoke throws off my sense of smell."

"Wonderful." I pull my hood back up. My phone vibrates against my belly. I take it out and check the text. "Dalia is here. She's at the coffee shop down the block. Hopefully, we'll have a little bit of privacy there. We need to talk to you about Haji."

"How is Haji? Have the two of you kissed and made up?"

"Kissed and made up? Where do you come up with these lines?" Mauve works insanely long hours as a network engineer at a boutique web hosting company located in the capital city to help keep her identity as a transdimensional dragon on the down-low.

"I watch television sometimes. It helps me fit in at work. Davis says I am eccentric in the best way."

Davis is one of her coworkers who I think she has a crush on.

"We haven't made up. Haji is missing. I'll fill you in at the coffee shop."

****

We find Dalia sitting on a stool near a window. The redolent aroma of freshly ground coffee beans wafts, and a milk steamer squeals over the soft buzz of conversation. Dalia slurps coffee out of a giant reusable mug—it's twenty ounces, maybe more. A single-serving container of half-eaten organic yogurt is on the tall circular table before my friend. She waves us over.

"Hey, do either of you want anything?" Dalia asks.

Joining her at the table, I shake my head. "Nah, I'm good."

"I do not require food." Mauve pulls up next to me. Her lithe draconic form takes up most of the café. Her serpentine tail passes through the bar where the baristas prepare custom beverages.

I raise an eyebrow. Both her human eyes and draconic apertures stare back at me. "We are in public.

You need to try a little harder."

Mauve's humanoid face flushes, and even her draconic face withdraws. "Oh, right. Sorry. I mean to say…I'm not hungry. Thank you."

I shake my head and exchange a knowing glance with Dalia. Light sparkles against her nose ring and neon pink hair.

Dalia sips her brew and shrugs. "Have you filled her in about Haji?"

"Not yet." We lean close together, and I give Mauve a whispered account of our concerns. "I think his disappearance might have something to do with his interest in…magic."

"Ah, I understand. Tanis and I are aware of his interest in magic," Mauve whispers.

Tanis broke her arm while battling Mark Cassidy, my mother's onetime superior, at The Grove of the Patriarchs inside Mount Rainier National Park. Cassidy may have broken Tanis's arm, but she along with Mauve and Dr. Radcliffe had feasted on his corpse. I haven't seen her since that horrifically memorable night.

"What do you mean aware?" Dalia whispers between quaffs of coffee. "I mean, hello? We know human magicians use…heroin to…what did Gore say?"

"Feel the magic," I say. Gore is the heroin addicted magician who tried to kill me twice at the order of Mark Cassidy.

"I assure you he didn't ask us for heroin," Mauve says. "He called me while I happened to be checking in on Tanis to ask about magic. He was interested if we thought he possesses magical ability. It was after he did that interview with Dalia's ex." She glances Dalia's way.

Dalia and I look at each other, saying in unison, "Devin."

"We should start by having a talk with him," I say.

Dalia pulls out her phone. "I'll message Keb. That's the best way to get in contact with him—through his indentured servant."

Am I to blame for Haji doing something stupid?

"We warned Haji off magic, but who knows what he did. You humans are so mercurial about some things, and Tanis did mention she suspected he might have untapped magical talent."

"Tanis said what?" I demand.

Dalia sets down her phone. "Why did Tanis say that?"

"Well, he did ask, and in her defense, she warned him off magic just a vigorously as I did," Mauve says.

I force a smile. "I suppose that's something."

"I'm so worried about that idiot. If my ex hooked him up with any drugs..." Dalia shakes her head, frowning.

"I sincerely hope he is not pursuing magic, and I assure you Tanis feels the same." Mauve turns her gaze on me. "Speaking of magic, shall we step outside so I can take another sniff? The coffee odor is strong in here."

"Sniff? What's that about?" Dalia asks.

"Someone has put a spell on me, probably my mother. She is a total control freak."

"I can imagine." Dalia gulps the rest of her coffee. "You don't think it could be...Gore?"

"Unknown," Mauve says. "But I personally believe Allison's assumption is correct."

"Is your mom going to show up looking for you?" Dalia looks at me quizzically.

"She better not."

Mauve shifts in her chair. Her dragon form stares down from the ceiling.

Dalia picks up two signs from beneath the table. "Before we go out, choose one, Mauve." Dalia holds up the signs. Both are red with bold black stenciling. One reads, *There is only one planet!* and the other states, *Be part of the solution.* She glances at me. "I only made two because you'll be taking pictures."

"Actually, there is more than one planet," Mauve says. "Even in this solar system, there are—"

"Well, you can be part of the solution then." Dalia checks the time on her phone. "We better get out there. Mauve can sniff you, and then it will be time for the march."

Outside the café, the streets are packed with people shoulder to shoulder. People chant, and in the distance are the beat of drums and the sounds of other musical instruments. A person with a bullhorn announces the march on City Hall will start in two minutes.

"Let's get the sniffing over with. I want to get a picture of you two holding the signs," I tell Mauve, but she's not paying attention to me. Both her golem and dragon form are staring into the mob crowding the street. "Mauve, what…" The words drown in my throat.

Weaving through the crowd is my mother in a midnight black power suit. Despite her diminutive size, people part for her like water. Is it magic or her predatory vibe that gives people the urge to step out of her way? Either way, people dodge her, even if it means colliding with other bystanders. Behind Mother trails my hapless dad. People don't bother moving aside for him.

Mother's eyes lock onto me. Dad bumps into a girl carrying a cup of coffee. She stumbles, and her boyfriend catches her by the upper arm, averting disaster. Dad stops, apologizing profusely.

Mother strides up into my personal space. I can smell the bloody residue of a raw steak breakfast on her breath. Dalia and Mauve back away. Mauve's golem is impassive, but her draconic form cowers. I hate Mother for how she scares my squad.

"Hi, Mrs. Lee," Dalia says shrilly. Her gaze alternates between Mother and me.

Mother ignores my pink-haired friend. "What are you doing here? We're supposed to be on the road."

"I have things to do." I point at my camera.

"You need to come with us right now," Mother says.

"No."

"No? " Her wide nostrils flare. "You dare defy me in public?"

"How did you know where to find me?" My free hand balls into a fist.

A growl rumbles in Mother's chest, and her hot breath blows over my cheeks.

I back up and turn my head away from her. "You need to brush your teeth!"

The stench is almost enough to make me double over, but it excites the sleeper, igniting its insatiable hunger for meat.

The peal of snare drums rings in my ears. People chant and scream all around me. I smell their sweat, their perfume, what they've eaten and drank. I want to taste their flesh and let their blood run down my chin.

"No," I whisper. "Never that."

"Maybe we should take the discussion elsewhere," Dalia says.

"I agree. Druk, you risk exposing us," Mauve says.

People march past us, many waving signs and some throwing us oblique glances.

"Do not speak to me about risking exposure," Mother says. "I will deal with my offspring as I choose without interference from you."

Mother turns her attention back to me.

"Mauve smelled your magic," I whisper through clenched teeth. "You put a tracking spell on me. You promised you wouldn't do that."

Mother sighs. "It wasn't active until you snuck away. I haven't been tracking all your movements."

"You promised."

"You did promise her," Dad says, leaning in close to us. "We all agreed she needs some freedom." Mother looks about ready to speak, but Dad puts a hand on her shoulder. "That doesn't change the fact you snuck off, Allison. I'm disappointed."

"At least, I didn't leave the security detail behind." The excuse even sounds lame to me.

"Oh, bravo, Allison," Mother whispers so softly I don't think Dad can hear her. "The skaag in you is growing stronger, but if you don't train, you'll never be able to harness its strength. If the skaags invade, you'll be as helpless as an infant while at the same time always dangerous, always on the verge of losing control…again."

The reminder I lost control is a slap to the face. "I have school. A life."

"You need to train," Mother insists.

"But—"

Dad raises a hand. "Let's have a compromise. Training is important, and so is school. Let's allow Allison to do her school project if she agrees to train tonight. How does that sound?"

Mother frowns. "She must promise to go without complaint."

"I promise," I mumble.

Mother nods and brushes past me.

Dad smiles. "Thank you for compromising, Allison."

I turn to find Mother whispering in Mauve's ear. Her draconic form has stopped flickering, becoming semitransparent as if she's about to emerge from the slipstream. I'm afraid they're about to duke it out in the middle of downtown Seattle, but then Dad is at Mother's side, wrapping an arm around her slender waist. He waves to me over his shoulder and guides Mother away. Soon I lose sight of them in the crowd.

I rush over to Mauve. The dragon is still semitransparent, gazing over the crowd. Probably tracking my mother's movements. "Are you okay?"

Mauve's humanoid form stares at me blankly, lips quivering.

"What's wrong?"

Mauve blinks, and her draconic form starts flashing in and out of existence. "She…she threatened to eat me."

"I'm so sorry." I embrace Mauve. To think, Mother claims I'm the one who needs to learn control. But I did kill a man. Turns out, I'm just like her.

Chapter 11

We join the raucous parade marching on City Hall. Mauve and Dalia wave their signs and participate in chants. I concentrate on photographing them and the surrounding marchers. I join in the catchy chants and start to feel the vibe down to my core. We can save the planet. All we have to do is make the people in power hear our pleas for justice. They won't turn a deaf ear to our despair and a blind eye to the ravaging of Mother Earth.

We turn down 4th Avenue, and in the distance stands City Hall. I weave my way to the edge of the crowd, taking snaps of protesters with the center of city government in the background. In the dense mob is Tammy Nguyen, a girl I know from elementary school and a fellow photographer. I almost wave but stop myself. I don't want to be recognized.

The mob trundles to a halt, and people start to mill around. Before the crowd, someone shouts into a megaphone.

"Do the right thing! Stand aside. We just want to deliver our demands to the mayor! Do the right thing!"

The protesters start chanting: "Do the right thing! Do the right thing!"

In the shadow of skyscrapers, I stare at the glass and concrete façade of City Hall, and my dreams for a sustainable world are run through a paper shredder. On the steps leading to City Hall stand black-clad riot police, ready to kneel on our necks to protect the status quo.

I take several pictures, then check the exposures on the back of my camera. The images are okay.

I turn to my squad. "I'm going to try to move closer to City Hall."

"We're coming with you," Dalia says. "They can't intimidate us."

I lead the way through the crowd, intent on reaching the frontline. If anything crazy will go down, that's where it will happen. That's where the Pulitzer Prize winning images will play out. I have to be there to document them. I have to.

Someone barges into my shoulder while I'm in midstride. I do a stutter step to stay on my feet but end up careening into a woman pushing a stroller. She lets out a cry and stumbles. For an agonizing instant, my gaze is one hundred percent focused on the woman, and the rumpus around me fades into the background. Her knee buckles, and she holds onto the stroller in a vain attempt to steady herself. The stroller's front wheel lifts off the concrete, the contraption on the verge of overturning.

I grab the woman by the upper arm to keep her from falling. The stroller's front wheel touches down, averting disaster. The woman stares at me, jaw unhinged, one hand gripping the stroller and the other going to her chest.

"I'm so sorry," I splutter. "Are you okay?"

"I should've known better than to bring him. You know, the crowd." She brushes back locks of hair from her eyes.

"We're here for his future," I say fervently. The cherubic baby swaddled in a blue blanket and strapped into the stroller by a five-point harness remains fast asleep.

The woman smiles, revealing tea-stained teeth. "Thank you."

I turn away, scanning the crowd for my friends to discover they have been swept away by the teeming mass. Mauve's draconic neck and head loom over the protesters fifty feet or so behind my position. I wave, and she bobs her head in return. Oh well. I can't wait for them. Time to take some prize-winning photographs. I set off and soon come face-to-face with the charming Drake.

"Hey, watch it, camera girl," he snarls like an angry raccoon. "You should apologize to me."

"Why?"

"You almost ran into me!"

Maybe Drake pushed me into the woman with the stroller. Maybe not. The streets are crammed with people. Regardless, I want to punch him in the smacker. I could knock him out with one wallop before he could even blink an eye, and boy would I enjoy it. But I remember what happened to the would-be kidnapper in my bedroom, and my intestines knot up like a giant ball of twine.

I take a deep breath. "Back off."

"Wait…I recognize you." Drake's eyes narrow. "You're that girl. You're—"

I lunge forward, grabbing him by the collar. He lets out a startled yip as I pull him down until his raccoon eyes are level with mine. He struggles, so I rattle his bones. If I shake him any harder, his eyes might fall out.

"Please, don't hurt me," he whimpers.

"You don't recognize me," I say, words staccato. "Understand?"

"Yes."

I release him, aware the scene is drawing more attention than I want. In his scramble to get away, Drake trips and lands on his butt.

"This is the Seattle PD," booms an announcement from a loudspeaker. "Do not attempt to breach the police line."

Like everyone else, I turn toward City Hall. I stand on my tiptoes but can't see much. The vanguard of protesters is within feet of the police line. When I turn back to where I expect to find Drake, he's gone. The march has slowed almost to a stop. People gather in small groups chanting and dancing. Sunlight glinting off her copper scales, Mauve towers above the crowd off to the left at least twenty feet behind me.

"We the people demand the mayor take measures to make Seattle carbon neutral now!" someone shouts into a bullhorn. "Come on, everyone. Let's make sure Mayor Andretti hears us! Carbon neutral now! Carbon neutral now!"

The chant reverberates through the crowd, growing into a roar. I join the chanting and shoot pictures of young people screaming and waving signs. I dart between people, desperate to take photos of the action up front.

"In fact," roars the voice from the bullhorn, "we want Seattle to be carbon negative! We want Seattle to be the capital of carbon capture technology! Invest in carbon capture technology now, Mayor Andretti!

Before it's too late!"

The mob repeats: "Carbon capture! Carbon capture!"

I weave between clusters of protesters, occasionally brushing against people. The screaming and sign waving are riotous near the frontline. I stop and snap more photos, zooming all the way out to 20 mm and getting up in peoples' screaming faces. A couple people give me offended glares, but most are too caught up in the moment to notice me. As I continue onward, I review the photos on the camera's LCD. A few are wicked. I can see teeth and spittle and tongues and wild eyes while still having a view of the seething mass all around. I smile when I break through the crowd to the frontline.

A handful of brave souls are yelling in the faces of stoic riot police lined up on the lower steps leading to City Hall. A tall man with a bushy beard, reflective aviator sunglasses, and a red bandanna wrapped around his head shouts into a megaphone, leading the crowd in climate protest mantras. Off to the left are the drummers, frenetically thumping on their instruments. I start shooting and keep shooting until my SD cards are full.

****

My cohorts catch up to me near the end of the march. A dozen or so diehards are still chanting or screaming at the police, but most people have already left. We head to a nearby coffee shop and order steaming black brew in gargantuan ceramic cups. Dalia and I slurp the black gold at a table next to a window looking out onto the street. Mauve, of course, does not partake in the repast. Her glimmering dragon form fills the space, passing through the ceiling, walls, furniture, and patrons. Outside the café, pedestrians walk straight through her shimmering tail.

"I thought Mayor Andretti was going to talk to us," Dalia says, shaking her head. "I mean that crowd. The vibe."

I take another sip of coffee. The dark roast is ambrosial against my tongue, but even that can't brighten my mood. "I know. There were so many people, and we were so peaceful. I can't believe how many riot police were at City Hall. I'm glad no one got pepper-sprayed or teargassed or whatever." I shake my head and place my mug on the table with a thump. "Today proves the mayor isn't for us or the planet. All we want are solutions for a sustainable future. Did she have a real conversation with us? No. All she does is send out the municipal muscle. As soon as I can vote, I'm going to vote her out!"

I seize the coffee mug and take a long gulp.

"Just another year. Then we can vote against her." Dalia retrieves her phone from her pocket. After staring at the screen for a moment, she sets the device on the table and looks up, smiling. "This will make you feel better."

"What? What is it?" I set down the mug. "Did Haji message you? Post on social media?"

"No, he didn't, but Keb messaged me. He says we can catch Devin Monday afternoon. I figure we can head over after school."

"Did you tell him Haji is missing?"

"Of course." Dalia sips her brew.

I cross my arms on the table and lean forward. "We need to blitz Devin. Have everyone come. You, me,

Leslie, Jason, and"—I glance at Mauve—"you're coming, right?"

"I can take Monday off…probably," Mauve says.

"Probably? Have you ever taken any time off?" Dalia asks.

"I did once. During The Incident." Mauve shakes her head. "Don't worry. I'll be there for Haji."

I nod. "Good. We need to bust down the palace doors and make Devin understand this is serious." I look Dalia in the eyes. "Do you think Devin could hook Haji up with heroin?"

She sighs. "Anything is possible with my ex. I don't think he ever used heroin, but he knows people who know how to get it."

****

When Dad pulls up to the trailhead for Poo Poo Point, a popular hang-gliding spot, it's nearly midnight. Unsurprisingly given the time, the hybrid is the only car in the dirt lot. As usual, when we left the house for my training, the security detail didn't follow us. I don't want to imagine what Mother might have done to the agents that made them blissfully ignore us after witnessing what her magic did to Devereaux.

"Love you, Daddy," I say as I get out. My breath fogs in the cold air. "See you in the morning."

Mother is already outside, pacing in the vehicle's headlights.

Dad rolls down the window. "What time do you want me to pick you up, honey? Is eight okay?"

Mother responds without breaking her stride. "Eight is acceptable."

I wave to Dad as he backs up and pulls away.

"Come, daughter. Stop wasting time."

I shut my eyes and take a deep breath. "Yes, Mother."

She waits at the trailhead like a runner at the start line of a race. All in black, leotards and windbreaker, she'd be invisible if it weren't for my prosthetics making the night seem like early evening. I'm wearing running gear too, which I have tons of, since before The Incident I ran cross country. I don't yearn for racing, but I do miss training with Dalia. I told her I'm still willing to train with her on the weekends, but she's never taken me up on the offer. Before the sleeper woke within me, she was always the faster runner. Now, she's afraid I'll whip her butt, which I might by accident.

"You want to race up the side of Tiger Mountain in the dark?" I ask, coming to Mother's side.

She nods.

"If you trip and fall, don't blame me."

"I might not be able to see as well as you in human form, but I can still see well enough to navigate the trail."

"If you fall and break a leg in human form, will your skaag form have a broken leg too?"

"I will not fall, daughter. I will defeat you, easily."

"Stop boasting," I grouse. She is faster and stronger than me even in human form, but the lack of light should give me the advantage.

"On your mark, get set, go!" Mother says, catching me flat-footed.

Her soles crunch over gravel and kick up dirt that flies straight into my nostrils and eyes. Blinking and coughing, I set off after her. I'm confident I can overtake her on the winding path through the woods. She'll have to slow down to avoid tripping over a rock or a tree root or slamming into a jutting branch. At least, that's the theory. She eats up the trail like she has a pair of booster rockets strapped to her shoes.

The narrow trail cuts a winding path uphill through a forest of mostly Douglas fir. The drone of crickets surrounds me, and soon a chorus of Pacific tree frogs enters the natural symphony. The scent of rotten wood fills the air when I pass a decaying snag. My labored breathing and the drumbeat of my shoes against the trail join the music. Mother reaches the top of a rise and disappears from view.

"No, you don't," I gasp, focusing inward on the skaag present below the surface. If I can brush against it, I can tap into a nearly limitless well of physical prowess.

My consciousness presses up against the skaag, and white-hot rage burns through me.

But there are other, more pleasing side-effects. My cramping leg muscles rejuvenate, and I blaze over the trail like a jet car. I crest the rise, seeing Mother in the distance before she disappears again around a bend. Dang, that woman is fast. Maybe she's been downplaying how good her night vision is in human form. That's Mother, always hiding a trump card up her sleeve.

I lope down the rise, hoping to make up ground, when a huge bird flies by, not more than a foot from my face. Its dappled brown and white feathers are magnificent as it glides between the trees. It's an owl, a great—

My toes slam into a rock, and I'm airborne, screaming as I plummet. My left knee hits first, and a shock of pain shoots through my leg.

After taking a moment to collect myself, I push myself up onto my butt, wincing. "I'll never hear the end of this."

I manage to stand without too much difficulty, which gives me hope I might be able to walk off the stiffness and pain. My body dispels that assumption. Just because unnatural strength courses through my veins doesn't mean I won't hurt myself if I run on a bum knee. Grimacing, I trudge down the path favoring my left leg.

Chapter 12

Sweat beads across my brow and dribbles down my face. A big droplet rolls into my eye, stinging. I scrunch up my apertures, about to spew invectives but gasp instead. An inferno ignites in my knee each time my left leg bears weight. Gritting my teeth, I put all my weight on my good leg. I gingerly probe my injured knee that feels like it has swollen up to the size of a cantaloupe. My body's supernatural healing isn't kicking in fast enough.

I stare up the steep trail. Through the trees is the telltale glow of distant urban sprawl. It's a testament to how fast we'd been running. I'm almost to the top. Even limping slower than a slug for the last quarter mile or so, I haven't been on the trail for much over thirty minutes. Taking a deep breath, I trudge onward, imagining Mother's infuriatingly smug expression when I reach her side. Undoubtedly, her conceitedness will soar to untold heights when she sees my bum knee.

A gentle breeze blows from the west, carrying with it the stench of human sweat and cheap alcohol down from Poo Poo Point. I go still as a granite statue, heart galloping. We've never encountered people before on our wilderness jaunts.

"Come on, stop hogging the booze," comes a nasally male voice from beyond the tree line.

I swallow a lump in my throat. What does Mother

have in store for the poor drunken fools? Will she frighten them or scramble their minds like she did to Agent Deveraux? Or will she do something worse? We are far away from prying eyes out here in the dead of night. Might she do something unspeakable? I remember all too well Ion's many threats to eat my squad and me, including our shoes. A near-perfect crime, she'd proclaim.

"I only had one sip. Share."

"Stop your whining," snarls a second voice. "I paid for it."

Two males. They sound about my age.

What should I do? If I stay hidden in the trees, I won't be able to restrain Mother from doing something drastic. But stumbling out into the open, attracting the attention of the drunks, might spur Mother to do something dire.

"If you ain't gonna give me a drink, I'm heading down."

Shoes scuff against pebbles. Light beams through the trees, bobbing up and down in time with the bearer's footsteps.

"Great," I murmur.

I scan the forest near the path for a likely hiding spot. On the left, a few feet off the trail, is a towering Douglas fir with lichen and vibrant green moss speckling its bark. I glance toward Poo Poo Point, my prosthetics adjusting to the bright spotlight illuminating the path's downward slope.

"Damn it," I whisper.

Out of time, I hobble for cover. The drunk's footfall sounds like a giant's. My left foot catches on a root hidden by dense ground cover. I clench my mouth shut tight to stifle a startled scream, but I can't silence the brush from shaking when I strike the ground. Pain blossoms through my leg with its epicenter at my bum knee. A soft whine escapes my lips, and tears join the sweat on my cheeks.

"Who's there? I hear you!"

The flashlight's beam jaggedly illuminates the trees and undergrowth. Grinding my teeth, I press my back against the tree trunk and hope the boy is too cautious to venture off the path.

"What are you shouting about?"

The light arcs back to the trail. "I heard someone."

"Heard someone? You dolt, who'd—"

A dragon's shriek reverberates through the woods, seeming to come from every direction at once.

"What was that?" whimpers the boy nearest to me.

A second shriek pierces my ears. I look up, expecting to see a shimmering serpent soaring above the forest's canopy, but there are only stars and clouds in the night sky.

The boy near me breaks out in a run, followed by his cohort at a lurching gait with a flashlight grasped in one hand and a fifth of whiskey in the other. Soon they disappear beyond a bend in the trail.

I try to stand, but my knee is not having it.

"Damn." I grimace and pull up the black leggings to expose the swollen, purple joint.

"An impressive injury."

I scream and would have jumped out of my skin if that were possible. Mother stands over me, smirking just as I had imagined.

"Not so loud, daughter. We don't want those boys to hear you."

"I didn't hear or smell you. How did you sneak up on me?"

"I have magic."

"The dragon call…that was you?"

Mother nods and kneels next to me, examining my injury.

"How long will it take to heal?" I ask.

"Not long, I think. You made it up here. You can move the joint. The injury is not bad."

"It hurts."

"Please, daughter, try not to be so…human."

I stiffen. "What? Don't you feel pain?"

"I do," she replies with a self-satisfied smile, "but you'll never hear me complaining about it."

****

We sit together next to the rectangular patch of artificial turf hang gliders and paragliders use to launch from out over Tiger Mountain's densely wooded slopes. To the north, beyond the wilderness twinkle the bright lights of Issaquah, one of Seattle's many suburbs. The night sky is salted with stars and the pale half disc moon obscured by wispy clouds.

"Are you going to call Dad?"

"I'm not calling your father." Mother stares out over the wilderness. I can't tell what she's looking at with her unnerving orbs. Maybe Cougar Mountain to the west.

"I can't train on my knee."

"If we leave now, how do you plan to get down to the trail?"

I toss my pride into a mulcher. "Maybe you can carry me down?"

The peal of Mother's laughter is unlike any sound I

have ever heard her make. She sounds genuinely mirthful, which is totally unlike her.

"What?" I demand.

"Allison, I'm not carrying you down the trail."

"But—"

"Relax, daughter. You will recover enough to train in a few minutes. You are half-skaag, after all."

I bite my tongue to restrain a snarky retort. Arguing will get me nowhere, and I'm already miserable enough. I hug my good leg to my chest and shiver.

About fifteen minutes later, Mother rises and looms over me. "Strip."

I stare, incredulous. Stripping requires I stand, which I doubt I can do. The only reason my knee is not a volcano of agony is I'm not moving it.

"I am speaking English, daughter. You can understand what I'm saying. Now, strip."

"I'll end up in the fetal position."

Mother reaches behind her back to produce a pistol.

My jaw goes unhinged. "Is that…doesn't that belong to one of the agents?"

"It does." Mother expertly flips the safety to off.

My mouth works soundlessly.

"Don't worry, Allison. I'll return it. I didn't damage anyone while procuring it."

"That's great. I have to know. What do you plan to do with it?"

"I'm going to shoot you, daughter. It's up to you if I shoot you while you're a human or a skaag."

"What do you mean you're going to shoot me?"

"Don't play dumb, daughter."

"Is this one of your jokes? It's not funny."

Mother grins, showing the barest hint of absurdly white teeth.

I scramble to my feet, relieved my injured knee is only stiff. By the time I'm halfway undressed, a fine drizzle mists everything. Naked and wet, I glower at Mother.

My teeth chatter as I speak. "Can I move my clothes under the trees?"

"Don't dally." Mother carelessly points the gun toward the trees.

I scurry to the tree line without limping, stowing my clothing at the base of a fir. I'm afraid it's already too late. On the hike down I'll be wearing damp clothes. If I get a chance to hike down. I wouldn't put it past Mother to shoot me in the head and shrug nonchalantly as I lay dead in the mud.

Steeling myself for the inevitable, I trudge back to Mother entirely unprepared for her motherly love. I stand before her shaking like a half-drowned cat. She points the gun at my head.

"Transform, daughter, or I'll shoot you in the kneecap." She aims at my uninjured knee.

My transformation is immediate and agonizing as my body folds and expands like origami paper, but I'm glad I'm not kneecapped. Hovering before Mother with all the power of my skaag form available to me, I note she seems fragile even with the gun leveled at my head. I could bite her in half or crush her under my prodigious bulk or vaporize her with a lightning bolt.

She pulls the trigger—bang! My vision flares white, and pain radiates between my eyes. Anger pulses through me, mine and the sleeper's. I blink to clear my vision and raindrops roll into my eyes, burning like acid. Bang! Bang, bang, bang! Fifteen more times pain sprouts over my face, giving me a skull-pulverizing headache. I hurt too much to even open my mouth to roar at the she-devil standing before me.

"Excellent," Mother declares, lowering the gun. "Your hide is as tough as I hoped. As soon as I transform, the real training begins."

****

I'm a zombie all day at school Monday and still am while waiting for the bus to Seattle downtown with Dalia, Leslie, and Jason. Only Mauve is missing. We still have our backpacks with us. My camera is stashed inside mine. When I informed Agent Deveraux Sunday night I wouldn't be coming home directly after school Monday, she rubberstamped my request without giving me any grief. I suspect her behavior is an aftereffect of what Mother did to her. It's yet another thing for me to feel horribly guilty about.

Dalia has her head buried in her phone. "Can you believe it? Mauve didn't take the whole day off. She only took the afternoon off, and now she's stuck in traffic. She's not going to make it."

"Oh, I believe it."

Dalia glances up at me. "What happened Saturday night? You've been acting zonked all day."

I lean close to Dalia and whisper. "She shot me."

"What?" Dalia exclaims.

"Not so loud," I say.

Leslie and Jason stop their conversation about an upcoming cross country meet and lean toward me. The other people at the stop, mostly commuters by their looks, take no notice of us.

"What happened?" Leslie asks.

I sigh. "Okay. I'll tell you. Just promise to keep your voices down." I look at each of my friends in turn for confirmation. Satisfied, I say, "My mother shot me. Sixteen times."

Jason rubs a hand through his thick hair. "What? You're not serious."

"As a heart attack."

Dalia takes my hand and squeezes.

"Wow," Jason says. "I don't know what to say to that. That's crazy."

"I thought I had issues with my dad," Leslie says. "Are you sure you're okay?"

"I'm fine. I wasn't…entirely human at the time."

The sleek electric bus pulls up to the curb, and we board, finding relative privacy at the rear of the bus since we're about an hour ahead of rush hour. We sit together in a tight knot and with some reluctance, I recount my latest night in the wilderness with Mother.

We disembark the bus near the intersection of Madison and 5th. High rises tower over the city streets in every direction, their peaks piercing the gossamer clouds dotting an azure sky. Automobiles whizz by, trying to beat the traffic lights.

The sedan of my security detail rolls by. Agent Haskell, in the passenger seat for once, watches behind dark sunglasses. I nearly flip him off but stop myself and wave instead. Agent Deveraux expects me to treat her underlings respectfully. I swear Haskell smirks at me.

"That the Federales?" Leslie asks.

"Unfortunately. They follow me around like a bad smell," I say.

The sedan parallel parks in a nearby loading zone.

"Let's roll," I say. "I can't stand those creeps watching me all the time."

Dalia leads the way down the sidewalk.

"He lives around here? On his own?" Leslie asks, glancing around at the real estate. She is every bit the golden-haired heiress in her preppy attire, looking chic and athletic at the same time.

"He does. Right there." Dalia points to a soaring glass and steel spire that might be the tallest building for blocks. "Like I said, he struck gold with the podcast."

"Wow," Jason says and whistles. "When you said he makes good money, I never imagined it meant he could afford a place in a building like that. Right, babe?" He looks at Leslie.

"This real estate is for high rollers," Leslie says.

"He lives in the penthouse," Dalia says.

"Don't remind me," I say, seething anger not entirely my own roiling in my gut. At the best of times, I'm annoyed Devin has turned his association with me into a multimillion-dollar podcasting empire. Looking at the massive edifice he lives inside makes me clench my jaw until my teeth hurt. He lives in a modern-day castle because of things he said about me. What a waste.

"I texted Keb," Dalia says, phone held before her. "He's expecting us. Let's head inside the lobby."

A gaggle of middle-aged salarymen and younger women in business attire exit the building as we approach. One woman, who looks like she's in her mid-twenties, gives me a double-take. For a second, I'm afraid she recognizes me as the monster girl despite my fire engine red hair.

"Julia! Is that you? Oh my God! Who would've thought?" Leslie says, coming between the adults and me. Jason stops with Leslie.

Dalia slows to join the conversation, but I take her by the upper arm. "Come on. I think Julia recognized me."

"Oh," Dalia says.

The monumentally tall glass door automatically slides open at our approach. As we cross the threshold, Leslie says, "The monster girl? Allison Lee? No, of course not. Are you crazy? I stay as far away from her as I can."

Leslie is feeding Julia and her posse lies, but the words still prick like needles. We enter the ultramodern lobby, and the door glides silently shut behind us. The faint yet pleasing scent of lavender permeates the air. Near the entrance is a display case showing off plaques declaring the building is net carbon zero. Before Devin became a podcast king, he was super involved in the local climate movement. That's how he and Dalia met.

"How is that even possible?" I say, pointing to the plaques. "A building like this is net carbon zero? No way."

Dalia shrugs. "Greenwashing, maybe? Beats me."

Outside, Leslie and Jason are disentangling themselves from the adults. A security guard behind a desk near the elevator watches us with a suspicious gaze.

"Can I help you girls?" she asks, making it clear by the way she says girls we have no business being here.

I'm ready to make a snarky retort when the elevator dings, and Keb steps off. He smoothly indicates we are with him, and the security guard relaxes. Keb wears purple horn-rimmed glasses and a white T-shirt prominently displaying a pride flag.

"Dalia," he declares extravagantly and gives my friend a peck on the cheek and turns to me. "Girl with red hair, whom I don't know." He winks at me, and we share a brief hug. "Oh, are they coming too?" He indicates Leslie and Jason with a graceful turn of his hand. "Come. Come."

He takes us to the elevator with the most massive control panel I've ever seen and punches the button for the 46th floor, the top. The elevator's interior is spacious, but not so much I don't smell everyone's BO. The ride is swift, and the elevator opens right across from a black door with a silver handle.

"Welcome to the dragon's lair," Keb says mysteriously and adds in a normal tone, "He's probably still at his workstation. Head straight in. You can't miss him."

That word, dragon, makes me wish Mauve is with us. Keb opens the door, which swings in silently. Dalia and I lead the way across a marble floor into a palatial room. In the room's center is a sprawling desk full of monitors and computer paraphernalia. Devin's purple hair pokes out above a monitor.

"Keb, where did you go? Get over here. I need your help."

That's Devin for you. Such a nice guy, great personality.

"Do you have to treat Keb like he's your slave? You don't even pay him," Dalia says.

Devin stands up from behind the computer equipment. His lips are stained orange like he has been eating crispy cheese puffs.

"Oh, no!" Devin yells and darts toward the hallway off to the left.

Chapter 13

Devin slips on the marble and belly flops with a loud slap. *Ouch.* That has got to hurt. His phone spins out of his hand across the floor. Scrambling to his feet, he disappears down the hall, and a door slams.

Dalia and I exchange quizzical looks.

"I think that tells us all we need to know," Dalia says, marching across the room to the monitors and computer equipment arrayed on the desk. "He knows something."

"Can he get away?" I ask Keb.

"Nah," Keb says. "That's the master bedroom and bath. He doesn't even have a panic room."

"A panic room?" I ask.

"He told me all about how they tried to sell him on one when he bought the place." Keb shrugs. "He didn't get one because it was too expensive."

"He's too cheap, you mean," Dalia says from behind the monitors. "Well, he had the wherewithal to lock the computers. Do you know his password, Keb?"

"Wish I did." Keb shakes his head.

I step deeper inside the opulent space and crinkle my nose. The unpleasant scent of stale chips and disinfectant hangs in the air.

Keb gives me with a mirthless smile. "Yeah, I swear Devin was born without a functional nose."

I force myself not to gag. Did a stink like this

permeate my bedroom before Mother did the deep clean? I hope not. How embarrassing.

Leslie and Jason walk by toward to the room's back wall that is all glass, providing a panoramic view of downtown Seattle, including the Puget Sound's dark blue waters and the whitecapped Cascades on the horizon.

"Listen," Keb says seriously, "I know y'all have an issue with Devin and his podcast, but I didn't let y'all in here to screw with that. That's my work too. You know that. Devin is exploitative sometimes, and I'm sorry for that, but this isn't about that. This is about Haji. Okay?" He looks at me and smiles apologetically.

I nod in agreement, despite wanting to transform into a skaag and fry all Devin's fancy computer equipment with a lightning bolt. For one thing, I doubt I can morph without crushing everyone into a bloody pulp.

"I thought," Dalia says, "you know, we might find some leverage on the computers to get him out here without busting down the door."

"Believe me, you ain't busting down the…" Keb glances at me. "Allison can bust down the door, but we're not going to need to do that. I got an idea, but you're not going to like it."

"What's the idea?" I ask.

"You didn't tell her it may come to this?" Keb turns to Dalia.

My BFF throws up her arms in an exaggerated shrug. "I hoped—"

"Come to what?" I stare at them.

Keb gestures expansively about the room with both hands. "Well, this is where he conducts—"

117

"Interviews," Dalia says.

"You want me to do an interview with him?" My pulse pounds behind my eyeballs. This is one of my greatest nightmares coming to horrifying fruition.

****

I methodically clench and unclench my clammy fists before the black door to Devin's bedroom. Keb stands with his ear pressed against the door as he negotiates with the podcaster inside.

"I can't believe you let them in. You're out of a job." Even muffled by the door, Devin sounds self-righteous.

"Technically, it's an unpaid internship. Plus, who else will do ninety percent of your research and sound editing for free?"

"Touché," Devin growls. "But you know they have it out for me."

Dalia leans close and whispers, "Can't you…I don't know…threaten him? Like, make him pee his pants? He's not brave."

Even Dalia doesn't know I killed the man in my bedroom. She's been fed the same lies as everyone else. How can I tell her I don't dare untether the beast within me without revealing more than I should? It's not that I don't trust Dalia with the truth. I do, but what Mother will do if she discovers Dalia knows I'm the killer scares the bejesus out of me.

"I don't want to be that person," I say.

"You're not that person, but you can pretend to be. We are dealing with my ex."

Dalia looks at the door like she can burn it down with her glare. What did she ever see in Devin?

"Devin, Allison is here to talk. She's even willing

to give an interview," Keb says.

After a long silence, Devin says. "Okay, I'll tell them what I know about Haji after I interview Allison. In addition to the interview, I have one condition."

I step up to the door, my fingernails cutting half-moons into my palms. "I'm listening."

"I need you to swear not to harm me."

"I'll hurt him," Dalia whispers. "I'll sock him in the nose."

Dalia will too. I hold a finger to my lips for silence.

"Did you hurt Haji?" I ask.

"No," Devin shouts, "of course not!"

"Alrighty, then. I swear I won't hurt you."

"Are you sincere? You don't sound sincere."

I sigh. "Devin, I'm not religious. I'm not going to swear on the Bible. I said I won't hurt you. I won't."

"This not hurting me pact includes Dalia and anyone else with you."

Keb nods his head and mouths "Smart."

Dalia rolls her eyes.

"I vouch for them, Devin. I won't let them hurt you. Not even Dalia."

The bedroom door swings open to reveal Devin in black silk pajamas a drug kingpin would wear.

Devin smiles and rubs his palms together. "Let's get this party started!"

"You haven't heard my conditions yet."

The smile slips from Devin's face. "What conditions?"

"Five-minute interview. Max."

Devin drops his hands to his sides. "Come on! Standard interview is twenty-five minutes."

"Second condition," I say.

Devin goes red in the face.

"Have you published the second interview with Haji yet?"

Devin mines zipping his lips shut, then flashes a smarmy smile.

"He hasn't," Keb says.

"Traitor!" Devin whines.

"They can easily confirm if it's published or not," Keb says.

"That's not the point. The point is not to cooperate."

I take a deep breath. Not having seen Devin since The Incident, I'd forgotten how truly despicable he is. "Devin, I want to listen to the interview, and then I want you to destroy it."

Devin shakes his head. "No way. Those interviews are my livelihood. Haji gave a great interview. A great one. I'll let you listen to it prerelease, but there's no way I'm deleting it."

"I want the interview deleted." My patience and the sleeper's wears thin.

"Devin, dude," Keb says, "this is Allison you're going to interview. It will be huge. Twenty-five minutes…five minutes…it doesn't matter. Your subscribership will go nuclear. I understand you not wanting to delete the interview with Haji, it's your work. It's our work."

"My art, you mean," Devin says.

"Art," Dalia scoffs and giggles.

Devin's expression becomes aggrieved.

Keb nods. "Your art. I totally understand where you're coming from. But how many times have you told me you'd do anything to interview Allison?"

Devin licks his lips and nods. "Keb makes a good point. Five minutes, but I won't tell you the questions beforehand. First though, I'll let you listen to the interview with Haji. There's nothing bad in the interview."

"Does my name come up or not?" I ask.

"Sure, but not in a scandalous way," Devin says. "All I'm asking is to listen to the interview with an open mind. There's nothing bad in it. Nothing. There's no reason to delete it. After you listen, if you really want me to delete it, I will."

****

I sit next to Devin by the computer equipment in the middle of the extravagant living room after listening to his interview with Haji. My guilt has entered hyperspace.

"Why do you want magic so bad?" Devin had asked Haji.

"Well…I don't know. I mean, it's kind of embarrassing," Haji said.

"Help me understand why. We both know most magicians with real magic are druggies."

"I know. That's a risk. It's just…if I have magic, maybe Allison, you know, will look at me differently. Pay more attention to me."

"Allison Lee? So love is driving to explore magic?"

"Yes—"

"Allison, are you ready?" Devin asks.

I blink and mentally reorient myself to the here and now. No matter how guilty I feel, I need to stay on my game or Devin will make a fool of me during the interview.

"Thinking about what Haji said? No worries, I won't ask about his pursuit of magic. I promise. As a thank you for not insisting I delete the interview."

Forcing a smile, I nod. Surprisingly, Devin had told the truth. The interview was anything but scandalous. I deserve to have it go out to the world as penance for how I had treated Haji. My gaze falls on two golden microphones in stands in between us on the table—the mics sparkle like real gold. I can't decide if the homage to overclocked consumerism is deadened or heightened by a crinkled bag of chips resting on the table between the mics.

Devin smiles smarmily. "The mics are plated in 24 karat gold."

"They're…amazing…wicked."

"Ten percent of my revenue goes to the planet. To fight climate change. That's a ton of green."

My immediate reaction is to bite his head off. Oh, thank you so much for spinning my life, my private life, my super personal emotional struggles into a multimillion-dollar business empire. *Thank you thank you thank you thank you.* You're a god.

But I don't. I know it's my guilt setting me on edge. Instead, I lean back in the chair, which is surprisingly comfortable, and survey the room. My team congregates near the window, Leslie and Jason canoodling on the couch while Dalia paces, her gaze alternating between the view and me. I'm not sure if she's worried I will hurt Devin or if she doesn't keep looking my way, she might miss the headline performance—me tearing his head off. Keb simply stares at me from the hallway with his hands in his pockets, playing with either loose change or keys.

"You can at least give me an attaboy," Devin grouses. "I was at the climate march this weekend."

"Me too. I'm sooo sorry I missed you."

His gaze drops to the table. "You won't give me a break, huh? Maybe I don't deserve one."

I don't respond.

Sighing, he leans back in the chair. "Shall we?"

"Let's get this over with."

"One second. Quiet on set, everyone. Quiet on set." Devin spins to face a monitor. He uses a wireless mouse to open a recording application, the kind with a jumpy bar graph providing a visual of the sound level. His fingers fly over a slick gamer keyboard. His index finger hammers on the enter key with gusto. "There"— he spins back to me—"we're recording. Are you ready? Just relax and move close to the mic."

I shimmy the chair closer to the table and lean toward the gold-plated mic until my lips nearly brush it.

"Not that close. There'll be feedback. Just relax."

I shift in my seat, knowing I'll never get comfortable.

"Better," he says and takes a deep breath and lets it out, then punches a button on the computer, starting a five-minute countdown timer. When he speaks, it's in a voice that's a podcast host and pitchman wrapped up in a sausage roll. "Welcome to a special edition of Skaags & Dragons, the most ginormous podcast in the world. Hell, maybe the entire universe! A big shout out to all my millions of fans listening from around the world. Without you, none of this would be possible. And when I say this is a special edition, I'm not bullshitting you. Sitting next to me in the studio is none other than the monster girl herself, Allison Lee. Do you have something to say to all the people around the world who idolize you, Allison?"

"Hi," I say through clenched teeth.

Devin waves his arms like a conductor indicating a fortissimo and mouths the words come on.

I unclench my jaw. "Peace and love."

"All righty then! Moving on," Devin says. "Why the fire engine red hair? I mean, I used to date your best friend. I know for a fact you love coloring your hair forest green."

"Ummm…it was time for a change." Lame. My gaze is drawn to the timer on the screen—four thirty-five.

Devin smiles. "So you don't know about monsterspotting.com?"

"I do." My cheeks flush. Four eighteen flashes on the monitor.

"You heard that, peeps, Allison Lee knows about monsterspotting.com! Is that why you changed your hair?"

"Maybe." My fingertips press into the chair's armrests.

"Ooooh. Hits a little close to home? Someone close to you posting snaps?"

I glare at Devin. "No."

"Ouch! I wish this was on video feed, folks! Then you'd see Allison give me a look that can kill! Moving on. I get a bunch of questions about this in the forums. People want to know, have you had sex while a skaag?"

Without warning, my eyeballs zoom in on his prominent nose until I can stare inside each pore. I'd like to break his nose.

"Devin!" Dalia exclaims.

"Hey! No comments from the peanut gallery."

I blink until my vision zooms out. I glance at the monitor; two forty-three to go.

"By your reaction, I'll take that as a ye—"

"No. Absolutely not," I say.

"You're sure? You can be honest."

I want to threaten to break his arms. "I am being honest."

"Haji indicated you might be up to that the first time I interviewed him. He was a little coy about it. I thought maybe he wasn't kissing and—"

I grab the crinkled chips bag and toss it in his face. Then, I draw my index finger across my throat.

"Hold on. Hold on. No need to get all salty. We're all friends here," Devin says, maintaining his suave podcast voice, but there is sweat rolling down his cheeks. "Last question. Is it true Dr. Radcliffe is the head of a multidimensional conspiracy to brainwash humans into being willing food stock for dragons?"

He winks at me, a conceited smile slashing his face. I nearly launch myself out of the chair at him. If he knew how close I am to knocking out his teeth, he'd be back cowering in his bedroom.

I take a deep breath. "No, that's not true. Dr. Radcliffe works tirelessly for the betterment of humankind. He doesn't eat humans. He loves humanity." I remember his tales about feasting on warriors sent to kill him. High-definition images of him, Tanis, and Mauve eating the skaag Mark Cassidy loop through my mind. "He's told me in his mind and in his heart, he feels as human as he does a dragon. I believe him. He's lived among us for hundreds of years and battled to protect us from the skaags. He put himself and his people at risk to protect us. This is his home."

I silently add, he's also a liar who had been ready to hand me over to Mark Cassidy, who planned to murder me, in exchange for information. Don't trust him. You'll get burned.

Devin beams and gives me two thumbs up. "All right! That's a wrap. I hope all of you out there across the world enjoy this interview with monster girl Allison Lee half as much as I enjoyed conducting it. This is Devin Montoya signing off. Love to you all."

Devin stops the recording. "See! That wasn't so bad. You told your side of the story. Put to rest all the rumormongering. You should be a regular guest on the show. What do you think?"

"That is my first and last interview."

My squad and Keb march over, clustering around Devin and me.

"No way! You're a natural," Devin says. "You should consider upping your media presence."

I roll my eyes.

"Don't push your luck, Devin," Dalia warns.

"Allison fulfilled her side of the bargain." Leslie stares down her nose at the podcast kingpin. "Tell us where Haji is."

Devin nervously smacks his lips. "Ahhhhh…about Haji. I don't know where he is."

Dalia snarls and lurches for her ex. Only Jason grabbing her around the shoulders keeps her from knocking him silly.

"You—"

Devin holds up his hands defensively. "But I can take you to someone who might know. Let me change, and I'll take you. Okay?"

My friends exchange looks. Keb shrugs.

"Devin, this better not be some BS move," Dalia says.

Chapter 14

Devin shows off how his SUV can parallel park by itself near the intersection of 15th and Republican. Everyone is duly impressed, including me. The gullwing doors are a nice touch, too, accentuating the vehicle's science-fiction suave. We gather on the sidewalk next to a single-story brick building housing a used book shop and other small businesses. A few parents with young children and dog walkers patrol the sidewalk, enjoying the relatively warm fall afternoon.

Across the street, right on the corner, is a brick building painted in garish rainbow colors. The purple sign above the entrance reads in lime green block letters: *ZEN MOMENTS*. An elderly couple exits the dispensary, one woman holding a white paper bag.

"This is the place?" I ask.

"Yeah, let me call her," Devin says and pulls out his phone.

I photograph the dispensary, documenting the scene like I imagine a private investigator might.

"Wait a minute," Dalia says. "Is Zen Moments owned by Zenobia? Why would she know where Haji is?"

"Zenobia?" Leslie and I ask in unison.

"Interesting name," Jason says.

"We ran into her once while we were dating. I didn't think she had enough brain cells to run a legitimate business of any kind."

"You're being a little judgy, Dalia. Zen is a top-notch business person," Devin says.

"Did she give Haji heroin?" My pulse goes supersonic.

"No! She's legit. She never pushed hard stuff even while she was dealing," Devin says. "Listen, I don't know what Keb told you all, but after the interview Haji wouldn't stop talking about wanting to use magic and needing heroin to do it. I told him I don't have access to that stuff, but Zenobia might. Honestly, I doubt she knows anybody with hard stuff like that. She probably told him to go to hell." Devin manipulates his smartphone with a thumb. He brings the device to his ear. "Yo, Zen! It's me, Devin. I'm outside. Come out."

With my heightened senses, I hear Zenobia's less than enthusiastic response, including a string of highly creative profanity that would've made me smile in a different situation. Devin smirks and nods like she'll be out any second.

"Listen, Zen, I have someone with me you'll want to meet." Devin winks at me. "Believe me, you want to meet her. Let's just say she's the subject of my podcast."

More profanity from Zenobia. I want to curse too. Why am I always the monster girl?

Devin ends the call. "Zen will be out in a couple minutes."

Five minutes stretches into fifteen, then thirty. My friends talk and play on their phones while I remain at the periphery. Haji could be strung out in a back alley somewhere, dying from an overdose, and here we are, standing around waiting. Doing nothing.

At some point, the security detail parallel parks across the street three cars down from Zen Moments. My prosthetics zoom in on the driver, who is none other than Agent Deveraux. This is strange. First, she lets me go on an outing after school without so much as a peep, and now she's following me around. I had always believed tailing me was beneath Deveraux. Maybe mother did fry her brain? Or she's giving Haskell his yearly performance review. What will she make of our confab with Devin's ex-pusher?

"Hey, is that her?" Jason asks, pointing across the street.

A tall broomstick of a woman with long stringy gray hair stands in front of the dispensary. She doesn't look so much like a drug dealer as a hippy reborn in bellbottom jeans and a tie-dye tank top with the dispensary's name emblazoned across the chest in giant bold print. Her exposed arms are all corded muscle.

"That's her," Devin says and waves at the woman. "Zen! Zen! Over here!"

Zen doesn't bother with the crosswalk, stepping right out into the street. A black truck with oversized tires squeals to a halt not half a foot from the hippie, horn blaring. Zen stands before the vehicle's massive grill and flips off the driver, then continues meandering across the street, somehow avoiding being run over.

Zen stands before us, fidgeting which causes the multicolored bangles she wears on her wrist to clatter together. I crinkle my nose from the earthy musk wafting off her that's almost enough to make my eyes water. Dangling around her neck by a lime green lanyard are glasses with thick lenses.

"Where is she?" Zenobia squints, eyeballing each

of us in turn.

"Come on!" Devin points at me. "The one who has red hair."

Feeling like a neon sign advertises my location to the world, I wave to Zen and give her a toothless grin. She squints at me, and her long-fingered hand hovers centimeters from my head. I back up a step, and she lowers her hand.

"This isn't her. I checked monsterspotting.com," Zen says huskily. "Wrong hair color."

"Put on your glasses," Devin says. "This is most definitely her," adding almost in a whisper, "Allison Lee."

Zenobia puts on her glasses, making her gold-flecked eyes look as large as ostrich eggs, and stares at me. I struggle to put up with her scrutiny. I keep reminding myself I'm doing this for Haji. After at least a minute, she harrumphs. "I suppose there's a resemblance."

"I changed my hair color," I say. "To be incognito. I don't need reporters hounding me every time I step outside my house."

"I should call Channel 5." Zen fishes a smartphone out of her back pocket. "I could use the free publicity."

I tense, tempted to snatch the phone out of her hand.

"Don't you dare call Channel 5." Leslie steps forward.

"Whoa! Easy, hon." Zen retreats a pace.

"Don't call her hon," Jason says.

Devin jumps in between Zenobia and us. He holds out his hands for calm. "Nobody is calling the news media. Relax."

"She said she's going to call channel 5!" Jason's brow furrows.

"Yeah, she did," Devin says, "but that was just talk, right, Zen?"

"I'm not calling anyone." Zen hammers on her phone with her thumbs. "I want to check out the latest picture on monsterspotting.com to confirm this girlie here is the genuine article." Zen holds up her phone, her gaze flicking between the screen and my face. She whistles. "I do see a resemblance. My, oh my, tinytim123 knows how to get some nice pictures of you, monster girl. Or, should I say, Allison Lee."

"He's my neighbor." I give her a tight smile. "Now, are you going to help us or not?"

"You bet. First, I need a selfie and"—she pats herself down—"I'll need to go back inside to get a sharpie. I want some autographs too. You do that, I'll tell you all about your friend. Let me tell you, Devin didn't do him any favors sending him to me. I know one pusher who deals top of the line…" She peeks around nervously and mumbles, "Heroin." She continues in a normal tone. "He ain't a nice guy if you take my meaning."

"Tell us—" I say.

"Pictures and autographs first."

"Don't you dare put any of the pictures on that website," Dalia says.

"Monsterspotting.com? Hell no! This is for my business website, zensensations.com. Move aside now, pink hair." Zen sidles up next to me. The marijuana stink permeating her makes me cringe. "Come on now, I want smiles, Allison. Like we're long-lost sisters reunited."

****

After I suffer through at least twenty selfies with Zen and autograph her jeans, tank top, and a poster advertising her business in exchange for her not-so-hot tip, we pile back into the luxury SUV. Everyone is talking about what to do next, coming up with a game plan. I'm too busy wallowing in guilt to listen. Maybe if I had been a little bit nicer to Haji, more understanding, we wouldn't be here.

Dalia, who sits next to me, pats my hand. "I'm going to text Mauve to tell her we're going to the club. We'll have to pick her up somewhere downtown."

"I doubt they're going to let us into an over twenty-one club," I say.

"I shouldn't tell you goody-goodies this," Devin says as he pulls into traffic. "I have an ID that can get me into the club...probably."

"I don't think we can trust him to go inside alone," Dalia whispers.

I shrug and pull out my phone to check the time. "Devin, drop me off at the rescue mission on Second Avenue."

"I'm not a taxi service," Devin gripes.

"Do you have to be a jerk about everything?" Leslie calls from the third row seats.

Devin argues about his character with Leslie and Jason.

"Joe?" Dalia asks.

"I need someone to run by everything that's going on," I say.

Hurt briefly flashes across Dalia's face. "Okay. The club opens at nine. We'll pick you up around eight?"

I nod.

"Devin, you are a taxi service," Dalia says shrilly, interrupting the argument over her ex's character. "Take us to the rescue mission. The club doesn't open until nine. We can drop off Allison and pick her up later. Plus, you need to pick up Mauve at Fifth and Pine at seven."

"Yes, your majesty," Devin grumbles.

****

The sun is low by the time Devin drops me off on 2nd Avenue. I wave to my friends as the SUV pulls away, emitting a soft hum to alert the visually impaired, which fades as the vehicle accelerates. I adjust the camera strap draped over my left shoulder and turn toward the rescue mission. Men congregate in front of the stairs leading to the portico. The younger men eye me up, perhaps salaciously, but I ignore them just as I attempt to ignore the crowd's odor permeating the air.

The men's shelter is the nicest building on the block. The other long brick buildings are rundown, some boarded up. There is a parking lot with more grass and weeds than concrete next to a graffitied building. I meander to the intersection of Washington and 3rd Ave and gaze at the mighty skyscrapers kissed by the sun's last rays in the distance. Diaphanous clouds decorate the dusky blue sky. The cityscape is simultaneously achingly beautiful and depressing. How can society have enough wealth to build such monoliths to consumerism yet be willing to leave so many lost in a concrete wasteland? Just thinking about it makes me feel like I'm going to burst apart at the seams. Humanity treats these men with the same concern given to the animal species going extinct every year. We pay lip service to how horrible it is, but we move on all in the name of that euphemism for compiling wealth at all costs we call progress. Still, the aesthetic splendor to the cityscape is undeniable.

I unsling the camera from my shoulder, pop off the lens cap, and compose a vertical image with the destitute buildings lining 3rd Avenue in the foreground and the icons to capitalism in the background. I meter off the sky, purposely increase my exposure and start shooting. Lowering the camera, I'm about to check the images on the LCD, expecting my exposures won't cut the mustard when a deep voice disturbs me.

"Hey, babe, what you doing?"

"Leave her alone!" someone shouts from the crowd. "She's Joe's friend, dumbass!"

Unperturbed, I face the man. The sleeper ripples inside me—ravenous and anxious to destroy any threat. But this man, despite his size and youth, is harmless.

"Oh, sorry. I thought you were someone else." He retreats back to the crowd.

I check my exposures on the LCD and smile. Replacing the camera on my shoulder, I walk to the alley behind the rescue mission. The narrow path is strewn with rubbish, and the stench of urine is enough to give me pause. A broad-shouldered man steps from the mission's back door located about twenty feet down the alleyway. He hoists up the lid of an industrial trashcan and tosses a garbage bag into the receptacle.

"Joe!" I run down the alley.

"Allison?" Joe squints, and a smile splits his face. "Allison! God, it's good to see you!"

His arms envelop me in a tight embrace. I hug him back, and he lifts me off the ground as if I'm as light as a snowflake.

He spins me but stops short of doing a three-sixty. "Oh. Damn." He sets me down gently. "Damn." Grimacing, he rubs his lower back.

"Are you okay, Joe?"

"Ah, I'm fine." He smiles and waves his hands dismissively. "Just my old bod reminding me I ain't twenty-five no more. Come on. Let's get inside. I assume you're here to help."

"You bet I am."

"Good. Good. I'll put you on the line serving the beans. We can chat all night after the dinner rush."

****

Joe and I sit together in the otherwise empty dining room. From the kitchen comes the clatter of pots and pans being washed.

"Eat up," Joe says between mouthfuls of beans. "It ain't much, but I can tell you're hungry."

To humor my friend, I eat a mouthful of beans and rice. The food tastes better than I expected, although only meat will satisfy my inhuman hunger. Between bites of food, I tell Joe about Haji, my guilt, and our ongoing attempts to find him. As I talk, Joe's expression turns dark as a thunderhead. He pushes away his plate with the food half-finished and leans back in his chair. When I finish the tale, he leans forward and stretches a big hand across the table, palm up. I take his comfortingly warm calloused hand. He squeezes my hand.

"First off, ain't your fault Haji is pulling this nonsense."

I open my mouth to speak, but Joe shakes his head.

"It don't matter what he said on some podcast. You

think on what I'm telling you. I spent fifteen years trying to drink myself to death after Afghanistan. I blamed all kinds of people for my plight. I blamed the war. I blamed the government. I blamed the military. Hell, I even blamed my mama. Now, maybe I do suffer from PTSD. I don't know. Never been properly diagnosed. But…I think part of my problem was guilt." Joe goes silent and takes a deep breath. "I had this friend back in Afghanistan. He was like my little brother. An IED got him. I was supposed to be on patrol that day but wasn't because some fool—don't even recollect his name no more—dropped a dumbbell on my foot. Broke all kinds of little bones. Anyhow, I never could shake the feeling it should've been me got blown up instead of my buddy."

Joe squeezes my hand again. He wipes away tears rolling down his cheeks.

"I'm so sorry. I never knew."

"It's okay." Joe thumps his chest over the heart. "Still hits me here, you know? Anyway, the day I gave up drink was the day I stopped feeling guilty over my buddy's death. It wasn't my fault. I didn't set the bomb or drop the weight on my foot. If I was going to be mad at myself, I might as well be mad at God. That's something my mama drilled into me. There ain't no being mad at God. I'm still messed up, but I'm way better off than I was. Take it from me. Don't go feeling guilty over something you have nothing to do with. That boy, he's old enough to make decisions and own them."

"I'll try," I murmur.

Joe nods. "Good. Now, what concerns me is this pusher you're talking about, this Ace. I've heard of him. He's bad, Allison. Real bad. I'm coming with you. I'll go inside the club with Devin."

"Joe, you don't need to. You saved my life. You don't owe me or any of us anything. I just needed somebody to talk to."

"Allison, saving your life is the best thing I've ever done. I mean that. It was on the recommendation of detective Hal Caine I got my job here washing dishes and a little apartment upstairs. Now, look at me. I'm the head cook. I have a savings account. With money in it! Maybe I don't owe you nothing, but you don't owe me either. I don't want that boy going into the club to face down Ace alone. He's a bad man. He'll eat that boy alive given half a chance, especially seeing as I figure this boy is or used to be an addict."

Chapter 15

My squad, Joe, and Devin stand on the sidewalk underneath a streetlight across the road from the club. Mauve is with us, too, having been picked up by Devin at a downtown bus stop. She is not dressed for the occasion, wearing pink sweatpants and a black sweatshirt several sizes too large for her. Her draconic form is magnificent, bathed in the blue neon light from the sign above the club's entrance, which reads in frightfully twisted calligraphy Discotheque West.

It's just turned nine p.m., and already scantily clad young women queue at the club's door—I swear they must be freezing half to death. I am, and that's with my heavy winter coat on. About an equal number of men are lined up, some with women on their arms and most ogling the opposite sex. A steady pulse of electronic music thrums from the club's entrance sandwiched between a seedy-looking bar and an art collective's gallery. A potent blend of flowery perfume, forest-inspired cologne, greasy food, and pheromones clog my nostrils. I'm glad I'm not the one entering the club. I'm afraid the overwhelming smells will make me pass out in a confined space.

A bouncer built like a keg, sporting a loose-fitting tracksuit, guards the club's entrance. He scrupulously checks the IDs of potential patrons before letting them inside.

"Well, I'll go line up," Devin says. "You coming, old man?"

Joe nods. "In a minute."

Devin shrugs and struts across the street like a banty rooster.

"Should I go too?" Mauve asks.

"You're not getting into the club dressed like that," Leslie says.

Joe breaks off from our group, heading across the street. Instead of joining Devin, he cuts in front of a couple near the head of the queue. The man complains loudly; Joe turns and whispers something. The man raises his hands and backs up a step, and his girlfriend blanches. The bouncer looks up from the ID he inspects, but not spotting a fight, returns his attention to the card.

"Wow," Leslie says. "That's ice cold. I didn't know Joe had it in him to pull a move like that."

"Neither did I," I say.

Joe is soon at the head of the line and talking to the bouncer while the man inspects his ID. Dalia is about to say something, but I wave a hand for silence, concentrating on listening in to Joe's conversation with the bouncer.

"Yeah, man, a kid with purple hair. Got a fake ID."

"Thanks for the tip. He won't be getting in," the bouncer says and hands Joe back his ID. "You're good."

Joe disappears into the club.

"I have a bad feeling about this," I say and tell the others what I overheard.

****

"What?" Devin exclaims as he and Dalia cross the

140

street to us. "You let him go into the club without me and point out the fact I have a fake ID? Jesus!"

He plunks his hands on the side of his head and paces.

"We didn't let him do anything, Devin," Dalia says.

"He just did it," Leslie says.

Less than fifteen minutes later, Joe emerges from the club followed by a rotund man covered in tattoos wearing an oversized baseball jersey and a ball cap on sideways. They walk together to the edge of the sidewalk, and Joe points across the street at us. The rotund man nods.

"Ummm…I think Joe found Ace," I say.

Ace lumbers across the street, squinting and lips curling into a sneer. "Devin! You purple-haired little shit!" The pusher slows and stops smack dab in the middle of the street. "I should've known." He rounds on Joe and shoves him in the chest. Joe stumbles but remains on his feet. "You're damn lucky. Damn lucky."

"I thought you didn't know this guy," Dalia hisses to Devin.

"Not well. Just acquaintances." Devin smiles sheepishly.

The outburst attracts the people queued at Discotheque West, including the bouncer who hands back the card he's inspecting to a girl who isn't more than a year older than me. The bouncer pulls out his cell phone.

"Don't go pushing me again, big man," Joe says.

"What? What you gonna do?" Ace snarls, reaching a hand around his back and shoving it underneath his oversized jersey.

My prosthetics zoom, momentarily throwing everything out of focus then bringing the gun's grip into dreadful clarity.

"He has a gun," I say, the sleeper's furious power supercharging every cell in my body.

Everyone talks at once, but I'm not listening. My prosthetics are zooming out, and I'm halfway to the pusher before he even finishes wrapping his hand around the weapon's grip. Physical prowess and insatiable hunger thrum through my body side-by-side with such intensity I fear the skaag will burst from inside me onto the street.

Joe holds his hands before him, palms outward. I reach for Ace, ready to crush every bone in the hand closing around the pistol. In my peripheral vision is the lambent glow of Mauve's flickering draconic form as she too closes in on the elephant seal of a man.

The disgusting reek of eucalyptus and menthol crashes into me like an avalanche, burying me under tons of rock. I'm no longer outside the club with the sleeper pulsating inside me. Instead, I stand on the grounds of Tahoma University that stormy night when Gore assaulted me, leaving me blind. My chest aches, rib cage collapsing as the air gushes from my lungs. I can't breathe. I can't twitch a muscle. I'm trapped by the detritus of past trauma, and worst of all, my inaction means Joe, who saved my life on that fateful night when the drug-crazed magician tried to kill me, will be shot at point-blank range.

Mauve's draconic form passes through me. The intense glow causes thunderbolts to shoot through my skull and shocks me back to the present. Mauve strikes like an interstellar whirlwind, insubstantial light and indomitable force intertwined. She is behind Ace with her hand locked onto his wrist, preventing him from drawing his firearm. Ace struggles against her, but he might as well be attempting to wrestle a bull to the ground.

I back away, anxious to escape the noisome menthol and eucalyptus stench of body spray known as Manscape Bodywhiskey. Why couldn't I save Joe? If Mauve hadn't been here, Ace would have drawn his weapon and…fired. I want to collapse on the roadway like a disintegrating paper towel and be washed down a storm drain into oblivion.

"Allison. Allison! Snap out of it."

Dalia stands in front of me with worry evident on her features, light from the streetlamp making her nose ring sparkle. Someone else takes me by my upper arm. It's Leslie.

"We need to go," Leslie says. "We're attracting way too much attention."

Devin has joined Ace, Mauve, and Joe in the middle of the road. He's talking rapidly, calming the pusher. People lined up at the club's entrance take an interest in the rumpus. At least half a dozen have cell phones out and are recording. The bouncer squints at us, expression severe. His fingers are poised to dial his phone.

Two figures march in our direction alongside the line of onlookers stretching down the sidewalk like an anaconda.

"Great," I mutter.

"What is it?" Dalia asks.

"Agents Deveraux and Haskell."

"The security detail? Here?" Leslie nervously

scans our surroundings.

"I told you they follow me everywhere."

We step onto the sidewalk, and Leslie releases me.

"Who follows you around everywhere?" Jason asks.

I point out the federal agents across the street. Despite knowing doing anything to piss off Agent Deveraux is moronic, I flip off the agents. What's Deveraux going do anyway? Confine me to base for using my expressive finger? Let her try.

"Allison! Don't."

Jason tries to knock down my hand, but I lower my arm before he gets the chance.

"Don't touch me." The sleeper's fury bubbles inside me. What's the point of having superhuman power if you can't protect those you love?

"Maybe you shouldn't antagonize the federal agents," Leslie says.

"Why not? They antagonize me. Sometimes you all antagonize me. Did you know that?"

The color drains from Leslie's face. Jason looks like he's inhaled spoiled food.

"Allison, take it easy," Dalia says, her fingertips brushing against the back of my hand.

I rip my hand away, knowing that doing so moves me one step closer to the precipice. I'm on the verge of losing it like I did in my bedroom after the kidnapper shot me, but I can't help myself. My rage must go somewhere. I can't bottle it up anymore. "Don't tell me to take it easy. They follow me around everywhere. Everywhere! I don't need their protection or surveillance or anything to do with them. I go home, and all I hear are the protesters out in the street screaming for me. I'm sick of it."

"We should go." Leslie takes Jason's hand. He nods in agreement with his girlfriend. "Good luck finding Haji. I mean it."

I bite down on my lower lip until I wince. I call after them. "Wait. I'm sorry."

Jason throws me a look over his shoulder, frowning and fearful. Leslie continues onward without a backward glance.

"Don't worry," Dalia says. "It's been a long day. Everyone's tired. We're all stressed. Right now, we need to keep our cool. Is the security detail going to interfere?"

Deveraux and Haskell eyeball us from across the street but don't approach even as Joe, Devin, and Mauve lead Ace over to the sidewalk.

"I don't think so," I whisper. "They probably didn't see the gun and don't realize Ace is a dealer. They'll just keep watching me like they always do."

"Where are they going?" Joe points toward Leslie and Jason.

I shrug, and Dalia remains silent.

Ace has calmed down and even smiles, gaze locking onto me like a wolf scenting prey. I brace myself for the odor of eucalyptus and menthol to wash over me again. I'll stay in control this time.

Ace reaches a hand into the front pocket of his baggy jeans. Dalia clutches my arm as I shove her behind me. Mauve grabs Ace's wrist again. Joe and Devin tense.

"Chill. Chill," Ace says, his smile never faltering. "Just my phone. Just my phone."

Mauve releases Ace, and he whips out a

smartphone. He holds up the phone, and the flash flares.

"What the hell?" I demand.

Dalia squeezes my hand. Maybe I am losing it, but maybe I want to.

"Yo. You're..." Ace whispers. He's manipulating his phone as he speaks. "You're Allison Lee. My daughter loves you. I have to text her your picture."

"The picture is for your daughter?" I ask.

"She's ten. She's gonna love this. You just made me father of the year."

I struggle to imagine this purveyor of poison as a father with a young daughter. What kind of example is he for the kid?

"You'll tell us about Haji?" I ask.

"Yeah. Of course. Let's get away from the prying eyes."

Ace leads us up a block and down an alley to a dark parking lot with about half a dozen cars spread around the forty or so stalls. Ace makes a show of looking around, muttering about privacy.

"Looks good. No one follow us?" he asks.

I listen intently, half expecting to detect the click and clack of shoes against concrete, but I don't. Maybe the security detail didn't follow us down the alley. I exchange a quick look with Mauve. "I don't hear anyone."

Ace smiles and nods. "Sensitive hearing and all that?"

I nod.

"Wow." He smacks his meaty hands together. "Okay. Let's get down to business. No worries about cameras here."

"How you know?" Joe asks.

"I own this lot," Ace says.

"Huh," Joe grunts.

"What? You think all I do is deal premium big H to those fools with dreams of being magicians? Nah. My business interests are diversified."

"Tell us about Haji," I say.

"Haji? Haji…" Ace places his hands on his wide hips and stares into the sky.

"A Pakistani male," I say. "Seventeen years old. You would've seen him earlier this week."

Ace looks at me and shrugs. "The kids looking to feel the magic"—Ace puts air quotes around magic—"are coming out of the woodwork. Like cockroaches. You can't expect me to remember one boy. I have dozens of clients like that every night."

"Come on, Ace," Devin says. "You said you'd tell us about him not five minutes ago."

"Now I'm saying I can't. I don't remember him."

"You said there are no cameras?" Dalia asks, glancing between Ace and me.

"Businessman like me needs privacy," Ace says.

"We can jog his memory. Make him talk," Dalia says with a sly smile.

"What do you mean by that?" Joe asks, backing up.

Ace points a finger as thick as a burrito at Dalia. "You will make me talk? Are you high on something? I still have my gun."

Mauve reacts first, moving in a blur of light and magically animated flesh. Her draconic form passes through the pusher. Before Ace can even reach around his back, Mauve is behind him, holding the pistol in her hand the way one might hold a dead rat.

"Hey. I wasn't going to shoot anyone," Ace says.

"We feel better with you not having a gun," Joe says.

"Now talk," Dalia says.

"Yeah, talk," Devin says.

Ace's cell phone, which he still grips in a meat hook, dings loudly. He looks at the screen, and smirks. "Why don't we head to my place? I have information on your boy Haji there."

"Something in that message jogged your memory, huh?" Joe frowns and steps toward the dealer.

"Personal space." Ace backpedals until he bumps into Mauve. "Come on, give me some space."

"Why does the text message you received state: give us twenty minutes then bring them here," Mauve says, who I suspect used her draconic eyes to read the message. Her head looms fifteen feet or more over Ace, but of course, he is unaware of that.

"I...I can explain," Ace splutters with an ingratiating smile.

Chapter 16

Ace's eyes swivel in their sockets.

"Spill the tea," I say.

The pusher darts to his left toward Dalia. Maybe he thinks she'll be the easiest to barge through since she is the smallest. I grab for him but stop myself. Dalia sidesteps, like a matador evading a charging bull. Instead of flourishing a red cape, she hooks his ankle with a foot. Ace momentarily defies gravity, then belly flops onto the concrete with a fleshy smack and doesn't move. His breath comes in wheezing gasps.

"Ace?" Devin says, going to the pusher's side and kneeling. "Ace? Come on, buddy. Sit up." He places a hand on the man's upper back across the name of a local major-league baseball player. "You can sit up, can't you?"

Dalia makes an exasperated sigh. "Give him a minute. He's not hurt...seriously."

Devin glances at his ex, the space between his eyebrows crinkling. "He's our best lead, and since when do we go around hurting people?"

Dalia balls her right hand into a fist and punches her left palm. "That's an appetizer of what he has coming to him if he doesn't start talking."

Devin furrows his brow and looks at Dalia like he doesn't recognize her, then turns back to Ace, gently rubbing the pusher's back between the shoulder blades.

Devin wasn't with us on the Olympic Peninsula, so he doesn't know about Dalia's sadistic side. Unless Haji told him. Dalia and I have, through an unspoken agreement, kept that detail to ourselves. Dalia had repeatedly kicked Gore's broken wrist to make him talk. He had tried to kill me twice by then, but still.

"Something's wrong," Devin says.

"Devin is right," Joe says, brushing past me. He kneels beside the pusher. "Ace? What's going on? Come on, big man, roll over."

Ace rasps a response. His breathing morphs into death rattles.

Devin leans in close to the pusher's head. "What was that? Say again."

"I think he said inhaler." I look to Mauve for confirmation.

Mauve shrugs. "Perhaps."

Joe turns his gaze on me. "He needs help. He's got asthma or something going on."

"Should I flip him? I can do that," I say.

"He ain't taking his inhaler until he's on his back or sitting up," Joe says.

I brush past Dalia, who is pale and gnaws on the tip of her thumb, and take a knee in between Joe and Devin.

"Give me some space," I say. Placing one hand under Ace's beefy shoulder and the other around his flabby midsection, I roll him onto his back, catching a whiff of body spray. I crinkle my nose. *Stay in control. Stay in the here and now.* Ace's halfway listless eyes are wild with fear. His lips move wordlessly as a meaty hand paws at his pants front pocket. "Is the inhaler in there?"

"Y...y...yes."

I move aside his trembling hand and fish the rescue inhaler from his pocket. His eyes bulge at the sight of the medical device, which I hand to him. His arm shakes so violently I'm afraid he might drop it before getting it into his mouth, but he manages. He depresses the cylinder, and there is a whoosh. His arm thuds against his massive chest. The inhaler rolls from his hand across his torso, and I catch it before it plummets to the parking lot's surface.

"Do you need another dose?" I ask.

"No," he murmurs. "Just...ne...need a minute."

I place the inhaler back in his pocket and stand. My arms tremble. We almost killed a man. I almost killed a man. Again. I quiver, whether from dread or the sleeper's pent-up hunger, I'm not sure. We're trying to save Haji, not hurt people no matter how much they might deserve it. And no matter what, I can't allow myself to kill again.

Devin and Joe resume kneeling beside Ace, asking the drug dealer if he's ready to sit up. Mauve leans so close I am inside the nebulous bronze shimmer of her draconic form. My prosthetics adjust to the intense glow.

"If this...Ace...is that his name?" the dragon asks, and I nod. "If Ace is out of immediate danger—"

"Hey, Allison, Mauve," Dalia says, "Look."

We turn to where Dalia points. Joe and Devin have Ace sitting up. He's still pallid as a snowcapped mountain, but his breathing slows to a regular rhythm. Joe walks over and motions for us to gather around.

He waits for Dalia to come close and whispers, "I think he's out of immediate danger, but you all need to go easy on him. He's asthmatic, and who knows what else." He gives Dalia a hard stare. "And that fall ain't doing him no good."

"He nearly ran me over." Dalia's cheeks flush.

"I'm saying go easy." Joe glances at Ace. "Either of you ever killed someone?" Dalia gulps and shakes her head. I make a non-committal sound. "I didn't think so. Don't go starting tonight."

"He needs to tell us what he knows," I say. "He was trying to lead us into a trap—at least, I think he was. I don't know." I throw up my arms.

Joe stares at the ground and scuffs his shoe against the concrete. He looks up at me with a deep frown. "Did you ever consider, Allison, maybe Haji don't want to be found? If Ace is trying to lead us into a trap, maybe it's best to let him loose. When Haji wants to be found, he'll come to you."

"No." Dalia shakes her head emphatically. "Haji might be stupid enough for some moronic reason to want to become a magician. He might even be loco enough to shoot up heroin to feel the magic, but he would never up and disappear without saying goodbye. Not if he could help it."

"People who shoot up heroin ain't right in the head," Joe says.

"Haji wouldn't leave without saying anything," I say.

"Okay. Okay. Talk to Ace. Just be gentle," Joe says.

"Allison, I have an idea," Mauve says.

I face my draconic friend and raise an eyebrow.

"I'm not as skilled as Frederick or—" Mauve nearly chokes up. "—Ion at manipulating the human mind, but I think I might be able to use magic to make Ace talk."

"Magic?" Joe backs away from us. "I thought you moved fast." Joe looks Mauve up and down. "You're one of those dragon people, aren't you?"

"I am. Since you are Allison's friend, I trust you'll keep that fact to yourself," Mauve says.

"Oh, man. I know I shouldn't be surprised. Oh, man. Lord have mercy." Joe wrings his hands.

"Joe will keep quiet," I say.

"Yeah, I will," he says.

"Hey, if you're done," Devin says, "Ace wants to talk."

We all turn to Ace, who still sits on the concrete. His color is improving, and his breathing sounds almost back to normal.

Ace heaves a heavy sigh. "You saved me. It is partly your fault I had an asthma attack, but...I figure I owe you." His voice is weak but is no longer raspy. "Your friend...Gore has him."

"Did you say Gore?" I ask, becoming as tense as a rubber band about to snap.

"Drug-crazed maniac Gore?" Dalia asks.

"Yeah, that's him. He used to be a client when he had the green. He's still a maniac, but drug-crazed?" Ace shakes his head. "Not anymore. He's like...a black ops commando. There are five of them. They got weapons and...magic, I guess. They have an ambush set up at my condo. He wants you, monster girl."

I suppress the urge to scream. Instead, taking a deep breath, I turn to Mauve. "What do you think? Can we take them?"

Mauve bends the barrel of Ace's pistol to a forty-five-degree angle as easily as if it's overcooked linguine and hands the weapon to the pusher. He stares open-mouthed at the gun.

Mauve nods. "Between the two of us, five magicians shouldn't prove difficult to deal with."

"Good." I smile, the sleeper's anticipation of a fight intermixing with my own. *We're coming, Haji. We're coming.* "Let's roll."

****

We're driving along a tree-lined street beside the waterfront when the security detail's sedan rolls up behind us. Their presence is expected, but it's still annoying as all get out. What if they interfere? Tip Gore and his goons off? We've already taken away Ace's cell phone, so he can't make any surreptitious texts or calls.

The sedan passes beneath a streetlight, giving me a crystal-clear view of the driver. Agent-in-charge Deveraux. I sigh.

"What is it?" Dalia asks.

My prosthetics zoom in on Agent Devereaux's face. Expression serious, she speaks rapidly to Haskell, who appears to be relaying her commands via a cell phone. I turn in my seat and face Dalia. She is a blur of pink and bronze as my prosthetics zoom out and refocus.

"It's the security detail. They're right behind us. I think they're up to something."

"Next left is the parking garage. Yeah, that one," Ace says from the passenger seat. The pusher faces me, his brow furrowed. "Security detail?"

"Don't worry about it," I say.

Ace raises an eyebrow. "Don't worry about it?

154

Security detail sounds like the police. I don't need police anywhere near my crib."

Devin slows the SUV to make a left turn into the well-lit parking garage.

"Too late to worry about them now," Dalia says. "We're already here."

"They're not following us inside. Nothing to worry about," I say.

"Whatever," Ace scoffs.

****

The elevator slides open with a ding on the condo complex's top floor. I'm glad to escape the stuffy compartment permeated by the stinking mixture of body odor and Manscape Bodywhiskey. We step out onto a hallway with a plush burgundy carpet. Doors to condo units line the hallway.

Ace trundles past me, heading left and pointing to a door at the end of the hall. "That's my place. They'll be waiting for you inside."

"Wait," I tell the pusher and face Mauve. "Do you sense anything?"

Her flickering draconic body fills the hallway, passing through the ceiling and walls and my companions with equal ease. Her dragon head projects out of the ceiling, forked tongue tasting the air as it fades in and out of existence. Both her human and dragon eyes stare at the door to Ace's abode. Her draconic form flares so bright I squint and throw a hand in front of my eyes. The radiance rapidly fades. Ace and Joe give me puzzled looks but remain silent.

"Magic was used here recently," Mauve says and brushes by me. She turns to Ace. "Lead the way." She looks at the rest of us, her gaze locking onto me. "Stay back."

I nod. I'll stick to the plan such as it is, but inside me, the sleeper stares at the door desiring to rip it from the hinges, force Gore to reveal Haji's location, and kill everyone else inside.

Ace leads us down the hall, sweat rolling down his neck. Mauve walks beside him as relaxed as if she's out on a Sunday stroll through a park. Behind me, the others murmur. We stop at the door. A key card reader is built into the handle. Ace pulls out a wallet from his pants and takes out a rectangular plastic card.

"You all ready?" he whispers.

"One sec," Mauve says.

I blink, visualizing the condo's interior in a rainbow of colors. My prosthetics switch to IR mode, and I study the heat signatures beyond the door.

"I count five people in total. Just like he said," I say.

"A nice-looking condo," Mauve says. "Hmmm...yes, I see them. I can understand why he calls them commandos. Very militaristic. Their weaponry looks exotic."

I turn to my friends, IR mode switching off. "Let Mauve and me deal with the magicians."

Ace stares incredulously at Mauve and me.

"Magic," I tell him.

"Making me wish I had some magic," the pusher says.

"Open the door," Mauve says.

Ace gulps and runs the card through the reader. A distinctive thud of a deadbolt emanates from the door. Mauve opens the door and strides inside. My body quivers with my twin desires to follow her. As agreed,

I'll wait for a ten count.

"Shoot her! Now!"

My breath catches in my throat. I recognize that voice although it's devoid of the whine I associate with it.

From inside the condo flashes crackling electricity like a dragon about to emerge from the slipstream. No! Mauve can't exit the slipstream now. She'll bring the roof down on top of us.

The skaag in me surges to the surface. I swear my muscles tear, sinew stretches, and skin bulges. I'm about to transform. My skaag form might be a malformed infant compared to Mother's, but I'm still enormous enough to crush everyone in the hallway.

"N...no!" the word emerges half-strangled, and I will myself with every fiber of my being not to transform.

Maybe the skaag listens, or I win the battle of willpower because the transformation stops. I'm still human, but with all my half-skaag prowess fueling my body. I rush into the condo. Behind me, my friends scream, the elevator dings, and someone barks commands.

I enter a lavishly furnished living room. Standing inside the room is Mauve. Her golem is as still as a Grecian statue.

"Mauve?"

Neither the golem nor the dragon responds in any way. The bronze beast is still translucent but no longer brightens and dims like thousands of fireflies in a dark forest. Wrapping around the dragon like fine netting are sizzling orangish-red arcs.

"Tranquilize her! Now!"

I tear my gaze from Mauve to the five paramilitary types spread out around the room. One holds a huge gun that wouldn't be out of place in the first-person shooter. Two carry short-barreled rifles aimed at me. Gore stands on the far side of a coffee table and creamy white sofa. He is not as cadaverously gaunt as I remember. Next to him is a petite woman with Asian features and quavering lips. White-hot anger not entirely mine pounding through me, I charge Gore.

Cracks echo in the room like the report of gunfire but softer. Something whistles past my face. I'm stuck in the neck by a needle. I paw at my neck, tearing away a syringe fletched with red feathers, tossing it aside without consideration. If I can capture Gore, his minions will surrender and release Mauve from the strange netting ensnaring her.

I leap onto the coffee table. Gore's leering face distorts like a reflection in a funhouse mirror, and my limbs are as heavy as diving bells. A second dart punctures my thigh. No worries. My body will metabolize whatever drug they're dosing me with before it takes full effect.

I leap, soaring over the couch, stretching my hands toward Gore like the talons of a raptor. His thin lips curl into a sneer.

"Kill them!" he shouts, backing away and pointing toward the condo's entrance.

My trailing foot catches against the couch, and I plummet to the floor, landing with a bellyflop. Air whooshes from my lungs. My first reaction is to bounce my feet, but my body feels like I'm weighed down by dozens of those lead aprons used in a dentist's office while taking x-rays. My vision blurs and darkens around the edges.

Gunfire reverberates through the room. I try pushing myself up to my knees, but something bony jams against the back of my neck.

"Inject her. Now, damn it!"

Gore's voice. The bony protuberance presses down until I'm gasping for air.

"Inject…her…before…it wears off!"

"I'm…"

The voices smear into the din filling the room. Screams. Bangs. A crash.

"Give it to me!"

A needle jabs my neck, and cold fluid rushes into my body.

Chapter 17

"The pink-haired one. Bring her. She and…"
The voice intrudes on my muddled mind, teasing at memories and emotions lost inside a lightless cavern. What's going on? Who…wait. I recognize the voice but can't place it. Who does it belong to? I know it's important.

Pink hair. Pink hair. Dalia! My BFF. The sister I never had. I cling to my memories of us running cross country and struggling through algebra and screaming our lungs out at climate protests and dancing the night away to Dark Matter Electrica's cosmic beat.

I try to get my bearings, but my eyelids might as well be sewn shut. It's so frustrating, I want to scream, but it's far more pleasant to float along in semiconsciousness until the current whisks me to slumberland. No. *No.* Do not go to sleep.

Someone pinches my left upper arm. I register pain, but it's distant, almost like it's happening to someone else. I pull away from whoever holds me, and fingernails dig into my skin. Someone grabs my right arm, and they drag me across the floor on my belly.

"Ahhh…let…go…" My voice is mushy and sounds as soft as a whisper.

"Chief, she's waking up."

Several people speak at once, male and female. A shrill scream. Harsh commands. Someone cries.

I force my eyes open to slits only to be assaulted by shattered light, but my prosthetics swiftly adjust. I'm staring at the room's wood floor, which two men drag me across. My gaze rests on a man in a black military-style uniform sprawled across the floor with a red pool spreading out next to him. My eyes zoom in on wet marks on his uniform—gunshot wounds.

What is going on?

"Dalia," I croak.

"Chief, she's talking."

"Dose her again."

"I've given her enough to kill an elephant." A female voice with a Southeast Asian accent.

"Give her more. If she regains her abilities, we're screwed! Dalia! Get over here, pinkie."

Gore.

Oh my God.

Gore who tried to kill me twice.

Gore whose wrist I broke.

Gore whom Dalia tortured.

I writhe in the arms of my captors. I should be able to throw them off me, crush them like ants, but my sense of the sleeper is shockingly distant. Although I feel the half-skaag's anger, none of its prowess fills me, and my limbs are ponderous millstones.

"Hold her still," the woman says.

I crane my neck toward the sound. She's petite with her hair up in a tight bun and wears the same black paramilitary gear as her male counterparts. In her hand she holds a syringe with coppery light sparkling along the needle.

That light. I recognize it. "M...Mauve!"

My dragon friend doesn't respond. I swing my

head up, searching.

"Keep her still," the woman says.

"She's stronger than she looks."

At the entryway to the condo, men in suits are strewn across the floor, bodies arrayed at unnatural angles. One man's ribcage juts from his sports coat like blood-spattered ivory tusks. My gaze locks onto a dusky woman, and I stop struggling.

Agent Deveraux, my adversary and protector.

Keening escapes my lips. Deveraux's neck is twisted around like a kitchen rag.

The needle pricks my neck. I stop fighting oblivion.

****

Discomfort through my forearms and across my shoulders drags me back to consciousness. My body aches, and my hands are numb. I'm strewn against something plush, keeping me halfway upright. A dull roar fills my ears. There are fainter sounds too. Talking maybe? I roll my shoulders and try to stretch my arms overhead. No luck. My hands are stuck behind my lower back. The restraints are cold against my wrists.

Moving causes pins and needles in my hands. I arch my back to give myself room to work the blood back into my appendages. My fingers prove as dexterous as crushed snails.

"She is waking up."

The pins and needles in my hands crescendo to a painful fever pitch. I slump and stop moving. Pushing aside my discomfort, I slog through possibilities of what is happening, but thinking makes my head throb like I'm repeatedly pounding it against a brick wall.

"Give her another dose."

My breath lodges in my throat. Gore!

"Don't you dare drug Allison!"

"Dalia? Dalia!" My mouth moves like I am choking on taffy.

"Allison! I'm here."

I ask where, but Gore's voice drowns out my question.

"Quiet, pinkie."

"You be quiet," Dalia snaps. "You'll regret this. You messed with Allison and Mauve. Allison's mother and Dr. Radcliffe will come for us. Just you wait."

"I don't need to listen to this," Gore mutters and says louder, "Tranquilize pinkie."

"No! No!" Dalia screams.

I turn my head toward the struggle, opening my eyes a crack. Gore and a small woman stand over Dalia, who is seated in a cushioned chair. A carpeted pathway about two feet wide separates us.

"Don't!" Dalia yells.

"Hold her still," the woman says.

"L…leave her alone," I slur.

Gore looks over his shoulder at me, and a smile splits his face. His teeth are straight and pristinely white. That's bizarre. I remember his stinking maw full of chipped yellow and brown teeth snapping centimeters from my face when he attacked me at a campground on the Olympic Peninsula. That had been the second time he tried to kill me. I was victorious in that encounter, breaking his wrist and forcing him to use magic to escape.

"Don't worry, Allison. I'll get to you in a minute." Gore turns away.

He grabs Dalia around the neck and shakes her

until she stops struggling. The small woman jabs a needle into my friend's arm. I expect the sleeper's power to surge through me like a tidal wave, but the limitless prowess never comes.

Dalia's head lolls listlessly, and I gasp. "No...why?"

Gore straightens and rounds on me. "What's wrong? All we did was give her something to help her sleep. She did far worse to me. Remember, Allison? She's lucky I don't rip her head off. Don't you agree?"

I gulp and silently scream at the sleeper. *Where are you?*

I don't sense the half-skaag.

Worse, I have no idea what that means other than I'm as helpless as a gnat in a tornado. Did Gore put a spell on me? My mother's magic had, unbeknownst to me, caged the sleeper for sixteen years. For all I know, if my eyes had never been replaced with prosthetics allowing me to see dragons, the sleeper might still be caged deep within the recesses of my being, and I'd be ignorant of my true nature. Gore, though, is not my mother. He might be a competent magician, even a great one, but that doesn't mean he is even a spluttering match compared to her. Tanis, Mauve, and Dr. Radcliffe are dragons possessing extraordinary magical abilities, and they acknowledge my mother as a masterful magician of immense power.

Shimmering memories of being injected with something at least once, perhaps twice, haunt me. That must be how they're keeping the sleeper at bay.

"How long will pinkie be out?" Gore asks.

"At least three hours, four on the outside."

Gore smirks. "Fantastic. I've had enough whining.

Now, for you, Allison."

I want to wipe the sneer from his face, but no matter how loud I scream into my mind for the sleeper, only my voice echoes through my skull.

"What are you waiting for? Give her the injection," Gore snarls at the woman, who cringes as if scourged.

"It is too risky." The woman shakes her head. "More might kill her."

Gore clenches his hands into fists and stares upward. I swivel my eyes to take in our surroundings. A curved ceiling. A long narrow pathway between rows of seats. The noise. No way. The rumble permeating the tubular space is the roar of aircraft engines. A chill starting in my chest shoots through me. Where is he taking us that requires a plane? And not just any plane, a jet with only the four of us as passengers.

"Nineteen hours. Nineteen hours in the air until we arrive. Plus, however long it takes to refuel. Do you have any idea what will happen if she regains her powers?" Gore begins pacing.

The woman stares at the floor, hands smoothing her black pants.

"Bring me the Juice," Gore says.

The woman looks up. "You only have one vial left."

Gore rounds on the woman with a scowl. "Bring it! We defeated a dragon. We've come too far to risk her escaping now."

Defeated a dragon? Dalia's words from earlier smother me: *You messed with Allison and Mauve.*

"What did you do to Mauve?" I whisper, tasting ash.

Gore squats beside me, placing his elbows on his

knees. "That one was Mauve? I didn't know."

The woman returns with a thin metallic briefcase. Gore takes the briefcase and places it across his knees.

"What did you do to Mauve?" My chest is so tight I might burst with each breath.

The latches click, and Gore opens the case, his head disappearing behind the lid.

"My new employer possesses some interesting weapons. I don't understand how they work in detail." Gore closes the case and sets it on the floor. In his right hand, he holds a syringe full of glowing orange liquid. The luminescence paints his face an eerie orangish hue. "All I know is these weapons are a synergy of magic and technology." He points an index finger at my eyes. "Just like your prosthetics."

"My prosthetics aren't magic."

Gore shrugs. "Maybe. Maybe not." He rolls up the shirt sleeve covering his left arm. I'm surprised how toned and muscular his forearm is. He is still super thin, and his dark eyes are insanely deep-set, but otherwise, he looks far stronger and healthier than ever before. "I'm not an expert on marrying technology to magic, but I work with people who are authorities on the subject."

He jabs the syringe into his arm near the elbow joint and injects the orange liquid. Gasping, he shuts his eyes and rocks back on his heels. Orange light forming fractal patterns gleams from underneath the skin of his forearm, shooting up and down its length then fading. A smile of pleasure alights his face. He withdraws the needle and waves the woman over to take it and the briefcase.

"What did you take?" I ask.

Gore's fathomless gaze bores into me. "The Juice. That's all you need to know." He places his left hand against my forehead.

I flinch and cry out. His palm is as searing as the surface of the sun. My skin must be crackling, oozing, blackening. I kick out with my legs, catching Gore on the knee, but there's no power behind the blow, and it doesn't even cause him to sway.

"Shhhh...don't fight it. Don't fight." Gore's tone possesses the stately timbre of a funeral march. "Sleep."

With each word, his palm grows hotter.

"Go to hell," I hiss while shrieking in my mind for the sleeper to wake.

"Stop fighting. Sleep." With each word, fractal patterns flare on his forearm, emitting an unnerving tangerine tint.

My eyelids droop.

"Sleep, Allison. Sleep."

A soporific undertow drags me down toward a lightless chasm.

Just before I enter freefall, Gore whispers, "Your friend Mauve. I killed her."

****

Gore's hand burns into mine as we queue at a checkpoint. I follow his lead, shuffling forward and standing idle with the flow of the people. Tall trees soar overhead toward the glass ceiling. In wavy patterns before the ceiling are blue and purple streamers of gossamer fabric. Beyond the glass is a bright, cloudy sky.

Arrivals are efficiently processed, and soon I'm standing before an official in a navy-blue uniform. As the official questions me, the heat from Gore's palm increases in intensity. I respond to the official without comprehending the questions or my answers.

After passing through the checkpoint, Gore releases me. Our surroundings assault me in a dizzying array. Sweet and savory smells waft from down a wide hallway. Over loudspeakers are announcements in English and other languages I don't understand. The airport's name is announced, but I've never heard it before, and it slips through my mind like smoke on a breeze. I want to run, but a lethargy grips my body unlike any I've ever known, and I can't flee without Dalia, who is still in line at the checkpoint.

Once Dalia and Gore's assistant are through security, Gore gathers us near him. "No funny business. I still have enough Juice in me to stop you. Got it?"

Gore lifts up his left sleeve to reveal several inches of forearm. Orange fractal patterns tattoo his skin. The glow doesn't seem as intense as on the plane, but I can't be sure.

I exchange a glance with Dalia, and we nod. At least we're together. For now, that's enough.

Gore's assistant leads us through palatial hallways lined with luxury boutiques full of shoppers. Down the center of the halls are huge planters teeming with colorful orchids, flamboyant birds of paradise, and other tropical flora I can't name. The floral displays include statues and kaleidoscopic works of glass art. All the displays are beautiful and whimsical and too much to take in. The magician trails behind us at my shoulder, always an arm's length or less away.

After a short hop on a jam-packed train, we disembark near the exit from the airport at an outdoor stop. Humid heat hits me like a punch to the gut.

Perspiration spouts from my pores, rolling down my face like waterfalls. Gore grabs me by the upper arm, guiding me to the open back door of a waiting sedan. His assistant forces Dalia inside first, and the impetus to balk drains from me.

We cram inside the back of the sedan. The cool air blasting from the vents feels wonderful after the humidity. As soon as Gore closes the door, the car pulls away from the curb into slow traffic. I try to take in our surroundings, but I'm sandwiched between Dalia and Gore, and the back windows are tinted so dark even my prosthetics struggle to gather enough light for me to see much outside. My friend takes my hand and squeezes. I squeeze back.

"Give me that." Gore reaches around behind my head.

"What are you doing?" I demand, then the needle punctures my neck.

****

The roar of engines and bouncing around like a racquetball drags me back to consciousness. I inhale exhaust and the sharp tang of the ocean. As I sit up, a wave of vertigo makes the world swirl. Moaning, I blink as my prosthetics adjust to the bright surroundings, and the world stops spinning. Heat and humidity surround me like I'm trapped inside a sauna instead of riding in a speedboat out on stunning cerulean water. A stocky man wearing shorts and a T-shirt with skin the color of a kaiser nut drives the craft. Dalia, pink hair bobbing in time with the boat's crash against the water, sits next to me in a daze. Gore stands over us, leering. There is no sign of the small woman from the plane.

Behind us is a forest of modern skyscrapers, including what looks like a massive luxury yacht floating atop three towers. Overhead is dull gray cloud cover similar to the ominous marine layer of home. The sun is a bright disc distorted by the clouds.

I turn to Gore. "Where are we?"

"Doesn't matter." He turns and points to a green island far in the distance. "That's where you'll meet my employers."

Chapter 18

The speedboat slows as we approach a rickety dock leading to a white sand beach and a dense jungle beyond. A darkly tanned youth waves to the boat from the pier. The pilot waves back and shouts something in a lilting language I don't recognize.

I glance at Dalia and bite my lower lip. She stares listlessly into the cloudy sky. Sweat sheens on her face and mats down her pink hair.

I place a hand on her shoulder and ask not for the first time, "Are you okay?"

Her eyes roll until she gazes upon me. Her lips move, but I can't understand what she says over the outboard engine's rumble. Unlike Dalia, who is progressively more out of it with each passing moment, I'm gaining clarity. I remember entering Ace's condo to discover to my horror Mauve captured in some kind of electric mesh. My chest aches. Gore claimed he killed Mauve. I don't want to believe that. She is a dragon, nearly impervious to harm, but I can't deny the possibility he hurt her. Not with the image of her helplessly bound in the netting burned into my mind.

I place a hand across Dalia's brow. Her skin is scorching. I glare at Gore. "She needs water."

"She'll get some soon enough," Gore says.

"I think she might have heat stroke."

"Serves her right."

"Please. The driver. He has water. Dalia is here to ensure I cooperate. She's no good to you dead."

On the pier, the youth picks up a coarse rope and tosses it to the pilot, who expertly snatches the line from the air while skillfully maneuvering the craft next to the pylons. He cuts the engine and scampers forward to tie the rope to a metal fitting at the bow.

Gore smirks, raises a hand, and snaps his fingers. "Water." He points at Dalia. "Doctor."

The youth on the dock nods and runs toward the beach, the planks clattering under his feet. The pilot grabs the half-full bottle of water next to the steering wheel, scurries across the deck, and kneels beside my friend. He dribbles water across her mouth until her lips part, and she starts swallowing the fluid.

"Get up," Gore says. "Let's go."

"What about Dalia?"

"They'll take care of her. The boy will bring a doctor. Don't worry. Like you said, she's no good dead."

I turn back to my bestie. Her eyes are closed, and she greedily guzzles the water.

"Dalia…"

She looks at me with an unfocused gaze.

A hand clamps down on my shoulder, fingers burrowing into my muscles.

"Let go of me," I cry.

Gore's grip tightens, and he bends down to whisper into my ear, "Come. I grow tired of asking, Allison. It was a long flight. You remember the flight, don't you?"

He's so close I breathe in his mint-sanitized exhale.

"I remember a woman drugged me…repeatedly. You used magic on me."

His fingers drive into me like nails. My muscles spasm, sending shocks of pain through my shoulder and up my neck. I suffer stoically, refusing to give him the pleasure of seeing me react.

"Let go. I'll come."

Gore grunts dismissively and releases me. Reluctantly, I stand and become acutely aware of the speedboat rocking in the waves. Up ahead, the white sand lurches drunkenly up and down. Dizziness and nausea claw at me. I shut my eyes until the wooziness fades to a tolerable level.

"After you." Gore points to a wooden ladder attached to the pier.

I trundle cautiously across the deck, worried my feet will fly out from under me or I will retch with every step. Relief floods me when I grasp the rough wooden ladder and climb. I pull myself up onto the dock and stand. The boards sway under my feet. Fortunately, the movement is far less than on the boat.

Gore climbs up behind me and barks an order to proceed to the jungle. A breeze off the water carries the ocean's scent and exhaust from the boat. Up ahead, coconut trees and other tropical flora gently sway. From the trees come the whistles and warbles of birds. A pigeon-sized brown bird with a yellow eyepatch lands on the planking ahead of us. It stares at us curiously, and for a moment I wish I had my camera to document this fascinating bird. The bird takes to the air, perhaps startled by Gore's thumping footfall, and disappears into the fronds of the trees.

When we reach the pier's end, I search for a way down to the white sand and find none. It seems like an easy drop. I turn to Gore for confirmation I should jump.

Sunlight gleams along the length of the hypodermic needle Gore thrusts at my neck. "No!"

I grab his arm. Gritting my teeth, I call upon my half-skaag might to crush his bones, but my silent cries go unanswered. With his free hand, he tears my hands away.

"Don't fight, or I'll use magic," Gore growls.

"Suck on it!"

I yelp as pain shoots through my calves, and I go airborne. Everything goes blank, then bright stars slash through my vision when my head slams against the dock. Gasping, I blink to clear my head. Gore sneers down at me. Before I can sit up, he straddles my waist and smashes my head against the planking.

"Don't." I slap at his arms, but he brushes aside my defenses.

****

"Is she awake yet? When will she wake up?"

The rapid-fire words wake me to muddled consciousness. My head feels like it was used as a bongo drum. Gore must have brought me here, wherever this is, after drugging me so many times I've lost count.

"She should be coming out of sedation soon."

A second voice, heavily accented and almost staccato.

"How soon?"

"Less than a quarter-hour. I can't be more precise than that. I don't have data yet on how her body metabolizes the carfentanil."

Something is odd with my prosthetics. I don't have any sense of light or shadow from beyond my eyelids, only nothingness.

My pulse quickens. Why can't I feel my prosthetics?

Stay calm. Stay calm. Whatever is happening is a side effect of the drugs or magic.

I'm leaned back in a chair, I think. My arms are on armrests, maybe? Something clamps down against my wrists. I roll my ankle to discover the movement impeded by a strap of some kind. Oh God, I'm strapped down like a dangerous psychiatric patient or a prisoner about to be executed.

Maybe I should break the bonds? I haven't heard Gore. Maybe he isn't here.

Where are you? I call to the sleeper.

The silence in response is deafening.

"Can you give her something to speed things along? I have places to be. We have a timeline to keep."

"As I told you before, Ms. Bergman, our understanding of her physiology is incomplete. The subject must be treated delicately."

I stiffen. The subject. The words remind me of the vitriol hurled at me over the past year. Abomination. Monster girl. Aberration and much, much worse.

"Hah. Allison Lee is most certainly not delicate, Dr. Rah. Missed deadlines won't be tolerated."

"She moved, Ms. Bergman."

Stay still. Don't even twitch.

"She's awake?"

Footfall against…tile?

"I believe so."

"Hah. She's faking? Wakie-wakie, Miss Lee. We have some questions for you."

I'm not awake. I am not awake. Go away.

"Miss Lee," Ms. Bergman says. "Stop feigning and open those peepholes, or I will have Dr. Rah clamp them open for you. You'd like to do that for me, wouldn't you, Dr. Rah?"

"I am happy to, Ms. Bergman."

Dr. Rah doesn't sound happy; she sounds deadly serious. Figuring I have nothing to lose and might gain some information through cooperation, I open my eyes.

And scream.

I keep screaming even when it feels like a serrated blade saws at my throat. I stare into the mouth of a black hole.

"Stop her screaming!" Ms. Bergman shrieks.

Tears dribble down my cheeks. They had better kill me before I regain my powers because I'm going to murder them for this. I'm not sure if I'll be able to see as a skaag, but I'm confident that won't matter. I'll smell them, and that will be enough.

"I have to do everything!" Ms. Bergman snarls. "Give me that!"

Something sharp and cold presses against my throat. I stop screaming and strain against the restraints, but all my skaag strength remains beyond my grasp.

"Careful now, Miss Lee. I wouldn't want to slit your throat by mistake," Ms. Bergman whispers into my ear. She's so close, her breath tickles my earlobe, and the scent of jasmine wafts from her.

"Why can't I see?" I demand.

"Dr. Rah removed your prosthetics. We have—"

I open my mouth wide and scream, despite the knife's tip pricking my throat, drawing blood. They need me alive. I'm a test subject, after all. Triumph blossoms in my breast when the blade is withdrawn.

"Give me back my pros—"

Fabric is jammed into my mouth. A hand grabs my jaw as the material is forced in deeper, stifling my words. I try to scream, but all I can manage is a pitiful gurgle. I thrash, arching my back, but the bonds hold me in place. I can barely breathe.

A hand clamps down over my face, fingers pinching my nostrils shut. I whip my head side to side, but the fingers tighten.

"Stop struggling, Miss Lee." Ms. Bergman's words ratatat like machine gun fire. "Do you want to pass out? I'll make you pass out, and then we'll do it again. Over and over and over until you stop fighting. Would you like that?"

I throw my head to the left, and the fingers release my nose—I suck in air. Metal clatters against tile. The aching in my chest lessens. The fingers pinch my nostrils shut again.

"Careful with my equipment," Dr. Rah says. "That will have to be sterilized before I can use it."

I lash my head about, but Ms. Bergman's fingers hold on like a crab's pincers.

"She almost head-butted me," Ms. Bergman says.

My nose aches from the pressure, and my lungs burn.

"Keep your face away from her."

I shout into the void of my mind's eye for the sleeper.

"Thanks for the advice. That never would have occurred to me."

I arch my back again and work my wrists against the bonds.

"This will go much faster and be less painful if you

stop struggling and promise not to scream," Ms. Bergman says.

To hell with her.

"Stop fighting, or I'll break Dalia's wrist."

Gore's words are like a hatchet to the head. I stop struggling, and my insides knot. Gore is here. Where did he come from? But without my eyesight and my heightened half-skaag senses, anyone could be here, and I'd never know. I don't even know where here is.

"Oh, right. You and the Chief have a history." The fingers release my nose. I breathe in deeply. "No screaming, okay?"

I nod.

"That's a girl," Ms. Bergman croons as fingers slither through my hair. "Now, we have some questions for you. You will answer those, correct?"

I nod again.

"Excellent. I'm going to remove the gag now. No biting."

Fingers tighten around my hair and wrench my head back. I tense, anticipating more torment, but instead the gag is yanked out of my mouth. I heave a breath.

The hand releases my hair. "Dr. Rah, do you want to ask the first question, or should I?"

A beat of silence follows.

"Guess I'm up," Ms. Bergman says. "Miss Lee, can you see dragons while they ride the slipstream?"

"Yes." My throat is so raw it stings.

"Why can you see dragons riding the slipstream? Humans can't. Neither can skaags, or so I'm told. Why can you?"

"I…" I clear my throat, which feels like

swallowing glass. "I don't know."

"You don't know. You don't know. How can you not know? Are you a magician? Do you know spells that can penetrate the slipstream?"

"I'm not a magician."

"Are you telling us the truth, Miss Lee? Your friend's wellbeing depends on it."

Dread splinters my voice. "I'm telling the truth! Don't hurt Dalia. Please."

"Your friend's fate is in your hands, Miss Lee. Dr. Rah, do you have questions?"

"Of course, I do, Ms. Bergman." Casters roll across the floor. "Allison, tell me about your prosthetic eyes."

"What about them?"

"Explain how the prosthetics allow you to see dragons riding the slipstream."

"I don't know."

"Are you certain you wish to answer with recalcitrance?" Dr. Rah asks.

"I couldn't see dragons before the prosthetics. Now I can. I don't know why."

"Are the prosthetics imbued with magic or not, Miss Lee?" Ms. Bergman demands.

"I don't know. I really don't."

"When's her next dose?" Bergman asks.

"Two hours," Dr. Rah says.

"We'll let her stew."

"Please, I need to see. Please."

Footsteps echo across the floor, fading. Hinges squeal. A door?

"Tell them what they want to know," Gore says. "I've seen what they do to extract information. You'll talk eventually. Everyone does."

The door thuds shut.

Chapter 19

I'm trapped in darkness with only my sour thoughts and bubbling panic for company. I try deep breathing to maintain a relative calm, but it's tough. Losing my sight is the most dreadful experience of my entire life. I never imagined I'd be forced to experience it again.

Deep breathing isn't working, so I think of anything besides my blindness. My thoughts swirl to the ambush at the condo. Gore and his thugs were ready and capable of taking on a dragon and a skaag. I shiver at the memory of Mauve held helpless in the electric netting. How could they have known she is a dragon?

I chew on my lower lip. Maybe they had pieced together Mauve's identity from the Internet. There are dozens, possibly hundreds, of pictures and videos of her in dragon form battling my mother. And what's all this talk about marrying magic and technology? Maybe they could see Mauve riding the slipstream, and if they can't, that explains why they're so interested in how I can see dragons. I hope Gore lied when he said he killed Mauve.

A sob wracks my chest. Mauve isn't my only friend who might be hurt. What about Joe, who came along due to some misguided sense of duty or owing me or both? I should've never burdened Joe with my problems in the first place. He might be dead alongside those poor agents. I never wanted or needed their protection, but it's still my fault they're dead. I cry softly as images loop through my mind. The worst is Agent Deveraux with her neck twisted like fusilli. She didn't deserve to die for just doing her job.

A mechanical clank reverberates through the chamber. I choke back sobs as hinges squeal. Who's coming for me? Ms. Bergman or Dr. Rah or Gore or all three of them?

"Who's there?" I say hoarsely.

"Remain here."

A new voice, precise and strong.

"Be careful, sir. She's due to be dosed in less than a half-hour."

Gore is shockingly respectful. Whoever this sir is must be a VIP.

"You better hope you didn't hurt Dalia," I splutter, despite knowing the wiser course is to keep my mouth shut.

"That's why you're here. To keep me safe." The words are followed by mirthful, resonant laughter. "The containment spell is active?"

"Stop ignoring me," I shout and grimace at a sharp pain in my throat.

"One moment, Allison. I'll be with you as soon as I finish speaking to the Chief."

He's respectful, borderline friendly, yet entirely commanding. For some reason, I want to trust this man. That makes me too stupid to live, but I can't help myself.

"I renewed the spell after we arrived on the island. We have no way of knowing how effective it is or how long it will last," Gore says.

"Relax, Chief. The tranquilizer is here. I'll give it to her myself if I have to, but I don't think it will come to that. You see, Allison, despite what you may think after the roughshod treatment you've received at the hands of Chief Gore and some of my associates, I'm not your enemy. Truth be told, neither are they."

Footsteps clack against the floor, coming toward me.

"You have a strange way of showing you're not my enemy. Why should I trust you? You haven't even told me your name."

"My name is Dr. Kihl, Allison. If you give me the opportunity, I believe I can prove I'm not your enemy."

"I have a hard time believing that."

"Do you know what I hold in my hand, Allison?"

"I'm blind."

"I hold your prosthetic oculus dexter."

Relief and hope make a heady concoction. "Let me see again. Please."

"I've read all about your prosthetics in various medical journals. Dr. Woolworth is a genius, and you are brave for undergoing experimental surgery. What I don't understand is how the prosthetics allow you to see dragons riding the slipstream. One of my areas of expertise is medical equipment. I have recreated your prosthetics and the nanobot treatment to the best of my considerable abilities. I believe the prosthetics I have created are an exact facsimile of yours. Yet I know the volunteers I have outfitted with prosthetics can't see dragons riding the slipstream. You must understand this poses quite a mystery."

I shudder. I suspect this doctor didn't put out a call for blind volunteers.

Dr. Kihl continues. "Why is that? I don't expect you to answer the question. I believe you have no idea why you can see the dragons riding the slipstream."

"What do you want from me?" I ask.

"Relax." A hand gently rests on my shoulder. "I'm going to install your oculus dexter." The hand releases my shoulder, and fingers gently probe around my right eye socket. "Our mission is to protect humanity. Understanding your abilities is the key to accomplishing that goal. Dr. Rah sterilized the interface area when she removed your prosthetics. Try not to move." Something round and cool fits into my eye socket. "I beg you to cooperate. I can protect you and your friend to some extent, but only your cooperation guarantees your safety and hers. My powers, I'm afraid, are far from absolute."

"What about Haji? Is he here?" I ask.

"Haji?"

"A candidate, sir," Gore says. "He arrived about a week ago."

"Ah, yes. I will ask after him, Allison, but I'm afraid his welfare is outside my direct control. You're going to feel some pressure. There. It will take a few minutes for the prosthetic to boot up. Once you can see again, the Chief will take you to the holding cell. I believe your friend is there. Isn't that right, Chief?"

"Yes, sir."

The doctor's heels clap against the floor, sound fading. "Wait. Dr. Kihl."

"We'll talk again, Allison. Don't worry. For now, relax and remember the only way I can protect you and Dalia is if you cooperate."

I blink as my vision returns to a whiteout. Like

total blizzard conditions. My head buzzes, and my right eye socket aches. The snowfield resolves into a sterile room, all white with strange equipment shining like polished stainless steel. Projecting from the ceiling by long arms is an insectile array of devices.

"Make sure Allison's basic needs are met, Chief. She'll be thirsty and hungry. Fluids are essential," Dr. Kihl says.

My wrists are secured by heavy manacles to the armrests binding me to the industrial-strength version of an examination chair complete with faux leather.

"Won't fluids flush the medication?" Gore asks.

"That shouldn't be a problem. Dr. Rah has prescribed regular dosing."

I crane my neck backward as far as I can and swivel my head, trying to catch a glimpse of Dr. Kihl. I'm rewarded with a spear of pain through my neck.

"Sir, she's dangerous. Don't let her petite build fool you. Even in human form, she went toe to toe with me while I was enchanted with superhuman strength. She broke my wrist. Later, she knocked me out cold with one punch."

Dr. Kihl laughs. "I know she's not human, Chief, but she is drugged and will remain so for the time being. Her true nature is held in check by your magic. Is there something you're aware of I don't know?"

"No, sir, but I wouldn't be doing my job if I didn't express my concerns."

"Your concerns are noted, Chief. I expect you to see to Allison's wellbeing."

"Yes, sir."

I arch my back, which allows me to twist my neck a few more inches. My depth perception is wonky, and it seems like half my field of view is cut off without my oculus sinister. A gray-haired man in a lab coat strides toward the doorway for a brightly lit hallway of nondescript white. Gore closes the door behind the doctor. I settle myself in the chair as Gore turns toward me.

"Just you and me now, Allison," the assassin says.

I don't respond.

"What's wrong? Cat got your tongue?"

"I could use some water," I say.

"Is that so?"

Combat boots thud against the floor. There's a crack of a plastic bottle being opened for the first time. Gore strides over to stand before me, scowling. He hefts a water bottle.

"Purse your lips," he says.

"Those end up in the ocean. Have you ever heard of the Pacific trash vortex?"

"Do you want water or not?" Gore shrugs. "Bottled water is all you're going to get here. They'll put you on an IV when you get dangerously dehydrated."

"I suppose refusing sustenance counts as being uncooperative."

A flash of white teeth. "Something like that."

"Can you at least let me out of the cuffs? My wrists are sore."

Gore's smile broadens. "As soon as I unlock those manacles, I'm going to zip-tie your hands behind your back."

I wish my prosthetics have a death laser function so I could burn through Gore's skull and the restraints.

"What? Feeling salty?" Gore raises the bottled water close to his lips. "Waste not want not, my mama always told me."

"Fine." I purse my lips.

Gore arches an eyebrow.

"I'll drink the water."

"Manners?"

"Please." The word escapes my throat as a gruff growl.

"That wasn't so hard, was it?" Gore presses the bottle's rim to my parched lips.

I gulp the lukewarm liquid like I've been out on a midday run through Death Valley. Even so, the water doesn't quench my thirst or relieve my scratchy throat.

"Easy. Easy." Gore withdraws the bottle.

Without thinking, I lurch forward, desperate for more fluid, but the restraints keep me in the chair. My stomach cramps and rumbles.

Gore chuckles. "Thirsty and hungry."

"I don't recall you providing me anything on the plane besides drugs."

"That's true." He shakes the water bottle. "Want the rest?"

I nod.

Gore holds the bottle upside down, splashing the water on the floor. I stare aghast at the waste and his pure nastiness. Smirking, he smashes the bottle in his hand and tosses it aside.

"The Pacific trash vortex just got a new member," he says.

Gore takes a set of keys from his pocket and unlocks the ankle manacles. My first urge is to kick him in the face, but I decide the better course is to bide my time until I regain my sense of the sleeper.

He straightens and leans close to me. "Don't try

nothing. I can always call the nurse to dope you up and drag you to the holding cell. Got it?"

"You're going to drug me anyway."

"This way, you can say hi to your friend and eat something first," Gore says.

The scent of coffee on his breath makes me aware of my pounding caffeine withdrawal headache.

"Do I get coffee?"

"What do you think?" Gore releases my right wrist from the manacle.

"I'll take that as a yes." I stretch out my arm and open and close my hand.

"That's what I like about you, Allison. You're always a comedian." Gore meets my gaze. His deep-set eyes are emotionless as a fish's. He could kill me without a second thought and no regrets. "No funny business, eh?"

"No funny business," I say and mean it because the sleeper is still dead to me.

Gore finishes freeing me and allows me to stretch my stiff joints.

"What's all this fancy equipment?" I ask, gesturing to the various apparatuses attached to articulated arms dangling from the ceiling.

"My area of expertise is security," Gore says dryly. "Turn around and put your hands behind your back."

Reluctantly, I comply and have my wrists zip-tied together. Without warning, a black hood is lowered over my head.

"What the hell?"

Gore takes me by my left forearm. "What? You expected the grand tour?"

A hand presses against the small of my back,

propelling me forward. Toward the door, I suppose. Hard to tell with the hood—all I can see are my sneakers and the floor. Luckily, I have my prosthetics— well, at least my oculus dexter, and it has infrared mode. Beneath the hood, I smile and end up with a dangling string in my mouth that I spit out.

The door clanks open. I visualize the world in a dazzling rainbow splash of color, but nothing happens. Gore roughly grabs me by the upper arm. His grip tightens until his fingers digging into my bicep cause discomfort.

"By the way," Gore whispers into my ear, "Dr. Rah disabled your IR. I don't know what else, but she's very thorough."

"What! She messed with my prosthetics?" I don't want to kill again, but I might make an exception for that malignant carbuncle of a doctor. I stop myself from taking the thought any farther. Why is rage burning so hot in my chest? Maybe this is the sleeper's way of telling me it's re-emerging?

Help me. Give me your strength.

Not even an ephemeral ripple tickles my consciousness. The rage must be mine, which frightens me almost as much as being blinded.

"Let's go."

Gore half leads, half drags me along.

In the distance off to the right is conversation in multiple languages. English for certain. I'm not sure about the other languages, perhaps Chinese and at least one more. I strain to make sense of the words. It's so damn frustrating not having the sleeper experiencing the world along with me. With my half-skaag enhanced senses, I'd be able to follow the whole conversation—at least, the English. Instead, I'm guessing at words. I give up trying to interpret the conversation as the voices fade into the drone of forced air and other ambient sounds. I swear the speakers were switching between English and Chinese while speaking, sometimes in midsentence.

I count my steps and note each turn. The floor at my feet remains starkly white. Gore puts an end to my mental map when he stops me without preamble and spins me around several times.

"What are you doing?" I demand.

He spins me in the opposite direction. "You're a smart girl. Figure it out."

This procedure happens several more times before we stop at what I guess is a door. Gore spends nearly a minute opening it.

"Watch your step." Gore thrusts me forward.

Even with his warning, I catch my foot on white painted metal. Squealing, I fall, heart booming at the realization I can't catch myself with my hands zip-tied behind my back. I twist to avoid doing a faceplant, and my shoulder smashes into the concrete floor. My teeth clack shut, but I avoid chomping down on my tongue.

Behind me, the door slams with a resounding boom followed by an echoing screech of metal. Wherever I am is different from the white hallway. It's dark, chilly, and quiet by comparison. Gore snatches me by my arms and hauls me to my feet.

"Get moving," he growls, shoving me.

I stumble along, too discombobulated by the fall to attempt tracking my steps or the turns. Abruptly, Gore grabs my arm and mutters to be careful, then we're descending stairs. One flight—two, three, four before emerging onto a narrow hallway. At least, I think it's a hallway because my shoulder brushes against the wall that is cold to the touch, and we move out dead ahead, no turns. Goosebumps rise on my skin beneath my shirt.

"Where are we? Where are you taking me?" I ask.

"I'm taking you to the holding cell. That's all you need to know."

The stagnant air smells musty like there's no ventilation down here in the bowels of whatever this place is. What do I know about this place? I'm on an island in the ocean close to a city on the mainland or a larger island. It took a long plane ride to arrive here. Really long. Definitely, an international flight. How did I even get on board the plane? I don't have a passport. Neither does Dalia, for that matter. As much as we both would love to visit Europe and Asia, we are far too concerned about the environmental impact of international travel to do so. Since we don't have passports, Gore had fake passports made or…

"How did you get us through security at the airport?"

"How do you think?"

"Fake passports? Magic? Both?"

"Stop here," Gore says. "You've arrived."

He spins me ninety degrees to the left. I see the tip of black combat boots, not half a foot from my sneakers.

"New arrival. See she gets food. I'm going to bring a nurse to shoot her up," Gore says.

The boots move from view, and hinges groan.

"Did you use fake passports or magic?" I demand.

"Let's just say you're not in Seattle anymore," Gore whispers into my ear. "Watch your step."

He cuts the zip tie binding my wrists. I roll my wrists and flex my hands, working the blood back into my appendages. He pulls off the hood, barely giving me enough time to take in the dark doorway ahead of me before shoving me hard in the back. I stumble forward into the cell, avoiding the concrete lip jutting from the floor across the doorway. The dank room reeks like a sewer. There are one, no two, occupants sitting up against the back wall, staring at me with blurry eyes. I'm ready to spin around to confront Gore, but I see Dalia's disheveled neon pink hair.

"Dalia!"

The door slams shut behind me.

"Allison…is that you?"

Chapter 20

I rush across the cell to my BFF, my shoes splattering in muck. She rises on shaky legs, squinting in the dim light, and we embrace. Her body quivers in my arms. Even with my pitiful human olfactory senses, she smells horrible, and I'm certain I'm just as ripe. But that doesn't matter. She is solid and real and alive.

"When they separated us, I thought I'd never see you again," Dalia whispers.

"I was afraid too." Tears roll down my cheeks. "You're shaking. What's wrong?"

"I don't know. I'm weak. The nurse thinks it's a reaction to the sedatives."

"Should we sit?"

Dalia nods. "Be prepared for your butt to be wet with…I don't even know."

We break our embrace, and Dalia lowers herself to the floor, leaning back against the wall with a sigh. Overhead is a single fluorescent tube recessed in the ceiling, emitting super faint light and a constant, almost imperceptible buzz as annoying as a housefly. I don't see any video cameras affixed to the ceiling or the walls, but that doesn't mean we're not being recorded. The equipment in the examination room is high-tech to the point of being exotic, so who knows what kind of spy gear these people have.

As I take in the room, I run through my prosthetic's

capabilities, determining Dr. Rah has turned off everything except the zoom function. Tucked into the room's right corner is a bucket—*ewww*. I don't even want to consider using the bucket, especially with a strange boy about our age in the room. I look at him and discover he's staring at me with wide, dark eyes. I swear something floats around him, fuzzy filaments reminiscent of dandelion seeds, only variegated. I blink, and the filaments are gone.

"Do you only stare, or can you talk too?" I'm entitled to my waspishness considering the last twenty-four plus hours have been ripped from Dante's *Inferno*.

"Oh, this is Jett. Jett, this is Allison," Dalia says. "I should've introduced you sooner. I'm still out of it."

"Hello, Allison," Jett says as melodiously as a K-pop star. I'm not sure which one. He is striking even with his grime-covered clothes stained to an indeterminate color. His charcoal skin contrasts stunningly with his pale blond locks that almost appear prematurely white.

"What happened to your eye?" Jett asks.

"Her eye?" Dalia squints at me. "Oh, what happened?"

I sit next to Dalia, so she is between Jett and me. I fill them in on what happened in broad strokes, leaving out references to magic, dragons, and skaags. Anyone might be listening.

"They removed your eyes." Jett shakes his head. "That's harsh. Your eyes are prosthetics? Did it hurt? When they took out your eyes?"

"I was unconscious when they did that. But it doesn't hurt. I've had it done before."

"Wow. That's awesome," Jett says. "You can take

your eyeballs in and out without hurting yourself."

"It's not like I take my eyes in and out. Ever."

Jett smiles sheepishly. "I didn't say you do. I think that's...I don't know...I'd like to be able to take my eyes out."

I shake my head. Are all boys dumb and gross? Jett is starting to sound like Haji. Yet there is something about him that's totally unlike my friend. Jett exudes confident masculinity opposed to Haji's sometimes inane goofiness. Where Haji is soft and gangly, Jett is filled out with toned muscle. Something about him makes me all fluttery inside, and he is undeniably mesmerizing. I blink and turn away before he notices me staring. Maybe I don't mind if he catches me staring. Now, there's a thought.

"They better give you your eye back," Dalia says.

"I hope so," I say.

"What kind of questions did they ask you?" Jett asks.

I shrug. "Background stuff."

"Like what?" Jett's gaze is intense.

We've discussed my eyes, but it's his that are disturbing. The pupils spill into the irises like spreading ink. The orbs are reminiscent of my mother's, but the sclera isn't unnaturally thin like hers. His eyes, along with the filaments that may or may not have been there, make me suspicious. I'm not sure about what. The vibe is odd like my undeniable attraction to him. Of course, my suspicions might be misplaced. Dr. Rah has fiddled with my prosthetic oculus dexter, perhaps causing me to hallucinate.

"I don't want to talk about it."

I'm about to ask Dalia about Haji, but the door

being unlocked echoes in the cell. A guard in black fatigues enters, carrying a plastic tray with a heaping mound of steaming rice. He sets the tray on the floor and turns to his comrade standing outside in the hallway to retrieve three steaming plastic cups. These he sets on the floor next to the tray.

"Eat. Chief says eat." He points at me. "You must eat. Orders."

The guard stares at me when I don't respond.

"Must eat."

"Don't antagonize them," Dalia murmurs. "They'll drug us."

Dalia looks even more listless than when I arrived. The food will do her good.

"Okay," I whisper and pat her knee. To the guards, I say, "I'll eat."

"Eat and drink. All," the guard commands.

"I'll eat." I nod.

The guard nods and backs out. His compatriot shuts and locks the door. The food smells innocuous, but I wouldn't put it past our captors to have spiked it with drugs.

Jett scrambles across the floor to the tray. He loudly sniffs the food.

"Are you sure we should eat?" I ask.

After wiping a hand across his grimy shirt, he gingerly picks up a few grains of rice—gross. Crinkling my nose, I glance at Dalia. She is far too listless to be disgusted by the proceedings.

"Gelatinous rice—still hot!" He licks every grain from his fingers, then carries the tray to us. "You must be a VIP. I've been here for...I don't know. I've never had food this good."

As Jett scurries back for the drinks, I eye the food skeptically. "Is there any meat in it?"

Jett returns burdened with the three plastic cups. Steam rises from the pale green liquid.

"Ohhh, so sweet." Jett sets a cup down beside each of us. He sits across from us and smiles. "Eat." He grabs a handful of rice and shoves it into his mouth. "Perfectly cooked."

Jett continues eating with gusto. If the food is laced with drugs, it's not affecting him in any discernible way. I wonder how dirty his hands are, but my stomach twisting with hunger overcomes my disgust. I reach for the mound of rice, the rising steam warming my fingertips.

"It's tasty," Jett says through a mouthful of food.

I take a handful of rice that's sticky and not quite hot enough to burn my hand. I raise it to my mouth, breathing in the starchy scent. I nibble at the small white grains. The rice is sweet as honey and gooey. I scarf down the handful and take another. The rice takes the knife's edge off my hunger, but I'm left unsatisfied. I crave meat. Maybe the sleeper hasn't entirely abandoned me, but I receive no reply when I inwardly call to the skaag.

"You should eat," I tell Dalia, who hasn't taken a bite of rice or a sip of tea. "It's delectable."

In between slurps of tea, Jett adds, "Yes, do eat. We might not get another meal like this again."

With more gentle encouragement, Dalia eats. With each bite, she's pulled from her funk and eventually remarks on the sweetness of the rice.

The teacup is hot to the touch. Even after blowing across the liquid, the tea scalds my tongue.

I set down the cup to let the beverage cool. "Have you seen Haji?"

Dalia shakes her head and asks between bites of rice, "Have you?"

"I haven't seen him, but Gore and Dr. Kihl told me he's here. Somewhere."

"He is?" Dalia perks up, even smiling. "That's great." She faces Jett. "Did I tell you about Haji?"

"Haji? No." Jett shakes his head and raises a teacup. "What does he look like?"

"He's our age," Dalia says. "Black hair. Tall. Skinny."

Jett looks thoughtful. "Like from India?"

"Yes! Maybe. He's from the United States, but his parents are originally from Pakistan." Dalia nearly bounces off the floor.

"He was here for a few hours…almost a week ago, maybe. He was out of it. Didn't say a word. The guards took him away. That's all I know. I'm sorry," Jett says and sips the steaming drink.

"That confirms it." Dalia looks between Jett and me. "Haji is definitely here."

Despite her disheveled hair and weary eyes, she almost looks herself again, bubbly and happy. I almost warn her not to get her hopes up. Gore and the doctor might be trying to manipulate me, and I trust Jett about as far as I can throw him without my half-skaag prowess. Honestly, I find myself wanting to be physical with him in more ways than one. It's strange. I've never reacted this way to a boy before, not even when I was still head over heels for Jason.

"Yeah." I force myself to smile. "So, where are we? It was a super long flight to get here."

"Jett told me...I don't remember," Dalia says, effervescence fading.

"Singapore," Jett says. "An outlying island, to be precise. Golden Shoal, I think, but I'm not certain."

"Golden Shoal?" I ask.

"That's the name of the island. It's hard to know though. Singapore has around sixty outlying islands. From what I remember...when those weird military types kidnapped me, this must be Golden Shoal. It's right at the edge of Singapore's territorial waters. Tourists aren't allowed to visit because the old World War II bunkers have unexploded munitions. That's what I remember from school, anyway. We might be in one of those old bunkers."

"The city with those three towers supporting a giant yacht is Singapore?" I ask.

Dalia nods, and Jett says, "That's right. That boat-looking thing atop the towers is a park—spectacular views."

"Wow. We're in Southeast Asia," I say. "Wow. Are you..." I wrack my mind for the correct term "...Singaporean?"

"Oh, yes. I have a national ID card," Jett says with pride. "Are you from Seattle too?"

"Born and bred."

"Born and bred?" Jett says quizzically.

"It means yes."

"Oh." Jett nods.

"Tell me, Jett, how long have you been here?" I ask.

Jett shrugs while sucking sticky rice off his fingers. "Couple weeks. Maybe a month."

"Do you have any idea where they're keeping

Haji?"

"No."

I give him a hard stare. "They called him a candidate. Does that mean anything to you?"

Jett lifts his teacup from the floor. "Candidate?" He shakes his head. "No."

I'm unsure if I should believe him or not, but I'm certain he's holding something back.

"You've been here for a month? Why did they pick you up?"

Jett gives me a blank look and sips his tea.

"The paramilitary types. Why did they pick you up?"

"I...I don't know."

"How can you not know?" I nearly yell.

Dalia places a hand on my forearm. "Take it easy. He doesn't know anything."

My fingertips hover near the teacup—maybe I should calm down. "He knows something."

Jett drains his cup. "Sometimes, they take me to a room. It's like this, but..."

He shakes his head, lower lip quivering. Is this an act or not? For the life of me I can't tell. I stand and march to the cell door. I try the knob. Locked.

"It's okay if you don't want to talk about it," Dalia says.

Jett takes a deep breath. "No. No. I'm good. I want to escape. I'll tell you what I know."

I back away from the door. "Where is this room they take you to? Do you know? Anything you can tell us might help."

Jett smiles wanly. "They put a hood over my head. Just like you."

"That's a convenient answer." I eyeball the cell's heavy steel door.

"Allison, what's with you?" Dalia asks.

"What do you mean?" I pace the cell's width.

"You're so aggressive."

I am aggressive. Angry. Maybe the sleeper wakes inside me, filling me with prowess I can't detect. I call to the skaag but receive no reply. That might be drugs or magic interfering with our connection. There's an easy way to find out.

I charge the door and throw my shoulder into it. I yelp as paralytic pain leaves my arm numb. Stumbling backward, I slip on the wet muck covering the floor. One instant, I'm staring at the door, and the next, the dim fluorescent flashes in my eye. Gritting my teeth, I twist to keep my smarting shoulder from slamming into the floor first.

Strong hands arrest my fall. Jett supports me, his body radiating heat like someone with a deadly fever. I want to cling to him and feel his hands all over me. That scares me.

"Let go of me." I shove him.

He releases me and backs off.

"Allison, are you okay?" Dalia asks.

I ignore my friend, glaring at Jett instead. "Don't touch me again."

"Next time, I'll let you fall."

Before I can retort, the door is unlocked. I back away, rubbing life back into my numb arm. Jett stands his ground, but I keep backing up until I'm next to Dalia and my back presses up against the damp wall. I grasp her hand; she squeezes back.

The door swings open, revealing Gore flanked by

the small woman I remember from the plane and at least two guards in black commando gear.

"Move aside, kid," Gore growls. "You don't want to interfere."

"No," Jett says flatly. "Leave us alone."

Maybe I'm dreaming, or it's a trick of the light, but I swear for a fleeting moment, uncertainty flashes in Gore's deep-set eyes. Why? Why? Jett is achingly handsome, but he's not as imposing as the assassin and his bully boys. Maybe it's Jett's stubborn defiance that takes Gore aback. The ex-junkie is probably used to his orders being followed due to his magic and underlings.

"Kid, last chance." Gore smacks a fist into his palm. "You're not gonna like it if I have to come through you."

"No way—"

Gore has raised a hand, looking ready to signal his men.

"Wait," I say.

Gore lowers his hand and smiles. My throat constricts. I don't want Jett hurt on my account.

"Jett, you don't need to be the hero," I say. "They're only going to give me a tranquilizer or something."

"It's not right," Jett mumbles and steps aside.

Gore and the nurse march up to me. The nurse holds a hypodermic needle.

"I suggest you sit," the nurse says.

Dalia holds my hand tighter. "Why are you doing this?"

"You know why, pinkie." Gore smirks. "Do as the nurse says. Sit."

I meet his stare, defiance bubbling alongside the

simmering rage. "Remember the campground? The one out near Forks."

His smirk curdles into a quivering frown, and he touches the wrist I had broken. "Remember why pinkie is here, Allison?" His expression oozes into a toothy grin, and he continues in a singsong voice. "Remember, remember…"

"Okay." I pull my hand free of Dalia's. "Just stop singing."

"Remember, remember…what? You don't like my singing?" Gore's laugh is the grating of a graveyard gate.

I slump to the floor and pull up the arm of my T-shirt, revealing my deltoid. The nurse steps forward, expressionless as a mannequin. Dalia, pink hair bouncing, jumps between the nurse and me.

"Don't do this, please…no drugs. We won't try to escape. We wouldn't even know where to go," Dalia pleads.

"You're so cute when you beg," Gore says. "Now, get out of the way."

Gore shoves Dalia aside, inserting himself between my BFF and the nurse. Dalia sobs, and Jett shouts something.

"Get in here! Beat that little shit down!" Gore barks.

There is the thump of boots and the din of a melee. Thuds resound in the cell. Dalia's shrill scream is piercing. I try to stand, but Gore grips my shoulders and forces me back down.

"Shoot her up! Now!" Gore yells.

The nurse turns back to me. Her gaze is downcast, and her hand trembles.

"Hurry," Gore urges.

The nurse kneels next to me. Over Gore's shoulder, I watch the struggle. A commando smashes a baton into Jett's temple. His eyes roll back as he sways on his feet. He tips, about to crash to the floor, but a guard catches him, and together the guards drag him from the cell.

The nurse jabs the needle into my arm and depresses the plunger. The drug surges through me like liquid ice, numbing everything it touches. Dalia screams, but her words are distant and indecipherable. A blurry figure stands and backs away.

Hot breath titillates my ear. "Tell them what you know, Allison. Tell them everything."

Chapter 21

I wake up feeling like someone is methodically pounding a two-by-four into my head smack dab between the eyes. The throbbing is unrelenting. I need a bottle of ibuprofen and a warm bed to sleep in. Whatever I'm on is definitely not a bed. It's eerily familiar to the examination chair I was strapped into earlier. I yawn, desiring nothing more than to drift back asleep.

"Miss Lee, so good of you to join the land of the living. I hope you understand we're not playing around, Miss Lee. Are we, Dr. Rah?"

My eyelids flutter, but all I see is blackness. My body goes icy cold.

"I never play games, Ms. Bergman."

"Dr. Kihl gave me back my right eye. Where is it? I want to talk to him." I try sitting up, but restraints constrain my movement. I struggle, screaming wordlessly for the sleeper to wake. The rewards for my effort are painful abrasions at my wrists and ankles.

"Don't hurt yourself, Miss Lee. You'll be ruining all the fun for Dr. Rah and me. Dr. Rah, should she be this together physically given the tranqs? I thought the drug is powerful enough to put an elephant under."

"Did the nurse administer the drug, Chief?" Dr. Rah asks.

"Yes, ma'am, per the schedule. A little late,

honestly. The prisoners resisted," Gore replies.

"Resisted? Naughty, naughty, Miss Lee. That behavior is unacceptable," Ms. Bergman says. "Don't worry, Chief, Allison won't be able to resist effectively while blind."

The anger and fear blossoming inside me bursts. "Give me back my prosthetics!" I scream and thrash, ignoring the pain in my wrists. "Give them back! Give them back!"

A hand slaps my face, whipping my head to the side. Blood trickles from the corner of my mouth.

"No outbursts. Do you understand, Miss Lee?" Ms. Bergman says.

Wincing, I nod.

"Good, Miss Lee."

A hand rests on my shoulder. For a moment, it's almost reassuring, then sharp nails dig into my skin. I gasp, and the hand withdraws.

"We've explained this to you before, Miss Lee," Bergman says, becoming more pedantic with every word. "Compliance is rewarded. Concrete rewards like I won't cut Dalia's head off. Or…" Her breath blows across my brow. I turn my head to the side. Calloused hands grip either side of my head and twist my neck until I'm facing forward. "No, no, no, Miss Lee. I want your attention front and center."

Light flickers before my right eye. Smudgy white resolves into muddy colors in the center of a bright gash.

"Can she see, Ms. Bergman?" Dr. Rah asks.

I squint as the muddy colors coalesce into a jowly face, tinged pink. The most prominent feature is a squashed nose angled to the left.

"Oh, I think she can see me just fine, Dr. Rah," Ms. Bergman says. Her mouth is enormous and opens wide as she talks, almost like a snake's. Her shoulders and arms bulge underneath a gray suit jacket. Her thick hands are as large and powerful as bear paws. "Now, Miss Lee, I'm going to ask you some questions. It's critical you answer them truthfully. Otherwise, Dr. Rah...well, you can guess what Dr. Rah will do if we decide you're non-compliant. Chief, bring the screen around, will you?"

She makes it sound like a request, but I know it's a command. Gore complies without complaint like a gopher who jumps at everyone else's whim. Do Ms. Bergman and Dr. Rah possess magic too? Is their magic even more potent than his? Where does Dr. Kihl stand in the pecking order? Gore treated Kihl as if the doctor is a superior.

Casters squeal as Gore pushes a tall cart with a widescreen LCD TV atop it. This room is similar to the one I was in before with my tormentors. It's stark white but lacks the accouterments protruding from the ceiling by segmented arms.

Without warning, Ms. Bergman lifts my head off the headrest and slams it back down. I gasp in startlement, and my gaze fixes on her meat cleaver of a face. "Eyes front...I suppose I should say, eye front and center, Miss Lee. I know you and the Chief have a long and sordid history, but I require your full attention. Can you give me that?"

"Why should I?"

Her right hand releases my head. I swing my head forward, hoping to clip her on her broken nose. Before my head slams into her, a bear paw of a hand slams into the side of my head above the ear. My vision goes from red to black, then clears as the fireworks booming in my skull recede. I'd have whiplash, but her left hand kept my neck relatively straight. Her right hand clamps down against the side of my head again, effectively locking me in a vise from the neck up.

"That," Bergman says matter-of-factly, "was for back talking. Maybe before I was too explicit with what I will do to Dalia if you refuse to cooperate. I am, Miss Lee, an expert in interrogation, especially the dark arts. Aren't I, Dr. Rah?"

"Some claim an artist, Ms. Bergman."

"You, Miss Lee, are valuable. You have information we want. Dalia does not. She is nothing to us except a means of extracting information out of you. Consider what I might do to her before I cut her head off if you don't cooperate."

Ms. Bergman sprays spittle all over my face with the last sentence. She leans back, and her lips curl into a broad, toothy smile that's almost motherly.

"Who are you people?"

"I represent part of your government, Miss Lee, that believes you and your dragon friend are the greatest threat to national security our country has ever faced. Now, you're going to watch a video. I want you to watch it closely because after this video I'm going to have some pointed questions for you, Miss Lee. Some very pointed questions." Ms. Bergman releases my head and steps aside. "Chief, start the video."

Gore points a remote at the TV, which flares to life with a newscaster sitting behind a desk before a pale blue background. White swishes in my peripheral vision. I turn toward the movement, hoping to get an eyeful of Dr. Rah since I don't have a clue what she looks like.

The newscaster begins: "What you are about to see is absolutely—"

"Pause the video, Chief. Pay attention to the video, Miss Lee."

I rotate my head until I'm staring straight ahead at the paused video. Dr. Rah has glided from my field of vision like an apparition. Ms. Bergman nods to Gore.

"—shocking. It was recorded earlier today by a pilot flying from Seattle to Japan."

The newsroom cuts to a blurred video of a Chinese dragon flying through the clouds. In the background, a man and woman mutter expletives. The man opines they should divert to avoid being attacked by the strange creature. The image might be blurry, but I have no doubt the beast is a skaag. Not only that, the skaag is my mother.

The video zooms in, becoming unsteady. Bergman orders Gore to pause the video and faces me. Her expression is as dark as a thunderhead. "Can you tell me what this is, Miss Lee?"

"I think you already know what it is, Ms. Bergman."

Bergman frowns and arches an eyebrow.

From behind me comes Dr. Rah's voice. "Now might be an appropriate time to use sodium thiopental, Ms. Bergman. What do you think?"

Bergman's frown whorls into a predatory smirk. "Why, Dr. Rah, great minds think alike."

"Sodium thiopental?" I whip my head side to side, failing to spot the doctor.

"Do relax, Miss Lee. It's only truth serum," Ms.

Bergman says.

"It's a skaag," I splutter. "A skaag, okay. Just like the videos on the Internet and on the news."

"That's odd." Bergman furrows her brow and looks beyond me. "Isn't that strange, Dr. Rah? Dr. Radcliffe claims all the skaags here on planet earth are dead. That is except for you, Miss Lee, but you're only a half-skaag, or so he claims. How is it possible a skaag was recorded flying over the Pacific Ocean a few hours ago?"

I swallow. "I don't know."

"You don't know? You don't know? Miss Lee, did you or did you not close the portal in the Grove of the Patriarchs?" Ms. Bergman starts pacing in front of the TV.

"I closed the portal."

"Did any skaags reach earth before you closed the portal?"

"No."

"Are you absolutely certain of that, Miss Lee?"

"Yes."

Bergman stops pacing and glares at me with eyes as wide as silver dollars.

"I mean…umm…I don't know. I don't think any came through. It's possible, I suppose."

"Did Dr. Radcliffe kill the skaag…what was the monster's name, Chief?"

"Mark Cassidy."

"Did Radcliffe kill Mark Cassidy?"

"Yes, he did."

"Well, Miss Lee, I wish I could take what you say at face value, but sadly I cannot. Dr. Rah, please."

A needle punches into my neck.

"What did you just give me?" I demand.

"Truth serum, Miss Lee. Do try to keep up." Bergman smiles condescendingly. Her gaze shifts to somewhere above my head. "How long before the serum takes effect?"

"About thirty minutes, Ms. Bergman."

"Excellent!" Bergman walks toward the door. "Gives us enough time to have some refreshments before round two. Chief, be so kind as to keep an eye on our guest. Oh, would you like some coffee? I heard a new shipment has arrived."

"I'd love some coffee." Gore waits until the women leave and the door thuds shut before continuing. "You're a big fan of coffee, aren't you?"

I grind my teeth, refusing to tell him I pine for a cuppa—strong, dark, and flavorful. I refuse to believe these people truly appreciate a good cup of coffee.

"Before I tried offing you the first time, Allison, I followed you and your little friends around. You were always at that artsy coffee shop…" He stares at the floor and snaps his fingers several times. He looks up and grins. "The Obsidian Roast. I even tried it once. It was okay. Overpriced. Self-important. Solidly Pacific Northwest. The cinnamon rolls are delicious. You like the cinnamon rolls, right?"

My nostrils flare. "I wish—"

Gore lurches forward, teeth snapping shut millimeters from my nose. "Wish what? That you killed me?"

Where are you? I need you! I call to the sleeper, but the skaag remains missing in action.

"Have you noticed they only know about Dr. Radcliffe?" Gore whispers. "They know Mauve is dead.

They don't know anything about Tanis or Tatsuo. Do you know what I think? I think Tanis and Tatsuo are alive. Shhhhh. Don't say anything. Not yet. We need some privacy first."

Gore mutters rapidly under his breath. I swear his skin briefly flickers with an eerie orange luminescence. He backs away from me, and I breathe easier.

"We can talk now." His left hand still emits faint orange light from fractal patterns etched into it.

"Why is your hand glowing? Did you cast a spell?"

Gore briefly admires his hand. "I put a simple illusionary spell in place. The cameras and other recording devices see and hear us reminiscing about our time together in Seattle and the Olympic Peninsula, etc., etc. Quite boring, really. Now, let's talk honestly. It's draining to hold the illusion in place. I have to know"—he points to the blurry image of my mother on the LCD—"is that Druk?"

Sweat beads across his brow.

"Why should I tell you anything?" I ask.

A globule of sweat rolls down his nose to dangle from its tip.

"I'm a survivor, Allison. If that's Druk, there's a fair chance she's hunting you. If she's flying over the Pacific toward Japan, she might end up poking around here. If Druk shows up here, people are gonna die. I don't plan on dying. Is that your mother or not?"

Ms. Bergman's grating voice echoes from nearby.

"Dammit. Leave it to them to be early," Gore whispers and wipes the sweat from his face with a sleeve of his black fatigues. "Don't tell them anything I told you. Understand? I can help you, but only if I'm alive."

I nod, but I'm not sure if keeping his secret is to my advantage. Maybe I should earn my captors' good graces by outing him as a traitor.

Gore backs away, and the glow fades from his hand.

The door opens, and Ms. Bergman calls, "Chief, we came back early to deliver your coffee!"

Chapter 22

Ms. Bergman tromps across the room and gives Gore a steaming cup. Dr. Rah follows her inside, and I catch my first real glimpse of the mad scientist. She is tall, slender, and has an Asian complexion. Her straight hair is cropped just below the ears. Underneath her lab coat, she wears a black knee-length skirt and a white blouse. What's striking is her severe expression, all grim annoyance verging on rage. Her face is so tight, I'm surprised her jaw muscles aren't dancing a two-step. Is she the one in charge? Maybe Bergman is her mouthpiece.

As the doctor steps behind me, Gore waves a steaming cup of black brew underneath my nose. The coffee smells ambrosial, reminding me I don't remember the last time I had a cup, and my caffeine withdrawal headache feels like an elephant systematically grinding my skull into the ground.

I purse my lips, and Gore withdraws the cup with a cackle.

He smiles and takes a sip. "Smells better than you expected, huh?"

"Much better." I'm unable to lie about coffee.

"How do you feel, Miss Lee?" Ms. Bergman asks and takes a long slurp of java.

"Like I need coffee."

"Did the Chief use magic while we were out, Miss

Lee?"

My heart palpitates. Do I betray Gore or not? Ms. Bergman stares at me like she can see straight into my soul and devour it.

"No." I shake my head. Betraying Gore will earn me nothing, but maybe, if he's not feeding me a line of bullshit, he might be able to help. "No, he didn't."

"He didn't?" Ms. Bergman says with mock surprise. "Did you hear that, Dr. Rah? Miss Lee told me the Chief didn't use magic while we were out."

"That sounds like a lie to me, Ms. Bergman," the doctor says.

My gaze flicks to Gore, who smirks in between sips of coffee.

"So the barbiturate hasn't taken effect?" Bergman asks.

"We are back early, Ms. Bergman," Dr. Rah says, "and I must remind you, the drug doesn't make it impossible to lie, only harder to lie convincingly."

Ms. Bergman pats me on the cheek, each touch of her calloused palm promising violence.

"Miss Lee, we have specialized equipment in this room that detects magic," she says and slaps my face so hard my lip starts bleeding all over again. "I don't appreciate being lied to, Miss Lee. In fact, I'm beginning to wonder if you care about Dalia."

"He said he'll help me escape," I say.

Bergman utters a grating laugh. "Is that what he told you?" She's laughing so hard liquid sloshes over the side of her mug. "Oh, damn." She stifles her laughter. "This coffee is too good to waste."

I feel a spark of superiority when I notice Ms. Bergman's spill is a light tan color, a sure sign the brew has been diluted by milk or creamer.

"That's what he tells everyone," Bergman continues. "Isn't that right, Chief?"

"Yes, ma'am," Gore says.

My body relaxes like I'm entering the liminal space between wakefulness and sleep. I fight to stay present, but I find I'm not motivated. I want to float on the calm water of an alpine lake and sink beneath the cerulean surface.

"Miss Lee, do you remember the video you were shown earlier?" Ms. Bergman asks.

Annoyance flashes through me. How dare she disturb my rest and relaxation? Then I'm giggling. "Yes."

"The skaag in the video. Do you recognize it?"

"No," I say between titters.

"Are you sure you don't recognize it?"

"Okay, yes." I'm laughing so hard I nearly snort. "Yes, yes, yes, yes. It's Druk. If she comes here…" I'm hooting so hard I'm shaking. "…she'll kill all of you!"

"Druk? How do you know her?"

"She…" I almost say she's my mother, but that's personal. Daddy always said never to share personal information with strangers. "She worked for Mark Cassidy."

Ms. Bergman rounds on Gore. "Do you have anything to add about this piece of intelligence, Chief?"

"No, ma'am. I never heard of this other skaag…Druk? I only had contact with Mark Cassidy."

The assassin's gaze darts around the room like he's looking for a way to escape. I nearly exclaim he's lying, but a presence nudges me out of the space between consciousness and unconsciousness. My situation isn't funny anymore.

Are you there? I ask the sleeper silently. *Help me!*

The sleeper fades.

No! Come back!

"Miss Lee, tell me all about Druk. How long has the skaag been here? Did it come through the portal in the Grove of the Patriarchs?"

My stomach becomes as hard as a rock. I'm alone again, but I'm no longer floating in semiconsciousness. I'm present.

"Answer the question, Miss Lee."

"The portal? No, Druk has been here for a long time. I don't know how long." I act loopy and giggly, but I'm not winning any awards.

Ms. Bergman's eyes narrow. "You're certain you've never heard about this second skaag before, Chief?"

"No, ma'am."

Ms. Bergman's jaw muscles twitch. "You worked for Mark Cassidy for how long, Chief?"

"Five years, ma'am."

"You killed for him on several occasions. You tried to kill Miss Lee. Obviously, he trusted you. He never once confided about a second skaag?" Bergman clenches and unclenches her fists.

"Ma'am, I was a drug addict. There's much from those years I can't remember and much I wish I couldn't remember. If Mark Cassidy ever told me about Druk, I honestly have no memory of it. However, I don't think he would have mentioned it. I was the hired help. Nothing more."

Ms. Bergman relaxes her hands and draws a deep breath. "And now you're addicted to the Juice. Heh."

"My head is clear now, ma'am," Gore says stiffly.

Bergman smirks while rubbing the tips of her pointer finger and thumb of her left hand together. "Take it easy, Chief. Your new addiction makes you a valuable, trustworthy asset. Isn't that right, Dr. Rah?"

"I wholeheartedly agree, Ms. Bergman. We all know, Chief, you would never do anything to endanger your access to the Juice."

"Exactly. You'd have to be an idiot to endanger your access to the Juice, Chief. We don't think you're an idiot. Do we, Dr. Rah?"

"No, we don't, Ms. Bergman...oh, what is that saying I often hear? Trust but verify. That's it. We trust you, Chief, but given this revelation about this skaag on the loose, we must verify."

Gore looks like he tastes bile.

A feral grin alights Bergman's face. "It would be irresponsible for us not to interrogate you at the earliest opportunity, Chief. You're dismissed. Remain confined to your quarters for now."

"I—"

"Is there a problem, Chief?"

"No, ma'am."

Gore marches from the room. The door thuds shut behind him.

"Now, back to you, Miss Lee." Ms. Bergman slyly smiles. "I do think, Dr. Rah, the barbiturate has already worn off."

Help me, I call to the sleeper.

"That is entirely possible, Ms. Bergman. She metabolizes drugs at several times the rate of a normal person. Might I suggest we use the alternative inducement?"

Deep within the recesses of my being are a spark of warmth and trickle of colossal rage that don't belong to me alone. I tingle with the anticipation of the limitless prowess accompanying the sleeper's waking.

Ms. Bergman nods. "Why, Dr. Rah, that's a lovely idea."

My vision goes black like someone flipped the light switch, instantly turning off all the lights in the universe.

Give me your strength, I tell the sleeper, but already the half-skaag is swept away by the flow of my consciousness. I fight to stay calm while my heart stampedes in my chest, and my breathing is rapid and shallow. I can't help thinking maybe this time that's it. Perhaps this time they won't restore my vision. This time, my hopes and dreams are flushed down the sewer forever. I chew ravenously at my lower lip. Tasting the coppery tang of blood in my mouth, I stop chewing before I do real damage.

"Relax, Miss Lee. I have a few questions about your prosthetics," Dr. Rah says. "Specifically, I want to know about Dr. Woolworth."

Fear pounds through my veins. I don't want these people going after those I care for. I don't want to put Dr. Woolworth at risk. If they go after her, will they track down my dad too? If Mother is rampaging around Southeast Asia, who will protect Dad? Mauve? My breath catches in my throat, and my chest becomes heavy and tight. Did Gore and his henchmen really kill Mauve? Don't think about that. It's too terrible to consider.

"Is Dr. Woolworth a magician?" Dr. Rah asks.

"A magician? No." Mother and Dr. Radcliffe

would be aware if Dr. Woolworth possessed one iota of magical power. Secondly, the woman has the good looks of a supermodel. I don't think I'd find track marks on her arms or between her toes.

"In her academic papers, she has many co-authors. Most often, the name Dr. Raymond Lee appears. That is your father, correct?"

"Leave my father out of this."

"Is your father a magician?"

My fear and anger coalesce into a seething pool of lava deep in my bowels. The volcanic fumes disturb the sleeper, and the beast stirs. Prowess seeps through me. I breathe in deeply. I can smell Dr. Rah's sweat. She's not more than three feet in front of me.

"Must I repeat the question?" Rah asks.

"I can't hear you," I mutter, slurring my words.

The doctor falls for the bait, heels clicking against the floor.

"Don't go any closer!" Bergman barks, and her heavy steps thump against the tiles.

Too late. With a surge of prowess, I jerk my right arm up and forward, snapping the restraint pinning the appendage to the armrest. I lurch upright as far as I can, my movements constrained by the bonds at my left wrist and ankles. My fingers home in on my prey like heat-seeking missiles. Dr. Rah screams before my fingers compress her throat, strangling her cry.

"Leave my dad out of this!"

Dr. Rah claws at my hand, attempting to wrench my fingers from her throat, leaving long scratches on my skin. Bergman's lumbering footsteps echo through the chamber. Something heavy and fleshy hammers into my right arm at the elbow joint. My arm collapses, but I maintain my grip on the doctor, dragging her forward.

"Guards! Guards!" Ms. Bergman bellows.

I can crush the doctor's windpipe or tear it out. With the half-skaag power coursing through me like rocket fuel, doing either requires as little effort as killing a fly. But I don't because I remember the dead kidnapper's glassy stare after I snapped his neck. Never again will I slay another and slip farther down the abyss ending with me becoming my mother, a killing machine capable of dealing out death without regret.

A fist smashes into my cheek, slamming my head to the side. With a snarl, I rip my left hand free and torpedo my fist toward Ms. Bergman. I miss. Her scurrying footfall announces her retreat. Dr. Rah continues trying to peel away my fingers, but each digit is like a stake driven into her throat.

"Guards!" Bergman hollers.

I release the doctor, who thuds to the floor like a discarded sack of potatoes. She coughs and gasps for air. I rip my left ankle free of the bonds. Before I can free my right ankle, the door bursts open with a clang followed by the clamor of the guards—two, no three...at least five. It doesn't matter. It can be one hundred guards, and they wouldn't be able to stop me. The restraint holding my left ankle fails, and I'm free. I surge to my feet, laughing.

Rage thunders through me as the lead guard approaches, breathing hard through his mouth. His compatriots are not far behind, spreading out in a half-moon formation. Let them come. I will make them pay for all they have done to me, to Dalia, to Mauve. My fist shoots forward like a battering ram with all my might behind it. What am I doing? I'll kill him. I pull my punch before my knuckles smash into the guard's jaw. In my mind's eye, the dead man in my bedroom stares at me; his neck is angled unnaturally.

My fist crashes into the lead guard's face, and bones snap under the blow, but he'll live.

"Tase her!" Bergman screams.

A trigger clicks, and I dive toward the door, sliding across the floor under the electrodes' trajectory. All around me, the guards make surprised sounds. Vaulting to my feet, I'm sprinting for the door. I skid across the tile to stop just before the doorway. An insatiable urge bubbles through me. Close the door. Kill them all. Make the doctor restore your eyesight, then…no, no, no! You're not a killer. A devilish voice rings through my mind. "Oh, yes, you are. Stop lying to yourself. You killed a man in your bedroom, and you can't wait to kill again."

Something clubs my legs behind the knees. My legs buckle. Before I can recover, I'm tackled from behind and forced to the floor. More weight piles on me, but I'm not worried. They'll learn the error of their ways.

"No," I snarl as a needle penetrates my neck.

I surge to my feet, throwing the guards to the floor, walls, and ceiling. I sprint down the hall, but soon I feel like I am running sideways and slow down. I'm woozy, and my body aches like I've been in a head-on collision with an eighty-thousand-pound semi. Worst and most telling of all, my sense of the sleeper drifts like a bit of wreckage sinking beneath the waves of a storm-ravaged sea.

My legs wobble. Windmilling my arms, I place a hand against the wall to keep my balance. From somewhere nearby come incoherent, startled voices. I slide down the wall like a wet towel.

Help me. Help me. Please, I call, but the sleeper is gone.

A meaty hand grabs my jaw and wrenches my head upward. "You're a naughty girl, Miss Lee." I smell coffee on Ms. Bergman's breath. "Bring me another tranq."

Spittle splatters my face. I want to resist, but everything hurts, and my limbs are leaden.

"Well, Miss Lee, you want to learn the hard way, don't you? You can't say I haven't warned you. Now poor, poor Dalia will suffer the consequences of your bad choices."

Chapter 23

Dampness soaking through my clothing shocks me awake. Moaning, I blink only to be greeted by darkness and buzzing from the light fixture inside the cell I share with Dalia and Jett.

"Dalia," I croak, pushing myself up with shaky arms. My palms press down onto the damp stone. With the stench of urine and defecation lodged in my nose, I don't want to consider the wetness.

"She's not here," Jett says.

"I can't see." I wish I could see him. "Are both my eyes missing?"

"Only your left eye is missing. What's wrong? Why can't you see?"

"Dr. Rah. Do you know her?"

"No. I've—" His voice cracks. "I've encountered nurses—at least two—sometimes they stitch me up…after…"

"After you've been tortured?"

"Yes." The word is a pained gasp.

"Is that what they did to you when they took you away?"

"They beat me, but not bad compared…compared to other times."

"Is that what they're doing to Dalia? Torturing her?" I demand, swiveling side to side and listening for any sound betraying her presence. I want to trust Jett, but Dalia might be strewn on the cell floor for all I know. When I don't detect any sign of Dalia, my heart burns in my chest like a dying star. "Where did they take her?"

"I don't know."

"You've been here for what? Weeks? Months? You must have some idea."

"The woman who came with the guards when they brought you. She told the guards to take your friend."

"Woman? What woman? Was it Ms. Bergman?"

"I...I don't know Ms. Bergman. The woman's name is Felicia. She tortures me."

I lurch to my feet. Trembling, I force myself to stand tall. "The woman. Felicia. Is she stout with a face formed by a sledgehammer and wearing a gray suit?"

"Yes, that's her."

Hello, Felicia Bergman. If that is her name. If Felicia Bergman isn't an alias. What I am certain about is I don't want Dalia in Felicia's presence one second longer. The mere thought my best friend might be suffering excruciating pain for my actions makes me feel like all the air is being squeezed out of me.

"Guide me to the door," I say.

"Why?"

"Because I'm going to pound on the door and demand they return Dalia."

"They won't respond."

"Don't help me then. I'll find the door myself." I have to do something, anything that might help Dalia. I call to the sleeper. *I need your help.*

Someone stirs, but it's not the sleeper. It's Jett.

"Wait. I'll help you."

His feet patter in the muck. A strong hand grips my

forearm. His cool breath caresses my ear. I lean against his chest, savoring the safety of his embrace. His breath tickles my cheeks, and I breathe it in. I gasp. He smells masculine and ambrosially exotic.

He pulls me closer until we are tangled together as one. His hands stroke my back, my hair, my shoulders, igniting wildfires with his fingertips. I catch his arm, gently guiding his hand to my hip.

Dust or something irritates my nose, causing me to sneeze, I imagine, in his face. I'd be flustered, but I don't have the opportunity because his hands slide sensuously over my hips. I'm nearly panting. I want more. I want him, but I'm also aware something is not right. This is going too fast. Weirdly fast. I barely know him. Why am I doing this when Dalia is being tortured by Bergman?

"Stop," I whisper.

"You want me to stop?"

"Yes…I have to help Dalia. I can't do this right now."

"Just one kiss?" Jett blows gently across my cheek.

"Yes," I say breathlessly.

His lips brush against mine. Ardor I've never known existed fires every nerve in my body, drowning out my doubt in pleasure. Since arriving on the island, I'm experiencing something other than pain and fear and anger for the first time. I want more. I don't want this to ever end. I press my lips into him, wanting to tantalize him with my passion. I wish I could experience this with my half-skaag faculties, which would make every sensation spark with a life of its own. There is the click of the door unlocking, and Jett pushes me away, the motion urgent and tender.

"They watch us," he whispers.

I cling to his hands as he backs away. It's not fair. I finally find something real, and already it's being torn from my grasp.

The door squeals. Our fingertips part, and I'm adrift. If I could see, I wouldn't have to imagine his expression is as stricken as mine.

"Allison," Gore says. "Dr. Kihl wants to speak with you."

Gore grabs me roughly by the upper arm and drags me along. When the door slams behind me, I know I'm in the hallway.

"You're back in action fast. I thought Felicia was going to interrogate you," I say.

Gore sets a fast pace my spasming legs can't keep up. Not that he cares. He drags me along.

"I wouldn't call Bergman that to her face. She did interrogate me, by the way, but it was perfunctory after your little display."

I laugh mirthlessly. "It was the least Dr. Rah deserved. Where have they taken Dalia?"

"I don't know."

"What do you mean you don't know? Aren't you the security chief?"

Gore shakes me like loose change. "Quiet."

The murmur of conversation in a foreign language drifts from nearby. A Chinese dialect, maybe? I don't have the ear for languages.

When the sound of conversation fades, I hiss, "Which side are you on?"

An open palm slaps the side of my head so hard I stumble and collide with the wall. If Gore wasn't holding me up, I'd be in a heap on the floor. His coffee breath blow-dries my face. God, I could kill for some caffeine to help clear away the drug-induced fogginess.

"I'm on my side."

****

"Stop here," Gore commands.

I comply. What else am I going to do? I'm blind and no matter how loud or long I scream in my mind for help, the sleeper doesn't respond. From somewhere overhead comes the soft drone of forced air. Off to my right is the buzz of a microwave, maybe, and a whiff of garlic. Lunchtime?

Hinges softly squeal.

"Inside."

"Have we arrived?" I ask.

"Inside."

Gore shoves me hard in the back. I stumble forward, jaw clenched in anticipation of tripping on the door frame or something. It wouldn't be the first time, after all. Miraculously, I remain on my feet, much to my relief.

"Ah, Allison. It's good to see you," Dr. Kihl says.

We're playing games. He's the good cop in a good cop, bad cop routine.

"Wish I could say the same," I say.

The door closes behind me, and I sense Gore beside my shoulder. I swallow a lump in my throat. Without my half-skaag prowess, he could garrote me, and I'd be unable to stop him.

"You refer to your lack of vision," Dr. Kihl says. "I'm sorry about that. Very unfortunate. Ms. Bergman and Dr. Rah are…overly enthusiastic at times."

"That's one way to put it."

"Chief, please help Allison to a chair."

228

Gore grabs me roughly by the arm and thrusts me forward. I stumble on my wobbly legs, but the manly man keeps me upright.

"Sit." He presses down on my shoulders.

I collapse into a plush and surprisingly comfortable chair. Footsteps approach me from the front. Fingers gently rest against my wrist. I go on alert like a rabbit spotted by a predator.

"Relax, Allison," Dr. Kihl says. "I have no intention of harming you. As I explained before, I don't want you or Dalia hurt, but—"

"I remember." I jerk my wrist from his fingers. "Powers beyond your control run things here."

"Yes, I'm afraid that is true. It's also true I don't want anything…unfortunate to happen to you. We want to understand your abilities. That's all. Our research is for the benefit of humankind."

"Sending Gore and his thugs to kidnap us is for the benefit of humankind? Please!"

Dr. Kihl sighs. "I understand your fear and frustration."

"Then prove to me Dalia is safe and restore my eyesight."

"There is something you should know about me," Dr. Kihl says. "I am a magician. A powerful one for a human. Like the Chief."

"I thought you were a doctor."

"Oh, I am." Dr. Kihl chuckles. "I haven't lied to you, Allison. I'm a medical doctor and an expert in constructing specialized medical apparatus, like your friend Dr. Woolworth. I followed her work intently, even before learning about you and your ability to see dragons riding the slipstream. Why is it you can see the dragons, Allison? Why?"

"I don't know. How many times do I have to tell you? I don't know."

"I believe you. I do. You have no idea why your prosthetics allow you to see the dragons. I also believe the dragons have no idea why this is the case. Otherwise, I'm sure Dr. Radcliffe would have prevented the prosthetics from being created."

I breathe in deeply, trying to stay calm. The doctor might give something away. I need to keep my anger in check and fight back against the fuzziness intruding on my mind from the tranquilizer. But it's hard to hold back the anger roiling in my stomach. I wish it wasn't only my anger. I wish it was the sleeper's, too.

"I'm sure you have discovered the dragons have their own agenda that doesn't necessarily have anything to do with the betterment of humankind."

I nod in agreement. There is at least a fifty-fifty chance that Dr. Radcliffe will give humans the shaft. After all, he had offered me up as a sacrificial lamb to Mark Cassidy without so much as blinking an eye. I don't trust Tanis either. If anything, she's probably less trustworthy than Radcliffe. What about Mauve? The dragon who has lived nearly her entire life among people, suppressing her draconic self to masquerade as human. The one being in the universe who might have an iota of an idea of what it's like to be me. Would she betray me? What if Dr. Radcliffe gave her an order to turn on me? Is it fair for me to expect her to ignore a directive from her leader?

Kihl is trying to manipulate me. He's a magician, a junkie like Gore. Maybe he doesn't use heroin, but I bet he uses the Juice. That glowing orange liquid is a drug.

"Allison."

A hand grasps my shoulder. The muscles in my upper back twist into painful knots.

"I'm going to reinstall your prosthetic," the doctor says.

"You are?" I hate myself for how tremulous I sound. He's going to give me back my life.

"Yes, I am. Now, lean your head back. Easy. There. First, I'm going to sterilize the skin around the interface area with an antiseptic cloth."

Moist material pads the skin around my missing eye. The cleaner smells astringent. "That's cold."

"We must eliminate any possibility of infection." Kihl continues dabbing the material into my eye socket. "There. I think that's good. I'm going to wait for your skin to dry before installing the prosthetic."

"Okay," I murmur, although I want to scream at him to restore my vision this instant.

"You're wondering what we are doing here," Dr. Kihl says and pauses as if waiting for a response. I nod in the affirmative. "As I have said, everything we do here is for the benefit of humanity. Humankind must be able to protect itself from the skaags and dragons. That is our greatest concern at the moment, but it's not our only concern. Magic married with technology is the key to advancing human civilization. Imagine what we could do by combining medical technology with magic. We might be able to cure cancer. We might even be able to conquer death. Consider that, Allison. Consider that."

Dr. Kihl speaks with fervor I haven't heard from him before. It's both disconcerting and enticing.

"Your skin looks dry. We can proceed. Are you

ready to see again, Allison?"

"Yes!" The doctor's zeal echoes in my voice. What is he doing to me? He's not winning me over, is he?

"Good. You'll feel pressure."

Something is pressed to my eye socket. "Ouch!"

"Apologies," Dr. Kihl says. "Just a little bit more. I almost have it."

His words are followed by more pressure, and the prosthetic slides into place.

"There! Excellent." Kihl pats me on the shoulder and walks away. There is a sound of casters rolling across the floor, followed by a squeak that might indicate someone sitting down.

"You said you'd restore my vision." Panic restricts my throat.

"I'm connecting to your prosthetics. Lights. Camera. Action."

Light flashes before my eyes. Relief floods me. I thank God and Buddha and every other deity I can think of as I blink, the bright light resolving into a white office. Dr. Kihl sits in front of me behind a broad desk with a wide-screen computer monitor offset to the left. I sit in one of two chairs in the minimalistly adorned space. Behind me, next to the door, is Gore.

"I want to tell you a story, Allison," Dr. Kihl says, removing his spectacles and placing them on the desk next to the computer monitor. He leans forward, resting his elbows on the desk. When he speaks again, his eyes are rheumy. "Twenty years ago, my wife died of ovarian cancer. It was detected late. Perhaps if it had been detected sooner...surgery might have saved her life. But...as I'm sure you know, there are inequities in healthcare. Even between the sexes. This is no different in my country than in the United States." He takes a deep breath. "I've always known I'm a magician. I was born into a coven. My mother, God bless her, was a witch. She taught me enough about magic to keep me safe and to keep me from…well, becoming addicted to heroin in the pursuit of it. I never once experimented with drugs until…" He sniffs and wipes at his cheeks. "I did everything I could to save my wife." He lifts up his right arm and pulls back his lab coat, then unbuttons the cuff of his white shirt and rolls up the sleeve to his elbow. He rubs the skin of his forearm with a hand. "I can't tell you how many times I shot up. Dozens. Hundreds." He shrugs. "All in the hope of saving my wife, my Jung Hwan." His voice cracks. "I failed. But now, we are closer than ever before to advancing human magic to levels never before imagined. The cure for cancer is within our grasp, Allison. We are so close to ending human suffering. With more potent magical power, we'll be able to protect ourselves from dragons and skaags. You can help us reach our goals. Can you do that?"

I don't respond. On the surface what he sells is attractive. Who wouldn't want to live in a utopia free of disease and the threat of monster aliens? I want to live in that world, but there's a catch. I must submit to experimentation like I'm a lab rat. That's not something I or anyone else or even rats should be subjected to. A utopia built upon the bones of an unfortunate few is nothing but a gaudy façade the filthy truth is swept under.

Disappointment flashes in Kihl's eyes. He glances at the computer monitor. "Your friend is back in the holding cell."

"Dalia? Is she hurt?"

"Enjoy your time with her. We are moving to the second phase. I'm truly sorry, Allison, for what is to come. Know it is for the benefit of humanity."

He sounds exactly like Dr. Radcliffe. "Second phase? What are you talking about? What are you sorry for?"

Dr. Kihl smooths his shirt sleeve and buttons the cuff. "Chief, please take Allison back to the holding cell."

"Tell me! What are you talking about?" I demand.

The doctor swivels in his chair, facing away from me.

"What about Haji?" I cry as Gore clamps his hands on my upper arms.

"The boy? I almost forgot about him," Dr. Kihl says. "I asked after him. He is a promising magician, Allison. You should be proud. He is transforming into a soldier capable of protecting humanity against any invader."

Chapter 24

I'm still reeling from the thought of Haji being transformed into a magic-wielding super-soldier as Gore escorts me toward the entrance to the office. Haji might be a fool for pursuing magic and a lousy friend for betraying my trust, but he's no soldier. I can't imagine anyone less suited for battling dragons and skaags. He's practically a pacifist—kind and quirky and funny. He doesn't have the killer instinct needed to protect humanity from anything.

I struggle against Gore. "Let go of me."

"Settle down," Gore growls, grip tightening.

I drag my feet, slowing down our progress toward the door.

"You can't do that to Haji," I shout at the doctor. "He's not a soldier. He's not a killer."

I don't add I know what it is to be a killer. I lost control, and the sleeper took over, but maybe that's an excuse. Maybe the sleeper and I are one and the same. Does it matter? Either way, a man is dead by my hands. Haji would never lose control like that. He'd never take another's life, no matter the circumstances.

"Not a soldier? Not a killer?" Dr. Kihl asks.

Gore stops, releasing me. Kihl still stares at the blank wall.

"That's right. He'd never kill anyone. Never. You should let him go. Him and Dalia. You let them go, and

I will do whatever you ask."

Dr. Kihl sighs. "You know I can't release your friends. They've seen too much." He massages his temples with his hands. "They must remain here until they can be fully indoctrinated. In fact, Haji is almost completely trained and shows a truly exceptional aptitude for magic."

"Indoctrinated? What are you talking about?" I demand.

"Chief, take her away."

"Come on." Gore grabs me by my upper arms.

I fight, but I need more than my human strength to resist him. At the door, Gore hefts a black sack, looking at me expectantly.

"Is this necessary?" I ask.

"What do you think?"

I lower my head, and he slips the canvas bag over me.

"Chief, one question," Dr. Kihl calls.

"Yes, sir?"

"It will be a day before we are ready to proceed to phase two. Are you capable of recasting the netting? I can do it if need be."

"No need to do that, sir. I'll handle it."

"Are you certain? The log shows you're near your quota of Juice for the month."

"For the net to hold for a day, sir, I only need a quarter dose to cast the spell properly."

"Good thinking, Chief. Thank you."

A hand in the small of my back prods me forward.

"Wait," Gore says.

I comply, giving into the fact the sleeper has abandoned me like my mother did seventeen years ago.

The door thuds shut, and I startle at the sound, despite myself.

Fingers slide in and out my jeans' front pocket, startling me.

"What are you doing!" I cry, one hand going to my thigh and the other reaching for the sack over my head.

"Keep the hood on and move."

"Did you molest me?"

"Don't flatter yourself. Now, move!"

Gore sounds flustered. I'm the one who had a weirdo reaching into my pocket. He shoves me in the back, and I stumble forward. My skin crawls with slithering snakes as he leads me through the hallways. By the time I've calmed myself enough to count my steps and track the turns, it's already too late. Gore takes me by the upper arms at the next intersection and spins me like a top until I don't know my left from my right. This treatment repeats at every intersection. When I start walking sideways from dizziness, his grip tightens on my forearm. Voices echo in the hallway more than once, but they remain distant. Gore discombobulates me so thoroughly I don't have an inkling of where I am until we are descending stairs to the dim, dank hallway with its mucky floor that stands in stark contrast to the pristine white we left behind.

Gore takes me roughly by the forearm, and we stop. He removes the hood from my head. I blink several times as my surroundings resolve into the door to the holding cell with two black-clad troopers standing guard.

"I need Juice," Gore says.

A guard nods and speaks rapidly into a walkie-talkie attached to his uniform at the left shoulder. I don't understand the language.

"Remove the prisoners," Gore says.

"Not scheduled, Chief?" a guard says in halting English.

"Magic. No interruptions. Understand?"

"Oh. Magic." The guard nods. "Now?"

"Yes, now," Gore says.

The guard opens the cell door, revealing the room illuminated by a single flickering fluorescent tube. The air seeping out is a miasma of urine and defecation, causing me to crinkle my nose. The guards enter, issuing terse commands in a foreign tongue.

"They want us to go with them. Don't resist."

"Jett!" I call, just the sound of his voice igniting a bonfire in my chest.

"Allison!"

My heart roars with relief. "Dalia!"

Tears well at the corners of my eyes at the sight of her battered face. Her right eye is blackened, nearly swollen shut, and her left cheek is a splotchy yellow and purple speckled with red abrasions.

"What did they do to you?" I cry.

"Ms. Bergman beat me," Dalia says as a guard guides her past me.

"Wait." I stretch an arm toward her, straining, but Gore pulls me back.

Jett exits the cell next, followed by the second guard. Our gazes meet, and I'm swallowed by his dark eyes. Everything else melts away, and he possesses me utterly. I fight against Gore's iron grip as Jett is led away. I crave to devour Jett with a kiss.

"Be strong," Jett says.

The guard drags him down the hall and out of

sight. Only then do I realize Dalia is already gone. Recrimination slams into me like a wrecking ball. Why am I losing my mind over a boy while Dalia and Haji are in danger?

"Inside," Gore says.

Blinking back tears, I scowl. "Why? Why did Bergman do that to Dalia?"

But even as I utter those words, thoughts of the kiss I shared with Jett linger like an enticing aftertaste promising more all-consuming sensual pleasures.

"You know why." Gore elbows me through the cell's doorway.

I slip on the slick floor, dropping to my knees to avoid doing a faceplant. The stench from the chamber pot is as intense as the off-gas from a primordial pool. Falling and the smell chase the lustful thoughts from my mind.

"It's me they want. It's me. Not Jett. Not Dalia. Not Haji."

"Then tell them what they want to know."

"I don't know the answers to their questions."

Gore laughs. "It's not like pinkie didn't deserve a stint as a piñata. She's lucky I'm not the one doing the beating. She'd look a hell of a lot worse if it was me. After what she did." Gore holds up a hand, rolling his wrist and opening and closing his fist. "Do you know how many surgeries it took to repair the damage you and Dalia did to me? I'm still in rehabilitation." He smirks. "Lucky for me, Dr. Rah is a genius with a scalpel."

"Will they hurt Dalia again?" I ask, trying to keep the tremor out of my voice.

"How would I know? That's not my department.

Bergman likes causing pain." He rolls up the sleeve of his paramilitary uniform, revealing puckered flesh of a fresh burn wound on his forearm. "She and Dalia should get along just fine. Bergman can give her some pointers for the next time she wants to torture someone."

"Dalia isn't anything like Bergman."

"She's not? Are you certain about that?" Gore asks, eyes hooded.

"Yes!" Dalia had tortured Gore, but that doesn't mean she's a sadist. She's a firm believer that the ends justify the means. Is that any different? Would Dalia be twisted into a pretzel with grief and recrimination if she killed someone? Or would she be able to justify it and go on living without a single regret? That's what I want. No regrets, and that scares me down to the marrow.

"Your friend Haji. He was sent to me to begin his advanced training this morning." Gore smirks.

"Advanced training? What is that? What is the indoctrination?"

There is a knock on the cell door.

His smirk turns into a full-on grin. "My Juice has arrived."

"What is the indoctrination?" I repeat, but Gore turns to the door, ignoring me.

Gore opens the cell door, his lanky frame blocking my view of whomever is outside.

"Give it to me," he says.

He turns so I can see the vial of orange liquid. He injects himself in the arm above the burned flesh. Orange tendrils course up and down his forearm. He hands the vial still partially full of liquid to whoever waits outside.

"You can leave."

Gore shuts the door and faces me, opening and closing his faintly glowing hand. Indeed, his entire exposed arm is covered in orange fractal patterns. I scuttle away, hands splashing in muck until my back is pressed against the cold wall.

"Don't make this harder than it needs to be, Allison." He walks toward me with slow, measured strides, combat boots thudding against the stone and sending up droplets of filth.

I clench my jaw so tightly my teeth might crack and call the sleeper.

He kneels beside me, and I turn away from him, clenching my eyes shut. He's so close his breath blows across my cheek and neck. He can do anything to me in the cell, and I'm powerless to stop him.

His hand squeezes mine.

"Look at me," he whispers.

"Just get it over with."

He squeezes so hard I wince in pain. Anger flashes through me, and the sleeper stirs deep inside me. I meet his gaze, ready to break his arm, but the prowess never comes. He holds my right hand in both of his.

"Check your pocket," he mouths, and begins chanting under his breath.

With the chant heat radiates from his hands. It's a gentle warmth at first, intensifying with every syllable he utters.

I cram my hand into the front pocket of my skinny jeans, fingers questing. I touch something, smooth and folded on one edge and jagged on another. Paper? My fingers capture it, and I start withdrawing my hand.

Gore squeezes my right hand, and I freeze in place. He pauses the chanting, taking a breath. The heat building at my wrist dissipates.

"Slowly," he murmurs. "We're being watched."

He picks up the chant, voice growing louder, cadence faster. I gasp, my hand and wrist stinging like I have a nasty sunburn. Pushing aside the discomfort, I remove my hand from my pocket, a crinkled scrap of paper clasped between two fingers. I scan the room, wondering where the camera is, or cameras are. I presume Gore obstructs any view of me, but I can't be sure. Camera placement is something he should know about as security chief, but I have learned his place in the hierarchy is not as high as I originally assumed and is precarious, to say the least. The burn mark on his arm is a reminder of that.

Gore digs his nails into my wrist. He looks meaningfully at the paper held between my fingers. My hand burns like I am holding it for too long over a lit candle.

I carefully unfold the scrap of paper on my thigh. Written in neat, capitalized block letters is the message: DON'T TRUST JETT. Don't trust Jett? I laugh and drop the note to the floor to join the other garbage. Don't trust him? How I felt when his lips pressed against mine is the truest experience I've had since arriving on Golden Shoal.

"This is another mind game," I hiss.

Gore finishes chanting and releases my hand. The pain alleviates, and my skin is unblemished except where his fingernails cut half-moons across my wrist.

"If it's all a game, make sure you're not the one being played."

Being played? Is Jett toying with me? No. Gore is sowing doubt, that's all.

Gore stands and rolls his neck and gives me an oily smile, shaking his head. Laughing to himself, Gore ambles from the cell. Even when the door slams shut, his laughter continues, dwindling until all I hear is the light fixture's incessant buzz.

Chapter 25

I stew inside the cell with only my thoughts for entertainment. Or torture?

Don't trust Jett.

Do I trust him?

How can I not trust him? We have a connection, and it's real. But I haven't known him for very long. Everything is moving fast. We're moving fast.

He's been tortured. He told us, but I never saw any physical sign of torture. Dalia's face was used as a punching bag, obviously. Gore has a fresh burn wound.

I bite my lower lip and shake my head to clear the cobwebs. All I accomplish is making myself woozy. I take a deep breath, hold it for a count, and let it out. Center yourself, Allison. Center yourself and consider all the facts. Gore is one of them. Bergman, Gore, and the doctors. They are the ones to distrust, not Jett.

I remember how haunted Jett was when he spoke about the torture chamber. The way his voice cracked with fear and the faraway look in his eyes like he was reliving something terrible. That was real. It can't be faked.

"This is what they want," I mutter. "They want me to doubt my friends. They'll try to turn me against Dalia next."

Of course, maybe I should expect to be betrayed by Jett. I trusted Haji, and he decided to go on Devin's podcast against my explicit wishes. I put my life in the hands of Dr. Radcliffe, and he offered me to a skaag, knowing full well the beast intended to kill me. Even my dad lied to me for sixteen years. If I didn't love him so much and have intimate knowledge my mother is the dictionary definition of a controlling monster, I'd never be able to forgive him for allowing me to believe Mother had abandoned me at birth. Oh, and he failed to mention I'm not entirely human. When I discovered my heritage and met my mother, I speciously believed Dad had been ignorant of her true nature. Well, stupid me. I was dead wrong. He'd been feeding me lies alongside my breakfast cereal. Maybe that's my lot in life—to be betrayed by everyone I trust. Maybe they'll even turn Dalia against me once she's been indoctrinated.

My thoughts lead inexorably to my first encounter with Jett. I vividly recall the colorful dust floating around him. A fleeting vision, gone in a blink. A blink of my prosthetic eyes. Prosthetics that allow me to see dragons riding the slipstream. Can I trust my prosthetics after Dr. Rah and Dr. Kihl messed with them?

I've lost track of how long I've been contemplating the relativity of reality when my eyelids grow heavy. I fight against sleep. I want to be awake when Jett arrives to hold him, to kiss him. Nevertheless, my shoulder sags and my head wobbles until I give in to the inevitable. At least this way, I can be with Jett in my dreams.

****

"Allison. Allison!"

I'm shaking.

I'm being shaken.

My heavy eyelids slide open like they're mired in

sludge. I don't know how long I've been asleep. My head throbs, and my thoughts are muddy. I chafe with irritation at being disturbed from a wonderful fantasy. I was at Poo Poo Point snuggled up against Jett's warm body under a night sky bejeweled with stars. My annoyance goes up in smoke when my prosthetics focus on the dark face before me—Jett as beautiful as an obsidian David.

"You're back," I gasp and throw my arms around his solid, warm body.

After a moment of hesitation, he envelops me in a tight embrace I don't want to end. I quiver as we snuggle in closer, ready for a kiss. He ruins the moment by wincing.

"Are you hurt?" I ask, trying to pull away, but his arms are unyielding and my effort halfhearted.

"Felicia visited me," he says nonchalantly.

This time I put real effort into freeing myself. Again, he refuses to release me despite gasping and screwing up his face in a pained grimace. Even that expression, teeth bared and creases spreading from his scrunched nose, hardly detracts from his innate beauty.

"Sorry! Did I hurt you? Show me your injury."

He releases me and meets my gaze. A spiderweb of orange veins accent the sclera surrounding the indigo center of his eyes. The orange webbing is eerily reminiscent of the Juice Gore injects even down to the faint glow.

For an instant, his glowing eyes flare bright, and blurry varicolored clouds swirl around him millimeters above his skin. I blink, and the glow and swirling colors are gone. The prominent orange and bioluminescent glow fades from his eyes. I'd put off what I saw to the tricks of a tired mind, if not for Gore's message and the monster within me stirring. The sleeper's wariness cannot be ignored even though its consciousness seeps into me in muddled fits and starts like a beast emerging from hibernation.

I scoot away from Jett, scanning the floor near me for the scrap of paper with Gore's message.

"What is it?" Jett asks. "Are you looking for something?"

Gore must have taken the scrap of paper with him. "No. It's nothing."

Jett smiles and raises an eyebrow. "Really?"

As he utters the word filaments stream from his mouth on the exhale. Dozens. Scores. Too many to estimate. They tumble through the air like colorful dandelion seeds and fade into oblivion like ephemera.

Help me, I beg the sleeper, but no half-skaag prowess fills me. To Jett, I say, "Are you going to show me your injury or not?"

"I don't want you to worry about me," Jett says.

"I'll worry more if you don't show me." Despite my growing suspicion, my concern for him is as genuine as my lustful desires.

"All right. All right."

Grimacing, Jett gingerly lifts his ragged T-shirt. His abdomen is as desirably chiseled as I imagined, and the swollen purple welt looks as horribly painful as his movements imply.

"Oh my God, Jett. Why did Bergman do this to you?"

Jett shakes his head. "I don't know."

On a whim, I gently trace the bruise on Jett's abdomen. Before I've even outlined a quarter of it, his face knots with pain, and he grits his teeth, not quite stifling a grunt. I snatch my hand away, feeling equally bereft at the loss of skin-to-skin contact and afraid I've hurt him.

"What did Bergman hit you with? A baseball bat?"

Wincing, Jett allows his shirt to fall back into place and maneuvers himself closer to me. "She uses her fists."

"Why, Jett? Why did Bergman do this to you?" I ask for a second time.

"She didn't tell me why or ask questions. She just started beating me."

"I'm so sorry."

"It's not your fault."

But I'm more than sorry. Ms. Bergman is using Jett as a whipping boy to punish me. I feel so guilty I want to cry, my tears held in check by my natural stoicism.

"Do you know what they did to Dalia?" I ask.

He shakes his head. "They separated us."

His words are knife thrusts to my chest. I stare at the filthy floor, vividly remembering the bruises and abrasions covering Dalia's cheeks. What will the woman do to my friend next? More beatings? Waterboarding? Will she hand Dalia over to Gore to do with as he pleases? The thoughts keep circling like ravenous turkey vultures homing in on reeking carrion.

Jett rests a hand on my shoulder and tenderly squeezes. "Don't worry yourself sick. Dalia will be fine."

"How do you know?" I scoot closer until our legs touch. Pleasant tingling shoots through me.

"I got to know her while you were gone," Jett says. "Dalia is tougher than she looks. She's strong."

"Maybe…maybe I worry too much."

The words sound wrong as they tumble from my lips. The sleeper stirs within me, still groggy from sleep or a magic-induced stupor—I can't tell which.

"No." I shake my head. "She's strong, that's true. But she can be broken like anyone else. I won't be able to live with myself if that happens."

Jett wraps his arm around my shoulder. I want him to be dangerous and trustworthy. Yet Gore's neatly printed warning is a pop-up window I can't dismiss.

"Maybe you can stop that from happening," Jett says.

"How?"

"Just"—he shakes his head and flashes a smile that strikes me as a wee bit condescending—"tell them what they want to know."

"I…" Oh my God. The variegated spindles pour from his mouth, tickling my cheeks alongside his breath.

I pull away, but his grip is a tire clamp.

"Let go—"

He speaks over me, voice taking on a mesmerizing intensity. "Tell them what they want to know."

The cell door squeaks as it swings open. A guard shoves Dalia inside. She stumbles, collapsing to her hands and knees. I turn on Jett, ready to demand he release me, but his arm falls away before I can get a word out. The shimmering filaments floating between us are already winking out of existence one by one. I reach for one, but as soon as I'm about to capture it between my fingers, it dissipates into the ether.

Despite clutching his abdomen, Jett surges to his feet, striding to Dalia. I stand and scamper toward my friend, only to stop halfway, swaying on my feet. Deep in the recesses of my body, the sleeper untwines like someone waking from a long, if not entirely restful, sleep. As it stretches, its sides press up against something unseen that nevertheless constrains it. The sleeper reacts with violent anger, body writhing like a crocodile performing a death roll only to become increasingly entangled in the invisible magical netting. Gore had re-cast the spell a few hours ago. Yet my sense of the sleeper's presence is greater than it's been in days. A riptide of rage intermingles with my own emotions. If I'm not careful, I could lose myself in the sleeper's anger. Physical prowess trickles through my veins. It's probably not enough for me to rip the door off its hinges, but I'm steady on my feet now.

I rapidly blink a dozen times, a score, in failing attempts to clear my vision.

Don't.

Trust.

Jett.

He has helped Dalia sit up and rubs her back. My friend looks worse than before: haunted eyes bloodshot, pink hair lacking its usual luster, and her bruised face has taken on a splotchy green and yellow cast like a side of meat growing mold. As terrible as she looks, it's Jett who sucks the air from my lungs. His skin is unnaturally black like spilled ink or the Mariana Trench's deepest depths. Floating around him like a swarm of gnats are sparkling spindles with fluffy pompoms on either end.

"Stay away from her."

Jett looks up at me with eyes transformed into an arresting indigo glowing around the edge of the irises with orange bioluminescence.

"What's wrong?" he asks.

"He's helping me." Dalia sounds like she's chewing on pea gravel.

I march up to them, placing my hands on my hips, and glare at Jett. "Take your hand off her."

Smirking, Jett removes his hand from Dalia's back, but he remains crouching beside her like a demon ready to pounce. The sleeper's primal fear, usually reserved for a multiplicity of dragons, twists my insides.

"Back off," I say.

"Why? I'm comforting her. This jealousy…" Jett shakes his head, smirk widening into a grin.

I offer Dalia my hand without taking my gaze off Jett. He stares back at me with the unblinking intensity of a predator.

"Come with me. Please," I say.

Dalia looks at Jett and me in turn. "Come where, Allison? We're locked in a cell. What is this all about?" She clears her throat, wincing. "You're scaring me."

"He's not human, Dalia. I don't know what he is, but he's not human. He's something else, and he's working with Bergman. With them."

Chapter 26

"Working with them? But…" Dalia gapes.

She turns her gaze on Jett, who is laughing. He sniggers until he doubles over, clutching his bruised abdomen. Groaning, he falls silent, nearly curling into a fetal position.

I reach a hand for Dalia. "We can't trust him."

Jett uncurls. "Of course, you can trust me." His tone is saccharine. "Allison doesn't know what she's talking about. You must forgive her." He smirks. "She's stressed out."

"Not so much I can't see through you."

Dalia stares up at me. "Allison, what are you talking about? Jett is one of us. All he's done is help us from day one."

Dalia's utterly guileless tone dumbfounds me. That's not my BFF, who has faced dragons and skaags and a heroin-addicted magician.

"What have you done?" I demand of Jett.

"Nothing." Jett rises without even the pretense of agony etched into his handsome face. "I've been comforting her. Haven't I, Dalia dearest?"

Inside me, the half-skaag undulates, conscious but groggy. "Move away from her, or I will move you."

"Is that a threat, Allison? It's so unbecoming. Don't you think…"

I rush him, soundlessly calling to the sleeper to

grant me strength. I can't allow Jett to continue manipulating Dalia into being someone she's not. I shriek my rage at everything that's happened to us in this supervillain lair.

Smashing into Jett is like running into a bull moose. Our legs tangle. He teeters backward, maybe tripping over Dalia. His expression curdles in surprise. It's perhaps the first genuine emotion he's shown to me. As he falls, his arms wrap around my torso, dragging me down with him. He's all sculpted muscle and sinew, strong as steel and fluid as water. He lands on his back with a spray of muck. His neck snaps back, and his head cracks against the stone floor. His arms loosen, and I break free of his grip, straddling him. I grab either side of his head and beat his skull against the stone.

Nearby Dalia screams at me to stop, but I ignore her. Jett's lips move, but I don't hear any words. I raise his head again ready to pulverize his lies into nothingness forever. The sleeper wants him dead. The beast fears and hates him for reasons I don't comprehend.

Jett claws my hands and arms, but's too late. I'm the half-skaag now, and I am powerful. He's betrayed me and manipulated Dalia. Now he's getting what he deserves. *You're going to kill Jett*, a voice murmurs through my mind, but I no longer see only Jett. Each time I lift his head to hammer it against the floor, I see the face of a different traitor: my mother, Dr. Radcliffe, my father, and even Haji.

My hands are slick, and Jett's struggling intensifies, forcing me to readjust my grip. Warm fluid coats my palm and seeps between my fingers. It's orange and faintly glows.

"What?" Glowing orange blood. His eyes glowed orange, so maybe it all makes sense, but I'm still missing too many puzzle pieces to interpret the whole picture. Perhaps my brain is too jumbled to tease it out.

"Ahhh!"

Sharp pain lances through my arms. Razor-sharp claws have extended from Jett's fingers, and he's shredding my limbs. I smash his head against the stone again. His hands slip from me, falling to the floor while claws retract into his skin. Through my legs, I still feel the rise and fall of his chest.

The sleeper wants him dead, and I do too.

I raise his head for the deathblow.

A hand smacks my cheek. I release Jett, ready to destroy the new threat.

"Allison, stop! Stop. You'll kill him!" Dalia screams.

The fight goes out of me. I can't hurt Dalia, no matter what. Tears stream down her bruised face. I look down at my handiwork in horror. Softly glowing orange blood pools around Jett's head. The mask obscuring his true self has slipped off. His features are less human and more animal, indeed feline in structure. I scramble to my feet and retreat from the cloud of colorful filament swirling around him.

"I was ready to kill him." Tears streak my face. Inside me, the sleeper shrieks for blood. "I was ready to kill again."

"Kill again?" Dalia stands on unsteady legs.

She sways, and I grab her. She falls into my arms and embraces me.

"What do you mean kill again?" Dalia asks, equal parts comforting and demanding.

At least, she sounds like my BFF again. I almost tell her the cancerous truth that's been metastasizing inside me. I'm truly my mother's daughter, a monster and a killer. I almost tell her, but instead, I take the coward's way out.

"Do you see that?" I gesture to the kaleidoscopic cloud floating around Jett.

"Yes. Yes, I—"

The door slams open, and guards thunder into the cell.

****

"Wake up, Miss Lee."

Bergman's grating voice intrudes on my consciousness. Honestly, I'd rather stay asleep than face her. If I rouse myself, I might kill her. I don't know if I could stop myself after what she did to Dalia and Jett. Jett…no, whatever she supposedly did to him wasn't real. At least, I don't think it was. That purple welt is fake.

I want to go back to sleep to escape my hell hole of a life for a few more minutes. Unfortunately, an itch between my eyes drives me bonkers. Something is attached to my head by a gooey substance in at least four places, maybe more. I try scratching the itch, but my arms are locked at my sides by some serious restraints and so are my waist and ankles. Something tugs at my fingertips when I attempt moving my arms. I must be hooked up to something, maybe? I won't know until I open my eyes, but I don't want to yet. Bergman isn't as observant as she pretends to be, or she would've noticed my attempt to scratch myself. Just by her breathing, I discern she is about five and a half feet away at about thirty degrees to my left. Maybe I can learn something if I fake unconsciousness.

Still, I'm tempted to escape. The only problem is even with my eyes closed I'm aware this room is different from any I've been in before. For one thing, I hear Bergman walking across what sounds like a *metallic* floor. All the other exam chambers I've been in have tile floors. I'm not sure what to make of this, but it can't be good.

Since I don't hear anyone else breathing or moving around, I'm about ninety-nine-point-nine percent certain Bergman is the only sadistic sicko in the room with me. I think I can overpower her, especially after what I did to Jett. Whatever he is, he's stronger than a human, but I handled him easily. Bergman can't stop me by herself, and if she calls for tranquilizer dart gun-toting guards, I'll transform. I'd like to see a dart pierce my skaag hide. But I'm not ready to escape. Not yet. Not when I have no idea where Dalia is or where I am. With my heightened senses, I can probably track down my friend but not before they hurt her or worse. I don't even want to consider what they might do to her to discourage me from escaping. And there's Haji to consider too. Is he already too far gone to be saved? No, I can't think like that.

I'll save them.

I'll save them both.

"I know you're awake, Miss Lee. The skaag in you is metabolizing the tranquilizer at an astonishing rate. The Chief did such a lousy job casting the spell keeping your inner skaag in check, I wonder if I should question him again."

Bergman's words are ever so slightly tremulous. Without my preternatural hearing, I don't think I'd detect it. Plus, she's not huffing and puffing in my face. She's nervous. Maybe I can use that to my advantage.

"You should go question him and leave me alone," I mumble, feigning tiredness.

I hear a sharp intake of breath and the heavy tread of Bergman striding across the room.

My eyes open. Bergman stands over me with her hand raised to deliver a slap.

"I wouldn't do that," I say.

The woman's blocky face contorts into a sneer. Her bear paw hits me full on the cheek. The vicious slap twirls my head to the side and echoes in the chamber. Groaning, I work my jaw that feels like she almost dislocated it.

"Ugh. That stings." I blink back unbidden tears. "Do I get a turn?"

Bergman's face goes fire hydrant red. She pokes me in the nose with her pointer finger. "That's just a reminder, Miss Lee. I don't tolerate cheek." She turns away, marching toward the door. She pauses about halfway and leers at me. "Consider for a moment what I might do to Dalia if you continue refusing to cooperate, Miss Lee."

"Don't you dare…ahhhh!" My entire body burns from intense heat radiating from the chair. The heat dissipates. I'm surprised my clothing didn't go up in flames.

"Felt that, did you, Miss Lee?" Bergman's eyes are full of maniacal glee. "Did you see that, Dr. Rah? Your latest contraption works admirably."

"As I knew it would, Ms. Bergman," the doctor's disembodied voice crackles from somewhere up high, perhaps a speaker in the ceiling.

"You'll receive your instructions after I leave the chamber, Miss Lee. You must follow the instructions. Dalia's life depends on it."

I strain against the restraints, and the chair heats up like a blast furnace again. I scream, and the burning sensation is gone.

"Patience, Miss Lee. Wait until I'm gone."

Bergman marches to the door and grasps the polished handle. The door, a foot thick of solid metal, opens inward on three industrial-strength steel hinges. Despite the door's size, it glides as if it's featherlight. Bergman steps out into a white hallway and closes the door behind her with a resounding boom followed by the thud of mammoth deadbolts sliding into place.

I crane my neck to take in the room, which as I suspected is unlike any I've been inside so far. Every surface is smooth, polished metal. The walls go up and up, fifty feet or more. It's almost like this chamber has been specifically designed to hold a monster. My lips twitch upward in a half-smile. We'll see about that.

I lean back in the chair and try to relax—to wait for my instructions. I suppose I should be happy I can still see. Dr. Rah has a track record of ripping out my prosthetics. With the return of my preternatural senses, maybe I don't need to see. My skin is so sensitive against the cold stainless-steel exam chair it's like it electrically tingles. Various sensors are attached to my fingers with wires traveling down the chair and out of sight. I'm guessing electrodes are attached to my head. Not wanting to be burned again by the fiendish chair, I tap down my urge to rip the devices from my body.

Buzzes and drones come from the walls, the floor, and the high ceiling. Without my heightened hearing, I wouldn't detect the sounds as distinct personalities. The hinges of the massive door are well oiled; I can smell the oil, but that's not the scent that makes the hairs on the back of my neck stand at attention and alarm klaxons echo in my skull. No. That is the rusty tang of blood saturating the air like a crimson drizzle. The scent is obscured by a miasma of bleach and other astringent cleansers, but the gory aroma is distinct. The smell explains why the floor is bowled with a drain at the lowest elevation. A fleck of color against the steel captures my attention. Without warning, my prosthetics zoom in until all I can see is the drain's grating and a red speck the cleaners had missed. Dried blood. Hunger pangs rip my abdomen. The sleeper roars through my body, roused by the desire for sustenance. The skaag's raw hunger for flesh intermingles with my body's needs so thoroughly there is no distinction.

I tear my gaze from the red flake, stomach lurching. I even taste a hint of copper on my tongue. As my vision goes out of focus, my entire body heaves, straining against the restraints. My prosthetics zoom out, and the glistening walls snap into focus. The only reason I manage not to throw up is my stomach is empty or practically so. My mouth waters with the yearning for uncooked meat—disgusting. I sniff the air, concentrating on the headache-inducing stench of disinfectants. The reek is enough to put the sleeper's usually insatiable appetite on hold.

The sleeper's prowess, along with a nearly overwhelming urge to break my bonds and escape, surges through me.

Escape this room.

Escape this stink.

Escape this island.

Oh, and rend flesh and sinew from bone along the way. Don't forget about that part. That's the fun part.

No. No! I scream at the sleeper, but cataclysmic images of death and flight spiral through my mind.

I strain against the restraints.

No. Not yet.

Metal screeches.

Stop. Stop. I don't know the locations of Dalia or Haji. If I try to escape, they'll hurt them.

Dalia is my friend, my sister, my love, not the sleeper's. Haji is…what is Haji? My boyfriend? Jett's enticing face flashes in my mind. My ex? Haji is my ex, but he's still in my squad. I won't allow anything to happen to him or Dalia. Even if that means remaining here as a prisoner and even…even cooperating. Just the thought of doing anything at the behest of Ms. Bergman is enough to make me gag.

The sleeper is having nothing to do with the not escaping part. The beast wants to be free, to take vengeance, and to fly. Holding the monster back feels like propping up a boulder on a crumbling precipice with a toothpick. Perspiration runs down my face, and my breathing is ragged as I battle the impulse to transform. Metal groans, and the restraint at my right wrist bends.

"No! No," I croak.

I'm losing myself, half-drowned in the primordial flow of the sleeper's rage and desires. Body thrumming with the sleeper's longing to emerge, I lift my head from the exam chair and swing it back into the unyielding steel. Stars flash in my vision. The pain rocketing through my head disrupts the sleeper, and I stop straining against the fetters, but the cravings to destroy and kill and fly free are still there.

"For Dalia. For Haji." My tongue feels bloated.

I wrench my head forward and swing it backward again.

Chapter 27

Fingers manipulating my head and scalp tease me awake. My head throbs like my brain is being rendered into mush. I keep my eyelids glued together and tolerate the probing without flinching, so I can surreptitiously listen to Dr. Rah speak.

"You shouldn't be here. She nearly transformed without inducement. I had anticipated needing to threaten her friend."

I don't sense the sleeper, not even in the recesses of my being. I'm not sure why—drugs or magic or my throbbing head. Regardless, operation bash my brain is a success, albeit a painful one.

"You worry too much," Dr. Kihl says.

Hands gently lift my head off the cold, metallic headrest. Fingers brush aside my gooey, matted-down hair. The movement feeds pure oxygen to the inferno rendering my skull to charcoal from the inside out.

"Look at this!" Kihl exclaims in the tone little boys use when they discover the thrill of burning ants with a magnifying glass.

"And your point? Scalp wounds tend to bleed profusely."

I hate being treated like I am a specimen. From deep within my core, the sleeper stirs, sending tendrils of prowess through my veins. Water douses the flames burning in my head. The fire is not out, but it's contained.

"A good-sized scalp laceration is needed for so much blood. Agreed?"

Stay calm, I tell the sleeper.

"Ah, I see what you mean."

A growl echoes through my skull, fanning the flames.

"No laceration. See this faint pink line. It's hard to see with all the blood and hair."

I'm not going to try anything until I'm confident I can rescue Dalia and Haji, I insist.

"I see it. A scratch. You don't think…"

"That is all that remains of the laceration," Dr. Kihl says. "Imagine if we can unlock the secret of her body's accelerated healing."

Of course, they want to unravel the secrets of my physiology for their benefit.

"Combine her accelerated healing with the Juice," Dr. Rah muses.

I force my eyes open to cracks. The bright light is like a laser beam vaporizing my brain. I only have a clear view of Dr. Kihl's shoulder and the soaring ceiling. He is still holding my head, so they can examine my nonexistent scalp wound. I wish my gray matter could recover as speedily from trauma as my skin.

"And our magicians will be unstoppable."

"Unstoppable?" My laughter sounds like the stuttering croak from a two-thirds dead frog. "Keep living the dream."

"Ah, listening in, are you?" Dr. Kihl chuckles and gently sets my head back against the headrest, which is icy cold after the warmth of his fingers.

Both doctors maneuver around to stand before me. Dr. Kihl smiles, shoulders hunched, vaguely avuncular, and mostly harmless. Dr. Rah stands taller than him, gaze intense and frown disapproving.

"You think unraveling the secrets of my physiology will turn your magicians into super soldiers?"

"Of course," Kihl says. "Dragons and skaags have innumerable advantages over us. Suppose we can unlock the secret to your accelerated healing, and with a combination of magic and technology impart that gift to magicians. We will level the battlefield or at least come one step closer to doing so."

I cackle even though it makes my head throb. "The skaag I was shown on TV. That's my mother. If you think accelerated healing will give your magicians a fighting chance against her, you're wrong. Accelerated healing won't do them a bit of good when she bites their heads off."

The doctors exchange a knowing look. Dr. Rah's lips perk up from a frown to a straight line.

Dr. Kihl nods. "The Chief informed us the skaag might be your mother. The feared Druk."

My jaw tightens. I shouldn't be surprised. I suppose spilling the beans about my mother is Gore looking out for number one.

"You of all people must understand, Allison, humans don't stand a chance against dragons or skaags with our current level of technology and magic. We must push the envelope no matter the cost or face extinction at the teeth and magic of our enemies," Dr. Kihl says zealously.

"Don't stand a chance?" I remember the strange

weapons used by Gore's henchmen to ensnare Mauve and the assassin's claim he murdered my friend. "The weapon Gore's men used on my friend worked—too well."

"You refer to the dragon Gore netted when he captured you?" Kihl asks.

I nod. Dr. Rah smiles toothlessly as pleased as a well-fed viper.

Dr. Kihl claps his hands together. "Ah, yes, that was a field test of the phase disruptor. I wish I had time to explain the technical details of marrying magic with technology." He shakes his head. "Alas, we don't have an abundance of time. Suffice to say, the test was a resounding success."

"Resounding success! My friend died!"

"The dragon?" Dr. Kihl's expression turns into a puzzled frown. He glances at Dr. Rah. "Odd. The Chief didn't include that in his report."

"I've often warned you the Chief holds back on the extent of his powers while under the influence of the Juice." Dr. Rah frowns. "But this story smacks of deceit. If he possessed the magical power to slay dragons, our allies would have detected it. Miss Lee lies or is retelling a lie told her."

I breathe easier, relief palpable. Mauve is alive. Mauve is alive! Or this is them toying with me?

Kihl shrugs. "I will speak to the Chief about this later. Now, Allison, we require you to transform into a skaag. Can you do that for us?"

"Never."

Dr. Kihl sighs, shoulders hunching forward even farther as if he carries the fate of humanity on his back. "I sincerely hoped it wouldn't come to this. Forgive me."

"Forgive what? Everything you've done to Dalia? To Haji? To me?" I snarl at the doctors as they retreat from the room.

As the door swings shut, a panel in the wall several feet above the door slides open, revealing a recessed LCD monitor. What in the world is this? Are they going to indoctrinate me—whatever that means precisely— like they have Haji? I can't stop myself from laughing.

"You think forcing me to watch a video will make me transform? Get out!" I crow.

My voice echoes through the chamber. I can't see any recording devices, but I know they're monitoring me.

"Show me your worst," I murmur, gaze boring holes into the LCD.

The monitor doesn't so much as flicker.

After five minutes or so, I hoot. "Technical difficulties?"

I shut my eyes and attempt to relax while strapped to a metal exam chair that feels like it's been recently dipped in a cauldron of boiling liquid nitrogen. Mauve lives, I keep reminding myself. That might be a lie, but it fills me with the warm glow like I sit beside a crackling fire surrounded by friends and family, so I hold onto it like a life preserver. Everyone is there around the fire, even Mother, but she's not harassing my friends by telling stupid jokes or demanding I go into the wilderness with her for training or tearing into a raw T-bone. Instead, she's a sentinel, watching over us. Most importantly, my squad is there: Dalia, Haji, and Mauve, all full of life and unmarred by the tribulations of the present.

My thoughts are upended by screaming and the snap of a whip shredding skin. I recognize the pleading voice. I keep my eyes scrunched up, knowing the horror playing out on the LCD will break me. The dam holding back the sleeper will crumble, and I will be swept away in the torrent of the skaag's maleficent desires. Once the skaag is free, I will escape this chamber, but I might not be able to save Dalia and Haji before…before…

Maybe death is preferable to what's being done to Dalia?

Maybe death is better than being indoctrinated?

But who am I to make those decisions for them?

An agonizing scream pierces my eardrums. My eyes are nearly propelled open by my rage. I want to know who is doing that to her—Bergman or Gore. I want to know who will suffer my savage vengeance. The sleeper feels my wants and understands them. The beast offers support with inhuman power. All I need to do is transform. My other half will spell out revenge in my tormentors' viscera.

"No!" I scream.

I won't endanger my friends. But Dalia's yowling indicates she's already in danger and in pain and…

"If I break free, she will suffer more."

Is there greater agony than what she's experiencing? I can stop her torment. Surely, once I transform, they'll stop. Only, once I give in to the sleeper, I won't be able to stop myself. People will die by my talons and fangs. I will become my mother.

The sounds of distress cut out, and Dr. Kihl's voice fills the room. "Allison, please, end this. All you need to do is transform. Please. Transform, and your friend's suffering ends. I promise you."

"No!" I spit.

"Very well," the doctor says.

Agonized sobs ricochet through the chamber again. I grind my teeth as I concentrate on holding back the sleeper's cravings. This lasts for a few seconds before the exam chair superheats, searing my skin. The pain is so shocking my eyes flare open. On the LCD, Dalia is chained to a chair facing away from me. Her shirt is torn to bloody shreds revealing slashes crisscrossing her back and shoulders. Gore stands behind her with a bullwhip dripping blood.

Steel squeals and bursts as the exquisite agony of having my insides twist and expand and tear explodes through me. As the skaag's oily hide subsumes my human skin, the burning from the chair lessens, then subsides completely when it is crushed under my monstrous form.

I shriek, and yellow lightning crackles over my serpentine body. Bolts fly from me in all directions, leaving behind black blast marks where they strike metal. One bolt shoots from my head, frying the LCD. The tortured mewling dies with the screen. I fly at the door like an arrow, the impact shaking the wall and my bones. Metal creaks under the strain. The door might be thick and strong, but it was made by humans, and I am beyond their imaginings.

I continue slamming my blunt head into the door to a melody of metallic groans. A battered depression forms where my thick skull crashes into the metal. When a heavy bolt holding the top hinge to the wall zings out of place, careening off the wall and floor, I'm almost free. The skaag knows too, and we throw ourselves against the door with revitalized vigor.

On the next strike, the door radiates heat. Perhaps the temperature is enough to deter a human, but it's not even an inconvenience to a skaag with a hide capable of withstanding dragon fire. I imagine the guards, the so-called super magicians, gathering outside the door, preparing to unleash a withering magical assault. Well, let them. My pelt will withstand their attack longer than they will mine. I will feast on their still warm flesh.

The part of me clinging to the last remaining hangnail of my humanity is revolted by the sleeper's desire, my desire to sink fangs into dead bodies, rip meat from bones, and enjoy hot blood sloshing over my tongue.

No. I'm human. I'm not a monster.

The sleeper ignores my begging. We beat our body against the door. A boom resounds through the room, followed by a crack of metal.

I'm not a monster.

We rear back, stretching our body up toward the ceiling, then swoop down and hammer our head into the door. The top of the door buckles outward. Orange light flashes through the gap, leaving behind a sooty stain where it strikes the wall. A ball of light hits us on the nose, stinging. The pain is no more than an aggravation, but the sleeper reacts with the wrath of a cornered animal, sending scorching lightning bolts through the gap. Thunderous crackling and death screams follow. The hangnail I cleave to tears, ripping loose skin revealing the skaag's dark hide.

Again, we crash against the door that surrenders to our assault, falling outward into a white corpse hall. Triumph fills us at the same instant the hangnail splits, and I am plummeting into a nebula of inky black punctuated by twisting electrical arcs.

Chapter 28

I've been falling for an eternity bereft of all sensation except the roar of rushing air when without warning I'm thrust back into reality. It's discombobulating, gut emptying. I'm wedged in something...in the wall...in the doorway. Oh, no, I'm stuck in the busted doorway in skaag form. My inclination is to writhe and force my way free, but the sleeper informs me that won't work.

That's why you allowed me to return. Because we're stuck, I tell the sleeper. The silence in response is reptilian cold.

The stench of smoldering fabric and charred meat fills my nostrils. The white hallway is pockmarked with black burns and littered with the dead. Some bodies are blackened slags of overcooked meat burned almost beyond recognition. Others are obviously the remains of super magicians based on the tattered fatigues. These dead men and women are covered in wounds—some blackened, some blistered and oozing blood.

What did you do? I demand, but I know what the sleeper did.

What we did.

What I did.

I killed them all. It's my fault. I knew as soon as I transformed this would happen. That I would become a monster sheared from the same cloth as my mother.

I hate her.

I hate myself.

I had promised myself never to kill again. So much for that promise. Worst of all, Haji might be a corpse burned beyond recognition. I'll never know if I killed my friend, the first boy I ever kissed. My heart feels like it is being torn asunder by hydraulic jaws. Part of me wishes I could drown in my blood to escape what I've done, what I am. But I can't do that; I don't deserve it. I can't hide from the destruction I have wrought.

Were the magicians indoctrinated? Unwilling slaves carrying out the instructions of Gore or Bergman or the doctors? Does it even matter? They were sons and daughters, fathers and mothers, people with lives before this, and I ended everything they were and everything they could be in an instant of rage. They never stood a chance against the sleeper, against me. Killing them was as easy as crushing ants underfoot. Mother might revel in power or at least be comfortable with it, but not me. I feel terribly guilty because even when the sleeper took over, part of me was aware of what was happening and could've said no. Instead, I had remained silent.

I'm still sick to my stomach when pragmatism forces me to try unjamming my body from the doorway. I twist until I can see my bulging form crammed between the broken metal. About one-third of my length passed through the opening before my chunkier midsection clogged the space. On the surface, the solution seems obvious.

I scan the opening for any obstructions that might harm me in human form—metal sheared to a spearpoint, that sort of thing. I turn to the left, then right, doing my best to account for the entire opening and surrounding debris.

Dim footsteps intrude on my preparation. I still, focusing my senses on the ambient environment. I smell the intruders' perspiration before I see them, detecting at least five distinct individuals approaching the causeway of death from the left-hand passage of an intersection roughly fifty feet away. Two scents are familiar. I should recognize them but only smell magicians, who are prey.

"Stop."

The voice is a faint whisper, but it's as if Gore stands next to me. But he is torturing Dalia. How is he here? Wait. Maybe he came with the guards I killed. Maybe he avoided the lightning somehow. He is a survivor, and I don't know how long I dropped through the abysmal blackness before the sleeper pulled me back or I chose to come back. Are the sleeper and I one and the same?

"Initiate 935, get up here," Gore hisses.

I lunge forward. My desire to murder the assassin clots cogent thought. Electricity arcs along my writhing body. Wreckage grinds under the strain, but I make no progress through the opening.

"Show yourself. Hurry up, Initiate."

"Yes, Chief."

I recognize the voice. The gangly boy scurries into the intersection dressed in the same paramilitary uniform as the guards. His once wavy hair is shorn short in a crewcut, and I hardly recognize his eyes. Those twin channels into the human soul are haunted and starved and crazed.

I call to Haji. My elongated vocal cords turn my intended words into a shriek. He startles and raises his hands. A pulsing orange ball shoots from his fingertips. The ball strikes my face, exploding into sparkling confetti. The impact mildly stings, but the attack steamrolls my heart. My implosion into human form is immediate and excruciating.

****

An electric hum startles me awake. My eyes shoot open to a blur of white. I blink until my vision resolves into a sterile room with a figure standing over me dressed in surgical gear, including a medical-grade mask and face shield. In the sawbone's gloved hands is an electric saw with a spinning circular blade.

"What the hell," I say, words tumbling out mushy.

I try to sit up, but my limbs are sluggish and heavy, and I'm strapped down to a medical bed. An off-white blanket covers me below the waist, leaving the rest of me nude.

Where are you? I demand of the sleeper, thoughts moving with the celerity of a stagnant pool. When the sleeper doesn't respond, dread rises through me like vomit.

The saw's whine diminishes, the blade slowing to a halt. Its wielder looms over me, tall and svelte.

"Wonderful. Miss Lee, I'm so glad you're awake. That will make this all the more satisfying," Dr. Rah says, a playful lilt to her usually staid tone.

"What are you doing?" My tongue is a dazed banana slug.

"I'm sorry, Miss Lee, but I don't understand you. I gave you several extra doses of tranquilizer after the Chief delivered you. He supposedly gave you a dose before dropping you off, but you're metabolizing the drug at an astonishing rate, and I no longer trust the Chief. I'm not sure I ever did. He never truly gave himself over to the cause. I shouldn't be surprised, I suppose. He is an addict, and addiction is a weakness. You understand weakness, don't you, Miss Lee?" Dr. Rah leans close. If it wasn't for her face coverings, I'd feel her breath against my lips. "Weakness is ripe for exploitation."

The doctor rears back and starts the saw, an electric whine filling the room.

Dr. Rah has never been half this talkative before. My life depends on keeping her talking—I wish we had something in common. I focus on not drooling while uttering. "Why?"

Dr. Rah powers down the tool. "What was that, Miss Lee? Famous last words? I didn't catch what you said. Say it again."

"Why? I don't understand—"

Dr. Rah makes an annoyed clucking. "Hush, Miss Lee, I can barely understand your utterances. Why, you ask. I assume you refer to your impending dissection?" The doctor hefts the bone saw. "Because you are too dangerous to live, Miss Lee. You escaped the containment chamber. Even our allies were surprised to learn of that feat. Well, almost escaped is more accurate, I suppose. Now I'm going to take you apart to learn how you work." She meets my gaze, eyes scrunching like she's smiling behind her mask. "Don't worry. We gathered terabytes of data when you transformed. We'll be studying the data for years."

Dr. Rah restarts the bone saw, bringing the spinning blade close to my face, turning it left and right.

I press my head into the bed. I'm entranced by the whirling blade's radiant gleam. The doctor turns away and leans over my chest. I lift my head up, watching in twisted fascination as Dr. Rah lowers the saw between my breasts. Without warning, my prosthetics zoom in, focusing on the spinning metal mere centimeters, no millimeters, from slicing into my skin. I hardly dare to breathe lest the saw bite into me.

"No!" My tongue stumbles over the word, so it comes out as a grunt.

To my surprise, Dr. Rah stops the saw and straightens. "I almost forgot, Miss Lee." She sighs. "Dr. Kihl wants me to inform you before…" She points at the saw with her free hand. "That your sacrifice will help ensure the continuation of the human species. You will be celebrated, and your name remembered, etc., etc., for generations to come." The good-natured cadence returns to her voice. "Let's get to it then."

Dr. Rah leans over me again when the door to the room opens. The doctor turns toward the entrance, blocking my view of the newcomer.

"What are you doing here?" Dr. Rah demands. "I'm busy."

The door shuts with a solid thud, followed by a squelching sound.

"What is the meaning of this? Put those away!"

Dr. Rah raises her arms defensively. I still can't see the newcomer.

"Dr. Kihl and the eld—" Rah's words morph into a shrill scream.

A sound like the beating wings of a gargantuan hummingbird recoils off the walls. A dark blur is visible behind the doctor. Her scream is cut off, and she teeters backward, dropping the saw and clutching her throat. She backs into the bed and collapses atop my midsection. The impact knocks the wind out of me, and my head slams back against the cushion.

"Dr. Rah?" I slur between gasps.

The doctor gurgles and convulses. I force my head up. Rah desperately attempts to dam the red current bubbling from the gash across her throat. Blood flows beneath her palms and over her fingers, staining her hands and shirt sopping red. She faces me and arches her back. Her usually cold eyes are wide with animal terror. Her death throes are fascinating but not as mesmerizing as her lifeblood forming a warm pool on my abdomen.

I tear my arms free of the metal restraints. The bonds' twisted remains clank against the bedside. I sit up, hands darting for the doctor. I smell and hear the newcomer, but the sight and scent of the doctor's blood awakens a ravenous hunger demanding satisfaction. Even as the spark of life seeps from Rah's gaze, she bats a bloody hand at my arms and the soles of her shoes squeak against the floor. She rolls her body away from me on a trajectory that sends her tumbling to the floor. I snatch her hand, but the slick appendage slips through my fingers. Rah strikes the floor with a wet smack.

Snarling, so voracious my body aches, I fling myself after her only to have my movements arrested by metal cutting into my waist and ankles. I grip the metal restraint at my midsection, ready to tear it aside. The doctor flops on the floor like a dying fish. I yearn to feed. Prey is always best while the heart still pumps.

Chapter 29

"Allison."

I freeze at the sound of my name. My gaze lingers on my red hand and the blood pooling on my abdomen. What am I doing? Was I about to…bile sours my throat. I lean over the bed's side and retch vile liquid, which splashes onto the floor and the doctor. Rah is supine, still except for fingers twitching at her throat. As death glazes her apertures, hunger pangs cramp my stomach.

Still warm.

Still fresh.

Eew. I lurch and retch again.

"Allison."

Wiping the vomit running down my chin, I look up, and my jaw goes unhinged.

I propel myself entirely onto the bed and pull the sheet over my nude torso. The warm moistness reminds me the sheet is soaked with Dr. Rah's vital fluids. Regardless, I'm not removing the sheet.

"Allison, you're—"

"What are you doing here?" I demand. The words are clear, but my voice cracks with…with fear. I'm not afraid of Jett. Am I? Even like this, he doesn't scare me. Or does he?

"I'm here to save you."

But the sleeper fears him. Does that mean I fear

him?

"Let me help you." He steps toward me.

"No." I hold a hand before me, palm outward. Frowning, he halts. "Stay back." I don't have time for introspection. My priorities are to find my friends and escape. Jett obviously wants to help for some reason. "I can free myself. Can you..."

Should I be embarrassed if he sees me naked? Whatever he is, he's not human. Not unless it's normal for people to sprout enormous dragonfly wings from their backs. But wings or not, feline facial structure or not, he is male—I think. He wears ragged, splotchy gray pants with the legs cut off at the knees, so I can't see his equipment, but his alluring musk of testosterone-infused sweat is decidedly male.

"Oh, you want me to turn around. Just a second. I brought clothes." He strides toward the door with a panther's predatory grace. A vortex of twinkling filaments surrounds him like a storm of polychromatic dandelion seeds.

With his back to me, his translucent wings emergent from between his shoulder blades are on full display. Hypnotic glowing orange veins and capillaries form fractal patterns throughout the membranes. The bioluminescent streams are evocative of the Juice Gore injects to power his magic. I remember the orange fluid staining my hands after beating Jett's head against a stone floor. The same color highlights his veins.

"I beat you pretty bad." I snap the restraint securing my waist and grab an ankle manacle, careful to keep the bloody blanket covering my chest. "You don't look hurt."

Jett kneels next to the doorway, retrieving a

bundle. His close-cropped hair is snow white in sharp contrast to his dark skin.

"I heal quickly," he says.

I swing my legs off the bed, allowing the limbs to dangle. I rub my aching abdomen, unsure if the discomfort is from hunger or the shackles. I clean the blood smeared across my belly as best I can with the sheet. The pungent stench of urine and defecation assaults me with every breath but does have the benefit of masking the scent of blood. Still, I'm careful not to look at the doctor, fearful the corpse will make me salivate.

Jett stands, bundle in hand. "Can I turn?"

I hold the sheet in front of me. "Yes."

I study him as he crosses the chamber. His angular features are a cross between feline and humanoid. His eyes are at least twice as large as a human's. The sclera is lined with orange veins, and the irises are startling indigo.

"What are you?" I ask.

He smiles, showing off triangular teeth, like shark teeth only smaller. His tongue, I swear, is pointed. Some of the dust particles enter his mouth as he speaks. More particles exit his mouth when he exhales. "Humans refer to my kind as faeries."

"You're a faery?" I raise my eyebrows. "So that stuff surrounding you is…"

"Faery dust." He offers me the bundle.

I take the bundle with my unstained hand, careful to keep the white fabric away from the blood-soaked sheet. I've heard about faeries before. Didn't Dr. Radcliffe or Tanis say something about them?

Jett arches an eyebrow. "Can you get dressed? We

can't stay here."

"Turn around."

"Just hurry." Jett turns away.

I wrack my memory for why his claim to be a faery seems so incongruous. After wiping off my bloody hand on the sheet, I slip from the bed, avoiding the crimson pool around the doctor's head. My stomach growls at the macabre scene, and I avert my gaze. I put on the clothes that turn out to be white scrubs, including a skullcap. The scrubs are at least two sizes too large, and I cinch down the waistband with the drawstring to keep the pants up. The long pant legs cover my bare feet. I bundle my hair beneath the cap as best I can, but I suspect a few fire engine red strands stick out.

"Okay, I'm ready."

Jett turns and looks me up and down with a critical gaze. "Good. You won't be recognized as long as no one looks at you too closely. Come on."

"Wait," I say.

"I told you we can't stay here. I have a spell in place. An illusion masks what we're doing to the people watching the cameras, but it won't last forever, and if the wrong person looks—Gore or Dr. Kihl—it's possible they'll see through it."

"I thought there's magic detection equipment monitoring the room?"

"Human magic, yes, but not faery magic."

"Where are we going? My—"

"Yes, yes." Jett irritably shakes his head. "I'll take you to Dalia."

"And Haji."

Jett hesitates. "Of course."

"I'm not leaving without Dalia and Haji."

"No worries."

"Good." I nod. "You know, Dr. Radcliffe told me faeries went extinct centuries ago."

Jett chortles. "Allison, the one inalienable truth in the multiverse is all dragons are liars."

"Oh, dragons are liars, and you're not?"

His smile broadens, revealing more disconcerting shark teeth. How many does he have crammed inside his mouth?

"I am a liar."

This might be the first time he hasn't lied to me.

"But for a good cause."

"What cause is that?"

His smile fades. "I promise I'll explain everything once you're safe."

"No, I want to hear an explanation right here, right now."

"We don't have time."

"Forgive me if I'm skeptical about the whole situation."

His eyebrows scrunch up into a white wiggly worm. "I…I…"

He points at the doctor.

"Thanks for that, but killing her doesn't change that you betrayed us."

He covers the space between us in two long strides. We're so close the faery dust tickles my cheeks and neck. Three desires burn through me simultaneously like nuclear reactors milliseconds from meltdown: run or strike with deadly force or throw myself into his arms and hope he kisses me again instead of ripping out my throat.

He reaches for my hand. I don't know if I'm going

to allow him to touch me or snap his wrist like a dry twig. As his fingertips stroke my hand, I'm struck by the urge to sneeze—perhaps it's the faery dust irritating my nose. I lose the fight to suppress the sneeze, spraying spittle into Jett's face. The saliva never hits him. He leaps into the air in a nearly deafening hum of beating wings, flying backward and landing next to the door.

"Sorry," I say.

"Don't be. We do need to leave. I'll explain what I can on the way."

I roll my eyes.

He takes a deep breath and continues calmly. "Rah was going to dissect you. You're the prize. If they're willing to dissect you, what do you think they'll do to Dalia?"

I shut my eyes. Trust him or not, fear him or not, I must go with him. I can escape without him, but I can't find my friends and escape without his assistance. Opening my eyes to slits, I wish I had magic to peel aside all the layers of deceit people build up like callouses. Then I could see straight to their inner truth. Sometimes I suspect my mother and Dr. Radcliffe have that power.

Jett's wings retract behind his back, and there is a loud squelch. He winces at the sound and bends side to side. The faery dust swirls around him like a variegated blizzard, rendering him a silhouette inside the flurry. Orange light flares from within the storm's eye. The dust cloud slows and dissipates until Jett stands beside the door, still exotic but entirely human in appearance without even a trace of faery dust floating in the air.

Boy or faery or whatever, he's wearing the mask

he thinks will make me the most malleable. Two can play that game.

"Won't they find it odd you're only wearing ratty cutoffs?" I ask.

"The people here are used to my appearance. They know I represent their allies, and I'm different, although not all know I'm a faery."

"All right. Who should we rescue first, Dalia or Haji?" I join Jett at the door.

"This is the riskiest part," Jett says. "The guards only expect Dr. Rah and I are capable of leaving the operating room. Even in disguise, you don't look like Rah."

He didn't answer my question. His evasiveness disturbs me. He'll help me rescue Dalia and escape, but he doesn't intend Haji to leave. Why is that? Is Haji hurt or...dead? Did I kill him? Everything that's happened to Haji is my fault. If something irrevocable has happened to him, I don't know if I'm strong enough to live with the guilt. Part of me is tempted to grab Jett around the neck and wring the truth from him, but I suppress the impulse. Save Dalia, then improvise.

His fingertips brush across my forehead.

I flinch. "What are you doing?"

Jett hesitates. "I'm going to push your hair under the cap. If they catch a glimpse of—"

"Just do it." I'm anxious to escape this room and him. The dichotomy of my reactions rips me in two. Do I want to throw myself against his muscular chest or cave in his rib cage?

Jett's long, dexterous fingers gently tuck the loose strands beneath the cap. "Keep your head down and keep moving no matter what. My magic will do the rest."

I nod. "Which way?"

"Head left. After that, I'll guide you."

His finger caresses the top of my earlobe, and I breathe in sharply, desiring his touch and battling the instinct to lash out. I'm not sure if the stroke was purposeful or not.

"Careful," I say, tremulous with craving and apprehension.

His smirk tells me he groped my earlobe intentionally.

"Ready?" he asks.

I'm not down with this whole "I'll guide you" business, but I give him a thumbs up and throw in a confident smile for good measure.

Jett opens the door, and I step out into the pristinely white passageway. The guards eyeball me as I pass them. Body odor and the herbal scent of black tea wafts from them. I swear the guard on the left is about to bark a command and stop me, but the door clicks shut, and Jett amicably speaks to the men. I continue down the hall, reminding myself not to run.

Jett guides me through the hallways past closed doors, some with guards who respectfully acknowledge the faery, and large rooms with wall-to-wall cubicle mazes. Conversation buzzes from within the cubicle labyrinths.

"What language are they speaking?" I whisper to Jett as we pass row after row of cubicles.

Jett whispers, "Most of the staff are Singaporean. The languages…"

A man in a pink polo shirt and tan slacks emerges from a cubicle row ahead of us. Jett smiles and exchanges a greeting with the man in a foreign language that sounds like Chinese. I'm certain the man will say something to me, but I keep my head down, and the moment passes.

Jett leads me to another corridor, thankfully free of people. He glances over his shoulder.

"I was speaking Mandarin to that gentleman. Most of the staff speak Mandarin and English. Some are fluent in Tamil," he says.

"I didn't know that. Languages have never been my strong suit. Where are we going? Isn't Dalia in the holding cell?"

"No, she's…"

"What is it? Stop holding back."

"Not so loud." Jett looks nervously up and down the hallway. "You need to stay calm and keep your voice down. Can you promise me that?"

I clench my teeth and nod. We come to an intersection, Jett leading me down the right-hand hallway.

"I want you to know"—he shakes his head in disgust—"I disagree with what they're doing to Dalia."

"Do what to Dalia?"

"She is the subject of an experiment."

I stop dead in the hall. "What? Where is she?"

Jett grabs me by the wrist, pulling me along. I wrench my arm free and keep moving. I want to run. Explode. Lash out. It's all I can do not to beat a hole into the wall with Jett's head.

"Stay calm. We have to stay inconspicuous. If they find out you've escaped before we reach Dalia, they'll move her. We'll never find her."

"What do you mean experiment on her?"

"She's being tested for magical ability by both Dr. Kihl and my people. None was detected. But Kihl and Rah have a hypothesis a subset of humanity has nascent, as yet undetectable, magical ability. They believe...I should say Kihl believes the doctor who made your prosthetics possesses such magic."

"Nascent magic? No way." I shake my head, remembering Dr. Rah asking me if Dr. Woolworth or my father are magicians. "No. That's crazy. Dr. Woolworth is a scientist, a medical doctor. She's a freaking genius. That's all."

"Nevertheless, Kihl believes that's why you can see dragons riding the slipstream. This new, undetectable magic infuses your prosthetics. He and Rah thoroughly probed your prosthetics for magic and found none. Nevertheless, he's pushing the nascent magic theory."

"Nascent." I consider the implications. "You mean, Dr. Woolworth and others like her possess magic without realizing it?"

Jett nods. "That's what Kihl believes."

"What are they doing to Dalia?"

Jett slows and cocks head to the side, listening to faint conversation from nearby.

"Tell me about Dalia," I insist.

Jett slows and holds a finger to his lips for silence and whispers, "They plan to give her the Juice. See if it awakens any power in her."

"What will that do to her?"

"Keep your voice down. It shouldn't hurt her."

I clench and unclench a fist at my side.

"The boy isn't a total waste?"

Ms. Bergman's voice comes from a side passage

maybe twenty feet up ahead.

"Not at all. Initiate 935 will make a fine magician. Might even be commando material," Gore says.

Initiate 935? They're talking about Haji. If I listen in, I might discover where they are keeping him.

"Come on," Jett hisses from the hallway to my left.

It belatedly dawns on me I'm standing at an intersection. I whisper, "They're talking about Haji."

"They'll recognize you."

"Let them. I can handle them."

"Not before they set off the alarm, and Bergman is more dangerous than you think."

"Whatever." There's no way she's as dangerous as me. Not now that the sleeper and I are one.

"We're almost to Dalia. You want the truth? I have no idea what the Juice might do to someone without magic. It might hurt her. We get her, and then I'll take you to Haji. I promise."

Gore and Bergman are so close it will only take me seconds to kill the assassin and force Bergman to take me to Haji. I want to do it. I want to kill Gore and…I shake my head. No. Save Dalia first, especially since the Juice might harm her, and I won't kill again, not even Gore.

Shaking my head, I follow Jett.

Chapter 30

"No guards?" I say, finding it odd since the door is to the room where Dalia is presumably held.

"All the guards are magicians. It's part of their military training. Fact is, there aren't nearly enough to guard every room." Jett opens the door. "And your friend isn't perceived as a threat."

"Gore might disagree," I mutter.

We enter a white room with an exam chair near the center with Dalia strapped down to it. Next to her, a stout woman in scrubs fiddles with tubing attached to an IV bag full of a faintly glowing orange fluid. The bag dangles from a stand beside the nurse.

"Get away from her!" I rush to my friend's aid.

Dalia is gagged. Otherwise, from her expression of horror, she'd be screaming her head off. The nurse looks up and starts talking, perhaps in Chinese. Her words turn into a scream as I close in. I shoulder into her chest, knocking her backward. Her legs tangle with the IV stand rolling across the floor on noisy casters. She staggers, the stand teeters, then both go down in a clatter of metal. The IV bag bursts, spraying the luminescent liquid over the floor and nurse.

"Dalia! Are you okay?" I rip the gauze from her mouth.

"What is he doing here?" Dalia looks past me.

My BFF doesn't look like she's been tortured

within inches of her life, and that is an incredible relief. The stifling terror I had felt at the mere thought of her wellbeing falls away. But it's strange. She still wears the same stinking, grimy clothes she arrived in days ago. The same clothing I had watched Gore use a bullwhip to reduce to bloody shreds along with her pale back. Dalia should be writhing in pain, her clothes in tatters, but that's not what I see. Are my eyes deceiving me now, or had I been deceived earlier?

"Are you going to unstrap me?" Dalia asks.

"Sorry," I murmur as dread scurries along my spine. Did I imagine Gore torturing her? What does that mean?

I unbuckle the restraint across her chest. When she sits up, I glimpse her back. The shirt isn't torn or bloody. I bite down on my lower lip. Am I going crazy?

"You can't trust Jett." Dalia sits up and loosens the bonds holding her ankles.

I peek over my shoulder at Jett, who corrals the blubbering nurse tangled in the IV tubing.

I turn back to Dalia. "It's okay. He's helping us escape."

"You don't understand, Allison. He's a monster." Dalia swings her legs off the exam chair. She adds in a whisper, "We should leave without him. He will betray us."

I'm tempted to agree. "I know he's a monster. He claims he's a faery. The important thing is he's going to help us rescue Haji."

"*Bù!*" The shrill scream pierces the air.

I spin toward the sound. Claws slip from Jett's fingertips. The nurse is on her side, one arm protectively cast before her face. He kicks aside the arm, pinning her wrist to the floor with a foot. His claws flash down, scraping a gash along her jaw.

"Jett, no!"

The nurse yowls and flails in a desperate attempt to escape, but he's too fast. His claws slash again, this time opening a bloody slash across the nurse's throat. A crimson waterfall stains the collar of her scrubs as she sinks to the floor. Jett kneels and casually cleans his claws on her chest, leaving behind red streaks.

"Why? You didn't have to kill her." I pity the nurse and am revolted by what he has done, and the metallic scent of blood makes my stomach ravenously twist.

He looks up at me, dark gaze lacking empathy. "She'd reveal our location. My magic is illusionary in nature. I can't make her unsee we've walked off with her patient." He inspects his claws before retracting them. "Besides, she's only human and not even a magician at that."

"Not a magician? What about Dalia? She's not a magician. Does that mean she's only human?" Am I destined to become like him? A monster gazing upon human life with disdain.

Jett stands. "She's your friend. I won't harm her. Human magicians will help us defeat the dragons and skaags. Ordinary humans are too weak to be useful in the coming war. Besides, humans are nothing if not plentiful. This one can easily be replaced by another."

"See." Dalia comes to my side, pointing accusingly at Jett. "A monster. There is a room...a cavern full of vats. Inside each vat is an infant—I don't know if they're human or not—hooked up to tubes and wires. The Juice...it's being pumped into them or out of them...I don't know. What I do know is, I saw him kill the infants with his claws."

Jett cocks his head to the side, staring at Dalia with unblinking eyes. The blood pooling around the nurse laps at his feet is still warm, mouthwatering.

"You should not have seen that," Jett says, claws extending from all his fingertips. His hands remain at his sides.

"Jett," I say warningly.

"How did you see that?" Jett lunges toward Dalia.

I head him off, and he stops before we collide.

"I was able to get away, briefly," Dalia says. "I made it to the chamber before they caught me. I saw what you did."

"You shouldn't have seen that." Jett shakes his head.

"What's going on, Jett?" I ignore the dying nurse's throes and my hunger pangs. "You're scaring me." I'm scaring myself.

"It was a kindness." Jett's eyes are rheumy. "I spared those children a short and painful existence." Faery dust materializes, swirling around Jett as his human features fade and wings tear from his back. Fractal patterns glow beneath his skin like rivers of lava. "She wasn't supposed to see that. I'm sorry."

Jett leaps into the air, wings humming. Dalia screams. I grab Jett's ankle as he flies over me. I'm nearly pulled off balance. With all my half-skaag strength, I swing him toward the floor. Dalia scrambles away as he writhes, wings flapping and claws slashing at my hands. He smashes onto the floor with a sickening smack and goes limp.

I release his ankle and stare, fearful I've killed him, but his sides expand and retract in time with his faint, raspy breathing. Maybe I've broken his ribs and punctured a lung, assuming his anatomy is somewhat humanoid. Faery dust floats around him, some settling on his translucent wings. Where the dust touches him, orange tendrils flare beneath the skin.

I tear my gaze from him and look at Dalia. "Do you know where Haji is?"

Dalia's response is cut off by the blare of a klaxon and a voice announcing, "Escaped prisoners in transfusion room nine."

****

We burst into the hallway. The alarm's electronic blast echoes down the passage. My hands, wrists, and forearms itch and are slick with fresh blood. My blood. The arms of the scrubs are stringy, red-stained rags after being clawed by Jett. My arms should be shredded messes too, but the wounds have already sealed even before the blood has dried, leaving behind pale pink scars fading before my eyes.

"Which way?" Dalia asks.

We have two options, left or right. The only problem: both ways are exactly the same, stark white and gently curving.

"I hoped you would know," I say.

"Left then," Dalia says.

"Just a sec," I say and raise a finger to my lips.

I shut my eyes, concentrating on all the sounds reverberating through the passage. The alarm is the loudest, its insistent shriek nearly drowning out all the other noise. But only nearly. I detect the faint whoosh of our breathing, the dull drone of forced air from vents in the ceiling, and the stomp of running feet coming from…the left.

I drop my finger from my lips. "No, the guards are coming from that direction. This way."

Dalia grabs my hand, her fingers like popsicles, as we race down the hallway. A disembodied voice interrupts the klaxon.

"Prisoners are nearing transfusion room six."

I tighten my grip on my friend's hand, pulling her along.

"Prisoners are at transfusion room five. Allison Lee, surrender immediately. You can't hide. We can track your movements throughout the facility."

Dalia slows, and I decrease my pace, considering throwing her over my shoulder in a fireman's carry. The extra weight won't slow me down. In fact, I could pick up the pace to a sprint. The other option is to allow my friend to slow us until the guards overtake us. I'm not sure how many are in pursuit, but it will only take a few tranquilizer darts to put me out of action. The best way to ensure a victory over the guards is to transform, but the hallway isn't large enough for me to change without crushing Dalia. Maybe I can send her up ahead on her own or have her shelter in one of the rooms we pass at regular intervals.

I drop back next to Dalia. Her cheeks are flushed, and she's breathing like she's setting a personal best at a cross country meet. I yell to be heard over the alarm, "Let me carry you."

"No, I can keep going."

I detect a disconcerting sound that makes goosebumps rise up my arms and neck. The distant thumping of boots up ahead, coming toward us.

I stop. Dalia keeps moving, tugging at my arm. Halting she turns toward me, face soured with desperation. "What is it?"

"More guards." I point in the direction we're headed, then to our rear. "We're surrounded."

"Miss Lee, I must insist you surrender." Ms. Bergman's husky voice booms through the hallway. "Surrender now, and your little friend dies quickly. If you continue this inane escape attempt, I'll make sure she begs for the sweet release of death, and I won't grant it."

"Never!" I shout at Bergman. "Never!" I turn to Dalia, my decision made. "That room." I point to a door to our right. It must be another transfusion room. "Get inside."

"But—"

The clomp of the boots amplifies. Bergman's rant rebounds through the hallway.

"Now, Dalia! I'm going to transform. I don't want to crush you by accident."

To my relief, Dalia nods and scampers to the door.

I close my eyes and prepare for the excruciating pain of transformation. I hope Haji isn't among the guards because I don't think I'll be able to stop myself from hurting him along with everyone else.

"Allison! Allison!"

I register Dalia's screams over the din. Opening my eyes, I face her. She stands in the doorway to the room I told her to hide inside.

"You have to see this," Dalia says.

"But—"

"No buts. You have to see this. It's a game-changer." Dalia enters the room.

Reluctantly, I follow her inside and seal the door. I see two individuals strapped down to exam chairs and hooked via tubes up to a waist-high rectangular device with an LED panel protruding from the top at a forty-five-degree angle. Next to the device is a set of drawers on casters. The alarm still goes off in the hallway, but the noise is muffled inside the room. Odd. The alarm isn't channeled into the room. A rhythmic thumping emanates from the device. Is one patient...test subject...a child? A wave of revulsion crashes into me, followed by the desperate urge to help her. Whatever is happening in this room, it's wrong, like everything else going on inside this villainous lair. The other chair is angled so I don't have a clear view of the subject.

Dalia meanders toward the room's center, head swiveling to gaze upon each patient in turn. A harsh stench like industrial grade cleaners fills the air strong enough to make me nauseated.

I turn to the door and run my hands over the cool metal. No lock. It figures. Coming in here was a mistake. I hastily search for an alternate exit—none, of course. It's like the transfusion room I rescued Dalia from. One way in and out. I can transform without crushing Dalia. We'll have to move the people in the exam chairs, so I don't squash them. We have to do that. There's no way I'm going to hurt a child even to save Dalia and myself. The one problem with the grand plan is I can't pass through the doorway in skaag form. I could blast the guards with lightning as soon as they open the door, but my control over my electrical discharge isn't fine-tuned. There's at least a fifty-fifty chance I'll fill the hallway and this room with deadly electrical arcs. I need a new gambit ASAP. I still hear the super magicians approaching, closer, closer.

"Allison," Dalia says excitedly, "you seriously

need to see this."

"Just a sec," I mutter, not listening.

Beneath the stench of cleansers are two scents. One aroma I recognize all too well as human blood as my salivating mouth attests, but the other scent is something else, reminiscent yet different. Reminiscent of what? I sniff, eerily aware I'm a predator scenting prey. I turn toward the exam chairs.

"Allison, look," Dalia says. "It's Dr. Kihl, and this girl looks like Jett. She must be a faery."

"What?" I maneuver until I have a clear view of the patients. "Get out."

Dr. Kihl, perhaps under the influence of an anesthetic, sprawls in one chair with the sleeve of his button-down shirt rolled up to expose his forearm. Two IVs run from his forearm to the rhythmically pumping device. One tube carries blood to the machine while the other tube transports blood highlighted by glowing orange streaks from the device into Dr. Kihl.

"That's the Juice, isn't it?" Dalia points to the orange lines. "That machine mixes the Juice with Kihl's blood. That means…"

"The Juice is her blood," I say. "Faery blood."

The IV jammed into the child's arm transports her glowing blood into the device. A hospital gown decorated with rainbows and unicorns is draped over her small, dark frame. Her hair is white, and a few delicate spindles of faery dust float around her. My heart aches for her. I can't imagine she's undergoing this procedure of her free will. My impulse is to disconnect her from the machine, but I don't know if doing so will harm her or not.

"We have hostages," Dalia says.

"Dalia, what are you talking about?"

"If the guards come in"—Dalia gestures to the doctor and girl—"we'll kill them."

I stare at my friend. She's breathing so hard she's almost hyperventilating. Her eyes gleam maniacally, and she runs her thumbs over her fingertips while bouncing on the balls of her feet. I swallow hard. Dalia is hyping herself up into a frenzy so she'll be able to carry out the threat.

"Dalia, you don't want to kill anyone."

The guards are at the door shuffling, preparing magic, checking weapons, readying themselves to burst inside. I press my ear to the door, listening intently, trying to get a count of how many there are. It's difficult with the din caused by the alarm and the pump. Men and women talk in Chinese—Mandarin, Jett had told me. They sound excited, impatient, puzzled, and disappointed all at once.

Dalia looks at me, smirking. "Don't worry. I'll do the killing. You don't have to get your hands dirty."

A year ago, I wouldn't have believed Dalia had it in her to kill someone in cold blood, but I'm not so sure anymore. I watched her torture Gore in the van. Even worse, as much as I don't want to admit it, at some level she enjoyed it.

Dalia rummages through a set of metal drawers next to the pump. She tosses a roll of medical tape that skates over the floor. Tubing and gauze bandages and needles follow the medical tape to the floor until Dalia straightens, holding a scalpel overhead like it's Excalibur.

The deadlatch slides out of place with a clank. I spin to face the door that is inching open. Lowering my shoulder, I smash into the door like a linebacker. A man grunts, and someone in the hallway shouts commands. Pressure builds on the door as the guards attempt to force it open, but my half-skaag prowess gushes through me. They won't be forcing the door open like that.

Carefully so I don't damage the door, I force it closed until it latches. Shouts come from outside, along with shuffling like they're clearing a pathway.

"Do you hear that, Bergman? We have hostages!" Dalia screams.

Boom. The door vibrates against me hard enough to rattle the bones in my wrist.

"Tell the guards to back off now!"

Boom. The door rattles. Chanting similar in cadence to Gore's voice when he casts magic comes from the hallway.

"I think they're using magic to break down the door," I call. "I don't know how much longer I can hold them back."

"We have Dr. Kihl! If those guards don't back off, I'll kill him!" Dalia screams.

Boom. The shriek of shearing metal is razor shrill. The door buckles inward. A bulge jabs into my ribcage. Boom.

"I'll do it! I'll slit the slimeball's throat, and then I'll kill the girl!"

My lip quivers. I dare a glance over my shoulder. Dalia leans over Dr. Kihl, bent back and shoulders hunched forward. Her disheveled hair is a pink curtain hiding her face. In a steady hand, she presses the scalpel against Dr. Kihl's neck.

"Dalia, no," I whisper, knowing if my friend

follows through with the threat, her start down the irrevocable path will be complete. I must warn her killing is the easy part, but living with yourself afterward is like having your heart and soul fed into a waste disposal bit by bit and ground into a soup of guilt as vast as the ocean.

Chapter 31

I should rip the scalpel from Dalia's hand, but as soon as I stop propping up the door, the guards will break it down and swarm into the chamber, and I will have to decide if our escape is worth all their lives.

I no longer hear the guards attempting to break down the door when the alarm abruptly stops. I relax, but I keep my body pressed against cold metal and listen. Footsteps. Fading ever so slightly. They're backing away from the door.

Ms. Bergman's acerbic voice pipes into the chamber. "I'm willing to negotiate."

Still bent over Kihl with the scalpel at his throat, Dalia looks at me with wild eyes. Her jaw works, but no words come out.

"What are your demands?" Bergman actually sounds reasonable. That's a first. "You know how negotiation works, don't you? You tell me what you want, and I either provide it or make a counteroffer."

"Say something," Dalia whispers.

"I thought you were the one negotiating."

"Now, now, girls, no need to argue. Just name a spokeswoman and let's get on with it," Bergman says.

"I…" Dalia says. "I can't talk to that woman and think straight at the same time. Look at my face. She did that."

I can't help wincing; her face is tattooed with

splotchy black, blue, and purple patterns. The abrasion along her jawline is an angry red, and she has raccoon eyes. I yearn to comfort her and break her tormentor.

"What's wrong, girls? Did you bite off your tongues?" Bergman asks.

"You're negotiating with me," I say and stop propping up the door.

A bolt the size of my thumb pops out of the wall, clattering to the floor. With a loud groan, the door teeters inward. I tense, ready to fling myself against the cold steel, but the door stills. With my hands held before me, I back away. When I'm about halfway to the exam chairs without the door collapsing, I relax a bit.

"I'm waiting, Miss Lee," Bergman says, her tone a serrated knife sawing through bone. "You know, Miss Lee, I will have justice for Dr. Rah."

"Talk to Jett. I didn't do anything to her."

I didn't kill her.

I didn't lap her blood.

I didn't sample her flesh.

"Oh, I intend to speak with Jett in great detail. Have no fear, Miss Lee. I will uncover how you manipulated the faery boy into helping you. Even after you beat him to near death…impressive. I never imagined you having ice water running through your veins. Perhaps that shouldn't come as a surprise. You are a cold-blooded killer. You and I, Miss Lee, we are very much alike."

"No, we're not! I'm nothing like you!" I'm not my mother's daughter. Raymond Lee raised me, and he wouldn't crush a cockroach.

"Weeeelll, Miss Lee, I'm not claiming we'll ever be besties, but I can't help feeling we are members of the same sisterhood. I say this as one killer to another. Did you feel like a goddess watching the life dribble from your victim's eyes? I always do. That's when I feel the most alive and powerful. It's wonderful, really."

"Allison, don't listen to her," Dalia says. "She's...she's messing with your mind."

"It was an accident," I whisper. "He was in my room. He shot me. I didn't mean to..."

"What's that, Miss Lee? If we're going to negotiate, you need to speak up."

Or maybe it wasn't an accident. Maybe I wanted to kill the kidnapper. The sleeper wished to, and I've come to understand we are mirror images. Opposing sides of the same coin. Even so, I hadn't intended on killing him. Even after the bullet tore through my shoulder, I had only meant to keep him from killing me, but I heard my father screaming from downstairs. I needed to save him no matter what. That's what drove my action, the desire to save my father. I didn't mean to punch the gunman with enough power to break his neck.

"Allison, snap out of it!" Dalia says. "She's up to something. She's manipulating you."

Dalia's voice claws me back from the dreadful reverie.

"Please," Ms. Bergman says. "I'm waiting for you to make your demands. If I wasn't, I'd have already sent in the guards."

"She's trying to distract you. She's buying time for something," Dalia says.

Buying time for what? I do a three-sixty, scrutinizing the floor, ceiling, and walls. Ms. Bergman continues speaking, her voice becoming more booming and insistent as I ignore her. Are they outflanking us? There's only one entrance that I can see. A secret entrance?

"Ah-ha," I growl, throwing my head back.

Directly above me is a foot square vent. It's difficult to see because the vent is a fine mesh and painted the same sterile white as the ceiling. Are guards coming for us through the airshafts? My prosthetics zoom in on the vent so close I can see grayish dust embossing the mesh. My prosthetics zoom even closer until I can clearly see a dangling cobweb, mere millimeters long, caught in an almost imperceptible airflow.

I turn my gaze to Dalia, vision momentarily going out of focus as my prosthetics zoom. It all makes sense. The guards backing off and Bergman trying to distract me. Gas. They're going to gas us. They're smart about it, doing it slowly because otherwise I'd immediately detect it with my heightened senses.

"What?" Dalia asks.

"Gas," I yell. Ms. Bergman falls silent. "Our first demand is you stop attempting to gas us. Turn off the forced air."

In the relative silence that follows, I focus my awareness on my sense of hearing. The drone of forced air is as soft as a butterfly's flapping wings, but it's present at the precipice of my perception.

"I'm waiting, Ms. Bergman. Does Dalia need to eliminate a hostage?"

"No! It's done. What—"

"Quiet. I need quiet." I magnify the vent. Bergman continues babbling, but it doesn't matter. She hasn't stopped the air. "Dalia." I turn to my friend, winking and hoping she gets the message. "Bergman is failing to meet our demands."

Dalia smiles, and her body tenses. Blood rolls down the doctor's neck from where the scalpel's blade has pricked his skin. Oh, no. She's going to kill him.

"Wait! Wait!" Bergman screams. "The air is off. The air is off."

Dalia relaxes, smile drooping into a frown. I let out a breath. A quick visual inspection of the vent proves this time Bergman is honest.

"Next, I want the hallways cleared of guards."

Bergman issues orders over the intercom. "Done. It will take several minutes for them to clear the hallways."

I listen intently to the distant patter from outside, confirming Bergman's orders are being followed.

"Now, I want Haji brought to us, unharmed. And send in a doctor or a nurse who can wake Dr. Kihl and the faery without harming them. I need them ready to move."

"I will send in the boy and a nurse to revive Dr. Kihl, but the girl must remain. We can't wake her."

Dalia shakes her head and mouths, "We need both of them."

"I don't believe you. I want the girl woken up and ready to move along with Dr. Kihl. Once they're awake and on their feet, and Haji is with us, the nurse will lead us above ground. I want the entire route free of guards."

After a brief silence, Bergman replies, "I need time to discuss the arrangements with my allies."

****

Dalia and I sit back-to-back near the chamber's

center. I'm nearly folded into a fetal position, my arms across my knees and my forehead resting against my arms. I'm exhausted and haunted by the reality I have killed. First the kidnapper, and now the guards. Maybe Bergman is right, and I am exactly like her and my mother. I shudder and sob. I've become my mother, a monster. I can't deny that horrible fate any longer.

Dalia shifts, her spine pressing into mine. "Are you okay? Allison, seriously, what's wrong? Is it what Bergman said? When she was messing with you? That was all psychobabble. Jett got what he deserves, and so did the man who shot you. Besides, you didn't kill anyone. I don't know where Bergman gets her information, but it's obviously inaccurate. You have nothing to feel bad about. You saw through her ploy with the gas. Haji is being released, and once Kihl and the faery are on their feet, we'll be able to walk out of here."

"No, I killed him. I killed him and didn't stop with him."

Dalia shimmies away from me, robbing me of the comfort of her touch.

"What are you talking about? Are you talking about the guy who shot you? Your mother killed him."

"No, it was me." I shake my head. "I did it. The story that my mother killed him is a lie. Dr. Radcliffe and Agent Deveraux thought it would play better in the media if the monster girl was saved by her protective mother rather than having the news full of stories about me being a bloodthirsty killer."

The scalpel clinks against the floor.

"You've been keeping this to yourself all this time? Why didn't you tell me?" Dalia throws her arms around me, embracing me from behind.

"I…I…" The truth is I don't have an excuse.

"Allison, talk to me."

"It didn't stop with the kidnapper. I turned into a skaag and killed guards. Dozens of them. One of them could've been Haji."

"Haji is alive."

"Unless they're lying."

Thump.

I tense. Dalia releases me and picks up the scalpel.

Thump.

My gaze locks on the door.

"Can you open the door?"

I'm on my feet and to the door as soon as Gore finishes his query.

"Bergman called off the guards. I have Haji and drugs to reverse the anesthetics."

I grab the door, and the twisted metal squeals as I tear the portal off its hinges. In the hall, Gore supports Haji, who looks like he'll collapse without support.

"Haji!" I toss the door aside and lurch into the hallway.

Haji is listless and doesn't reply.

I glare at Gore. "What did you do to him?"

"I didn't—"

I grab Gore around the neck, strangling his lies.

The bullwhip cracks, flaying Dalia's skin.

I lift the assassin off his feet as he claws at my hands. Without Gore to lean against, Haji teeters.

The whip cracks again. Dalia yowls.

Haji collapses to the floor.

"Haji!" I scream, the sight of his writhing body pulling me back into the here and now.

Gore's face turns purple from lack of air. I'm killing him to avenge an act he didn't commit. I'm worse than my mother. She's just a monster, but I'm out of control. I fling Gore into the chamber. He slides across the floor, not stopping until he collides with the base of the exam chair Dr. Kihl reclines on.

I rush to Haji's side and kneel. "Haji? Haji!"

He is unconscious and convulsing like an asphyxiating fish.

"Haji!"

I might as well be talking to a brick wall. My pulse thrums as my helpless panic grows. It's my fault he's here, maybe dying. If I hadn't driven him away, he never would've pursued magic.

I bite down hard on my lower lip until I taste blood. *Snap out of it.* Setting my hands on his shoulders, I'm shocked by the violent strength of his spasms. I talk soothingly, concentrating on my tone opposed to the words. Nothing is working.

"Help!" I shout. "Help!"

Every second is an epoch.

"Haji, wake up. I'm sorry. I'm so sorry for everything."

He continues shaking. His eyes are scrunched up, and his head scythes side to side with frightful speed. Footsteps thud from the doorway. Gore appears, moving slowly with one hand massaging his bruised neck. His glare could drill holes into my skull.

"Can you help him?" I demand.

He nods once and trundles to my side. His knees bend, then buckle, and he's kneeling next to us. I shiver. I've never been this close to him without him trying to kill me or me trying to kill him or while I'm under the influence of drugs and magic. I don't like it one bit.

"Take…me"—Gore wheezes—"with…you."

"You want to come with us?"

The assassin nods. "Ber…Bergman…is watching." He gestures to Haji. "On…purpose…withdrawal."

"Okay. You can come with us. Just help him!"

Gore opens a pocket on the chest of his paramilitary uniform and pulls out a hypodermic full of Juice. He uncaps the needle and stares at me with loathing.

"The Juice will help him?" I ask.

Gore smiles slyly. "Trust me. Brace…his…head."

"Trust you? You've tried to kill me twice. I almost killed you."

"We can't…get enough of each other."

"What? You're a comedian now?"

"Your…mother…is in Singapore. She'll find…this place."

My heart palpitates. "She's here?"

Gore nods, smiling even wider.

"You're sure she's here?"

Gore clears his throat. "I've seen the footage."

"You're signing your death warrant by betraying Bergman. Is that a move a survivor would make?"

Gore's smile warps into a glower. "Bergman might try…to kill me. Druk will kill me unless…I can…convince her otherwise. You're my bargaining chip."

"Fine. Hurry up and inject him, or I'll do it myself."

I don't want to trust him, but what choice do I have? He can lead us out of here, and his words ring true. When my mother finds this underground lair, people will die, and I never bet against her in a fight.

I brace Haji's head. He squirms in my hands, but my grip remains firm. "If you're lying…"

Gore winces while he laughs and jabs the needle into my friend's neck.

Chapter 32

"You agreed to let him come with us?" Dalia demands. Her eyes bulge and her arms are folded across her chest. She turns her gaze on Gore, who jabs away at the control panel for the medical pump with his index fingers, presumably shutting it down.

"What was I supposed to do?" I'm sitting on the floor next to Haji, who is laid out near the exam chairs. The injection of Juice stopped the convulsions, but he's still unconscious, and a sheen of sweat glistens on his face. "We need his help."

"Do we?" Dalia snaps and takes a deep breath. "Why does Gore want to come with us?"

The device powers down with a fading electrical hum. Gore rifles through the drawer next to the pump.

"He said my mother is here, in Singapore, and it's only a matter of time before she finds this place."

"And you believe him?"

"I don't know what to believe anymore. I saw Gore strip the skin off your back with a bullwhip."

"I'd like to see him try."

"Anyway, Bergman showed me news reports of my mother flying over the Pacific. Maybe I shouldn't believe those reports. Maybe it's all a trick. But I wouldn't put it past Mother to track me down here. I just wish she had done it sooner."

"The video you saw of me torturing Dalia," Gore

says, still raspy. "It was a deepfake."

"A deepfake? So every video I've seen is fake."

"I think the video of your mother flying over the Pacific is real. But who knows," Gore says. "Bergman told you she's a spook, right? Works for part of the government that doesn't want anything to do with dragons. Here we go."

Gore holds up a bandage roll and gauze.

"She did," I say.

"The deepfake stuff is one of her pet projects." Gore sets the bandage and gauze on top of the drawers. He faces Dr. Kihl and starts removing the IV. "I'm sure you realized by now Jett has magic. He can create illusions. Convincing ones. Orders of magnitude better than what I can do, and he does it with ease. Believe me, holding an illusion for long is draining for a human magician." Gore clears his throat and pauses his work, massaging his neck. "Bergman has a team of computer geeks working with the faeries to combine deepfake tech with magic."

I frown.

"What?" Gore asks.

"It's something Jett said. He said creating illusions are difficult and easily seen though by magicians."

"Maybe." Gore shrugs. "I'm no expert in faery magic. But combine faery magic with tech..." He shakes his head. "...even I can't tell the difference in what Bergman's geeks are producing and the genuine article."

"Why are they making deepfakes?" Dalia asks.

Gore shrugs. "I don't know, but I can guess. Remember the deepfake of the president a couple years ago?"

We nod.

"It was pretty good, right? Convincing?" Gore turns back to Dr. Kihl. "Now, consider a deepfake so perfect even the computer geeks with all the know-how and fancy software can't debunk it as phony. Consider the chaos Bergman can create with a few videos." He flashes me a smile. "The violence."

"But to what end?" I ask.

"How should I know? Like I have said before, do you tell the hired help everything? As for your mother, she is in Singapore," Gore says. "We listen in on the military chatter. She was spotted by the Air Force two days ago. Dr. Radcliffe is in the city too. It's all over the news. This base is being evacuated as we speak."

"Dr. Radcliffe is here?" I say, exchanging a look with Dalia. Hope gleams in her eyes. Radcliffe being here means the city will be crawling with Draconic Task Force agents. If we can find an agent, they'll take us to Dr. Radcliffe. Undoubtedly, the massive dragon, who is a magician to boot, will be able to keep us safe. Tanis and Mauve might even be here. My heart nearly crumbles at the thought of Mauve. "Did you kill Mauve, the dragon in Ace's condo?"

"No. I didn't have time to eliminate the dragon."

I smile. I always suspected the claim was a lie, but him saying so obliterates the dread plaguing me. Dalia smiles too.

Blood tinged with orange highlights squirts from Dr. Kihl's arm, barely missing Gore's face. The assassin curses as he tosses aside the IV and slaps gauze over the puncture wound.

"Do you know what you're doing?" Dalia asks.

"More or less." Gore wraps a bandage around the

gauze. "Some of the early subjects"—he nods toward the faery girl—"weren't cooperative."

"What do you mean weren't cooperative?" I ask.

"Would you willingly undergo an experimental medical procedure you didn't volunteer for? When I was recruited, the experiments had already been going on for years. Some doctors and nurses had been injured by faeries, several killed if the rumors are true, so the medical staff started refusing to carry out experiments involving live faery subjects." Gore sets the bandage roll on the doctor's thigh. He removes a hypodermic from the pocket of his cargo pants and jabs it into Kihl's arm. The doctor gasps and mutters incomprehensibly. "It will be a couple of minutes before he starts talking sense and several more before he's ready to move."

Gore discards the needle and grabs the bandage and remaining gauze and maneuvers to the faery girl. He places the gauze and bandage roll on the exam chair beside her tiny form.

"The chamber I saw with all the infants in the vats. What will happen to the babies? Are they going to evacuate them?" Dalia asks.

"You saw that, did you?" Gore removes the IV from the girl. "Those will be destroyed."

"Destroyed? We have to stop it," Dalia says.

I nod in agreement. "We have to save them."

Glowing orange blood blossoms from the faery's forearm. Gore places gauze on the wound and starts wrapping it with a bandage.

Gore laughs mirthlessly. "They're not alive. No brains. One of Kihl's and Rah's innovations."

"All those infants..." Dalia says, her face

congealing in revulsion.

"Blood donors," I say. Simply imagining a cavern full of babies in vats like a scene from a B-grade sci-fi makes me nauseated and—*ugh*—sets my mouth watering.

"Sacks of Juice," Gore says.

"Is she alive?" I ask, tamping down the urge to sock Gore in the face for the crass statement.

"Oh, yes, she's what they're trying to re-create. Well, minus the brain. They'll evacuate her. Everything else can be reconstituted at a secure location."

"She's coming with us," I say.

Scoffing, Gore finishes with the bandage.

"She's not a willing subject, is she?" I ask.

"No, she's not," Gore says, "but I can guarantee you there's no way you're leaving the island with this kid. Bergman won't allow it."

"Bergman won't have a choice," I growl.

"Good luck explaining that to her."

"How many faeries are there?" Dalia asks.

"Yeah," I say, looking between Dalia and the faery girl. "All I've seen are Jett and her."

Gore shrugs. "Don't know. I've seen a few now and then, but never more than three at once. Beyond the cloning chamber is a section of bunker no one is allowed to enter. I suspect there's a bunch of them down there."

"Would he know?" I hook a thumb at Kihl.

"I don't think so. Bergman and Jett are intermediaries. When there's a big decision to be made, Jett has to run it past the Elders. Bergman gets on the horn to the higher ups. That's all I know."

Dr. Kihl sits up in the exam chair, gasping. Mouth

hanging open, he looks around, squinting, confusion and dismay writ large across his face.

"Where…" Kihl says.

Dalia reacts first. She hops onto the exam chair, forces the befuddled doctor back in the chair with a forearm, straddles him, and presses the scalpel to his Adam's apple.

"Keep him quiet," Gore says as he retrieves another hypodermic from his cargo pants. "He has enough Juice in him to vaporize us with a spell."

"What…what is going on?" Kihl regards me, squinting. "Allison—"

"Maybe I should slit his throat and get it over with." Dalia draws blood.

Kihl whimpers and falls silent.

"Don't kill him!" What I don't say: you don't want to become like me, Dalia, detritus awash in a sea of self-recrimination. "He's a bargaining chip."

"Allison is right. We need him alive for now." Gore injects the faery with the hypodermic. The girl shudders, eyes fluttering open, and gulps air. Gore backs up.

"Chief! Help!" Kihl cries.

Dalia slaps the doctor across the cheek and thrusts the scalpel deeper. Kihl falls silent, lips quivering.

"Not another peep, Doc," Dalia warns. Red rivulets run down Kihl's neck.

The faery girl sits up, muttering something that sounds like language, but nothing I've heard before. She stares at Kihl, her lips curling into a snarl revealing triangular teeth. A feral growl, surprisingly deep coming from such a small body, rattles her chest.

"Can she understand us?" I ask.

"Some." Gore backs up until his legs press against the exam chair where Dalia pins Kihl. "Bria, calm down. He can't hurt you. We're going to leave. Escape."

"Her name is Bria?" I ask.

Gore nods. At my side, Haji stirs as if the tension as choking as dragon smoke is finally enough to rouse him.

"Haji is waking," I say.

Bria hisses, claws extending from her fingertips.

"He's dangerous." Gore doesn't take his gaze off Bria. "He's fully indoctrinated. He might attack."

Bria stands, the hospital gown, at least three sizes too large on her petite frame, puddling around her ankles. Ripping flesh and tearing fabric sounds come from her back as her semi-transparent dragonfly wings extend from her shoulders.

"Indoctrinated? What does that even mean?" I ask.

"Brainwashed with faery magic. It takes several days, sometimes weeks to complete, and is very thorough. I've placed some spells on Haji that might counteract the indoctrination. Emphasis on might." Gore extends his arms out toward the faery. "Bria. Relax. We're going to escape. Dr. Kihl won't experiment on you ever again."

Jett told me faery magic can't brainwash people. It seems Jett told only lies when speaking about the extent of his magical power. I want to ask more about counteracting the indoctrination, but Bria hisses and slashes the air with her claws. Next to me, Haji groans and blinks.

"Haji, are you okay?" I ask.

"Haji is awake?" Dalia asks.

"Yes. His eyes are open! Haji. Haji!"

Haji regards me with cold intensity before scrambling to his feet, lips moving.

"Haji, what are you doing?"

"Soldier!" Gore's voice slices through the air like a sickle. "Attention!"

Haji halts so abruptly he slips and falls onto his butt.

"Bria, no!" Gore shouts.

The hum of faery wings fills the room.

"Yes, Chief!" Haji bellows and stands on shaky legs at attention, gaze unblinking.

Dalia screams, and there's a dull thud of a body striking the floor. I come to my feet, turning to the exam chairs. Dalia is on the floor. Bria is on the chair kneeling over the doctor, who pleads for his life. The faery holds a quaking clawed hand centimeters from his throat. Gore speaks soothingly to Bria, reaching a hand toward her.

I glance at Haji. He still stands at wobbly attention. In a different situation, he'd appear comical in the black fatigues so big it's like he's wearing a garbage bag. I focus my attention on Bria. Rainbow-hued flecks of faery dust float around her, one coming to a rest on her back between her wings. If I'm stealthy, maybe I can grab her from behind before she harms Kihl. Of course, I'm not sure if I want to catch her. In a struggle, I might end up hurting her. Maybe we should let her slay the doctor. He won't be casting magic then, and she might calm down after he's dead.

"No," I murmur, shaking my head. "We're not killers. We can't condone that."

Dalia clasps Bria by the ankle, pulling hard. A

shrill scream echoes through the chamber. The faery topples from the exam chair, landing hard on her side next to my friend. Kihl rears up from the chair, hands aglow. I spring forward to my friend's aid. In my peripheral vision, I see Gore chop the doctor in the neck. Kihl falls back into the chair, clutching his throat; the glow is gone from his hands.

The tang of blood fills my nostrils as I close in on Bria and Dalia. They roll across the white floor grappling, leaving behind red and orange streaks. My stomach growls, my body tormented by acid hunger. Half of Bria's top left-wing juts sideways at an unnatural angle, orange fluid leaking from a tear in the membrane. Dalia's wrists are crisscrossed with red slashes.

"Stop," I growl, as much at my desire to taste human flesh as at the combatants.

I lunge into the fray, hands locking like steel manacles around Bria's upper arms. Her wings beat, buffeting me as I haul her off Dalia. Orange liquid splatters across the floor and me. The wings are stiff yet flexible like leather belts, making each blow a lash. Bria writhes in my arms and shrieks, but my grip remains firm.

"Bria," Gore shouts, dragging Kihl around to face her. The doctor's cheeks are flushed, and he still clutches his throat. "Prisoner. He is our prisoner. We can escape. Understand? Escape."

Bria's struggles decrease until she is nearly limp in my hands.

"Escape?" she says thickly as if her tongue is unpracticed forming the word. Her claws retract into her fingers.

"Escape." Gore nods and looks me in the eyes. "Release her."

"Are you sure?" I ask.

"Yes. She's done fighting. Watch the doctor." Gore releases Kihl, who spills onto the floor, breathing raggedly. "He's still dangerous. I need to help Dalia."

My gaze goes to Dalia sitting on the floor, wincing as blood runs freely from the slashes up and down her forearms and hands. I salivate, and white-hot anger pulses through me. Feed. Taste the blood, the flesh. *No. No!* I tamp down my ravenous urges, which allow rage tinged with fear to burst to the fore. I tighten my grip on the faery child instead of releasing her. I can crush her bones to dust with my bare hands.

"Don't hurt her, Allison," Dr. Kihl says. "Bria is a child. Her attack on me is justified. I've done her great harm. She attacked Dalia out of fear, not malice."

"If I kill her, it will put your research back years."

Bria goes as taut as a rubber band about to burst, but she doesn't struggle.

From Dalia's side, Gore says, "We need her. Bergman is still monitoring us. If anything happens to Bria, I guarantee you she will move against us."

"The base is evacuating," I say. "She's probably already left."

"No," Gore says, "she's watching."

"What you say is true, Allison," Kihl says. "Killing Bria will set my organization back years, but she is still a child."

A child. I'm about to kill a child. I can barely live with myself after accidentally killing a man who shot me. How can I continue living if I kill a child in cold blood? How can I even consider it?

I release Bria, who sinks to the floor, drowning in the torn and stained gown covered in rainbows and unicorns.

Chapter 33

Gore leads us through the white hallways at a jog, pulling Dr. Kihl alongside him. Bria is behind them, ahead of me, with her hospital gown pulled up to her knees. Beside me jogs Dalia with a perpetual grimace plastered on her face. I struggle to ignore the scent of the blood staining the bandages covering her forearms and hands. Haji brings up the rear, shambling along on unsteady legs. Occasionally, people emerge from doorways or run by us in the hallway, but they ignore us.

Despite Gore's assurances Haji won't attack us, I can't shake the feeling I'm going to be blasted by magic in the back. The emotionless boy from the transfusion chamber is not the Haji I know, and the way he jumped to attention at Gore's command is bizarre. He's no longer the card-carrying member of my squad I've known for most of my life or the boy I dated on and off in the aftermath of The Incident. Maybe the Haji I know is buried beneath the magic brainwashing him, but I honestly don't see him. Coldness as chilling as an arctic gale has replaced his warmth and goofy good humor.

At an intersection, people in hazmat suits nearly collide with Gore and Dr. Kihl. They shout at us to run in broken English and continue their pell-mell sprint. Bria turns down the hallway from where the workers had come.

"No," Gore says. "This way."

Bria shakes her head and continues down the hallway.

"There's nothing you can do for them!" Gore calls hoarsely.

"They were never alive, Bria," Dr. Kihl says weakly.

The faery girl pauses, regarding the doctor with large eyes brimming with unfettered loathing. Her lips curl, showing teeth, and she hisses. Hiking up the hospital gown above her knees, Bria takes off at a run.

"Bria, wait." I follow. "Wait. Bria."

"Must...see," Bria says.

"See what?"

Bria keeps running. I follow, unwilling to force her to stop. An acrid stench clogs in my nostrils. There is a chemical undertone to the smell, making me wonder if we're breathing something toxic. We round the corner to discover a dark haze filling the hallway. The smoke emanates in black wisps from around a double door at the end of the hall.

The air is bitter on my tongue and burns my throat. "We should turn around."

Bria ignores me. Instead, she increases her pace. I follow at a jog, choking back coughs. From behind me echoes the patter of running feet, probably my people.

"Stay back," I call. "The smoke is getting worse."

I catch up to Bria at the double door, determined not to allow her to enter the room beyond. The smoke is thick, nearly overwhelming.

"Bria..."

She slams aside the doors, revealing a cavern full

of writhing flames and smoke as black as pitch. Vats burn, each containing a small body suspended in fluid and pierced by tubes.

"Oh no," I murmur, shocked by the scope of the revolting research. "Bria, I'm so—"

Bria ululates and slams the doors shut.

"Bria," Kihl hacks as he approaches us from behind with Gore, "they were never truly alive."

The faery rounds on Kihl and Gore, who stands at the doctor's shoulder. Her hand flashes toward Kihl's neck. Blood blooms, and the doctor falls to the floor, his neck a gory ruin. Bria looms over him, hissing, as the panic fades from his gaze along with his life. Red droplets drip from Bria's claws onto his pallid face.

"Let's go. Now," Gore says. "Run!"

Shaken from my stunned stupor, I follow Gore and Bria back to the intersection where Dalia and Haji wait.

****

Going up a metal staircase that creaks and shudders at every step, I take the lead. The higher we ascend, the more pungent the air is with the smell of brine.

"If this is the way out, where is everyone?" Dalia asks. "I thought they were evacuating."

"This will take us to the boat launch," Gore says.

"You didn't answer my question," Dalia gripes. "Where are all the people?"

"There are multiple ways off the base," Gore snaps.

They continue bickering, voices rising. I call for quiet and listen intently. A gust of wind. We're close. Two flights of stairs separate us from the outside.

"We're almost there." I sprint up the remaining flights to where the staircase terminates at a hatch in the ceiling. A rusted ladder built into the wall allows access to the hatch.

I don't wait for the stragglers to catch up. I scramble the ten feet up the ladder to the hatch and grab the cold steel wheel in its center. After a moment of resistance, the wheel turns with a grating squeal. After several turns, I force the hatch out and open. Warm rain falls from a dark sky, enormous drops battering my skin, and the wind howls, blowing palm trees nearly horizontal. I scurry through the opening into a jungle dancing to monsoon winds. I'm about to shout a warning down the hatchway when half a dozen figures with glowing eyes emerge from the dense foliage.

"Stay back," I snarl, the skaag in me ready to lash out with deadly force. I stare hard into the dense vegetation, surmising I'm surrounded by at least twenty faeries.

Jett steps forward from behind a leaf almost as large as he is. He is bruised and battered but otherwise seems to have recovered from our last encounter.

"Allison, we're here to collect Bria."

Overhead brilliant lightning flashes between thunderheads. Less than a second later comes the roll of thunder, and I swear the ground shakes. The rain increases to a squall, so hard the droplets sting. The wind howls through the jungle, shaking leaves. Somewhere off to my left is a sharp crack followed by the crash of foliage and a thump.

Jett slinks closer. His wings jut out above his shoulders and below his lower back. The rain mats down his white hair but appears to have no effect on the faery dust swirling around him.

I back up toward the hatch, straining to hear my

friends and allies over the din. I breathe in sharply. Gore and Dalia are arguing, judging by their tones. They must be at the ladder.

Jett stops three feet from me. My heart palpitates as intensely as the thunder overhead. Jett is handsome while masquerading as a human, but as a faery, he is astonishingly beautiful, a near-perfect synergy of man and beast.

"Give us Bria, then the rest of you can leave," Jett says.

"What if she doesn't want to go with you?"

"Why wouldn't Bria want to be with her people?"

"Because you experimented on her."

I take another step backward. Jett raises an eyebrow and smirks, showing a hint of his serrated teeth.

"I didn't experiment on her. None of my people did. That was all Dr. Kihl and Dr. Rah. The Elders authorized the experiments. But Bria isn't a specimen, Allison. Far from it. She is our savior. The salvation of my people is hidden in her blood. With blood like hers, we can create an army of magicians—human magicians—capable of defeating the dragons and skaags."

"Human magicians beholden to you? I've seen what your magic did to Haji. He's brainwashed. It's like you've…you've turned him into a zombie."

Jett shrugs. "He's a loaded weapon. Guns have safeties. So do our magicians."

"What about Gore?" I demand.

"Until recently, he was a trusted lieutenant," Jett says.

I take another step toward the hatch. My options

are limited. I'm not seriously considering handing over Bria, especially since I'm positive she won't want to go with Jett. Plus, I don't believe for an instant he's going to let us waltz on out of here. I can transform, but then I'd only have two options: fight or flee. Fighting means killing the faeries, and that's something I'd prefer to avoid. I don't want their deaths on my conscience, and there's no guarantee I can win a fight against twenty or more faeries. Also, my friends might be hurt either as combatants or collateral damage.

Jett smiles broadly, shifting to gaze beyond me. "Chief, you treacherous goat, we were just talking about you. Come out along with everyone else."

"Treacherous? I wasn't the one who murdered Dr. Rah," Gore says and comes up beside me on my left.

Jett raises his voice. "Come out, and you won't be harmed. If I have to send my people in to fetch you...well"—Jett turns his smile on me—"it wouldn't go well for you."

I bite my lower lip to keep from telling my friends to run. I've seen how Jett can move. There's no way they can outrun the faeries. I must transform for us to escape, but as Dalia and Bria scamper up beside me, I don't see how I can without squashing them. I don't see Haji, but I think he is standing next to Gore. If I can turn into a skaag without killing everyone, I can carry them to safety. My legs are short and powerful like a crocodile's. It's probably asking too much for everyone to hop aboard, especially when my skaag form ignites panic in humans, and the faeries will, in all likelihood, start blasting me with offensive magic.

Jett turns his gaze on Bria and vocalizes melodiously in a combination of hums and hisses.

327

Beside me, Dalia takes my hand and squeezes.

"Get ready," she whispers so softly her words are almost lost in the gale-force wind.

I don't even dare to swivel my eyes toward her out of fear Jett or his cohorts will spot something.

Bria replies to Jett by hissing like an angry cat. He lunges toward her, and she slashes at him, claws extended. He leaps backward, wings buzzing and buffeting the undergrowth, landing ten feet away. The faeries surrounding us utter angry hisses, and a handful stalk closer, extending claws.

"She doesn't want to go with you," I say. "You can't force her."

Jett glowers at Bria and hums. The vocalization is deep and commanding. The faeries approaching us halt but don't retreat. One slightly off to the left smiles predatorily, revealing teeth which she runs her tongue over.

"There's no need for violence," Jett says. "Give us Bria, and you may leave unmolested."

"Don't trust him," Gore says. "As soon as they have her, we're dead."

"Chief. Why so disingenuous?" Jett says. "You and I both know you want Bria for her blood. You're addicted."

Gore stiffens. "I never denied it."

"Why would I ever harm Allison? I murdered Dr. Rah to keep her safe. Without my intervention, the doctor would be weighing and measuring her innards right now."

"Why did you save me?" I ask, the memory of his touch as sweet as honey and sharp as the bone saw Dr. Rah had been ready to use on me.

Jett's smile fades. "You know why, Allison. We have a connection. Don't deny it. Join us. My people won't judge you. We'll accept you as one of us. Like you, we're not human and have been repressed. Like you, dragons have used us, manipulated us. Like you, skaags have hunted us."

His words are a siren's song and a slap to the face. A connection. I can't deny it. My body longs to be near him, and I desire the acceptance he offers. Yet, at the same time, our connection is something vile. We're both killers. That's part of my past I'd sooner never occurred and yearn to forget. I recall his indifference after he murdered Dr. Rah and the nurse. Only human, he had said. I will never become like him. My humanity is the best part of me.

"Don't listen to him," Dalia says, squeezing my hand reassuringly.

"I'm not," I say firmly. Jett hadn't needed to kill Dr. Rah or the nurse. He could have overwhelmed them with his superior physicality or magic and taken them captive. Instead, he killed them with the same indifference as a kid crushing an ant. That is something I will never accept.

Jett frowns. "That is an unfortunate choice." His head swivels to my left toward Haji. "Soldier, bring Bria to me unharmed. If the others resist, you may use deadly force."

"Yes, sir," Haji bellows and steps forward.

Chapter 34

My pulse roars like whitewater rapids. I don't want to hurt Haji, but I can't allow him to injure anyone or take Bria against her will. One punch. I'll knock him out with one punch, but I won't hit him hard enough to break his jaw or…or…my lips curl up into a snarl. I've never hated anyone so much as I do Jett.

I release Dalia's hand in preparation for violence, but she squeezes my hand even tighter and drives her thumbnail into my palm until my sneer becomes a wince. Haji marches before us toward Bria. When he is in front of Jett, his hands light up with orange flames, and he spins toward the faery. A softball size fireball spews from Haji's hand toward Jett.

"Get down!" Gore shouts.

Dalia pulls me down through damp undergrowth to the muddy ground. Hisses and screams join the typhonic winds as orange light flares, illuminating the underside of palm fronds.

"Call Druk!" Gore shouts.

I face the assassin kneeling next to me, hands glowing orange from wrists to fingertips.

"What?"

Gore ducks seconds before a gout of scorching flame blazes over our heads. The stench of ozone and smoke is thick in the air.

"Contact your mother," Gore snarls. "She'll sense

the magic. She might be looking for its location. Call out to her. Bring her to us."

Gore screams wordlessly and leaps to his feet. Orange light flares, so bright I'm momentarily blinded. Beside me Dalia trembles. I need to do something before we're overwhelmed by the superior force, but I don't dare stand while under the withering magical assault. In skaag form, my thick hide will offer some protection, but I'll be cooked while human.

Call my mother, he says. I've never contacted my mother telepathically while in human form. I can while a skaag, but that was always at close range and within line of sight. Even if I could call to her as a skaag, there's no way I'm transforming without crushing my friends to a pulp.

"Your mother! Call her!" Dalia screams. "That's the plan! Call your mother!"

"I can't," I say. "It only works when I'm a skaag."

"What about while you were in the hospital? You told me she spoke to you."

That's true. Mother had communicated telepathically with me while I recovered in the hospital after being nearly killed by Gore. While I lay in the hospital bed blind and weak as a kitten, she projected her voice directly into my mind. She transmitted her thoughts to me again in a farm field near Ashford, Washington, when I threw dirt clods at her to keep her from killing Mauve. Wait. I did reply to her during our second encounter. I told her I had been on the beach where she had killed Ion in response to a query she posed. Mother didn't give any indication my thoughts had reached her, so I've always assumed it was a one-way transmission. Mother has never said anything to disabuse me of that notion.

Unsure what to do, I call silently. *Mother, help.*

I receive no response from Mother.

A strident yowl cuts through the din. Haji. In pain.

We need Mother's help now. I scream into the void again. Nothing.

"I can't reach her."

"You have to!" Dalia screams as fireballs crackle all around us.

"I can't." I shake my head. "Haji needs help. He's hurt."

Dalia tightens her grip on my hand. "No. You contact your mother. I'll help Haji."

I nod. Dalia low crawls through the undergrowth toward our injured friend. A fireball whizzes overhead, uncomfortably close. I press myself down into the slick mud. Taking a deep breath, I drop the firewall between the sleeper and me.

Our consciousness becomes one.

I become whole.

Mother, I roar into the void.

Her presence crashes into my awareness like a meteor. My vision blooms white then withers to black. I grab the sides of my head. This isn't like at the hospital or the farm field.

Daughter, where are you?

I... My brain is a liquefied tomato. I can't remember the island's name. Mustering all my willpower I say, *Singapore. An outlying island.*

There are over sixty outlying islands, daughter.

Magic. Magic is being used.

I feel it, but I'm too far away to locate it precisely. The name, daughter.

I wrack my brain for the name. Jett had told me. But did he lie? It's almost impossible to think while drowning in Mother's presence.

The name, daughter.

Golden...Golden Shoal.

I'm coming.

Come quickly, or the faeries will kill us! I mentally scream, but she's gone.

How long until Mother arrives? Can we hold off the faeries long enough? Can I transform without killing those I want to protect? Each question hurls itself into oblivion without an answer.

"Haji! Are you hurt? Haji!" Dalia screams.

Fireballs sizzle by in every direction. Somehow Gore and Bria hold the faeries back, despite being outnumbered and surrounded. The rain beats down in a deluge, pinging against the foliage like machinegun fire. I crawl on my hands and knees through the thick undergrowth to Dalia's side. Haji is on his back, groaning. The stench of burned fabric and charred meat is thick, intermixing with the ever-present noxious aromas of smoke and ozone.

"How bad is it?" I ask.

Dalia faces me. Her eyes are bloodshot. "I don't know."

Dalia scuttles aside, allowing me to inspect Haji's wound when a fireball blazes above us. We duck even lower. The ball of flame flies by so close I'm amazed my hair doesn't ignite.

Tendrils of smoke rise from Haji's right shoulder. The fabric of his fatigues is burned through, the material singed around a grapefruit-sized hole. I clench my teeth at the sight of angry red skin and bulbous blisters. Sweat covers Haji's face, and his lips tremble as he whimpers.

"What do we do?" Dalia asks.

"I…I don't know."

An explosion cracks from nearby. The percussive sound directionless. I drop to the ground next to Haji, tugging Dalia with me. As I fall, I spot a faery dropping from the air impaled by a splintered length of a tree trunk.

"We have to do something. He's in shock."

"I don't know how to treat burns like this," I say. "Gore might."

Gore crouches back-to-back with Bria, springing up to send fireballs toward the faeries and ducking for cover.

"Cover the…wound…with something…" Haji mummers.

"What did he say?" Dalia asks.

"He said to cover the wound with something wet," I say.

"Won't a covering stick or something?" Dalia says.

I don't understand Haji's reply because a buzzing from overhead distracts me. A faery descends toward us, her wings a blur and arms ablaze with fire. Every part of her body not covered with clothing is highlighted by glowing orange veins forming fractal patterns. The faery dust around her is thick and swirling.

I leap upward. The faery's expression curdles in surprise as I rush up to meet her, certain I'll be engulfed in an inferno, but the flames never come, and I latch onto her legs with my arms. Even with my added weight, she starts ascending while bending over at the waist, bringing her fiery hands to bear against me. In desperation, I grab for the blur that is her lower right wing. I find purchase on the wing, which is moist and malleable. Pulling as hard as I can, I rip the wing from her body and fling the membrane into the jungle. We plummet to the ground, the faery wailing the entire way.

We land with a bone-jarring thud next to my squad. I scramble over the faery, who howls like a wild beast in abject pain. Her body is still aglow with fractal patterns, but I'm relieved the fire is gone from her hands. She struggles as I straddle her and raise a fist to knock her out with one punch before she has the wherewithal to incinerate us with magic.

"Stop! Stop!" Jett screams.

I hesitate, so hyped up my fist shakes. The faery stops struggling, and her screams reduce to whimpers. The flashes of orange light stop, and the sizzle of fireballs fade. Angry hisses come from all sides. Off to my left, Gore and Bria crouch still back-to-back, the assassin trying to look everywhere at once.

"Hand over Bria," Jett shouts over the rain and wind. "Surrender her, and you can go. No one else needs to get hurt or die."

I stare at the whimpering faery, who is going into shock. The ground glows faintly where her blood puddles. Faery dust gathers near the wound. Deciding she's no longer a threat, I lower my hand and raise myself up until I see Jett. The right side of his jawline and neck is puckered pink, leaking pus and blood in places. The faery dust floating around him coalesces over the wound.

"Please, hand over Bria, and this ends. You can all

go home," Jett says.

Bria hisses in reply. Hums and hisses come from all sides.

"I'll give you one minute to consider," Jett says. "If you don't surrender Bria…"

I turn to Dalia. "I have an idea."

"What?" my BFF whispers.

I scurry over to Dalia. Haji clenches his jaw in evident agony. His wound is covered with cloth torn from the arm of his fatigues.

"I'm going to jump and transform in the air, so I won't crush you," I whisper into Dalia's ear.

"They'll blast you with magic," Dalia says.

"Don't worry. Once I'm a skaag their magic won't hurt me."

Dalia looks incredulously at me.

"At least not very much. I need you to make sure everyone mounts me."

"I don't know, Allison—"

"Let her try," Haji says, pawing at Dalia with a shaky hand.

I meet Haji's gaze and nod. He manages a fleeting smile that morphs into a grimace.

I take a deep breath, muscles tensing, and spring upward. Heartbeats after I go airborne, I concentrate on transforming. The agony is immediate and all-consuming as my body rips and expands, organs rearranging as if an angry God remakes me in an instant as long as the lifespan of the universe. Flames sear my morphing form. Distantly, a small part of me not gnawed to the bone by torment comprehends something is wrong.

The pain is gone, and I'm a skaag, my tail end

slamming against tree trunks without ill effect. My left foreleg hangs limply at my side, and when I move the limb, a hot poker of pain lances through it from foot to shoulder. I shriek in rage and agony.

Fireballs fly toward me, stinging where they strike but not causing discernible damage. The rain burns like acid when it runs into my eyes. The droplets striking my hide are reminders I can't hold my breath underwater or swim while a skaag, and even a small body of water can be the death of me.

I descend toward the jungle floor, battling the urge to lash out at the faeries with lightning for fear of killing my friends. Dalia is on her feet supporting Haji and rallying Gore and Bria to her. Fortunately, the faeries concentrate their fire on me. Dalia and Haji scramble to my right foreleg, and I scoop them up. Gore grabs my left foreleg, and the pain is so intense I nearly fall to the ground. My piercing shriek forces him and the faeries to their knees. I twist my neck around until I'm staring at him and open my abyssal maw. He takes the hint and scrambles along my side to my hind legs, pulling Bria with him. Once Gore and Bria are secure, I shoot skyward, clutching the humans and faery tight to protect them from the fireballs zooming past and the jungle canopy above us.

I burst from the jungle into a typhoon. The rain blinds me, and a gust of wind sweeps me off course. Once I level out, I blink until my vision clears. Across a storm-battered sea dotted with bobbing cargo ships is a glowing neon jewel. I speed toward the dazzling light. Fireballs strike my body from below. Errant fireballs continue upward until they reach their trajectories' peaks, then fall in lazy arcs to the ocean, hitting the water with hissing plunks.

I twist to put my bulk between the magical assault and my passengers. My useless foreleg sears like it's been dipped in magma at the maneuver, forcing me to straighten. It's either that or plummet into the water. Flying higher is out of the question since lightning still arcs between thunderheads.

I should be able to outrun the faeries, but every time I call upon my body to undulate faster, nearly paralytic agony shoots through my injured foreleg. Never before have I felt so weak in skaag form. I shriek with frustration and have my call answered with a bone-rattling battle cry of the ultimate juggernaut of death, my mother, the feared Druk.

Mother descends from the lightning-streaked clouds with yellow electrical arcs coursing over her black body. She disappears inside a roiling mass of thunderheads. The bright yellow flash of her electrical discharge burns a jagged after image into my mind.

Gore whoops. "That thinned their numbers!"

More fireballs streak past me. From their shouting, I gather Gore and Bria are returning fire. Ahead, the neon lights have resolved into a forest of glittering spires and causeways and quays. Three massive rectangular buildings support what is, for all appearances, a yacht flying above a bay.

A golden dragon as massive as a jumbo jet rises out of the city. The scales of its underside sparkle kaleidoscopically in the city's radiance. Its broad green wings propel it toward me at an accelerating pace. My panic is short-lived for it is Dr. Radcliffe, who is my benefactor and betrayer.

A fireball bursts against my back. Unlike the

previous impacts, it hurts like it might've done actual damage to my hide. I want to turn and fight. An electrical discharge will send my attackers in a pell-mell retreat, but I can't do that without frying my friends. Clenching my jaw, I redouble my pace.

Dr. Radcliffe flies stunningly fast for such a colossal beast. He shoots past me, roaring so loudly I wince. Crackling boils behind me. I slow, coming to a stop. Levitating, I look behind me. Dr. Radcliffe beats his wings rapidly to hover as he spews dragon fire at the dozens of pursuing faeries. Most veer like fighter jets to escape the flames, but some are caught in the inferno and rendered to ash. The remaining faeries retreat from the fiery onslaught, heading toward Golden Shoal far in the distance.

Above the island, lightning flashes and fire flares. My mother is surrounded by scores of faeries, their battle illuminated by bursts of yellow and orange light. My chest tightens with worry for my mother. That's new. I've lost count of how many times I've sincerely wished her dead.

Dr. Radcliffe growls as he flies by me toward the city. Clutched in a foreclaw is his humanoid golem. I follow him, taking solace in the fact Mother is a deadly monster and will survive the faeries. Radcliffe leads me to a broad promenade populated by a few people who run screaming at our approach. A bay abuts the promenade on the left. On its right are low-slung buildings. Behind the esplanade are a stand of trees and a fish statue with the head of a lion spouting water from its mouth. Across the bay are the triple towers supporting the sky yacht.

Dr. Radcliffe swoops in first, his massive body

taking up most of the seafront. He sets down his golem, and lightning crackles along his dragon form. The dragon fades, becoming translucent, and Dr. Radcliffe the man animates, shouting at people to stay back to give me room to land safely. Dr. Radcliffe strides to the promenade's edge near the water, the translucent dragon following him like a loyal dog.

I hover over the landing site, slowly lowering myself toward the ground when something strikes my back, burning along my body's length. I writhe as my vision goes black.

Chapter 35

I'm falling. Every nerve in my back is aflame. My vision clears to the concrete rushing up to meet me faster than I imagined. My friends and allies! They'll be crushed beneath my bulk on impact. I spin like an Olympic diver, embracing the pain from my damaged limb and screaming back. The agony is so intense an involuntary shriek bursts from my mouth, but even so the physical torment is nothing compared to the fear I'll squish Dalia and Haji like slugs run over by a bicycle tire.

I strike the ground, back pressing into red hot coals. I see white, and stars flood my vision, obscuring the topsy-turvy cityscape. The coals burn through my protective hide to blacken the sensitive skin beneath. I want to throw myself over onto my belly, but I don't dare out of fear I'll crush my friends.

A roar reminiscent of a jet engine, but not quite as loud, rumbles from overhead. Blinking, I watch Ms. Bergman descend. What the hell? I squeeze my eyes shut and open them. Bergman touches down with a thud. She's encased in a mechanized exoskeleton that leaves her face twisted in a rictus smile visible behind thick glass. Her right arm is a gun with three different barrels stacked on top of each other. In her left hand, she grips a sword with glowing orange fractal patterns etched into the blade. With a whirl of gears, Bergman raises the sword overhead and charges.

I'd be a fool not to believe the sword isn't enchanted with faery magic and can slice through me like a red-hot knife through melting butter. Through the noise of pain like TV static turned up to the max, I don't feel anyone against my body. They must've escaped…I hope, because I shoot to the air, up and away from Ms. Bergman, narrowly avoiding the slashing blade.

Dr. Radcliffe stands like a granite monument at the edge of the promenade near the water. His translucent dragon form looms over the golem encased in the same fine orange mesh that had ensnared Mauve at the condo. Gore, carrying Haji in his arms, hustles toward the fish lion statue. Dalia and Bria trail behind the assassin, both limping.

Bergman raises her gun arm. A stream of white-hot plasma shoots from the top barrel. I bank left to avoid the blast. Even so, my hide feels seared from the heat.

"I told you I'd have justice for Dr. Rah, Miss Lee," Bergman declares, her amplified voice tinny over the speakers.

I want to tell her I didn't have anything to do with the psychotic doctor's death—it was Jett. All I can manage with my elongated vocal cords is a sound between a shriek and a growl.

"Oh, don't worry, Miss Lee. I haven't forgotten Jett did the deed. At your behest, of course. I'll make sure he gets his comeuppance as soon as I rid the world of you and Gore, and take Bria, that ungrateful little faery, back to where she belongs."

Bergman lifts off into the air with a rumble, flames blasting from the soles of the exoskeleton's feet and leaving behind scorch marks on the concrete. I'm tempted to summon an electrical discharge and see how Bergman's suit reacts, but instead, I soar higher. As the strength of my electrical attack has grown, my control has lessened to basically zero. I don't want collateral damage, especially my squad.

"Fleeing, Miss Lee? No worries. I love hunting down prey!" Bergman cackles and fires off another plasma shot.

The blast flies past well wide of me. Bergman snarls a string of curses. I catch something about overheating in between the vitriolic phrases. With the roar like afterburners, Bergman accelerates upward, her sword pointed toward me like a lance.

I fly even higher despite my body burning from my injuries and pure exhaustion. Every time I glance downward, Bergman is gaining on me. I summon the electricity and am rewarded with excruciating pain up and down my back. I falter, and my body stops undulating. For a breath, I'm suspended in air, then I'm nosediving like a freight train derailing from an overpass.

Bergman and I rush closer and closer. The pain lashing through me is so intense I'm ready to surrender myself to death. I'll never drown in guilt again or have to listen to people proclaim me an abomination day after day. By barging through death's door, I will finally find the freedom of obscurity I have yearned for since The Incident.

A maniacal funhouse grin warps Bergman's features, and I slam death's door. The spook won't stop at killing Gore and me. She'll murder Dalia and Haji too, sniggering the whole time, and I can't allow Bria to fall back into her hands. I know what it's like to be experimented on. I can't doom Bria to that fate.

Focusing my mind, I fire an electrical pulse. Yellow lightning lashes out in all directions from my body. A sizzling bolt strikes the exoskeleton in the shoulder of the arm holding the sword. The suit tumbles sideways, black smoke puffing from the shoulder joint. The sword spins out of Bergman's grip and is lost in the city's neon glow.

I fall toward the bay too weak to transform back into human form to keep from drowning. I accept my impending demise, hoping I've done enough to protect my people.

****

Saltwater gushes down my throat. My body heaves and limbs flail. A fiery lance pierces my left arm from my shoulder to the tips of my fingers. Thousands of leafcutter ants strip my back with their mandibles. My lungs are full to bursting with lukewarm liquid.

My eyes burst open to watery murk in all directions. I can't tell which way is up to life-giving air. Not that it matters. I don't know what form my body takes. If I'm skaag, I'm doomed because I can't hold my breath or swim. If I'm human, I'm gnawed to the quick with nothing left to give.

Hands seize me under the armpits. A bolt of pain scorches my left arm. I try to scream but choke on water. I want the agony to end. I need a saw to sever my limb.

My head ruptures the water's surface, and I'm being pulled to who knows where. I hack, each cough feeling like my esophagus is ripped out through my mouth and wrung out. I want it to end, but my body fights to live even as I surrender.

My vision resolves into a world of darkness and bright swirly light. From somewhere nearby, people scream, and in the distance are distorted sirens. The hands release me, and I flop down. Something hard cuts horizontally into my back at regular intervals.

"You owe me, Allison," Gore says.

****

Familiar beeping and buzzing along with medicinal odors shock me into consciousness. My eyes shoot open, and a growl rips through my chest. I'm in a hospital, again—not an experience I ever wanted to relive. As the brightly lit room resolves into gold-tinted walls and the side of a hospital bed, I'm comforted by the fact I'm not blind this time. Oddly, though, I'm lying on my belly. That's different. Also, why are there two men with submachine guns positioned by the door? No way. Is a green wing protruding from the soldier's chest?

"Allison." Dr. Radcliffe greets me as avuncular as ever.

I shift my head until I can see Radcliffe's human form sitting in a chair near the foot of the bed, elbows on the armrests, hands steepled, glasses he doesn't need perched on his nose. The real Radcliffe, the dragon riding the slipstream invisible to everyone except me, fills the room and beyond with its bulk.

"Why am I on my stomach?" I ask.

"You were badly burned while in skaag form. Your entire back is…well, be glad this hospital has an excellent burn unit and for your body's preternatural healing ability. Your left shoulder is badly burned too. It is worse than the rest. The doctors believe you will need to undergo cosmetic surgery. I have assured them you will satisfactorily heal on your own and only need supportive care. They, however, remain dubious."

I sit up. My left arm trembles from the effort, and my back is tender.

"Careful." Radcliffe stands. "Your wounds are not completely healed."

I wave off his warning and arrange myself cross-legged on the bed. The skin on my back feels like it's stretched almost to the point of tearing. "What about my friends?"

Radcliffe sits. "Dalia is recovering from a broken arm, taken in the crash landing. A minor injury, considering. Do you remember crashing?"

"What about Haji? And Bria?" I demand.

Radcliffe shifts in his chair and pushes his glasses higher up the bridge of his nose. His massive draconic head emerges from the ceiling, his tubular mustache drooping from his snout. "They have been evacuated, back to the U.S., for their safety. Really, it is for the best."

"Evacuated? What are you talking about? How long have I been here?"

"You have been here for a week."

"A week!"

"Like I said, your burns are quite bad. You might recall, I was caught in a magical netting—the same magic that ensnared Mauve, I believe. I observed the battle between you and Felicia Bergman. Not all of it, mind you, but enough. After I freed myself from the netting, I found you under the care of Dalia and Bria. I worried you might succumb to the burns, but Bria was able to stabilize you using magic."

I grimace. I'm glad to be alive but dislike magic being used on me under any circumstances.

Dr. Radcliffe waves a hand dismissively. "Do not worry about the magic she used. It is not mind-altering. They told me Gore pulled you from the water. After that, they lost track of him. Do you know what happened to Gore? I have many questions to ask him about the faeries and the operation on Golden Shoal."

I shake my head. "I remember him pulling me from the water. That's it." I cross my arms before my chest. My tender skin stretches across my upper back. "You told me faeries are extinct. Habitat destruction, you said."

"I told you the truth." Dr. Radcliffe folds his hands in his lap, his expression stern. "Clearly, I was mistaken."

Clearly, dragons lie, but as usual, I can't decipher if he's telling the truth or not.

"Have you visited the base on Golden Shoal?" I ask.

"I have. There is not much to be learned there. Everything of interest was taken or destroyed by fire. Once you are fully recovered, I will need to debrief you. I am sure various government agencies will also want to interview you."

Just the anticipation of being interrogated by overly officious government bureaucrats who have nothing better to do than to pry into my business gives me a headache. Inspiration strikes, and I ask for coffee. I haven't had a cup of the black brew in forever. A hit of caffeine will beat back the worst of my headache. Dr. Radcliffe requests a soldier to order coffee. The soldier does as he is bidden without comment.

"Did you ever find Bergman?" I ask.

"No, but knowing Felicia Bergman, she is in the wind."

"She tortured us. Dalia and me. I can only imagine what she did to Haji. He was indoctrinated. Brainwashed with faery magic. She claimed she is part of the U.S. government that doesn't approve of dragons or me."

"She worked for an alphabet soup of intelligence agencies in various capacities until going ghost about a year ago. I do not have any details about her service, but I plan to start digging."

"What about my mother? Did she uncover anything?"

"I have had no communications from your mother. The last she was seen she was battling faeries over Golden Shoal."

"Seriously?" Maybe I shouldn't be surprised Mother has disappeared. If she were around, she'd be in this room. Not to check up on me or anything vaguely motherly. No, she'd be here to tell me if I'd taken my training with her seriously, I never would've been captured by Gore in the first place, and none of this would've happened.

"Do not worry," Radcliffe says. "Your mother is likely tracking down the faeries and their allies as we speak."

"I'm not worried. Her not being here is par for the course."

The door swings open, and a soldier enters carrying a ceramic cup with steam rising off the contents. The aromatic scent of coffee sets my mouth watering as he strides to the bedside.

"Thank you." I take the brew.

The soldier returns to his post by the door.

I blow across the black liquid and take a sip. Hot and flavorful, exactly how I like it. I glare at Dr. Radcliffe through the rising steam.

"You still need to tell me what evacuation back to the U.S. means for Haji and Bria."

Dr. Radcliffe frowns. His dragon head retreats through the ceiling. "I will tell you, but first, I have a request. I need you to stay calm."

I lower my cuppa. "Stay calm. You say that and expect me to stay calm."

Dr. Radcliffe's frown deepens.

I sigh and take a swig of coffee. "Fine. I'll do my best."

Chapter 36

"Oh, yes, I see what you mean. What are the doctors' names again?" Dr. Woolworth taps furiously on her tablet with an index finger. She smells faintly of perfume and is dressed in formfitting black pants and a matching turtleneck. Even with her glasses perched low on her nose, she'd look like a movie star, except her blonde hair is disastrously hacked.

"Dr. Rah and Dr. Kihl." I sit at the dining room table back at home. I've been back for nearly three weeks, and I've been anxious to have Dr. Woolworth fix up my prosthetics since day one. I'm not entirely sure what the doctors' fiddling with the devices might have done to my vision. Well, Dr. Woolworth received approval to make a house call yesterday. Apparently, everyone I come in contact with is subject to scrutiny. Ironic, considering it was a thoroughly vetted bodyguard who tried to have me kidnapped.

"Well, they disabled almost everything. Fortunately, all I need to do is turn it back on. First, I'd like to remove the prosthetics and give them a once over," Dr. Woolworth says.

My fingers dig into my thighs.

Dr. Woolworth lowers the tablet and scrunches her eyes. "What's wrong, Allison?"

I relax my hands. "Nothing."

But that's a lie. Dr. Woolworth might be a

magician and not even know it. Even more disturbing, my prosthetics might be imbued with undetectable magic woven into the electronics by Dr. Woolworth without her conscious knowledge. So far, I've kept that bit of intel from Dr. Radcliffe and the government interrogators. If I let anything slip, they'll turn Dr. Woolworth's life upside down. She doesn't deserve that.

Besides, Rah and Kihl didn't know what they were talking about. They didn't understand how my prosthetics work, so they made up a specious story about Dr. Woolworth being a magician without knowing it. It's only because of Dr. Woolworth's genius that I can see.

"Daddy! Can you come in here, please?"

Dad appears in the doorway to the kitchen. In one hand, he clasps a scientific journal, and in the other he holds a half-eaten apple. "What is it?"

"Can you hold my hand while the prosthetics are removed?"

"Sure, Allison, sure," Dad says.

I look up at Dr. Woolworth. "That's okay, right?"

The doctor smiles kindly. "Of course, Allison."

****

I wave to Dalia as she walks down the path to a silver sedan parked next to the sidewalk. She's only one of my friends I have been able to see on a regular basis. I haven't even been able to visit Joe yet. He's recovering from gunshot wounds received in Ace's condo, but at least he's alive. I have to keep reminding myself of that. Devin and Ace possess the devil's luck, both surviving the condo incident without so much as a scratch. Sometimes, I wish they had been shot instead

351

of Joe. Guess I really am a monster. In the end, I wish none of us had been there in first place.

Parked in the street on this cool Pacific Northwest evening are at least eight vehicles belonging to my newly expanded protection detail, which includes soldiers from Joint Base Lewis-McCord patrolling the neighborhood. I'm glad they aren't patrolling inside my bedroom. On the plus side, the increased security has dramatically cut back on the protesters since I returned. I don't know if it's because the word is not out on the street I'm back home or if the added security is intimidating my fanbase.

Dalia's arm is still in a sling, but at least she's been able to return to school. Haji and I still aren't allowed to attend school in person. I've just started online classes this week. I like not having people staring at me and asking about my prosthetics and calling me a monster behind my back, but I miss seeing Dalia every day, and I yearn for the energy of being in school surrounded by my peers.

At the end of the path, a man wearing a conservative suit and an earpiece stands next to the sedan. He politely greets Dalia and opens the back door. Dalia blows a kiss to me before sliding inside, and I return the gesture. That's right. Even Dalia has a security detail now. She even has a bodyguard following her around at school—*ugh*.

****

I sit cross-legged on my unkempt bed leaning over my laptop. I'm in a group video chat with Mauve and Dalia. We're careful about what we discuss. Undoubtedly my laptop and Dalia's are loaded with undetectable spyware, recording everything from audio to our every mouse click for government minders.

"Where is Haji?" Dalia asks.

"He was released from confinement yesterday," Mauve says. "Maybe he wants to spend time with his parents."

"I texted him, and he promised to be here. It's not like him to be late," Dalia insists.

I agree with Dalia. How much has Haji recovered since escaping Golden Shoal? I doubt his recent confinement on Joint Base Lewis-McCord helped in that regard, and now from what we've gathered from the texts exchanged between him and Dalia, he's under house arrest like me. He's super extroverted, so I imagine that's quite an adjustment for him.

"Mauve, have you heard anything about Bria?" I ask.

A silence follows almost long enough to be uncomfortable. Presumably, the government snoops know Mauve is an associate of Dr. Radcliffe, but she still has to be careful what she says.

"Bria is still held on base. I've been told Tanis has built a rapport with her."

"That's great," I say, despite being unable to imagine Tanis building a rapport with anyone. At the best of times, the ancient dragon, who masquerades as an elderly woman, is as thorny as a briar patch, and as trustworthy as Dr. Radcliffe. She is as likely to dissect Bria as help her.

The computer pings, announcing Haji connecting to the video chat. His head appears in a fourth box in the top left-hand corner of my screen.

"Haji!" Dalia and I exclaim in unison.

Mauve smiles and waves.

Haji looks worse than I expected. He's always been thin, but he's never looked gaunt until now. His bloodshot eyes roll in their sockets, never still. Instead of a goofy smile his expression is bleak.

"Hi, everyone. Good to see you." Haji looks over his shoulder, and whispers. The background is blurred, so it's impossible to see to whom he is speaking. He turns back to the screen. "Sorry about that. Listen, they don't want me using the computer except for school."

"Why?" Dalia asks stridently.

Haji shrugs. "They're afraid…sorry. I can't say."

"Haji, what's wrong?" I ask.

"Listen, I can't talk more." His lips tremble, and a tear rolls down his cheek. "I have to go. I just popped on to say hi. That's all. I'm okay. I'm glad everyone is okay."

I say, "Wait, Haji—"

"Sorry, I have to go," Haji says.

"Haji, don't—" Dalia says.

Haji disconnects.

I'm too disturbed to say anything. We're home. We're supposed to be safe, free, but that's not the case for me and certainly not for Haji.

"Mauve, what is going on?" Dalia asks.

"I'm not privy to Haji's home situation," Mauve says.

"Is he even at home?" I ask.

"Yes," Mauve replies a little too quickly.

Mauve's response reminds me that despite being our friend, she is a dragon with a draconic agenda she will never fully share with us.

****

I slam my laptop shut after a particularly long

session of online school. The virtual classroom's novelty has already worn thin. My favorite class by far is photography, and it's not a virtual offering. Rubbing salt in the wound is the fact I adore Mr. Eldridge, Cascadia Prep's photography teacher. Now, I wonder if I'll ever see him again. Last summer, he had nearly died of lung cancer, and earlier this school year he looked like a dead man walking.

Footsteps thump in the hallway, followed by a knock at the door. I spin in my study chair to face the door. "What do you want?"

I can tell it's probably my dad. The bodyguard stationed inside the house twenty-four hours a day is usually one of several female agents. They have a lighter footfall than the male agents and Dad.

"It's your father, Allison. Can I come in?"

"Fine. I'm done with school for the day."

Dad opens the door and steps inside. Dark bags are beneath his eyes, and his shoulders are hunched. Worry about Mother and me keep him awake at night. Typically, he runs every day, five miles or more. He's only been out once or twice since I returned. He complains about having to slow his pace, so the security detail can keep up.

"It's been a week. What's the verdict?" he asks lightly.

"Verdict on what?"

"Virtual school."

I roll my eyes and lean back in the chair.

Dad smiles. "Not that bad then."

The smile almost makes Dad look like himself, but quickly fades, and he looks ten years older again.

I take a deep breath, and my nose twitches. What is

that smell? Alcohol? "Daddy, did you sleep at all last night?"

"Don't worry about me. Are you hungry? I'll go start something for dinner."

"Wait." I sniff the air again. "Why do I smell alcohol on your breath? Since when do you drink?"

"What business is it of yours?" Dad steps into the hall.

I leap from the chair and dash into the hallway before he can turn toward the stairs. I throw my arms around him in a tight embrace.

"What's wrong, Daddy?"

After a beat, he hugs me back. We stand in companionable silence, then he starts trembling. To my shock, he's fighting back tears. Dad is not a crier.

"What's wrong?"

Dad leans down and rests his chin on my shoulder. His hot breath blows across my earlobe.

"Your mother hasn't contacted me for over a month," he whispers.

"How do you stay in contact with her?" I ask.

"Shhhh…not so loud. They record everything since you came back."

"Okay. Are you using cell phones or what?" It makes sense he wants me to keep my voice down. He doesn't want to the blow cover story Dr. Radcliffe crafted to explain Mother's absence.

"Not cell phones. Magic. We have a system. We contact each other once a week. I've reached out to her. I've cast the spells. I wait. But there's only silence."

"Cast spells? Daddy, what are you talking about?" I know exactly what he's talking about, but I don't want it to be true. I don't want to find out he's been hiding more truths from me.

"Your mother is an expert in skaag and human magic, Allison. Who do you think taught her human magic?"

A word about the author...

Dan Rice pens the young adult urban fantasy series The Allison Lee Chronicles in the wee hours of the morning. The series kicks off with his award-winning debut, Dragons Walk Among Us, which Kirkus Review calls, "An inspirational and socially relevant fantasy."

While not pulling down the 9 to 5 or chauffeuring his soccer fanatic sons to practices and games, Dan enjoys photography and hiking through the wilderness.

To discover more about Dan's writing and keep tabs on his upcoming releases, visit his website: https://www.danscifi.com and join his newsletter.

Thank you for purchasing
this publication of The Wild Rose Press, Inc.

For questions or more information
contact us at
info@thewildrosepress.com.

The Wild Rose Press, Inc.
www.thewildrosepress.com